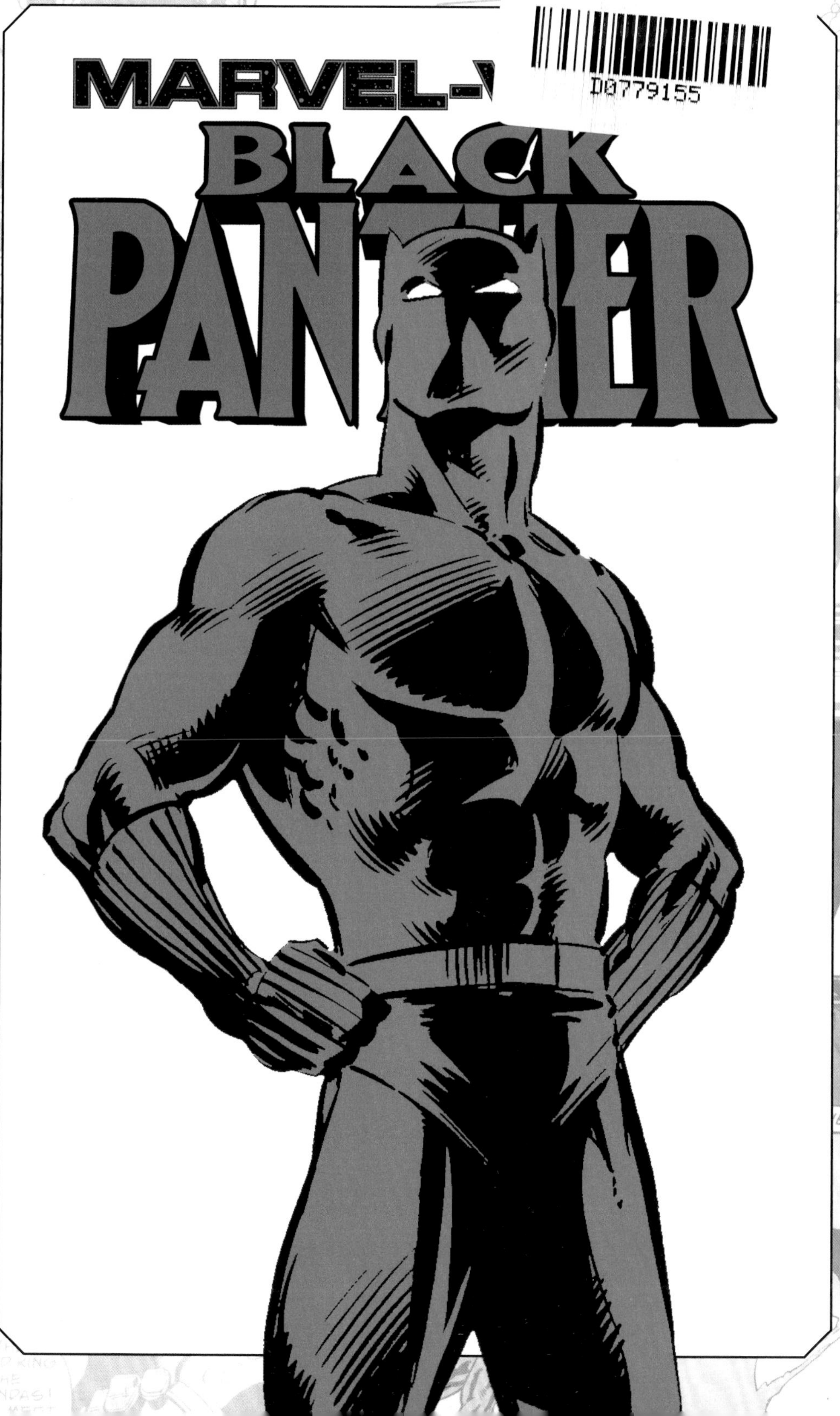
MARVEL-V
BLACK
PANTHER

# MARVEL-VERSE
# BLACK PANTHER

## MARVEL ADVENTURES FANTASTIC FOUR #10

## BLACK PANTHER #14-15

WRITER: **ED HANNIGAN**

PENCILER: **JERRY BINGHAM**

INKER: **GENE DAY**

COLORISTS: **NELSON YOMTOV** (#14) &
**GEORGE ROUSSOS** (#15)

LETTERERS: **RICK PARKER** (#14) &
**CLEM ROBINS** (#15)

EDITORS: **ROGER STERN** & **JIM SHOOTER**

WRITER: **JEFF PARKER**

PENCILER: **MANUEL GARCIA**

INKER: **SCOTT KOBLISH**

COLORIST: **SOTOCOLOR'S**
**ANDREW CROSSLEY**

LETTERER: **DAVE SHARPE**

COVER ART: **CARLO PAGULAYAN,**
**JEFFREY HUET** & **CHRIS SOTOMAYOR**

ASSISTANT EDITOR: **NATE COSBY**

EDITOR: **MARK PANICCIA**

CONSULTING EDITOR: **MacKENZIE CADENHEAD**

# IRON MAN ANNUAL #5

**SCRIPTER/CO-PLOTTER:** PETER B. GILLIS
**CO-PLOTTER:** RALPH MACCHIO
**PENCILER:** JERRY BINGHAM
**INKER:** DAN GREEN
**COLORIST:** BETH FIRMIN
**LETTERER:** DIANA ALBERS
**EDITOR:** MARK GRUENWALD

# SHURI #1

**WRITER:** NNEDI OKORAFOR
**ARTIST:** LEONARDO ROMERO
**COLOR ARTIST:** JORDIE BELLAIRE
**LETTERER:** VC's JOE SABINO
**COVER ART:** SAM SPRATT
**ASSOCIATE EDITOR:** SARAH BRUNSTAD
**EDITOR:** WIL MOSS
**EXECUTIVE EDITOR:** TOM BREVOORT

**BLACK PANTHER** CREATED BY **STAN LEE** & **JACK KIRBY**

**COLLECTION EDITOR:** JENNIFER GRÜNWALD   **ASSISTANT EDITOR:** CAITLIN O'CONNELL
**ASSOCIATE MANAGING EDITOR:** KATERI WOODY   **EDITOR, SPECIAL PROJECTS:** MARK D. BEAZLEY
**VP PRODUCTION & SPECIAL PROJECTS:** JEFF YOUNGQUIST   **BOOK DESIGNERS:** ADAM DEL RE WITH JAY BOWEN

**SVP PRINT, SALES & MARKETING:** DAVID GABRIEL   **DIRECTOR, LICENSED PUBLISHING:** SVEN LARSEN
**EDITOR IN CHIEF:** C.B. CEBULSKI   **CHIEF CREATIVE OFFICER:** JOE QUESADA
**PRESIDENT:** DAN BUCKLEY   **EXECUTIVE PRODUCER:** ALAN FINE

**MARVEL-VERSE: BLACK PANTHER.** Contains material originally published in magazine form as MARVEL ADVENTURES FANTASTIC FOUR (2005) #10, BLACK PANTHER (1977) #14-15, IRON MAN ANNUAL (1970) #5 and SHURI (2018) #1. First printing 2019. ISBN 978-1-302-92360-0. Published by MARVEL WORLDWIDE, INC., a subsidiary of MARVEL ENTERTAINMENT, LLC. OFFICE OF PUBLICATION: 135 West 50th Street, New York, NY 10020. © 2019 MARVEL No similarity between any of the names, characters, persons, and/or institutions in this magazine with those of any living or dead person or institution is intended, and any such similarity which may exist is purely coincidental. **Printed in Canada.** DAN BUCKLEY, President, Marvel Entertainment; JOHN NEE, Publisher; JOE QUESADA, Chief Creative Officer; TOM BREVOORT, SVP of Publishing; DAVID BOGART, Associate Publisher & SVP of Talent Affairs; DAVID GABRIEL, VP of Print & Digital Publishing; JEFF YOUNGQUIST, VP of Production & Special Projects; DAN CARR, Executive Director of Publishing Technology; ALEX MORALES, Director of Publishing Operations; DAN EDINGTON, Managing Editor; SUSAN CRESPI, Production Manager; STAN LEE, Chairman Emeritus. For information regarding advertising in Marvel Comics or on Marvel.com, please contact Vit DeBellis, Custom Solutions & Integrated Advertising Manager, at vdebellis@marvel.com. For Marvel subscription inquiries, please call 888-511-5480. **Manufactured between 11/22/2019 and 12/24/2019 by SOLISCO PRINTERS, SCOTT, QC, CANADA.**

10 9 8 7 6 5 4 3 2 1

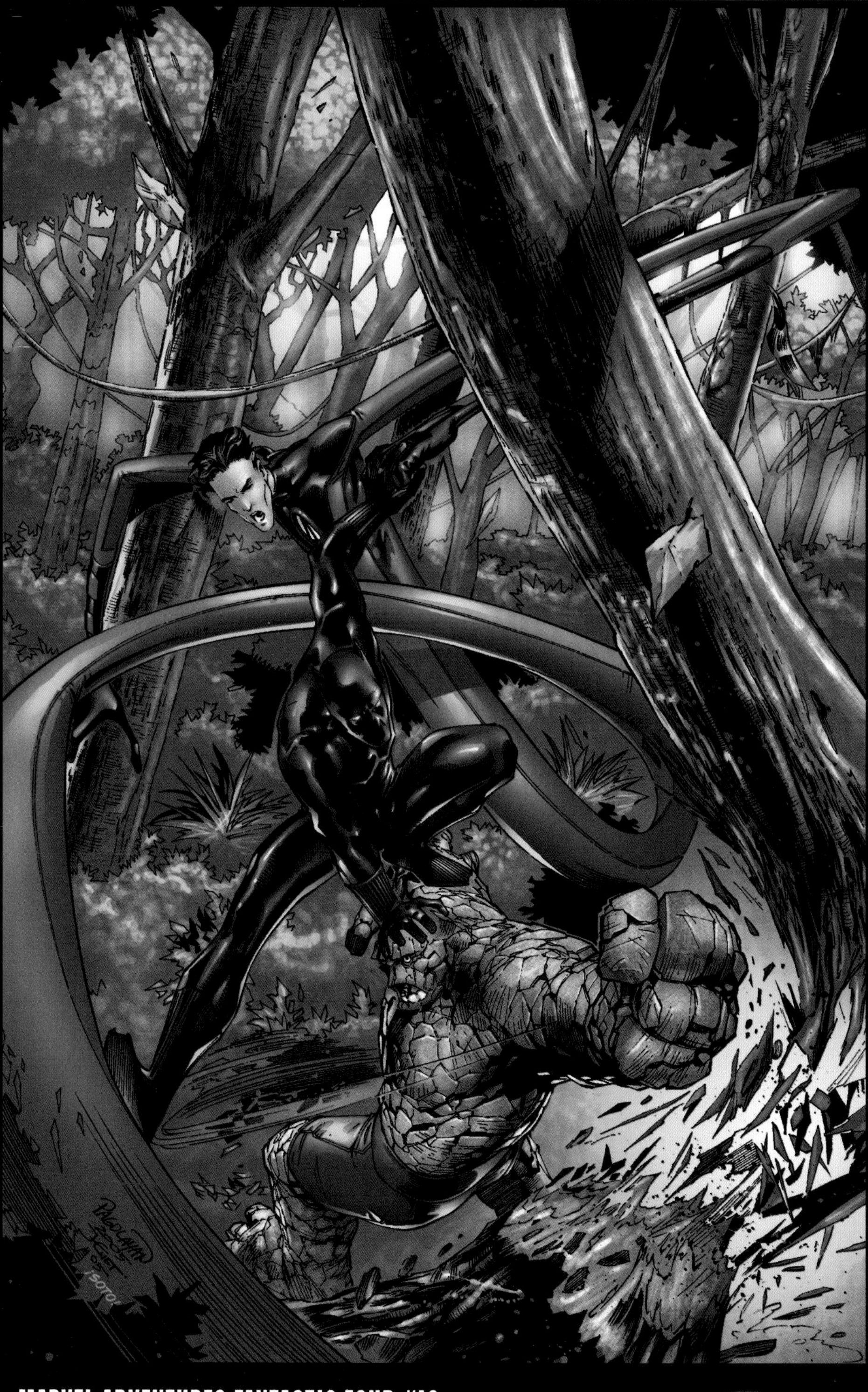

## MARVEL ADVENTURES FANTASTIC FOUR #10

THE FANTASTIC FOUR MEET THE BLACK PANTHER WHEN THEY ACCIDENTALLY STUMBLE INTO A VIBRANIUM-SMUGGLING OPERATION.

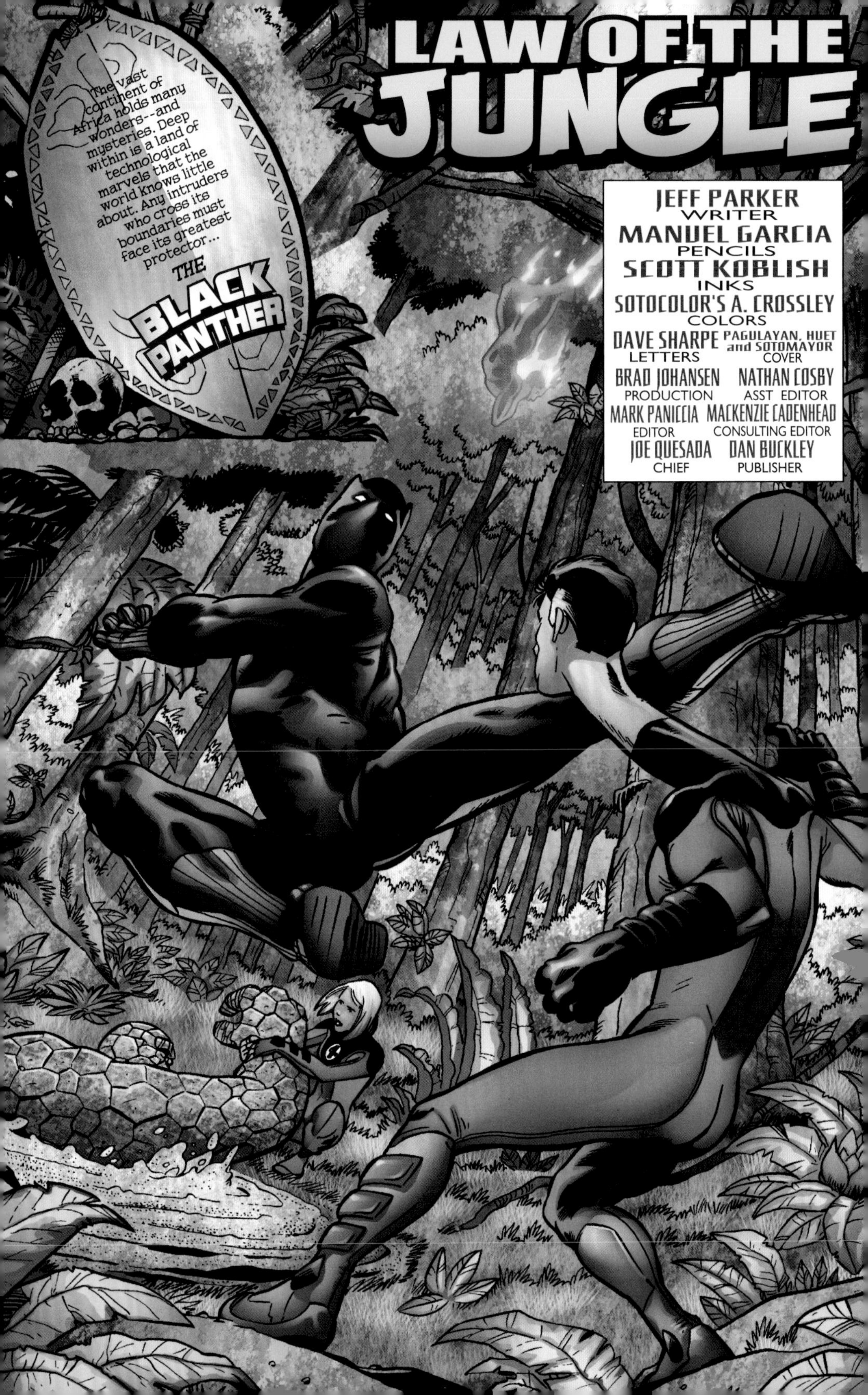

LAW OF THE JUNGLE
The vast continent of Africa holds many wonders--and mysteries. Deep within is a land of technological marvels that the world knows little about. Any intruders who cross its boundaries must face its greatest protector...
THE BLACK PANTHER
JEFF PARKER WRITER
MANUEL GARCIA PENCILS
SCOTT KOBLISH INKS
SOTOCOLOR'S A. CROSSLEY COLORS
DAVE SHARPE LETTERS
PAGULAYAN, HUET and SOTOMAYOR COVER
BRAD JOHANSEN PRODUCTION
NATHAN COSBY ASST EDITOR
MARK PANICCIA EDITOR
MACKENZIE CADENHEAD CONSULTING EDITOR
JOE QUESADA CHIEF
DAN BUCKLEY PUBLISHER

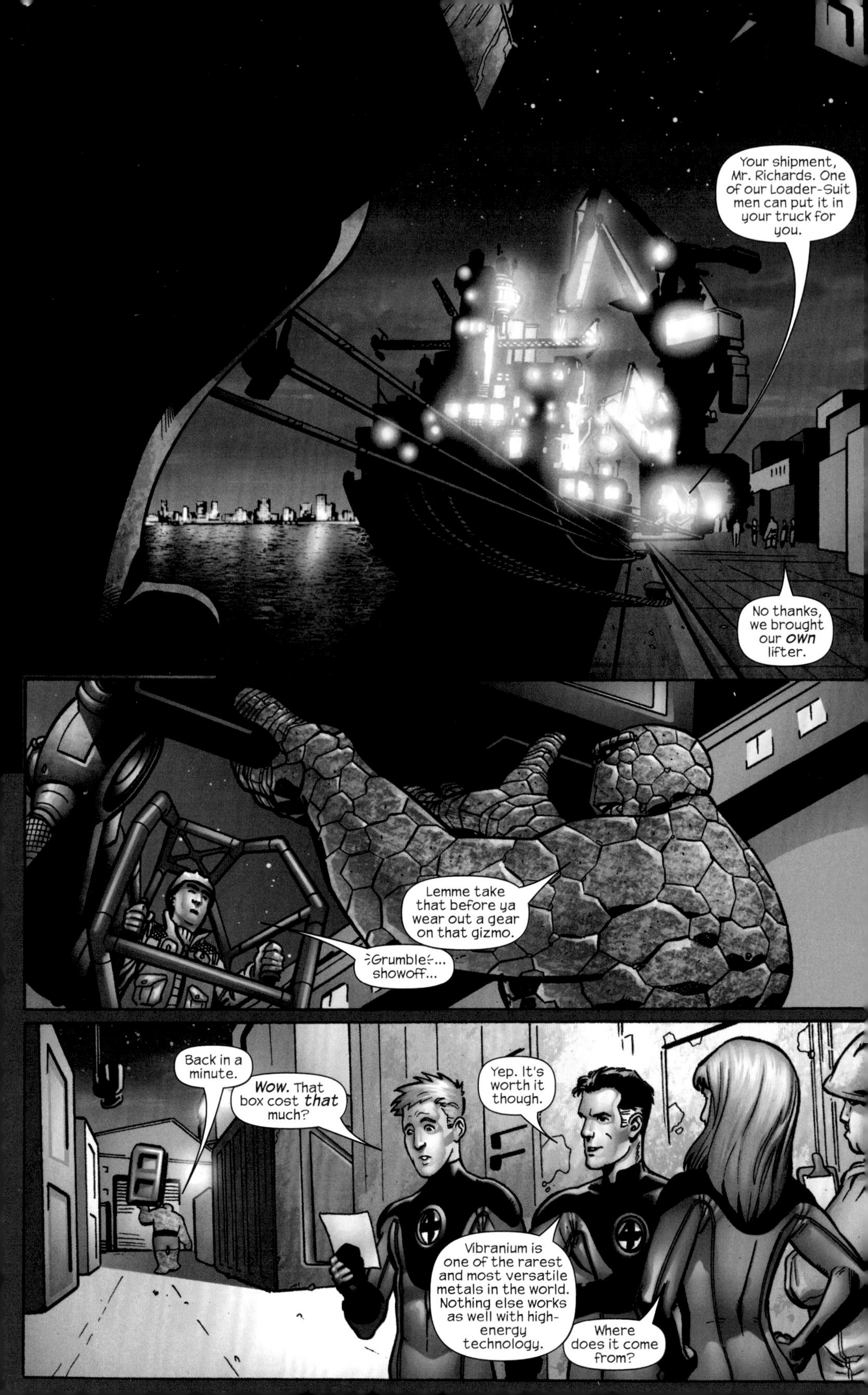
Your shipment, Mr. Richards. One of our Loader-Suit men can put it in your truck for you.
No thanks, we brought our *OWN* lifter.
Lemme take that before ya wear out a gear on that gizmo.
*Grumble*... showoff...
Back in a minute.
*WOW.* That box cost *that* much?
Yep. It's worth it though.
Vibranium is one of the rarest and most versatile metals in the world. Nothing else works as well with high-energy technology.
Where does it come from?

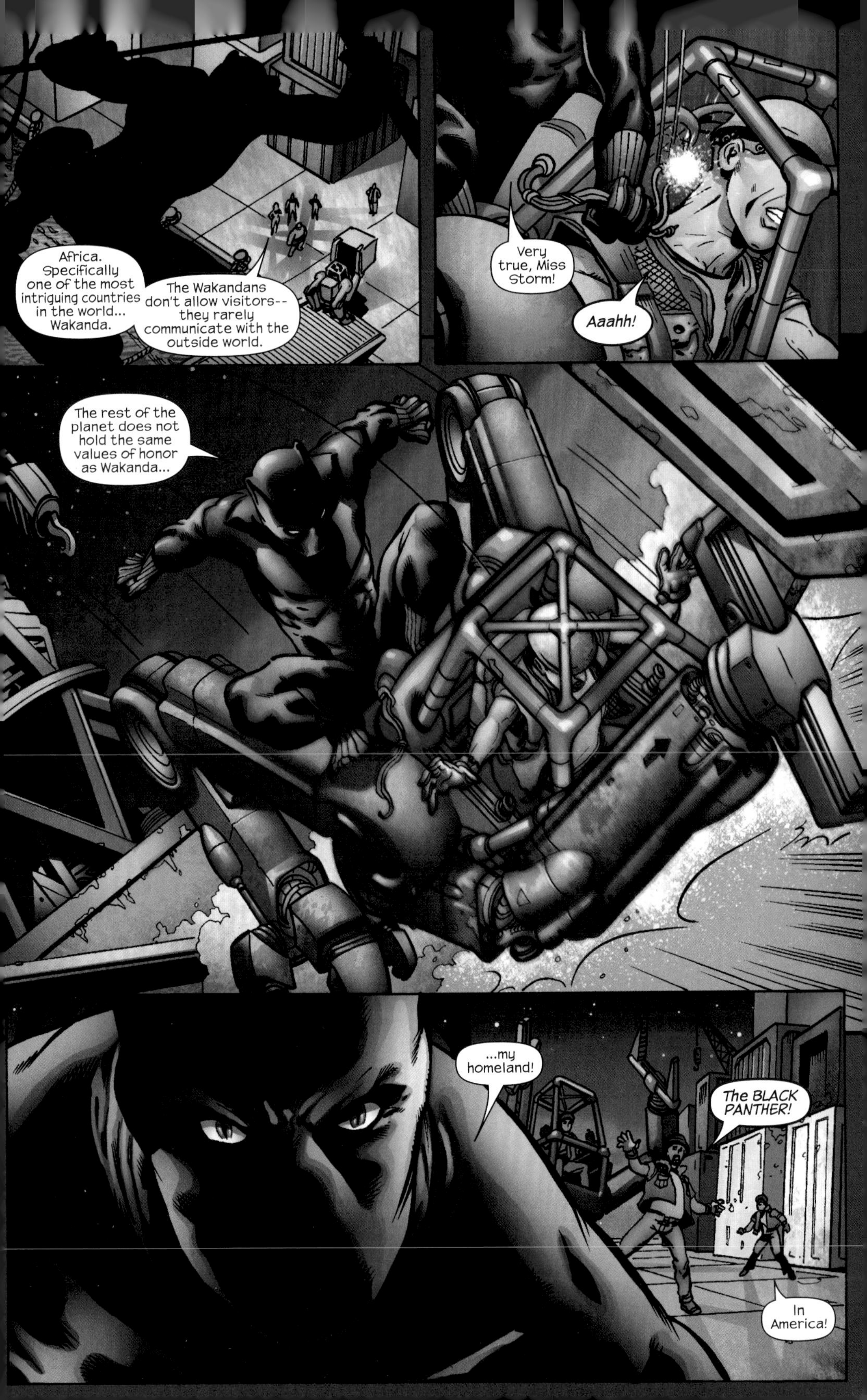

Africa. Specifically one of the most intriguing countries in the world... Wakanda.
The Wakandans don't allow visitors-- they rarely communicate with the outside world.
Very true, Miss Storm!
Aaahh!
The rest of the planet does not hold the same values of honor as Wakanda...
...my homeland!
The BLACK PANTHER!
In America!

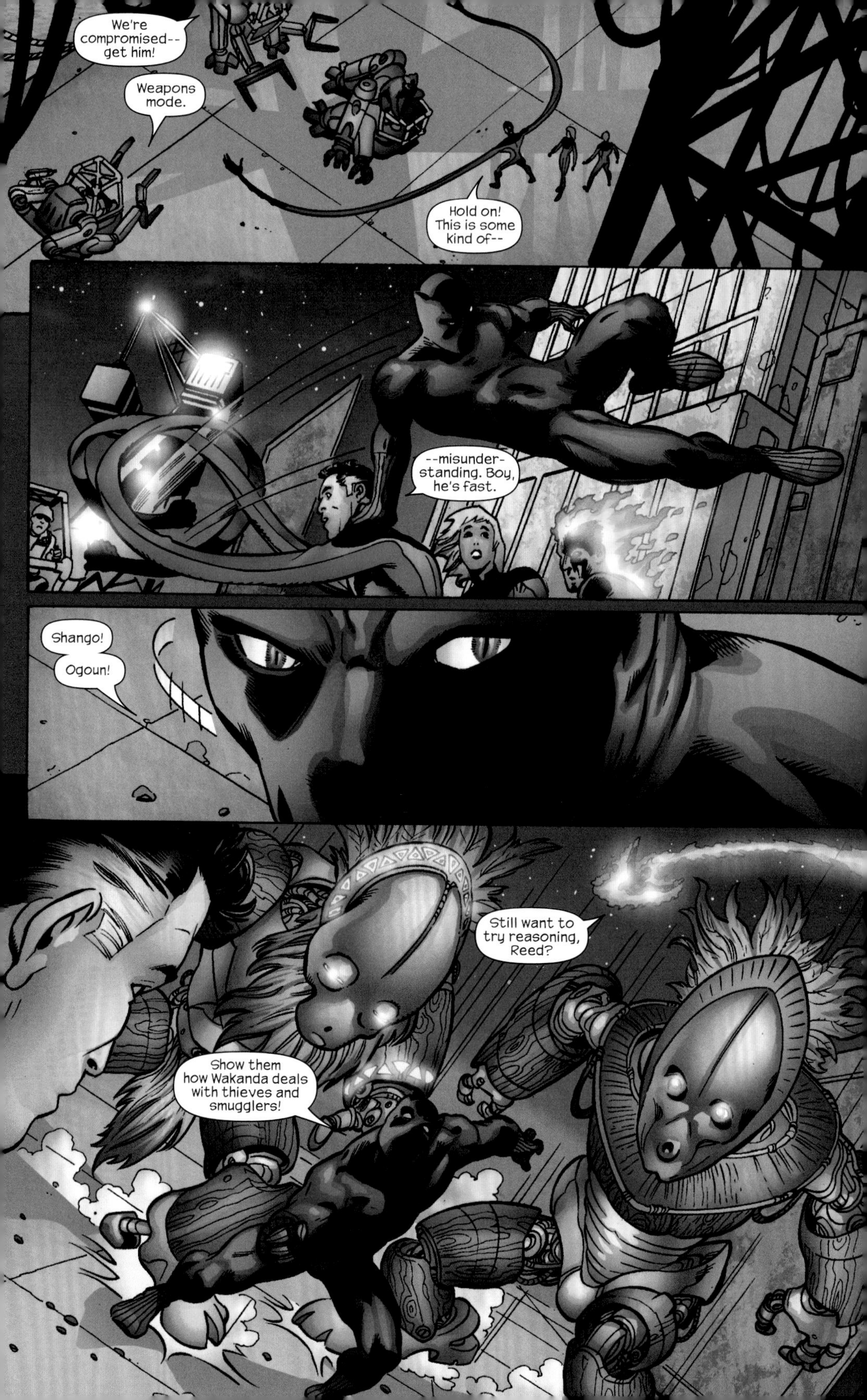
We're compromised-- get him!
Weapons mode.
Hold on! This is some kind of--
--misunder-standing. Boy, he's fast.
Shango!
Ogoun!
Still want to try reasoning, Reed?
Show them how Wakanda deals with thieves and smugglers!

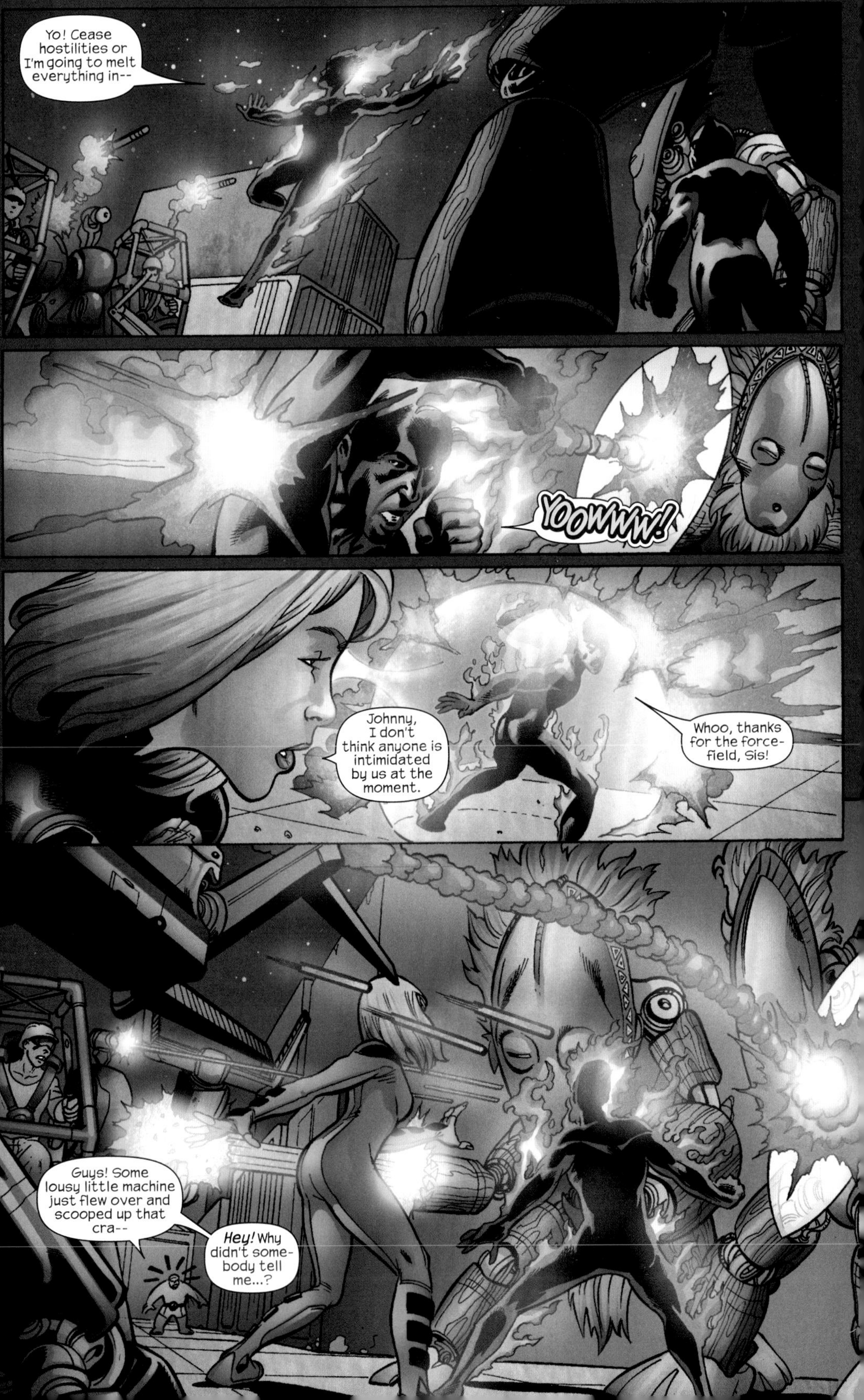
Yo! Cease hostilities or I'm going to melt everything in--
YOOWWW!
Johnny, I don't think anyone is intimidated by us at the moment.
Whoo, thanks for the force-field, Sis!
Guys! Some lousy little machine just flew over and scooped up that cra--
Hey! Why didn't some-body tell me...?

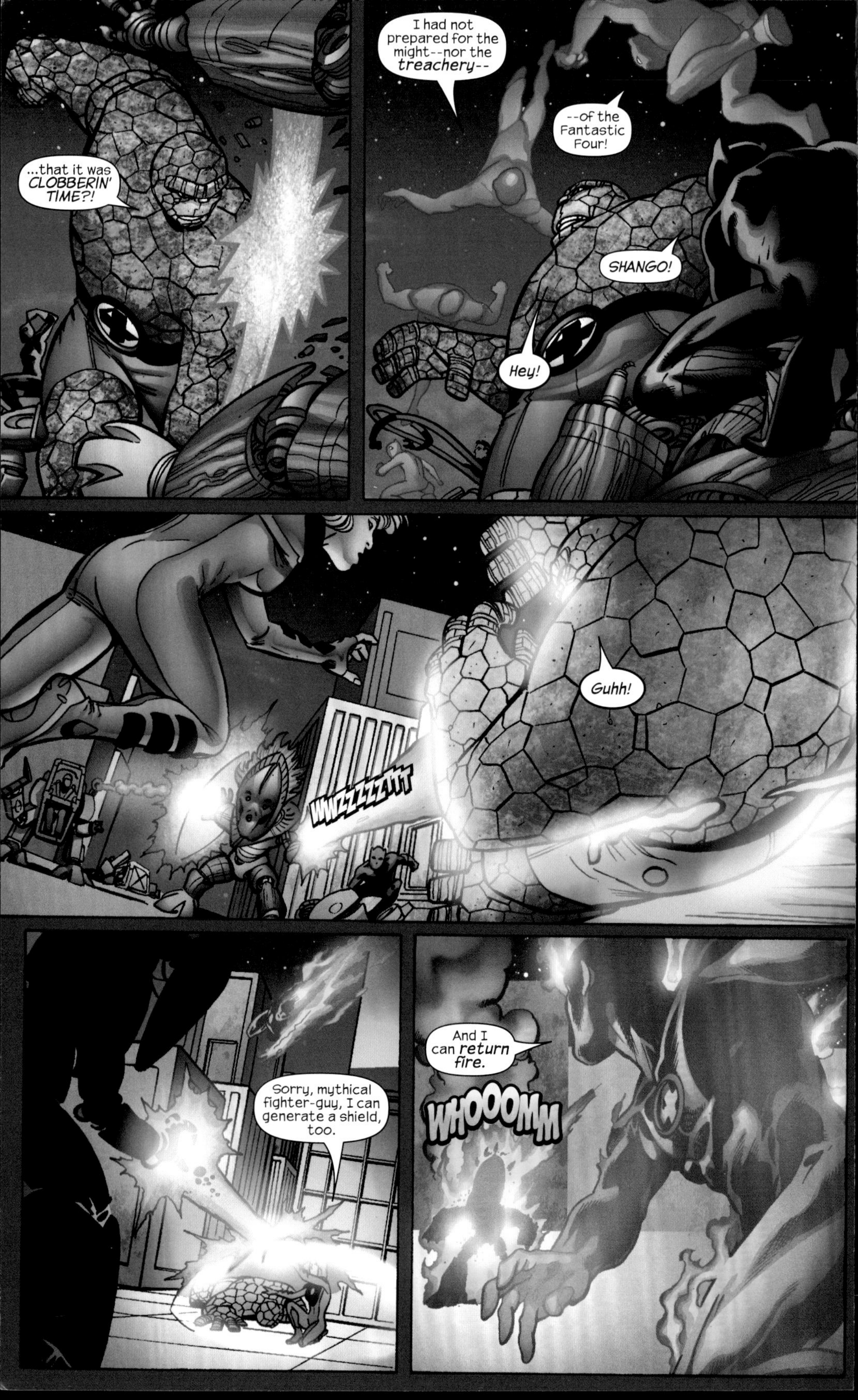
...that it was CLOBBERIN' TIME?!
I had not prepared for the might--nor the treachery--
--of the Fantastic Four!
SHANGO!
Hey!
Guhh!
WWZZZZZTTT
Sorry, mythical fighter-guy, I can generate a shield, too.
And I can return fire.
WHOOOMM

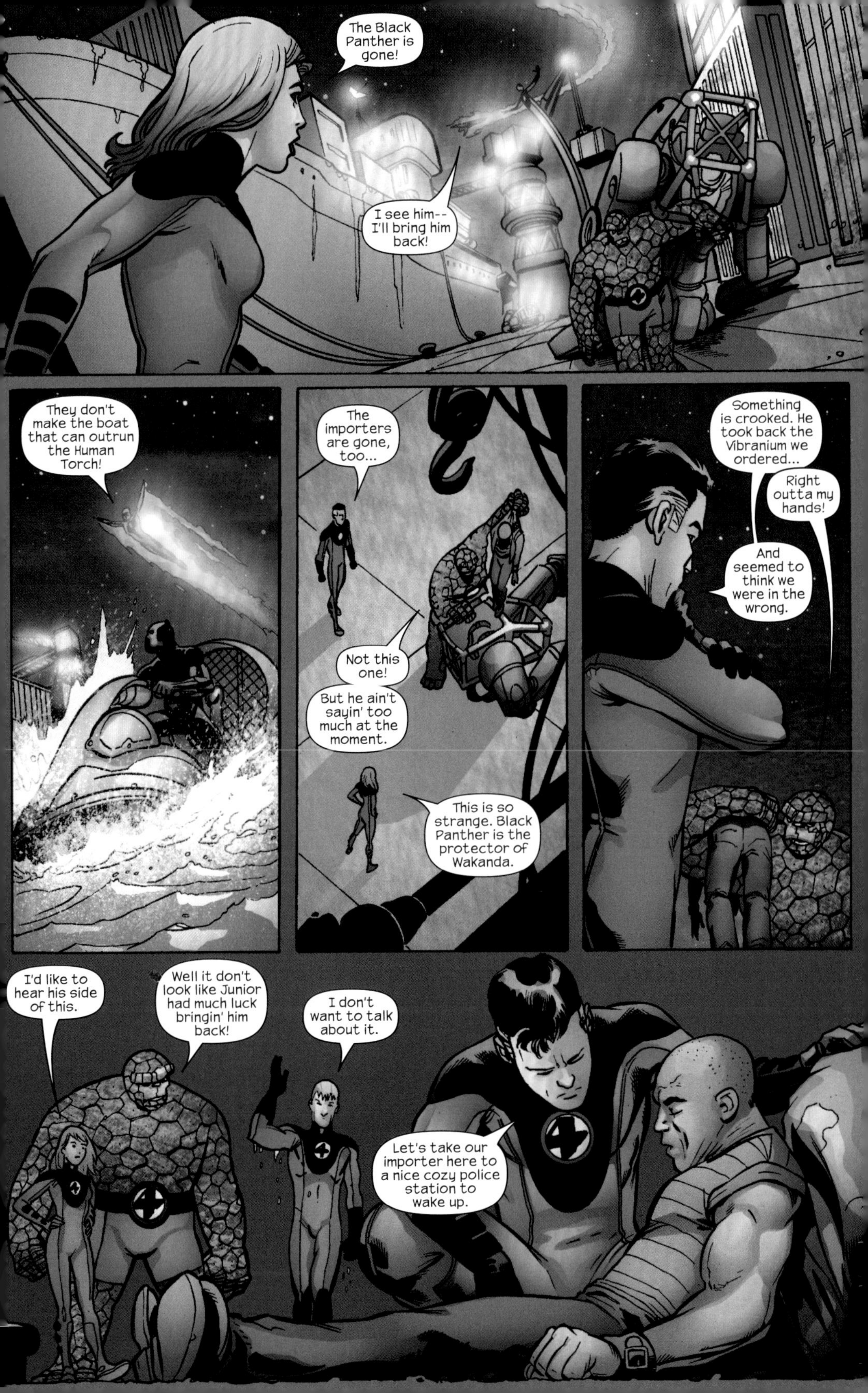
The Black Panther is gone!
I see him-- I'll bring him back!
They don't make the boat that can outrun the Human Torch!
The importers are gone, too...
Not this one!
But he ain't sayin' too much at the moment.
This is so strange. Black Panther is the protector of Wakanda.
Something is crooked. He took back the Vibranium we ordered...
Right outta my hands!
And seemed to think we were in the wrong.
I'd like to hear his side of this.
Well it don't look like Junior had much luck bringin' him back!
I don't want to talk about it.
Let's take our importer here to a nice cozy police station to wake up.

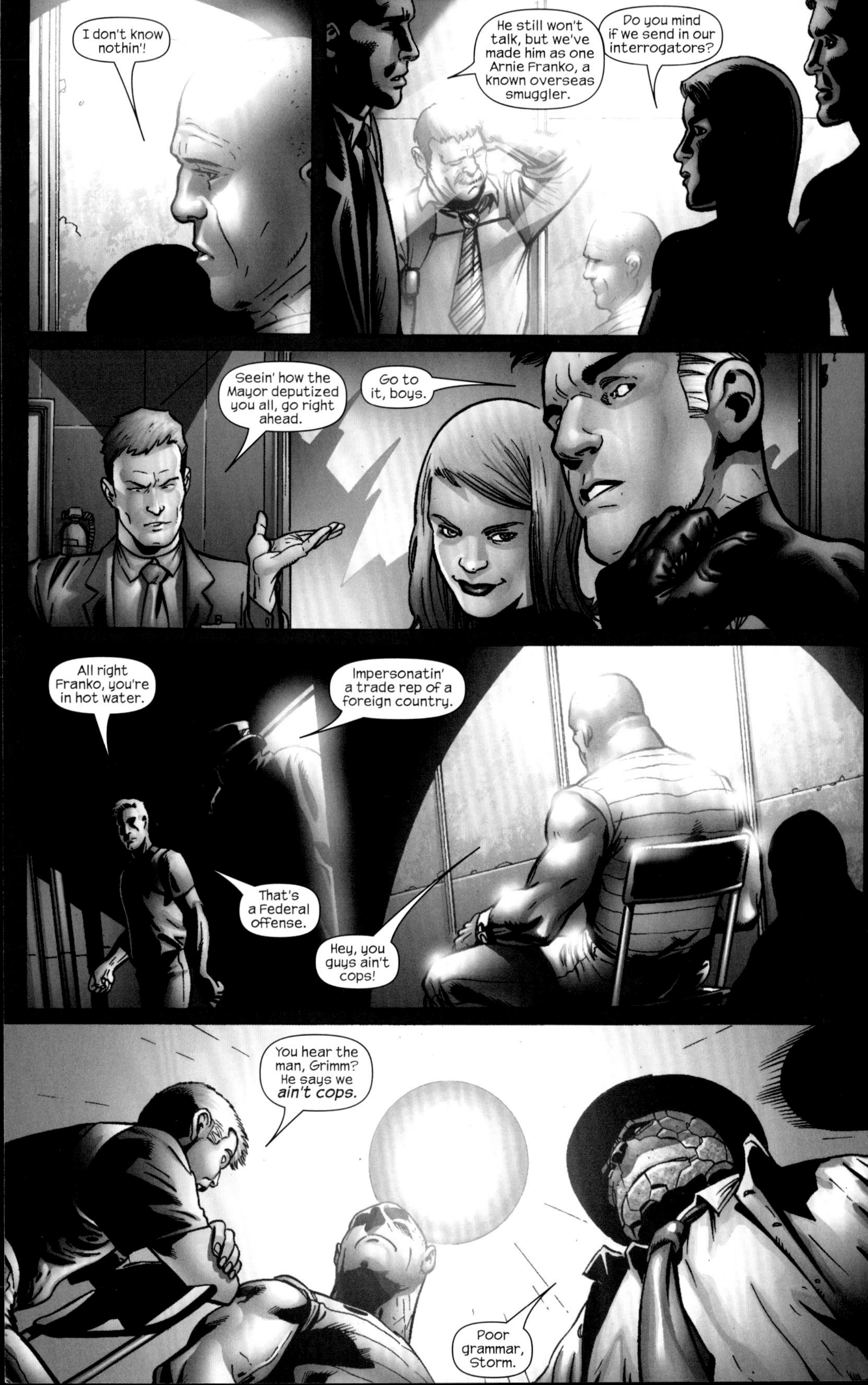

I don't know nothin'!
He still won't talk, but we've made him as one Arnie Franko, a known overseas smuggler.
Do you mind if we send in our interrogators?
Seein' how the Mayor deputized you all, go right ahead.
Go to it, boys.
All right Franko, you're in hot water.
Impersonatin' a trade rep of a foreign country.
That's a Federal offense.
Hey, you guys ain't cops!
You hear the man, Grimm? He says we *ain't cops.*
Poor grammar, Storm.

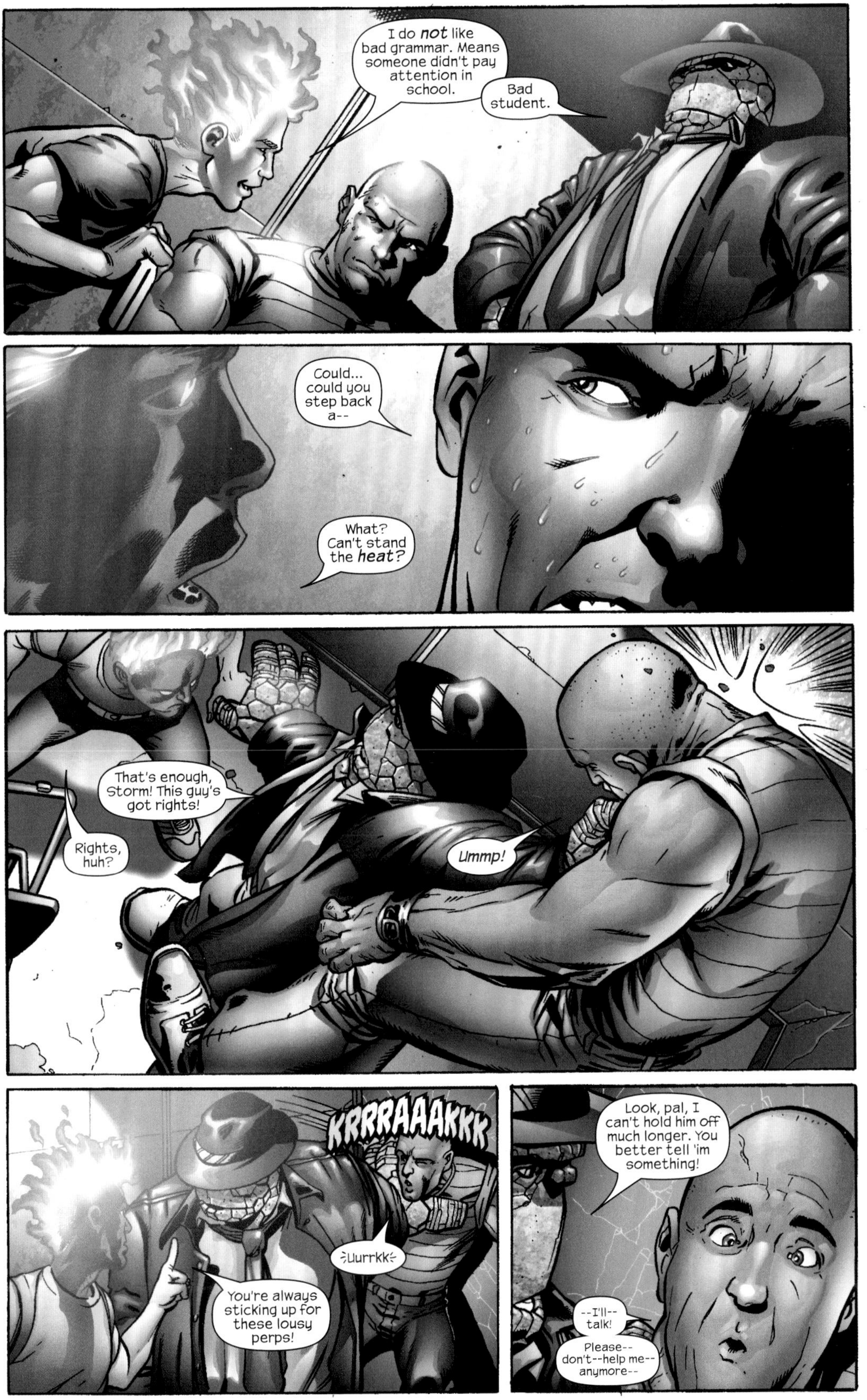

I do not like bad grammar. Means someone didn't pay attention in school.
Bad student.
Could... could you step back a--
What? Can't stand the heat?
That's enough, Storm! This guy's got rights!
Rights, huh?
Ummp!
KRRRAAAKKK
Uurrkk
You're always sticking up for these lousy perps!
Look, pal, I can't hold him off much longer. You better tell 'im something!
--I'll-- talk!
Please-- don't--help me-- anymore--

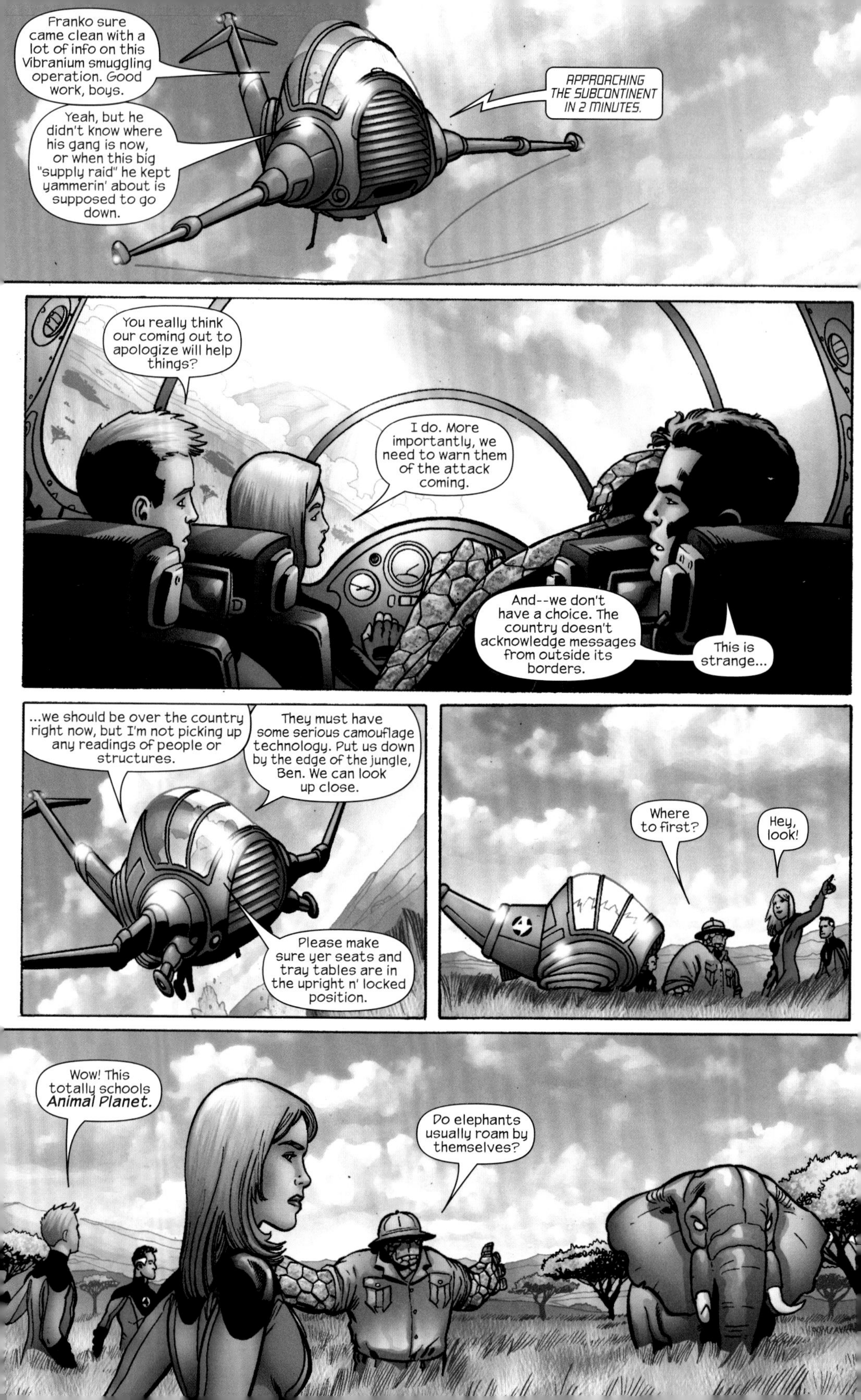
Franko sure came clean with a lot of info on this Vibranium smuggling operation. Good work, boys.
Yeah, but he didn't know where his gang is now, or when this big "supply raid" he kept yammerin' about is supposed to go down.
APPROACHING THE SUBCONTINENT IN 2 MINUTES.
You really think our coming out to apologize will help things?
I do. More importantly, we need to warn them of the attack coming.
And--we don't have a choice. The country doesn't acknowledge messages from outside its borders.
This is strange...
...we should be over the country right now, but I'm not picking up any readings of people or structures.
They must have some serious camouflage technology. Put us down by the edge of the jungle, Ben. We can look up close.
Please make sure yer seats and tray tables are in the upright n' locked position.
Where to first?
Hey, look!
Wow! This totally schools *Animal Planet*.
Do elephants usually roam by themselves?

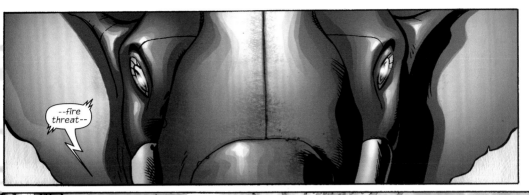

--fire threat--

--coat with non-combustible gel--

Ahgh! I'm always getting gooed!

Hey, that's no--

--elephant-- whoa! All right, buster, you're askin' for it!

Arrrhhh!

ZZZAAPPZZZAAP

Whew!

Let him go, Ele-bot!

Every-one, into the jungle!

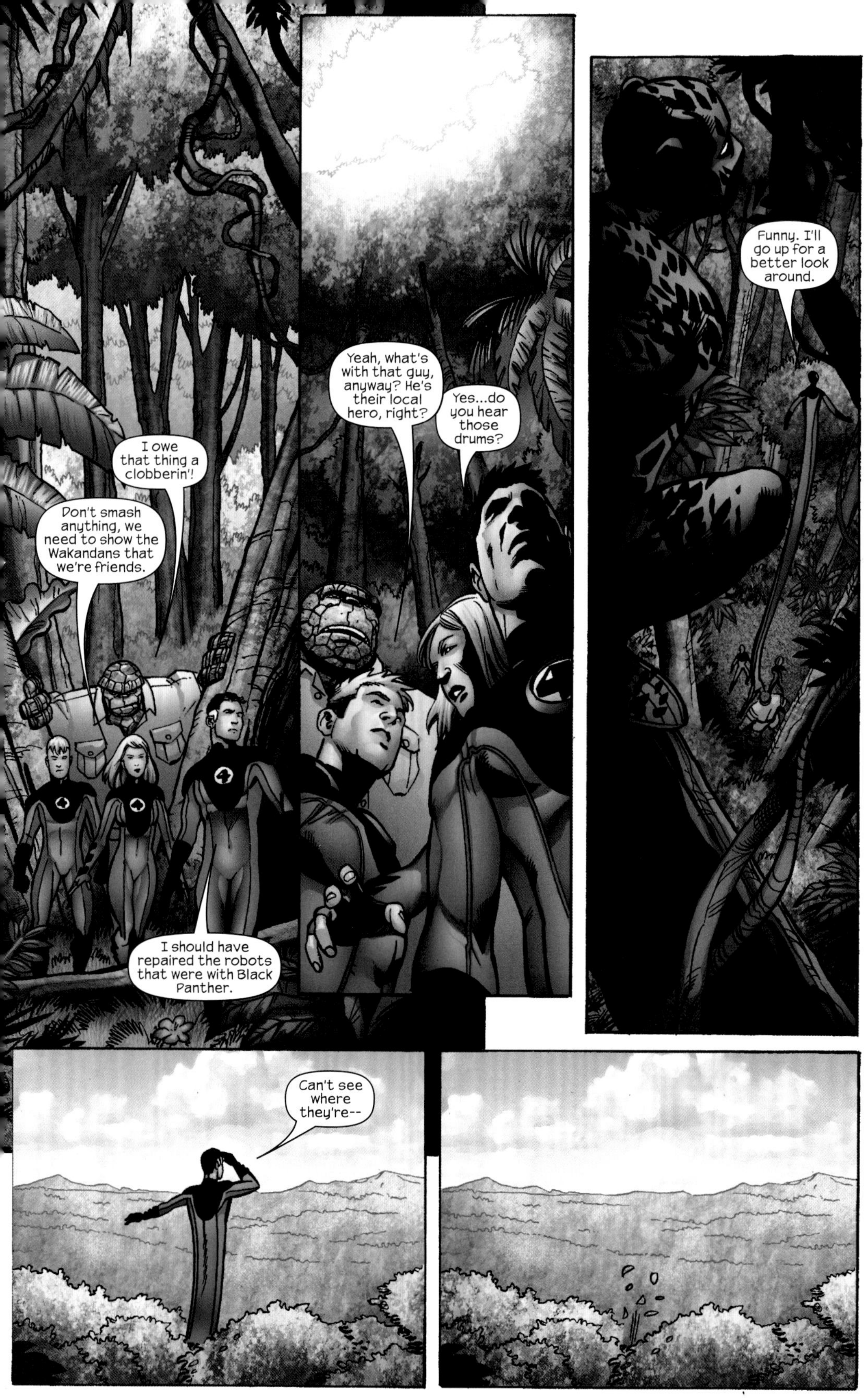
I owe that thing a clobberin'!
Don't smash anything, we need to show the Wakandans that we're friends.
I should have repaired the robots that were with Black Panther.
Yeah, what's with that guy, anyway? He's their local hero, right?
Yes...do you hear those drums?
Funny. I'll go up for a better look around.
Can't see where they're--

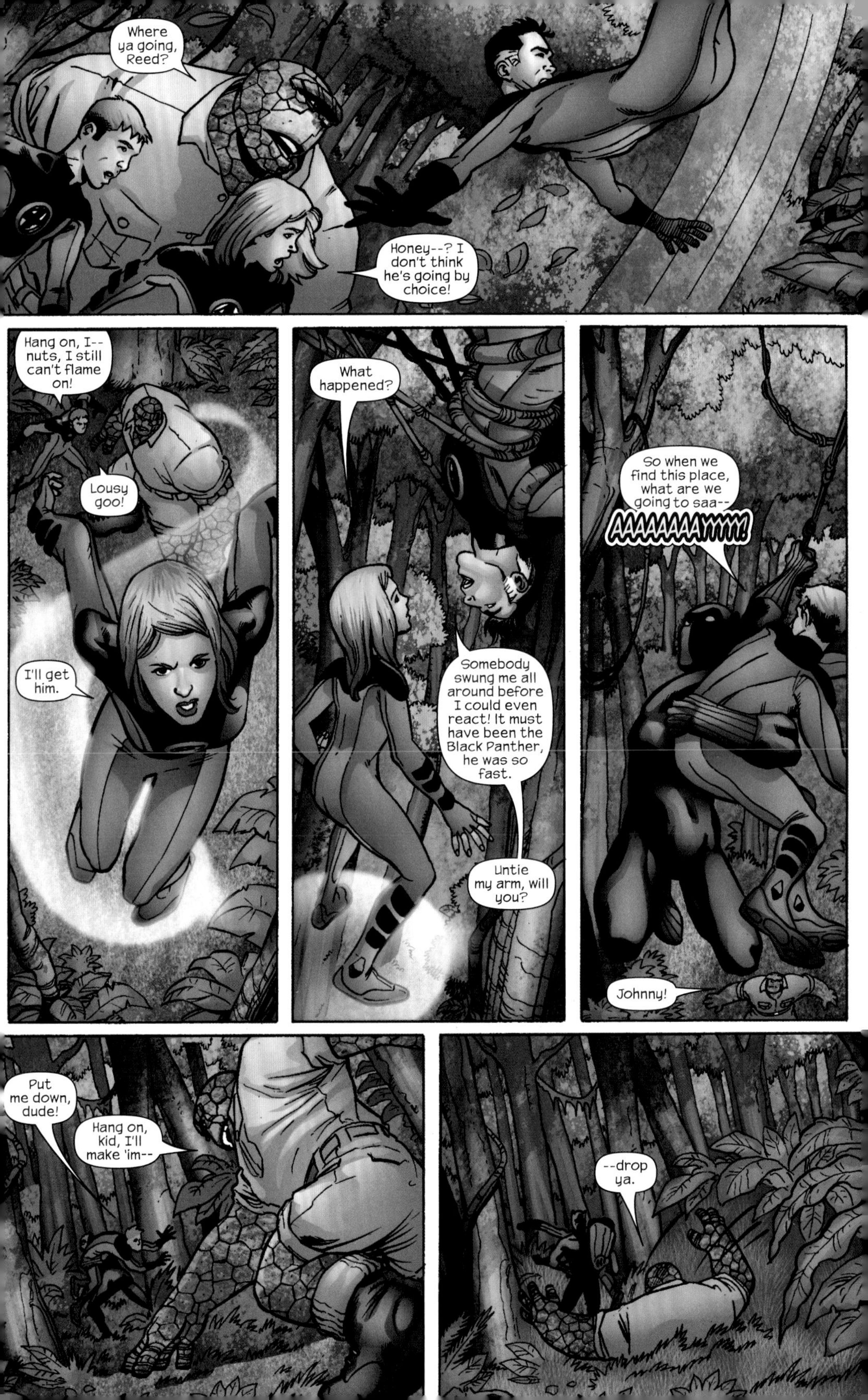
Where ya going, Reed?
Honey--? I don't think he's going by choice!
Hang on, I-- nuts, I still can't flame on!
Lousy goo!
I'll get him.
What happened?
Somebody swung me all around before I could even react! It must have been the Black Panther, he was so fast.
Untie my arm, will you?
So when we find this place, what are we going to saa--
AAAAAAAAYYYY!
Johnny!
Put me down, dude!
Hang on, kid, I'll make 'im--
--drop ya.

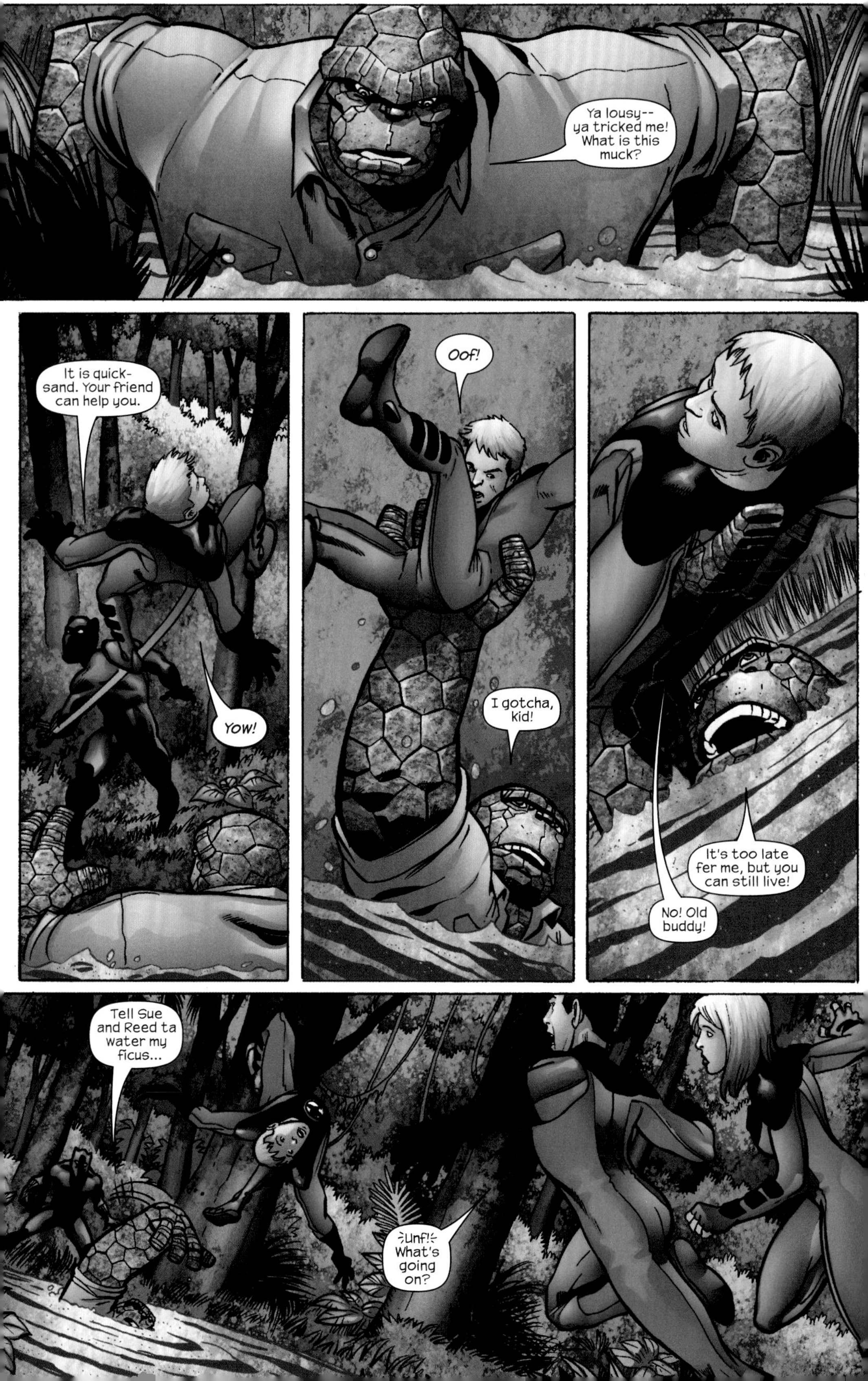

Ya lousy-- ya tricked me! What is this muck?
It is quick-sand. Your friend can help you.
YOW!
Oof!
I gotcha, kid!
It's too late fer me, but you can still live!
No! Old buddy!
Tell Sue and Reed ta water my ficus...
Unf! What's going on?

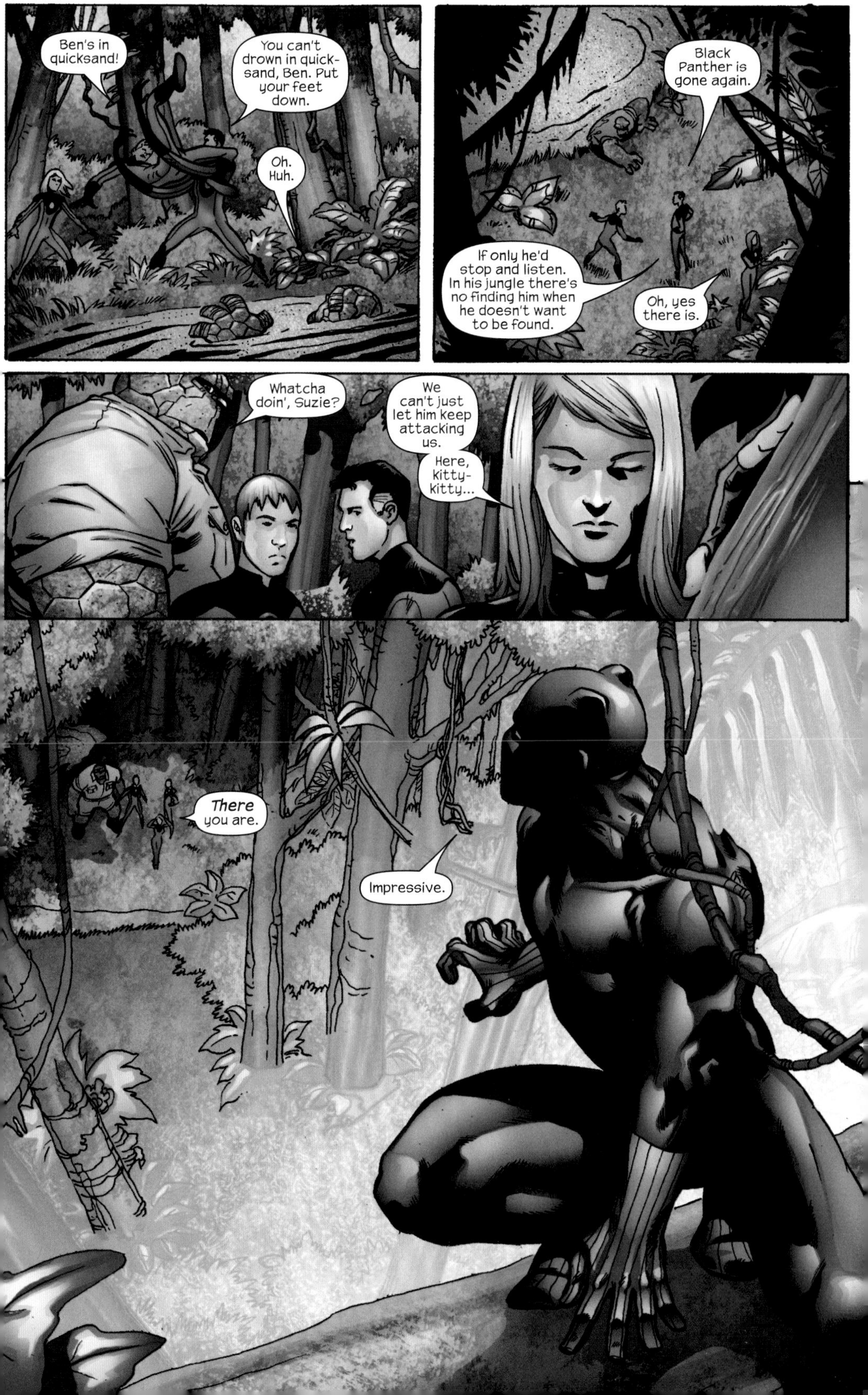
Ben's in quicksand!
You can't drown in quick-sand, Ben. Put your feet down.
Oh. Huh.
Black Panther is gone again.
If only he'd stop and listen. In his jungle there's no finding him when he doesn't want to be found.
Oh, yes there is.
Whatcha doin', Suzie?
We can't just let him keep attacking us.
Here, kitty-kitty...
There you are.
Impressive.

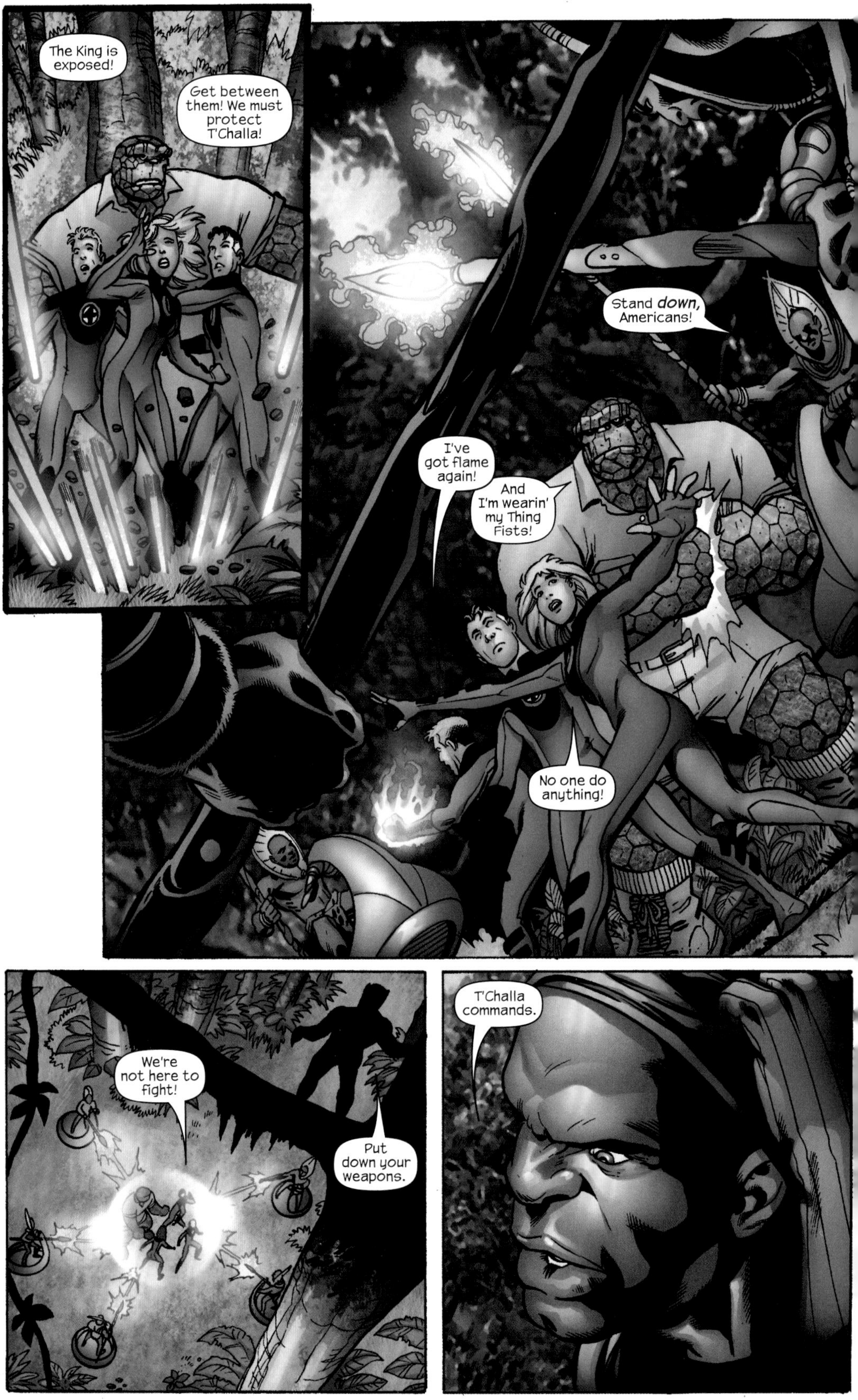
The King is exposed!
Get between them! We must protect T'Challa!
Stand *down,* Americans!
I've got flame again!
And I'm wearin' my Thing Fists!
No one do anything!
We're not here to fight!
Put down your weapons.
T'Challa commands.

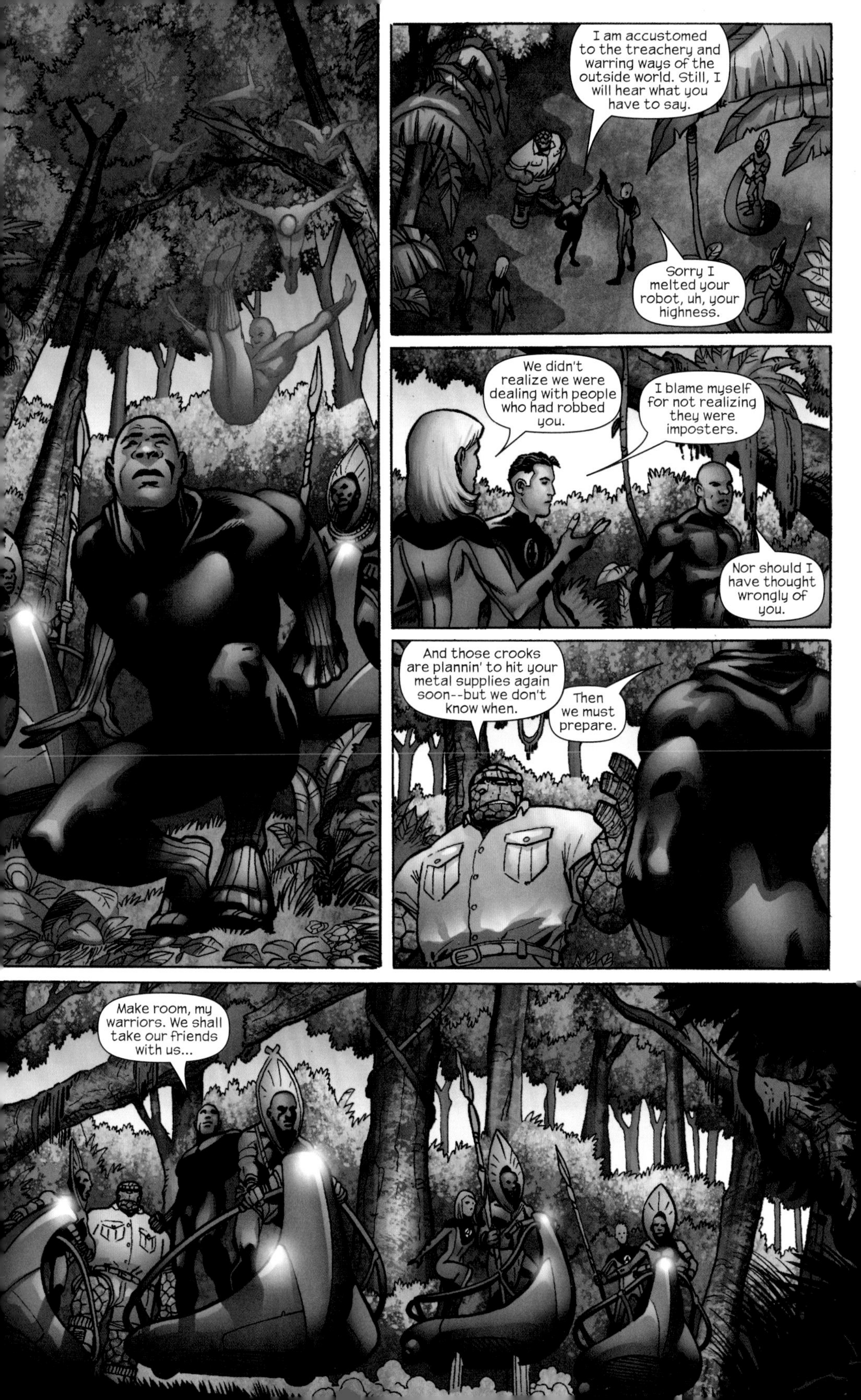
I am accustomed to the treachery and warring ways of the outside world. Still, I will hear what you have to say.
Sorry I melted your robot, uh, your highness.
We didn't realize we were dealing with people who had robbed you.
I blame myself for not realizing they were imposters.
Nor should I have thought wrongly of you.
And those crooks are plannin' to hit your metal supplies again soon--but we don't know when.
Then we must prepare.
Make room, my warriors. We shall take our friends with us...

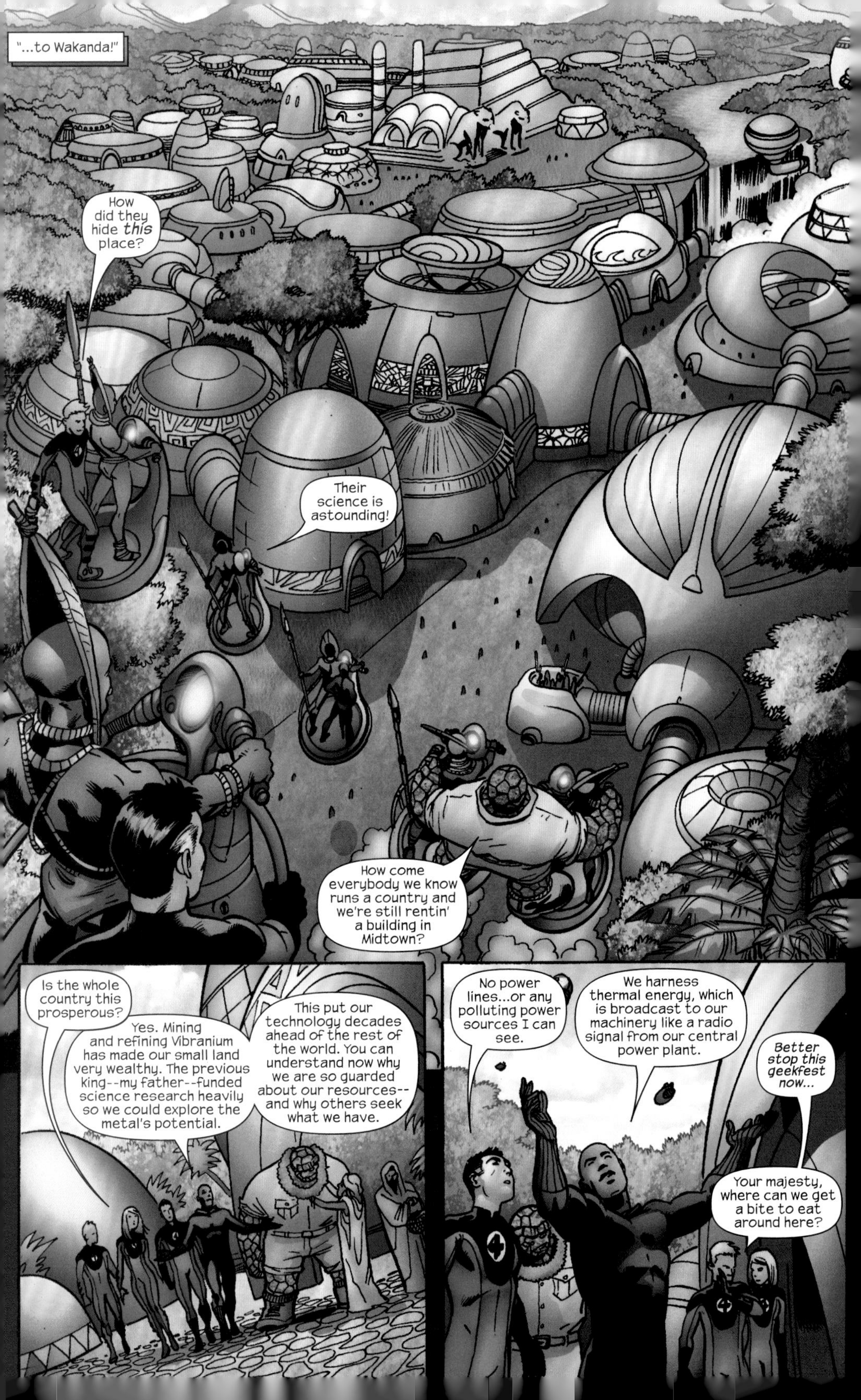
"...to Wakanda!"
How did they hide *this* place?
Their science is astounding!
How come everybody we know runs a country and we're still rentin' a building in Midtown?
Is the whole country this prosperous?
Yes. Mining and refining Vibranium has made our small land very wealthy. The previous king--my father--funded science research heavily so we could explore the metal's potential.
This put our technology decades ahead of the rest of the world. You can understand now why we are so guarded about our resources--and why others seek what we have.
No power lines...or any polluting power sources I can see.
We harness thermal energy, which is broadcast to our machinery like a radio signal from our central power plant.
*Better stop this geekfest now...*
Your majesty, where can we get a bite to eat around here?

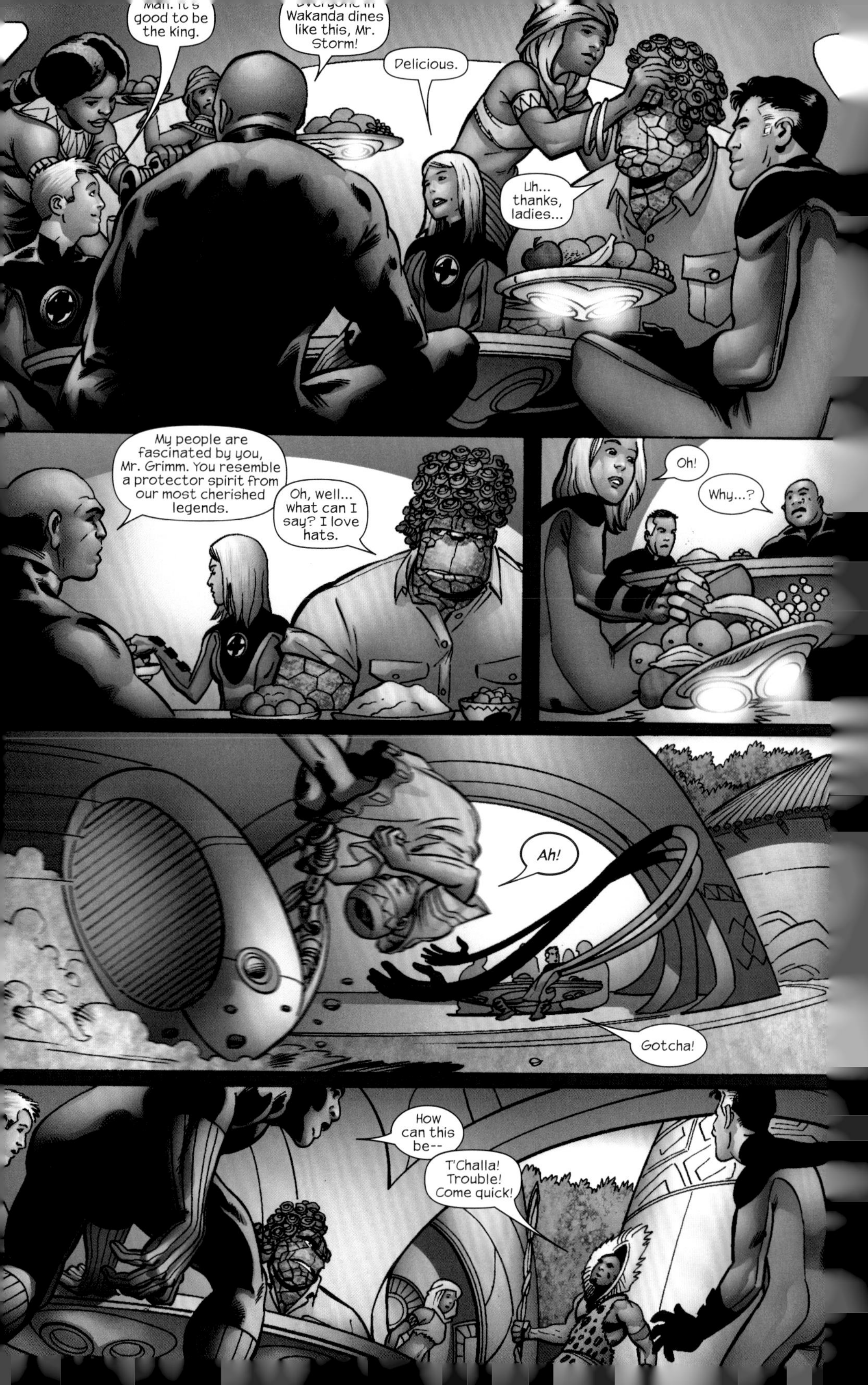
good to be
the king.
Wakanda dines
like this, Mr.
Storm!
Delicious.
Uh...
thanks,
ladies...
My people are fascinated by you, Mr. Grimm. You resemble a protector spirit from our most cherished legends.
Oh, well... what can I say? I love hats.
Oh!
Why...?
Ah!
Gotcha!
How can this be--
T'Challa! Trouble! Come quick!

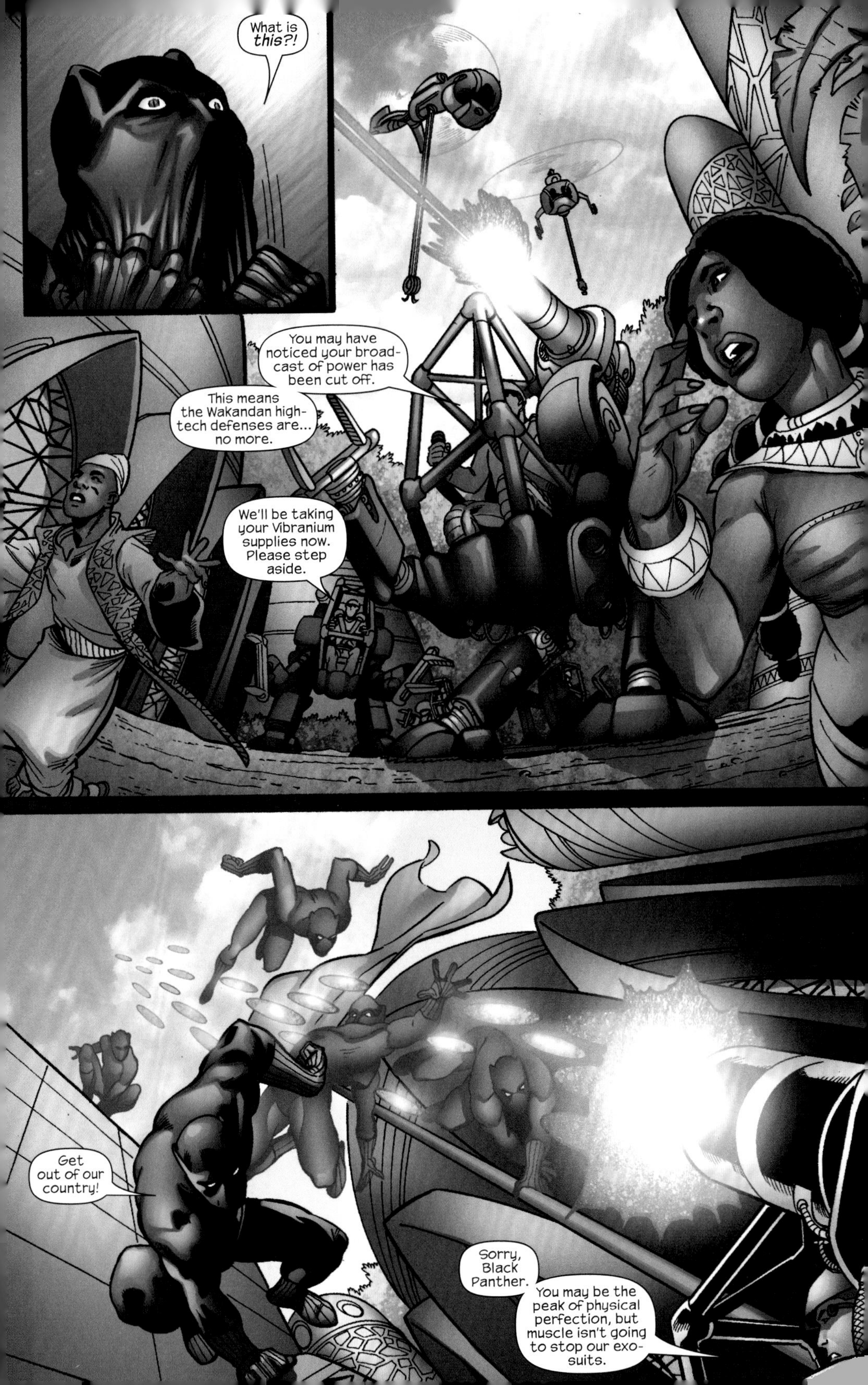
What is this?!
You may have noticed your broad-cast of power has been cut off.
This means the Wakandan high-tech defenses are... no more.
We'll be taking your Vibranium supplies now. Please step aside.
Get out of our country!
Sorry, Black Panther.
You may be the peak of physical perfection, but muscle isn't going to stop our exo-suits.

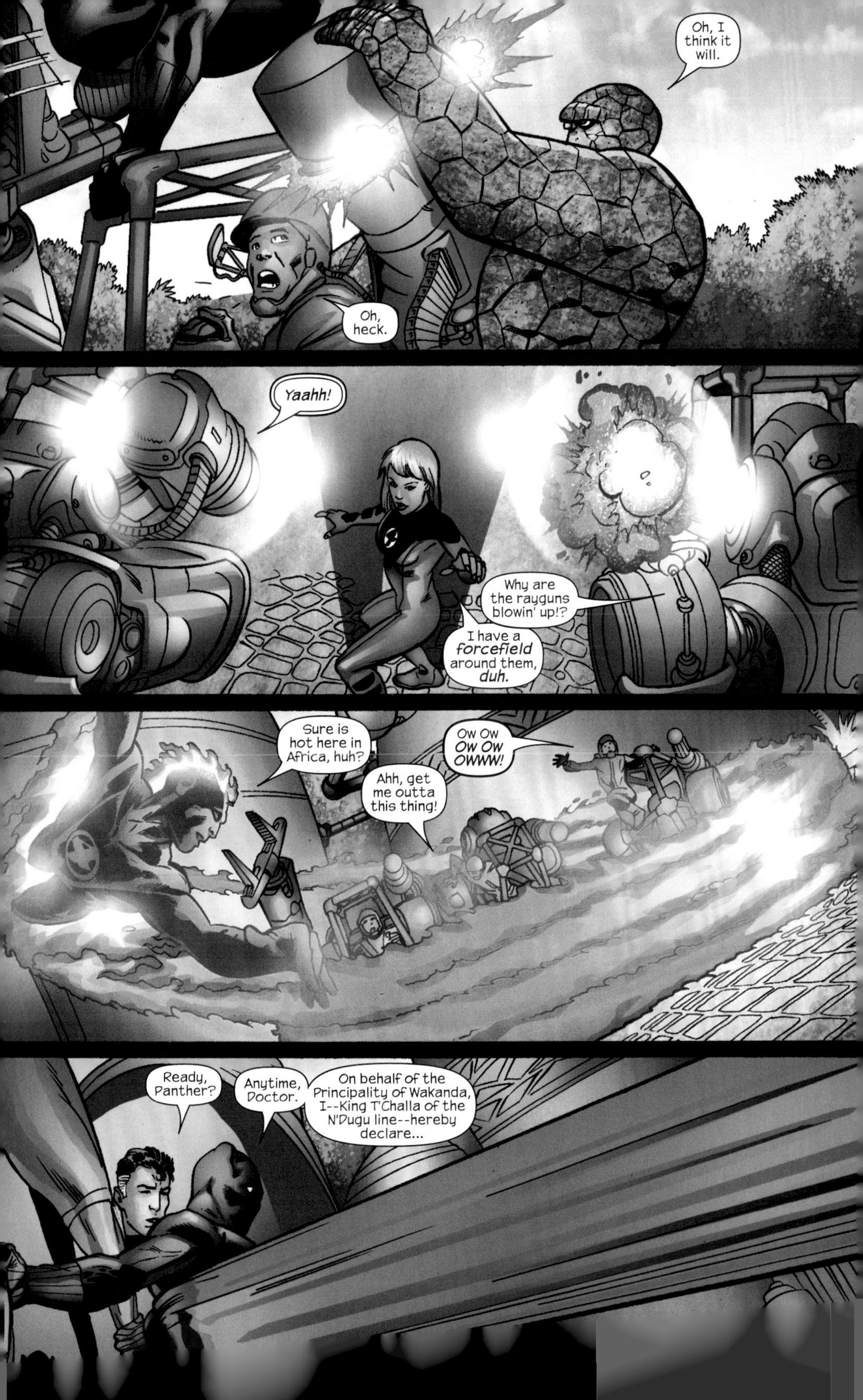

Oh, I think it will.
Oh, heck.
Yaahh!
Why are the rayguns blowin' up!?
I have a *forcefield* around them, *duh.*
Sure is hot here in Africa, huh?
Ow Ow *Ow Ow OWWW!*
Ahh, get me outta this thing!
Ready, Panther?
Anytime, Doctor.
On behalf of the Principality of Wakanda, I--King T'Challa of the N'Dugu line--hereby declare...

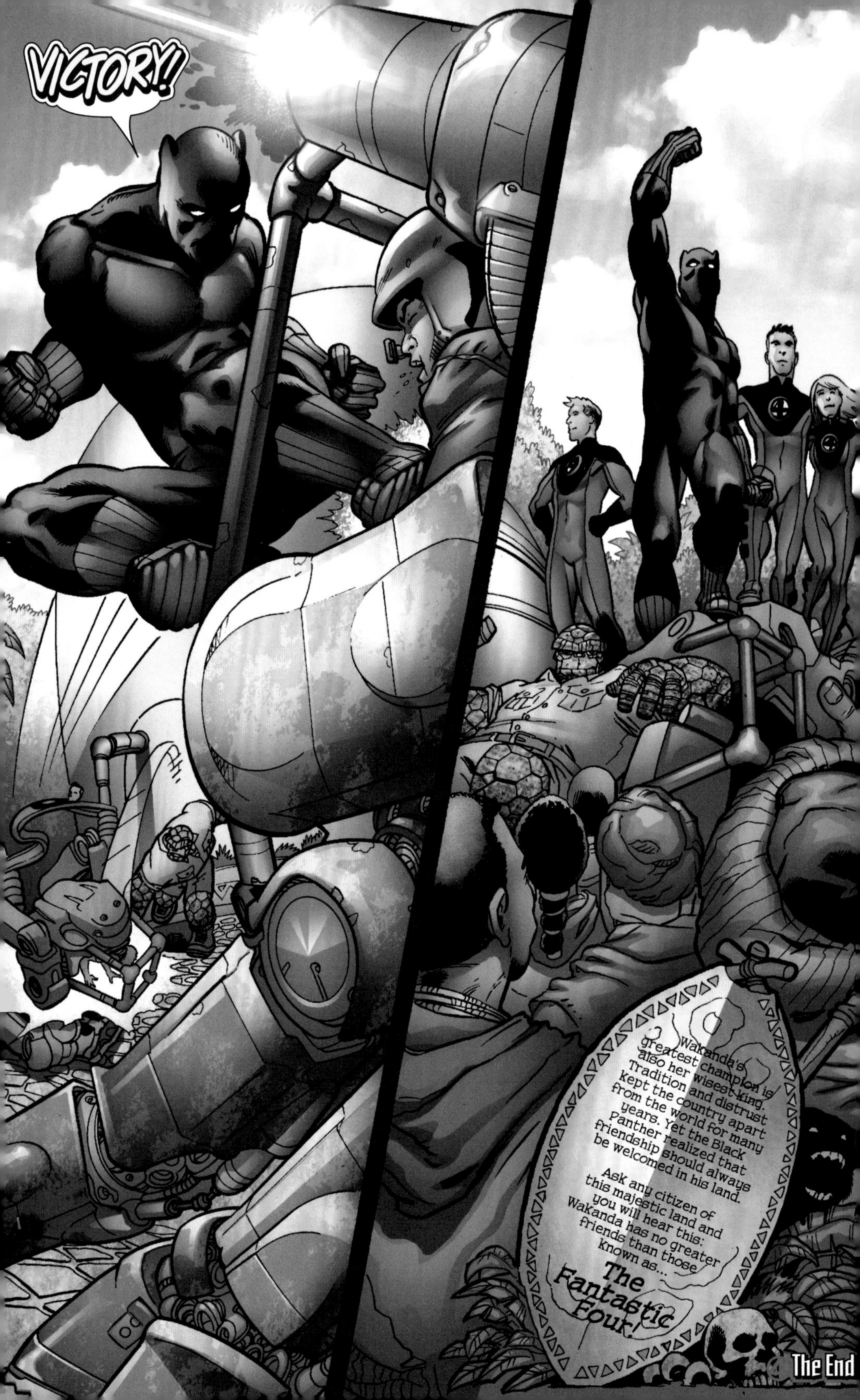
VICTORY!
Wakanda's greatest champion is also her wisest king. Tradition and distrust kept the country apart from the world for many years. Yet the Black Panther realized that friendship should always be welcomed in his land.
Ask any citizen of this majestic land and you will hear this: Wakanda has no greater friends than those known as...
The Fantastic Four!
The End

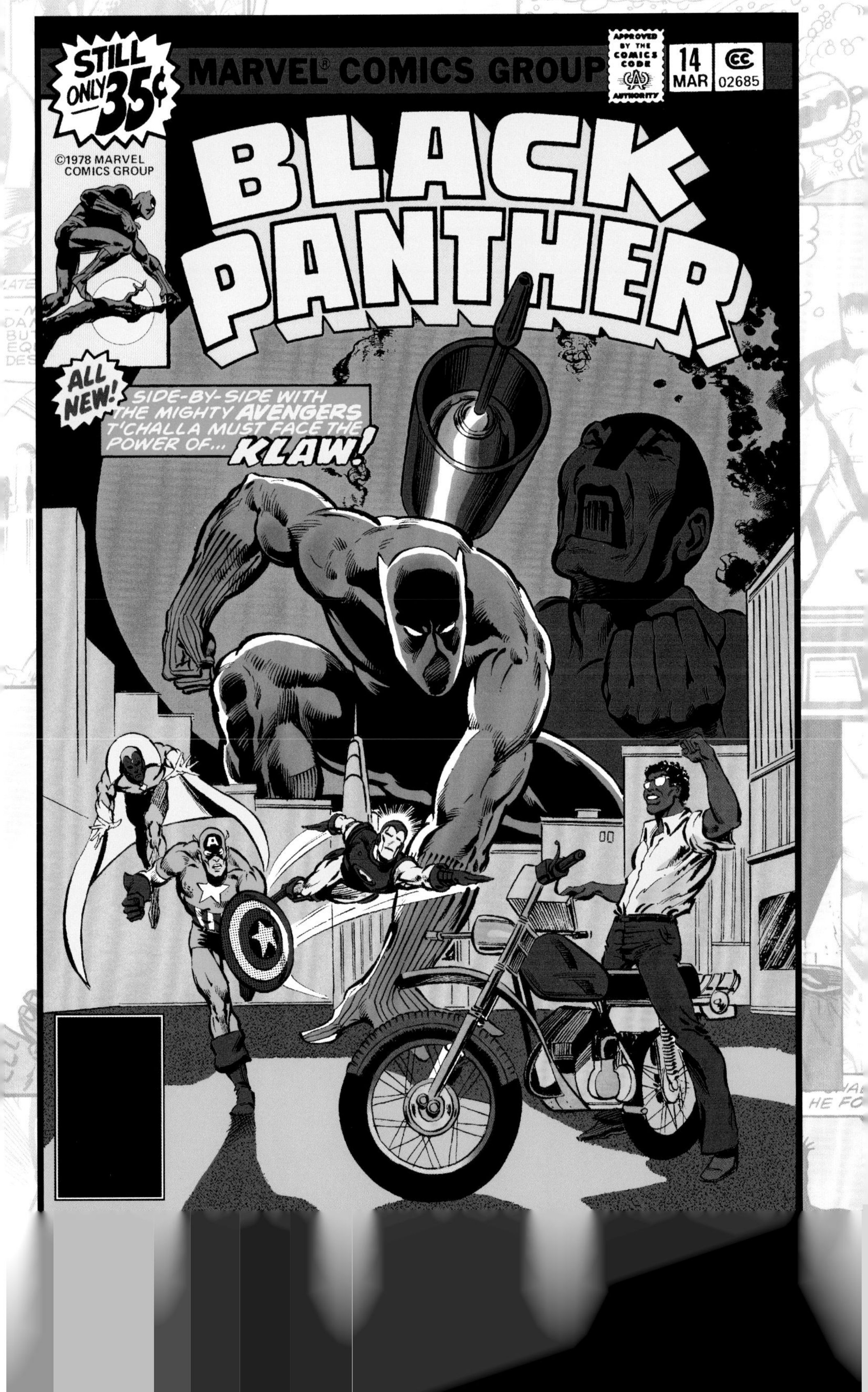
STILL ONLY 35¢
MARVEL® COMICS GROUP
APPROVED BY THE COMICS CODE AUTHORITY
14 MAR
CC 02685
©1978 MARVEL COMICS GROUP
BLACK PANTHER
ALL NEW!
SIDE-BY-SIDE WITH THE MIGHTY AVENGERS T'CHALLA MUST FACE THE POWER OF... KLAW!

With the sleekness of a jungle beast, the Prince of Wakanda stalks both the concrete of the city and the undergrowth of the veldt, for when danger lurks he dons the garb of the savage cat from which he gains his name!

# Stan Lee PRESENTS: THE BLACK PANTHER!™

ED HANNIGAN WRITER / JERRY BINGHAM PENCILER / GENE DAY INKER / RICK PARKER letterer / NELSON YOMTOV colorist / ROGER STERN EDITOR / JIM SHOOTER ED.-IN-CHIEF

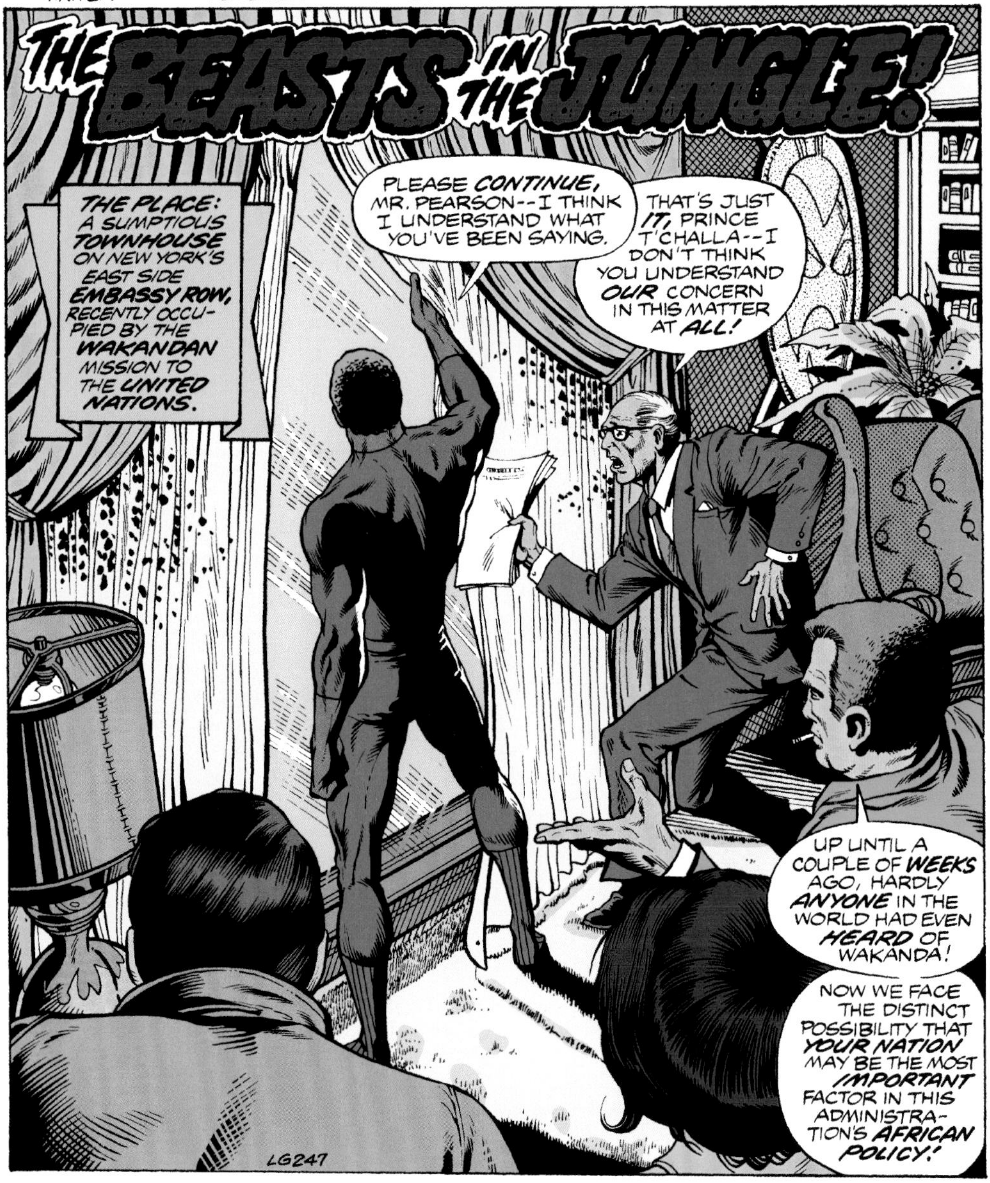
THE BEASTS IN THE JUNGLE!
THE PLACE: A SUMPTIOUS TOWNHOUSE ON NEW YORK'S EAST SIDE EMBASSY ROW, RECENTLY OCCUPIED BY THE WAKANDAN MISSION TO THE UNITED NATIONS.
PLEASE CONTINUE, MR. PEARSON--I THINK I UNDERSTAND WHAT YOU'VE BEEN SAYING.
THAT'S JUST IT, PRINCE T'CHALLA--I DON'T THINK YOU UNDERSTAND OUR CONCERN IN THIS MATTER AT ALL!
UP UNTIL A COUPLE OF WEEKS AGO, HARDLY ANYONE IN THE WORLD HAD EVEN HEARD OF WAKANDA!
NOW WE FACE THE DISTINCT POSSIBILITY THAT YOUR NATION MAY BE THE MOST IMPORTANT FACTOR IN THIS ADMINISTRATION'S AFRICAN POLICY!
LG247

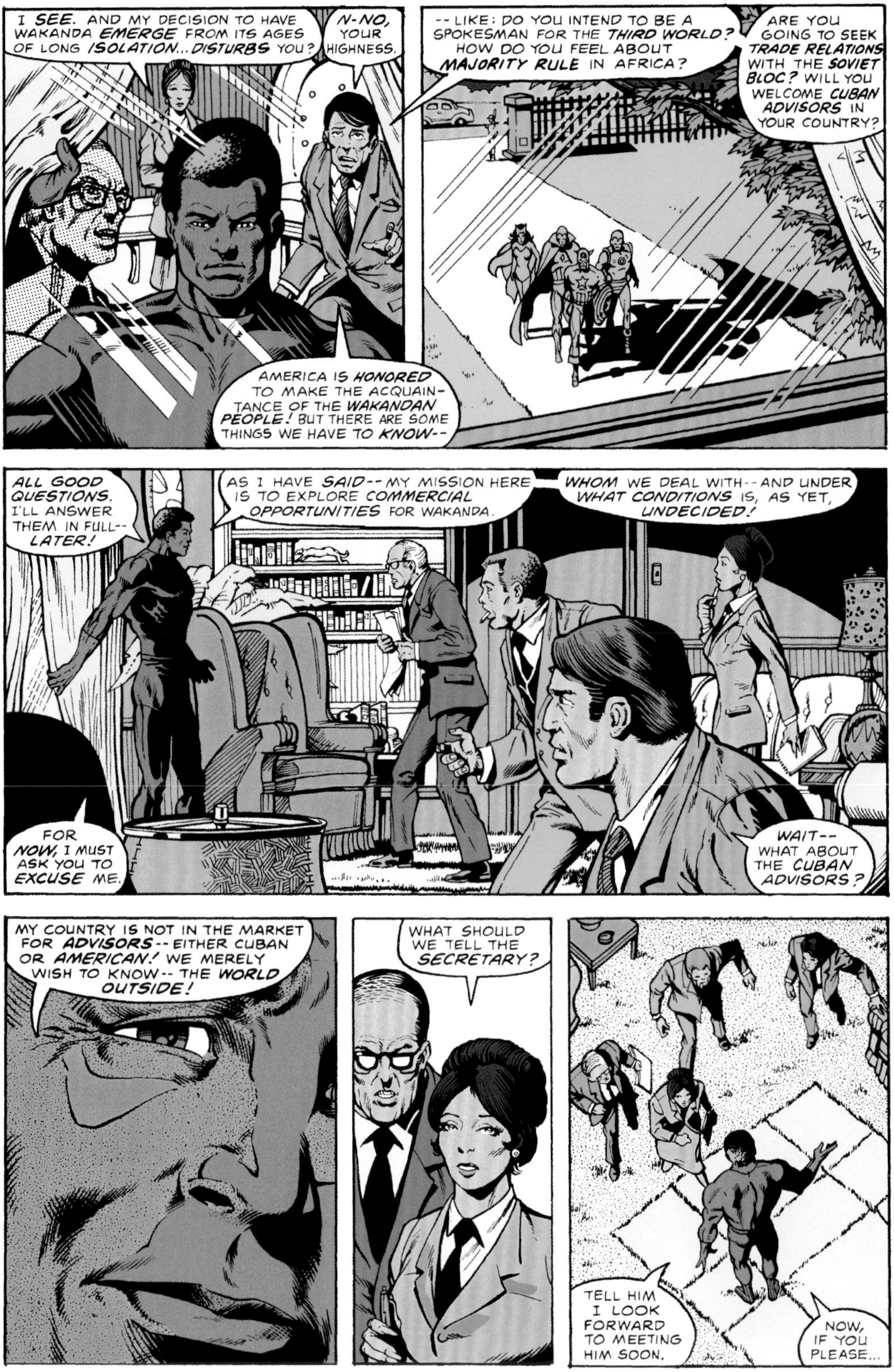
I SEE. AND MY DECISION TO HAVE WAKANDA EMERGE FROM ITS AGES OF LONG ISOLATION... DISTURBS YOU?
N-NO, YOUR HIGHNESS.
AMERICA IS HONORED TO MAKE THE ACQUAINTANCE OF THE WAKANDAN PEOPLE! BUT THERE ARE SOME THINGS WE HAVE TO KNOW--
--LIKE: DO YOU INTEND TO BE A SPOKESMAN FOR THE THIRD WORLD? HOW DO YOU FEEL ABOUT MAJORITY RULE IN AFRICA?
ARE YOU GOING TO SEEK TRADE RELATIONS WITH THE SOVIET BLOC? WILL YOU WELCOME CUBAN ADVISORS IN YOUR COUNTRY?
ALL GOOD QUESTIONS. I'LL ANSWER THEM IN FULL-- LATER!
AS I HAVE SAID-- MY MISSION HERE IS TO EXPLORE COMMERCIAL OPPORTUNITIES FOR WAKANDA.
WHOM WE DEAL WITH-- AND UNDER WHAT CONDITIONS IS, AS YET, UNDECIDED!
FOR NOW, I MUST ASK YOU TO EXCUSE ME.
WAIT-- WHAT ABOUT THE CUBAN ADVISORS?
MY COUNTRY IS NOT IN THE MARKET FOR ADVISORS-- EITHER CUBAN OR AMERICAN! WE MERELY WISH TO KNOW-- THE WORLD OUTSIDE!
WHAT SHOULD WE TELL THE SECRETARY?
TELL HIM I LOOK FORWARD TO MEETING HIM SOON.
NOW, IF YOU PLEASE...

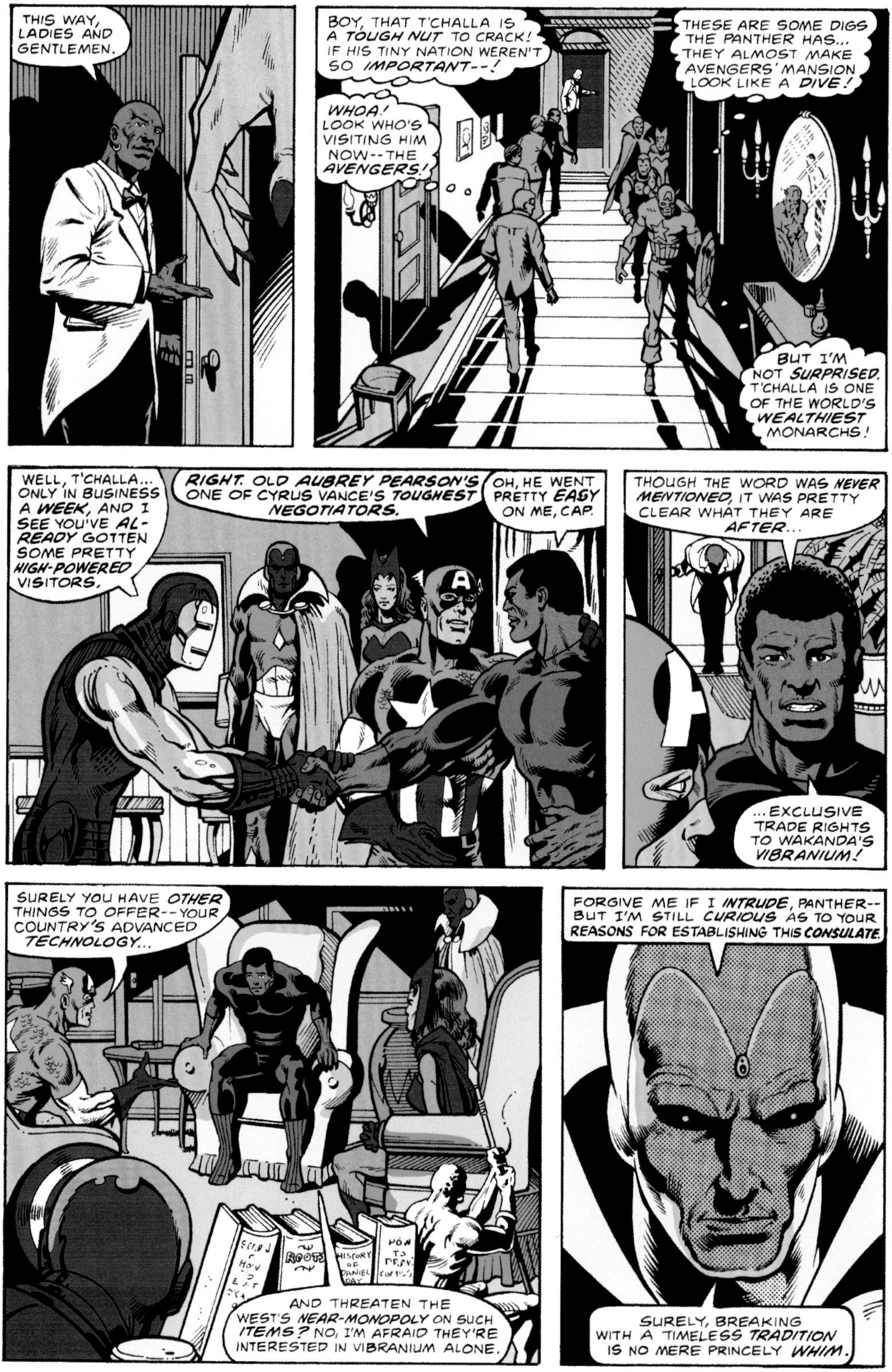
THIS WAY, LADIES AND GENTLEMEN.
BOY, THAT T'CHALLA IS A TOUGH NUT TO CRACK! IF HIS TINY NATION WEREN'T SO IMPORTANT--!
WHOA! LOOK WHO'S VISITING HIM NOW--THE AVENGERS!
THESE ARE SOME DIGS THE PANTHER HAS... THEY ALMOST MAKE AVENGERS' MANSION LOOK LIKE A DIVE!
BUT I'M NOT SURPRISED. T'CHALLA IS ONE OF THE WORLD'S WEALTHIEST MONARCHS!
WELL, T'CHALLA... ONLY IN BUSINESS A WEEK, AND I SEE YOU'VE AL-READY GOTTEN SOME PRETTY HIGH-POWERED VISITORS.
RIGHT. OLD AUBREY PEARSON'S ONE OF CYRUS VANCE'S TOUGHEST NEGOTIATORS.
OH, HE WENT PRETTY EASY ON ME, CAP.
THOUGH THE WORD WAS NEVER MENTIONED, IT WAS PRETTY CLEAR WHAT THEY ARE AFTER...
...EXCLUSIVE TRADE RIGHTS TO WAKANDA'S VIBRANIUM!
SURELY YOU HAVE OTHER THINGS TO OFFER--YOUR COUNTRY'S ADVANCED TECHNOLOGY...
ROOTS
AND THREATEN THE WEST'S NEAR-MONOPOLY ON SUCH ITEMS? NO, I'M AFRAID THEY'RE INTERESTED IN VIBRANIUM ALONE.
FORGIVE ME IF I INTRUDE, PANTHER--BUT I'M STILL CURIOUS AS TO YOUR REASONS FOR ESTABLISHING THIS CONSULATE.
SURELY, BREAKING WITH A TIMELESS TRADITION IS NO MERE PRINCELY WHIM.

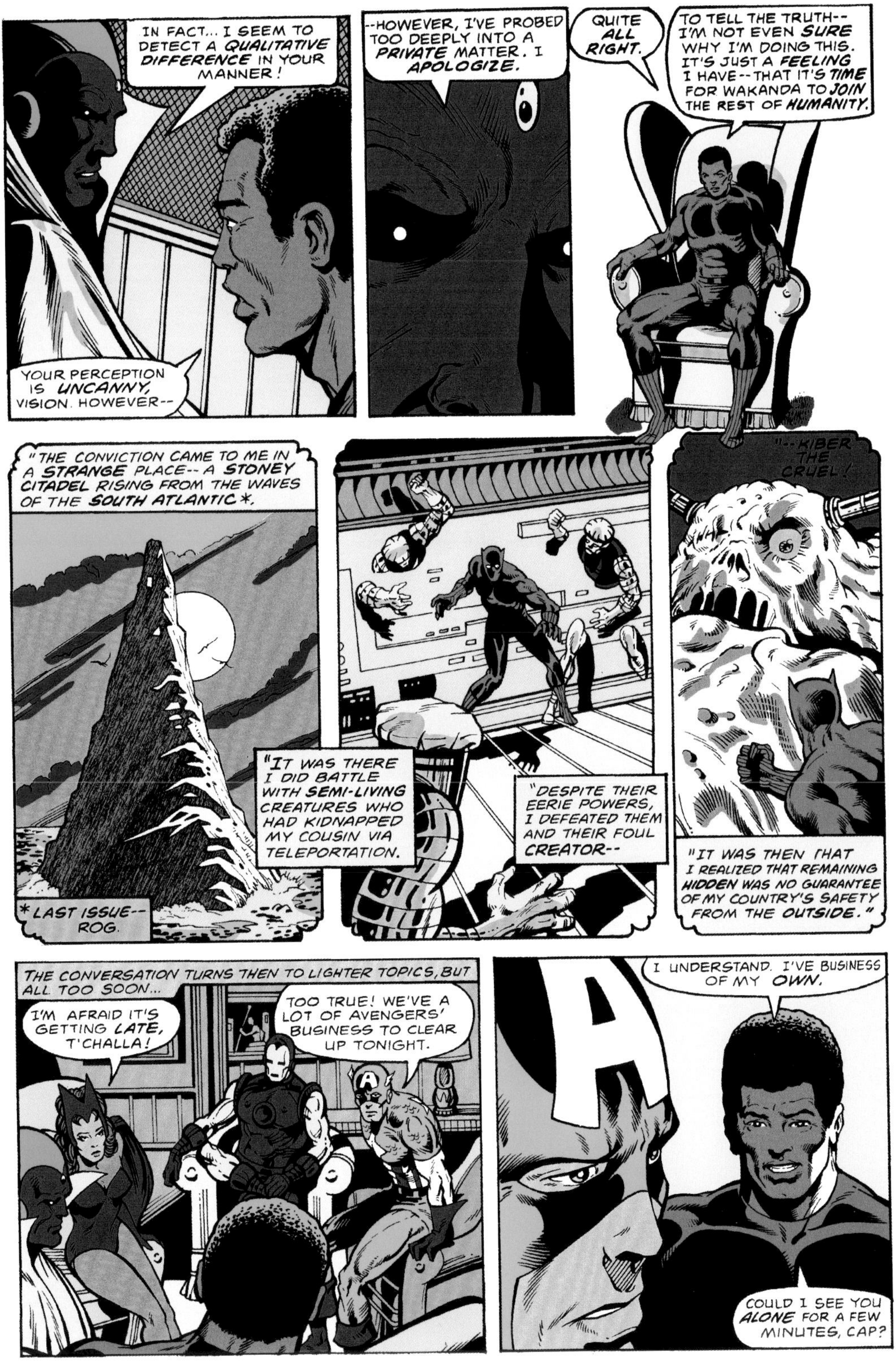

IN FACT... I SEEM TO DETECT A QUALITATIVE DIFFERENCE IN YOUR MANNER!
YOUR PERCEPTION IS UNCANNY, VISION. HOWEVER--
--HOWEVER, I'VE PROBED TOO DEEPLY INTO A PRIVATE MATTER. I APOLOGIZE.
QUITE ALL RIGHT.
TO TELL THE TRUTH-- I'M NOT EVEN SURE WHY I'M DOING THIS. IT'S JUST A FEELING I HAVE--THAT IT'S TIME FOR WAKANDA TO JOIN THE REST OF HUMANITY.
"THE CONVICTION CAME TO ME IN A STRANGE PLACE-- A STONEY CITADEL RISING FROM THE WAVES OF THE SOUTH ATLANTIC*.
"IT WAS THERE I DID BATTLE WITH SEMI-LIVING CREATURES WHO HAD KIDNAPPED MY COUSIN VIA TELEPORTATION.
*LAST ISSUE-- ROG.
"DESPITE THEIR EERIE POWERS, I DEFEATED THEM AND THEIR FOUL CREATOR--
"--KIBER THE CRUEL!
"IT WAS THEN THAT I REALIZED THAT REMAINING HIDDEN WAS NO GUARANTEE OF MY COUNTRY'S SAFETY FROM THE OUTSIDE."
THE CONVERSATION TURNS THEN TO LIGHTER TOPICS, BUT ALL TOO SOON...
I'M AFRAID IT'S GETTING LATE, T'CHALLA!
TOO TRUE! WE'VE A LOT OF AVENGERS' BUSINESS TO CLEAR UP TONIGHT.
I UNDERSTAND. I'VE BUSINESS OF MY OWN.
COULD I SEE YOU ALONE FOR A FEW MINUTES, CAP?

WHAT'S UP, PANTHER? I COULD SENSE YOUR *UNEASINESS* ALL EVENING.

THE *VISION* ALMOST PUT HIS FINGER ON IT. I *HAVE* UNDERGONE A *CHANGE*...

A CHANGE THAT WAS BROUGHT ABOUT BY WAKANDA'S RECENT *VIBRANIUM CRISIS.**

*B.P. #7-10 --ROG.

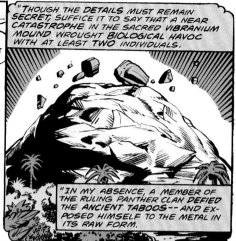

"THOUGH THE *DETAILS* MUST REMAIN *SECRET,* SUFFICE IT TO SAY THAT A *NEAR CATASTROPHE* IN THE SACRED *VIBRANIUM MOUND* WROUGHT *BIOLOGICAL HAVOC* WITH AT LEAST *TWO* INDIVIDUALS."

"IN MY *ABSENCE,* A MEMBER OF THE RULING PANTHER CLAN *DEFIED* THE ANCIENT TABOOS -- AND EX-POSED HIMSELF TO THE METAL IN ITS RAW FORM."

"ITS UNEARTHLY EMANATIONS TRANSFORMED THE UNWARY FOOL INTO A *RAMPAGING MONSTER.*"

"IN THE MIDST OF OUR *FINAL BATTLE,* I WAS ALSO EXPOSED TO THE RAW ORE. * "

*ISSUE #10 --ROG.

AS A RESULT, MY NATURAL IN-STINCTS WERE...*HEIGHTENED.* IT'S NOT LIKE TELEPATHY OR CLAIRVOYANCE -- I JUST... *FEEL* THINGS, SENSE *CRISIS POINTS.*

ARE YOU TRY-ING TO TELL ME YOU HAVE THESE *FEELINGS* -- ABOUT *WAKANDA?*

YES! WAKANDA, AFRICA -- AND THE *WORLD.* THINGS ARE GOING TO *HAPPEN,* AND THE *NEXUS* OF THE CRISIS IS *HERE* -- IN *AMERICA!*

IT'S A *NEW TIME,* CAP-- THE *OLD* RULES NO LONGER *APPLY!*

THOSE COULD BE *DANGEROUS WORDS,* T'CHALLA -- COMING FROM A MAN *LESS TRUSTWORTHY* THAN YOURSELF. WE *BOTH* KNOW WHAT IT'S LIKE TO BE *NATIONAL SYMBOLS*...

...BUT YOU'RE ALSO THE *SPIRITUAL LEADER* OF YOUR PEOPLE! LET'S JUST HOPE THE *VIBRANIUM* DIDN'T CREATE *TWO MONSTERS!*

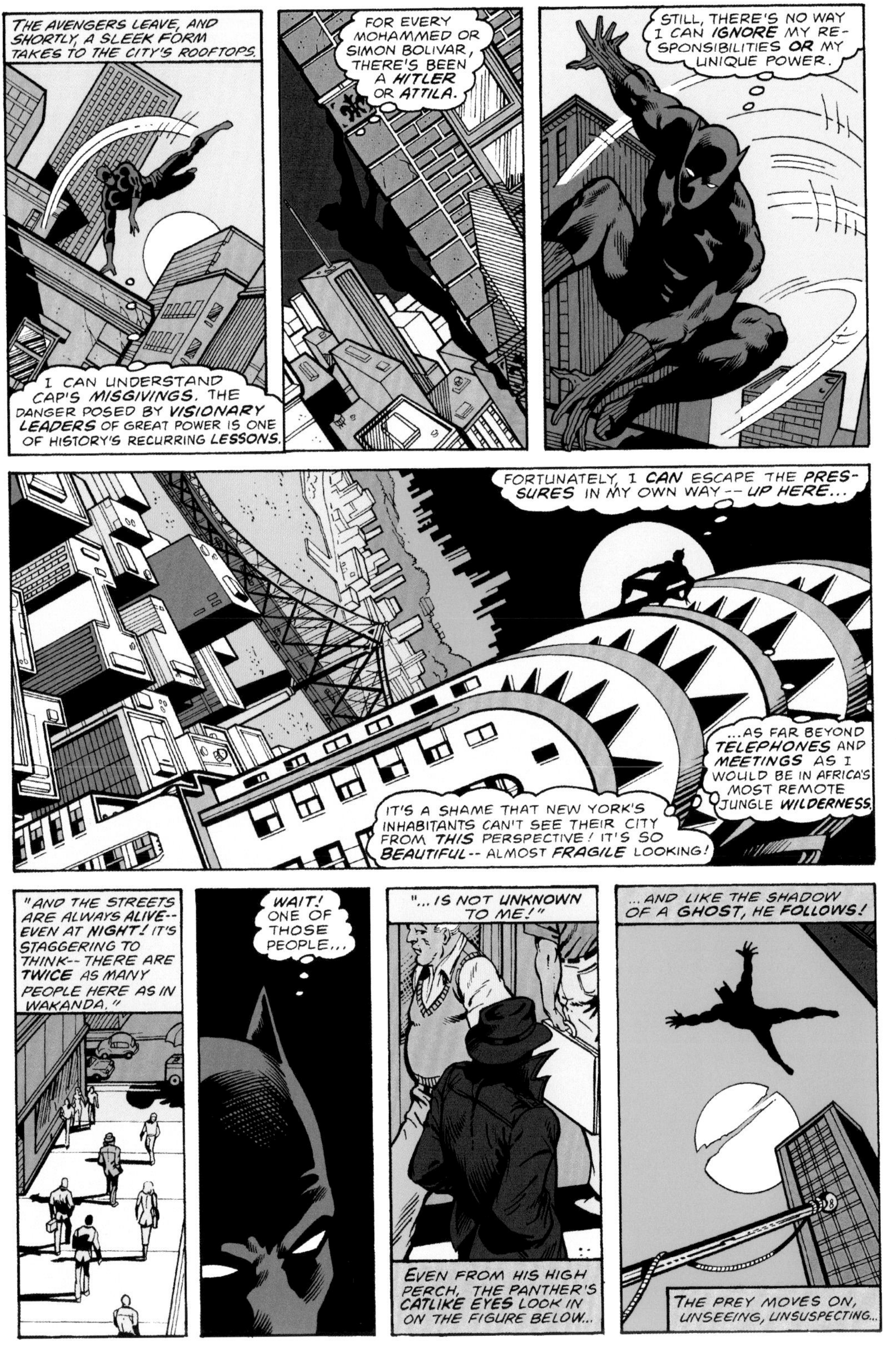
THE AVENGERS LEAVE, AND SHORTLY, A SLEEK FORM TAKES TO THE CITY'S ROOFTOPS.
I CAN UNDERSTAND CAP'S MISGIVINGS. THE DANGER POSED BY VISIONARY LEADERS OF GREAT POWER IS ONE OF HISTORY'S RECURRING LESSONS.
FOR EVERY MOHAMMED OR SIMON BOLIVAR, THERE'S BEEN A HITLER OR ATTILA.
STILL, THERE'S NO WAY I CAN IGNORE MY RESPONSIBILITIES OR MY UNIQUE POWER.
FORTUNATELY, I CAN ESCAPE THE PRESSURES IN MY OWN WAY -- UP HERE...
...AS FAR BEYOND TELEPHONES AND MEETINGS AS I WOULD BE IN AFRICA'S MOST REMOTE JUNGLE WILDERNESS.
IT'S A SHAME THAT NEW YORK'S INHABITANTS CAN'T SEE THEIR CITY FROM THIS PERSPECTIVE! IT'S SO BEAUTIFUL-- ALMOST FRAGILE LOOKING!
"AND THE STREETS ARE ALWAYS ALIVE-- EVEN AT NIGHT! IT'S STAGGERING TO THINK-- THERE ARE TWICE AS MANY PEOPLE HERE AS IN WAKANDA."
WAIT! ONE OF THOSE PEOPLE...
"...IS NOT UNKNOWN TO ME!"
EVEN FROM HIS HIGH PERCH, THE PANTHER'S CATLIKE EYES LOOK IN ON THE FIGURE BELOW...
...AND LIKE THE SHADOW OF A GHOST, HE FOLLOWS!
THE PREY MOVES ON, UNSEEING, UNSUSPECTING...

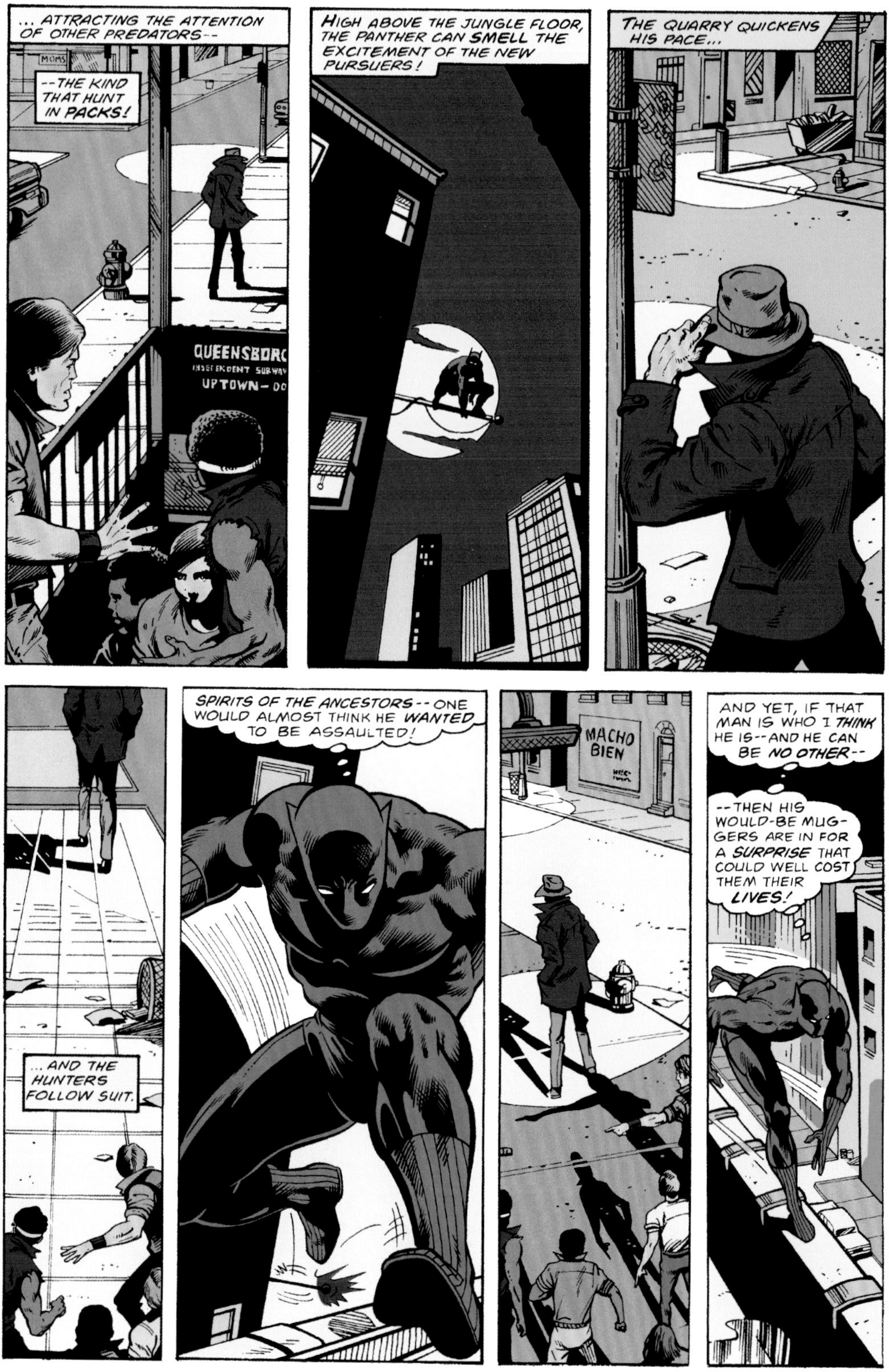
... ATTRACTING THE ATTENTION OF OTHER PREDATORS--
--THE KIND THAT HUNT IN PACKS!
MOMS
QUEENSBORO
INDEPENDENT SUBWAY
UPTOWN-
HIGH ABOVE THE JUNGLE FLOOR, THE PANTHER CAN SMELL THE EXCITEMENT OF THE NEW PURSUERS!
THE QUARRY QUICKENS HIS PACE...
...AND THE HUNTERS FOLLOW SUIT.
SPIRITS OF THE ANCESTORS-- ONE WOULD ALMOST THINK HE WANTED TO BE ASSAULTED!
MACHO BIEN
AND YET, IF THAT MAN IS WHO I THINK HE IS--AND HE CAN BE NO OTHER--
--THEN HIS WOULD-BE MUGGERS ARE IN FOR A SURPRISE THAT COULD WELL COST THEM THEIR LIVES!

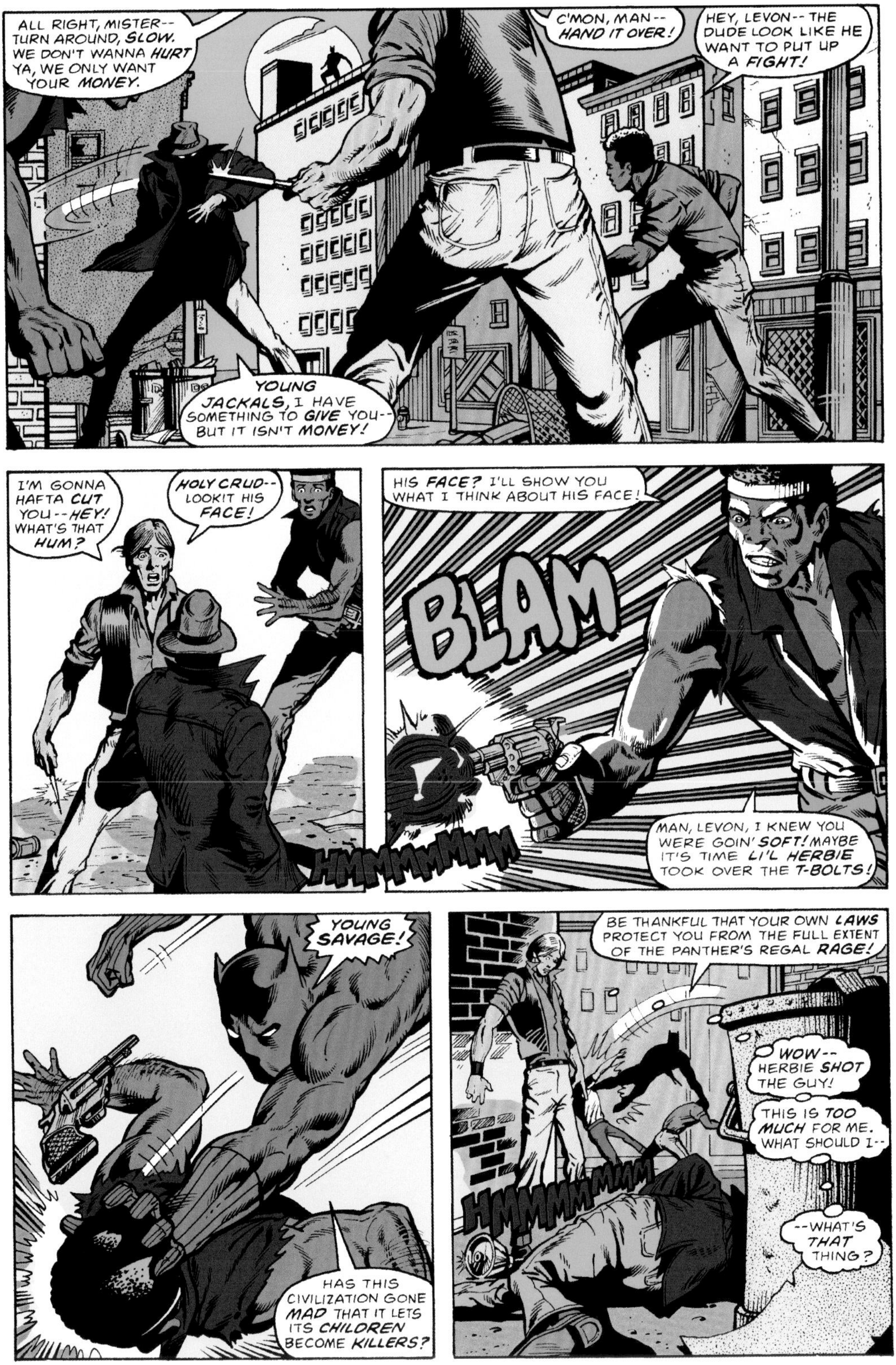
ALL RIGHT, MISTER-- TURN AROUND, SLOW. WE DON'T WANNA HURT YA, WE ONLY WANT YOUR MONEY.
C'MON, MAN-- HAND IT OVER!
HEY, LEVON-- THE DUDE LOOK LIKE HE WANT TO PUT UP A FIGHT!
YOUNG JACKALS, I HAVE SOMETHING TO GIVE YOU-- BUT IT ISN'T MONEY!
I'M GONNA HAFTA CUT YOU--HEY! WHAT'S THAT HUM?
HOLY CRUD-- LOOKIT HIS FACE!
HMMMMMMMM
HIS FACE? I'LL SHOW YOU WHAT I THINK ABOUT HIS FACE!
BLAM
MAN, LEVON, I KNEW YOU WERE GOIN' SOFT! MAYBE IT'S TIME LI'L HERBIE TOOK OVER THE T-BOLTS!
YOUNG SAVAGE!
HAS THIS CIVILIZATION GONE MAD THAT IT LETS ITS CHILDREN BECOME KILLERS?
BE THANKFUL THAT YOUR OWN LAWS PROTECT YOU FROM THE FULL EXTENT OF THE PANTHER'S REGAL RAGE!
WOW-- HERBIE SHOT THE GUY!
THIS IS TOO MUCH FOR ME. WHAT SHOULD I--
HMMMMMMM
--WHAT'S THAT THING?

I-IT'S SOME KIND OF WEIRD **HORN** THAT CAME OFF HIS **ARM!**

IT'S STILL VIBRAT-ING--

HMMMMMMM

-- MAKING ME FEEL LIKE I SHOULD... **USE IT!**

IN A NEAR CATATONIC **DAZE**, LEVON SLIPS THE ODD OBJECT ON HIS HAND, AND--

VREEOOOOOOO

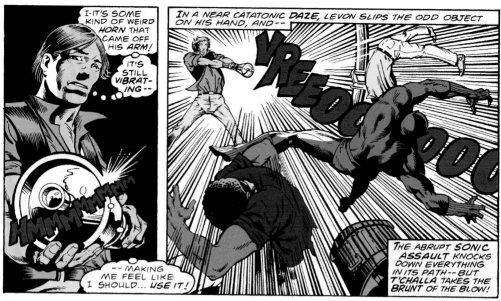

THE ABRUPT **SONIC ASSAULT** KNOCKS DOWN EVERYTHING IN ITS PATH--BUT T'CHALLA TAKES THE **BRUNT** OF THE BLOW!

THUS, WHILE THE **OTHERS** QUICKLY **RECOVER...**

I'M GONNA--!

NO, HERBIE-- HE'S **ALREADY DEAD!** WE GOTTA GET OUTTA HERE-- **NOW!**

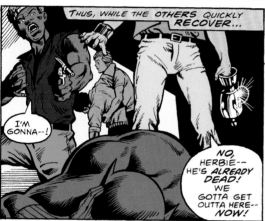

WHETHER LEVON INTENDED TO SAVE A LIFE, NEITHER THE PANTHER NOR WE WILL EVER **KNOW.**

PROBABLY, LEVON **HIMSELF** CANNOT BE SURE.

BUT, AFTER SEVERAL AGONIZING **MINUTES**, THE JUNGLE AVENGER STIRS...

... AND **RETURNS**, PAINFULLY, TO **LIFE.**

UHNNN... MY HEAD IS STILL **RINGING**-- BUT AT LEAST I **SURVIVED!**

THAT'S **SURPRISING** IN VIEW OF WHAT THEY DID TO THEIR INTENDED **VICTIM!** I'D BETTER SEE TO HIM. SEE IF IT REALLY IS--

--YES! KLAW, THE **MASTER** OF **SOUND**-- MY OLDEST AND MOST DEADLY **FOE!**

THERE'S NOT A **MARK** ON HIM--BUT HE SEEMS TO BE IN A **COMA!**

THAT'S NOT **LOGICAL,** THOUGH. KLAW CAN'T BE HARMED BY A MERE **GUNSHOT!**

WHATEVER THE *EXPLANATION*, I DON'T INTEND TO LET KLAW GET AWAY NOW THAT I FINALLY HAVE HIM!

AND THE *BEST* PLACE TO *SECURE* AND *STUDY* HIM IS--

"--AVENGERS' MANSION!"

WELL, THAT'S A *FIRST!* A BIG, BAD *SUPER-VILLAIN*... THE VICTIM OF A *MUGGING!*

A MUGGING HE WENT *LOOKING* FOR, IF MY *HUNCH* IS *CORRECT!*

THE TESTS SHOW NO EVIDENCE OF A *WOUND*-- BUT KLAW'S BODY STRUCTURE IS SO *DIFFERENT!*

AMAZING AS IT SEEMS, HE IS COMPOSED OF *SOLID SOUND ENERGY!* THE BULLET MUST HAVE PASSED RIGHT *THROUGH* HIM!

AND THE *SHOCKWAVE* FROM THE BULLET PUT HIM INTO THIS *STASIS*, EH?

IT'S A *THEORY.* THE *EXPERTS* IN *WAKANDA* WILL MAKE THE *FINAL ANALYSIS!*

IN *WAKANDA?* AFTER ALL THESE *YEARS* YOU WANT TO TAKE HIM BACK THERE?

*YES!* IT'S ABOUT *TIME!* WAKANDAN SCIENTISTS WILL FIND A WAY TO *REVIVE* KLAW, AND HE CAN STAND *TRIAL...*

"...FOR THE MURDER OF MY *FATHER!*"

"I WAS NOT YET OF *WARRIOR* AGE WHEN T'CHAKA FOUGHT HIS LAST BATTLE FOR OUR HOMELAND!"

"KLAW *INVADED* WAKANDA WITH THE INTENT TO STEAL CONTROL OF THE *SACRED VIBRANIUM MOUND!*"

"HE WAS BUT A MAN THEN, OF *FLESH* AND *BLOOD*--"

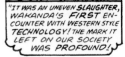

"--BUT HIS MERCENARIES SEEMED LIKE *DEMONS* AS THEY *MOWED DOWN* OUR MEN!"

"IT WAS AN UNEVEN *SLAUGHTER,* WAKANDA'S *FIRST* ENCOUNTER WITH WESTERN STYLE *TECHNOLOGY!* THE MARK IT LEFT ON OUR SOCIETY WAS *PROFOUND!*"

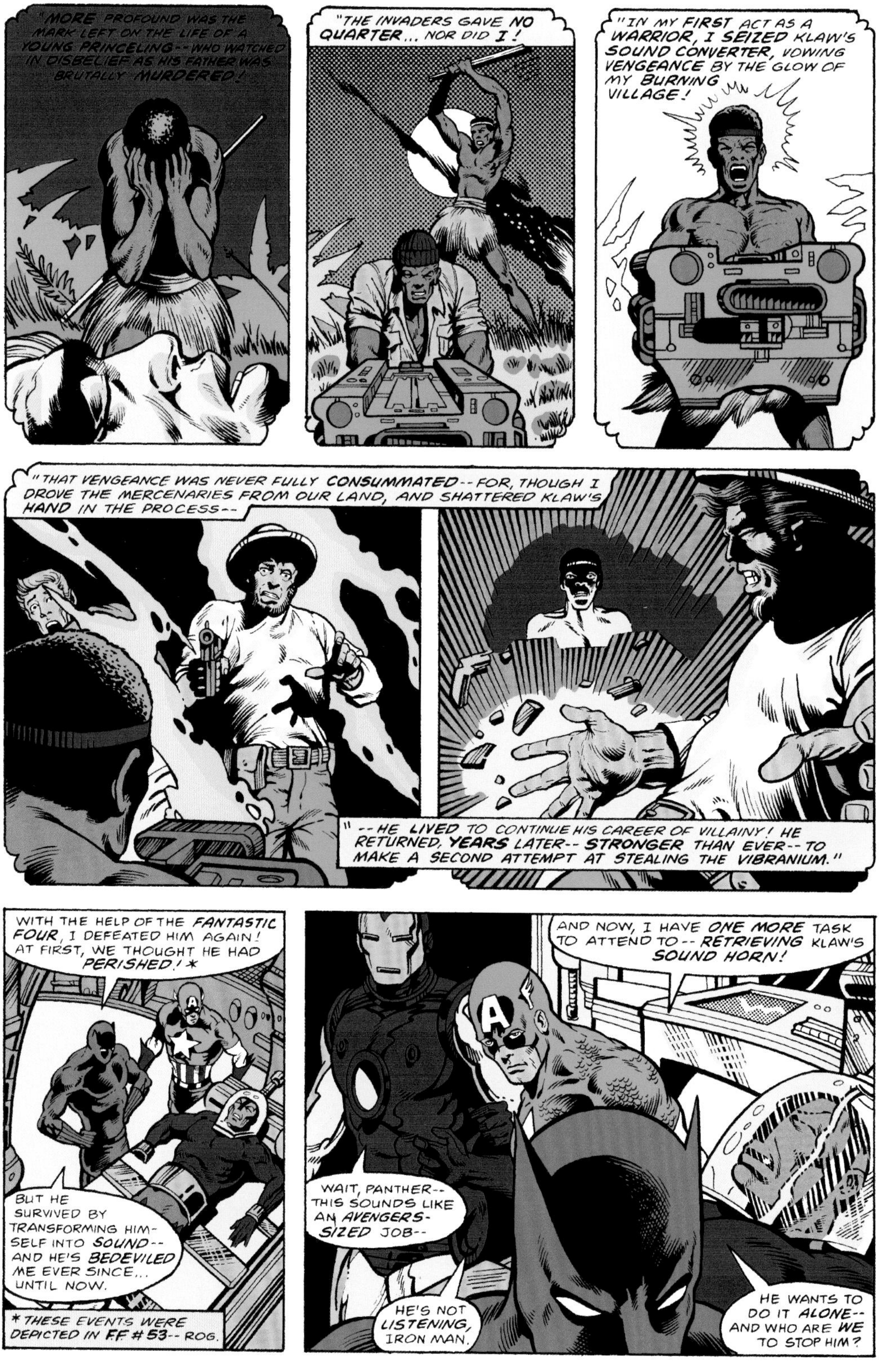
"MORE PROFOUND WAS THE MARK LEFT ON THE LIFE OF A YOUNG PRINCELING--WHO WATCHED IN DISBELIEF AS HIS FATHER WAS BRUTALLY MURDERED!
"THE INVADERS GAVE NO QUARTER... NOR DID I!
"IN MY FIRST ACT AS A WARRIOR, I SEIZED KLAW'S SOUND CONVERTER, VOWING VENGEANCE BY THE GLOW OF MY BURNING VILLAGE!
"THAT VENGEANCE WAS NEVER FULLY CONSUMMATED--FOR, THOUGH I DROVE THE MERCENARIES FROM OUR LAND, AND SHATTERED KLAW'S HAND IN THE PROCESS--
"--HE LIVED TO CONTINUE HIS CAREER OF VILLAINY! HE RETURNED, YEARS LATER--STRONGER THAN EVER--TO MAKE A SECOND ATTEMPT AT STEALING THE VIBRANIUM."
WITH THE HELP OF THE FANTASTIC FOUR, I DEFEATED HIM AGAIN! AT FIRST, WE THOUGHT HE HAD PERISHED! *
BUT HE SURVIVED BY TRANSFORMING HIMSELF INTO SOUND--AND HE'S BEDEVILED ME EVER SINCE... UNTIL NOW.
* THESE EVENTS WERE DEPICTED IN F.F. # 53--ROG.
AND NOW, I HAVE ONE MORE TASK TO ATTEND TO--RETRIEVING KLAW'S SOUND HORN!
WAIT, PANTHER--THIS SOUNDS LIKE AN AVENGERS-SIZED JOB--
HE'S NOT LISTENING, IRON MAN.
HE WANTS TO DO IT ALONE--AND WHO ARE WE TO STOP HIM?

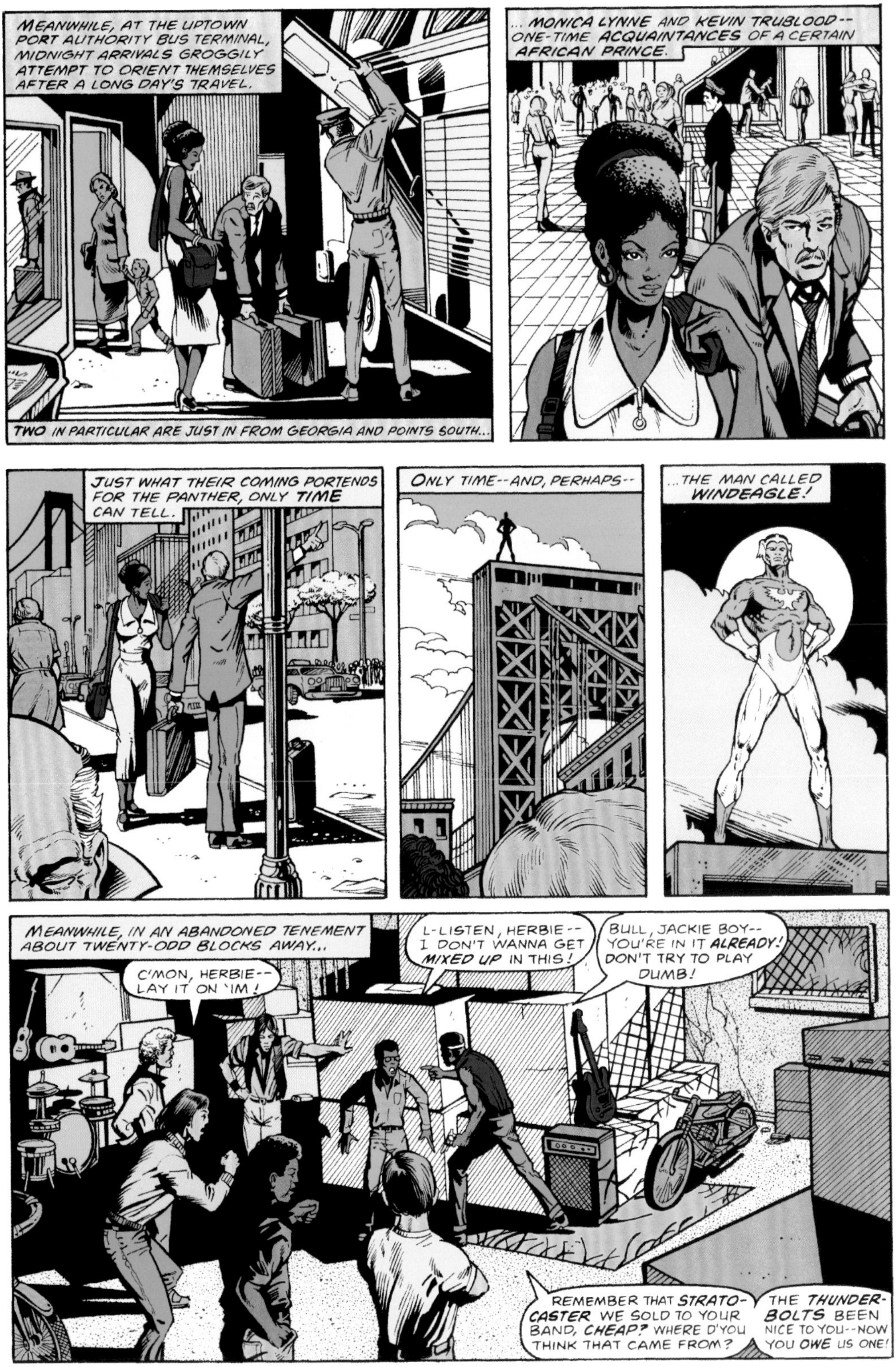
MEANWHILE, AT THE UPTOWN PORT AUTHORITY BUS TERMINAL, MIDNIGHT ARRIVALS GROGGILY ATTEMPT TO ORIENT THEMSELVES AFTER A LONG DAY'S TRAVEL.
TWO IN PARTICULAR ARE JUST IN FROM GEORGIA AND POINTS SOUTH...
... MONICA LYNNE AND KEVIN TRUBLOOD -- ONE-TIME ACQUAINTANCES OF A CERTAIN AFRICAN PRINCE.
JUST WHAT THEIR COMING PORTENDS FOR THE PANTHER, ONLY TIME CAN TELL.
ONLY TIME -- AND, PERHAPS --
... THE MAN CALLED WINDEAGLE!
MEANWHILE, IN AN ABANDONED TENEMENT ABOUT TWENTY-ODD BLOCKS AWAY...
C'MON, HERBIE -- LAY IT ON 'IM!
L-LISTEN, HERBIE -- I DON'T WANNA GET MIXED UP IN THIS!
BULL, JACKIE BOY -- YOU'RE IN IT ALREADY! DON'T TRY TO PLAY DUMB!
REMEMBER THAT STRATO-CASTER WE SOLD TO YOUR BAND, CHEAP? WHERE D'YOU THINK THAT CAME FROM?
THE THUNDER-BOLTS BEEN NICE TO YOU -- NOW YOU OWE US ONE!

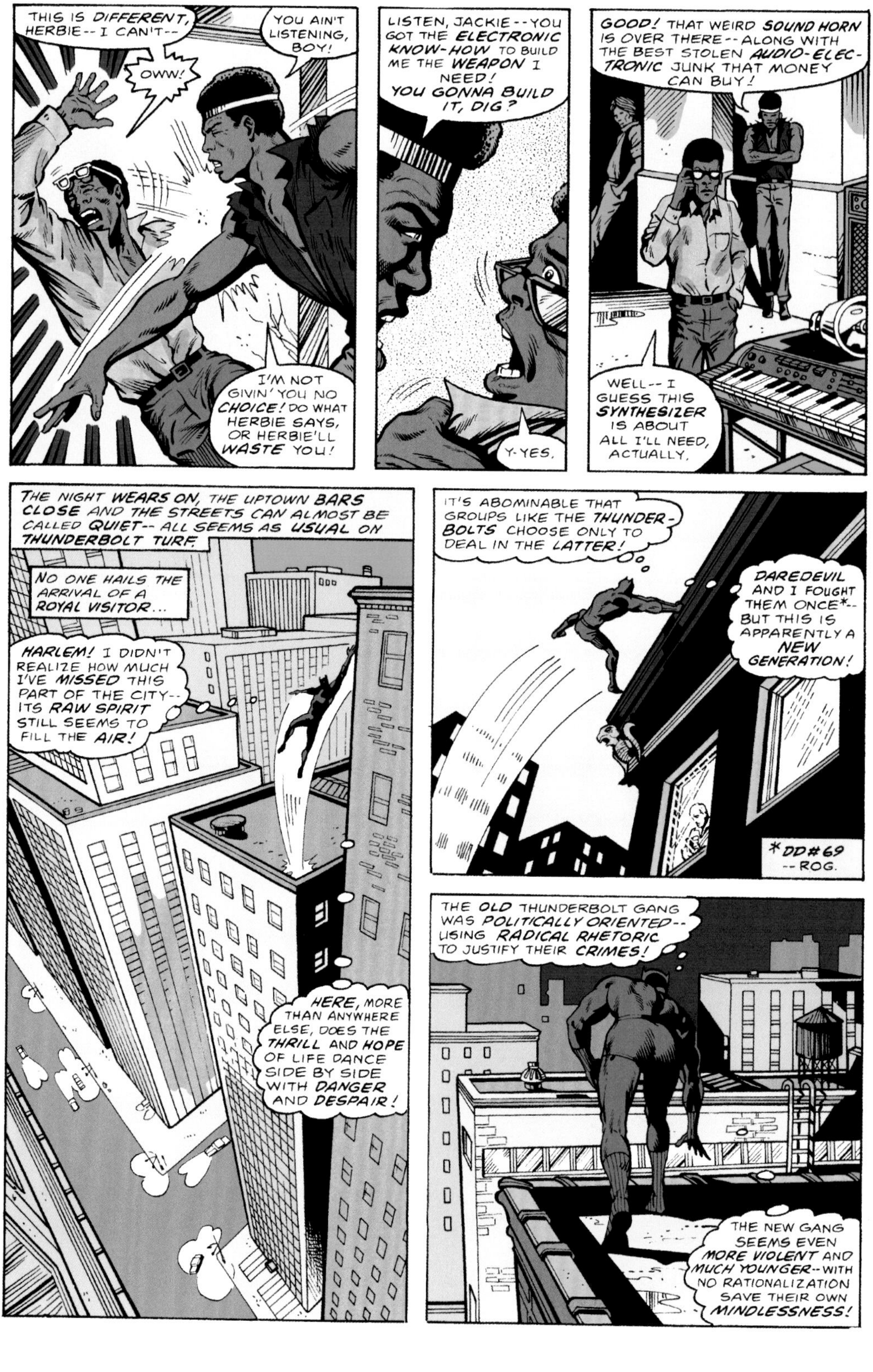
THIS IS DIFFERENT, HERBIE-- I CAN'T--
YOU AIN'T LISTENING, BOY!
OWW!
I'M NOT GIVIN' YOU NO CHOICE! DO WHAT HERBIE SAYS, OR HERBIE'LL WASTE YOU!
LISTEN, JACKIE--YOU GOT THE ELECTRONIC KNOW-HOW TO BUILD ME THE WEAPON I NEED! YOU GONNA BUILD IT, DIG?
Y-YES.
GOOD! THAT WEIRD SOUND HORN IS OVER THERE--ALONG WITH THE BEST STOLEN AUDIO-ELECTRONIC JUNK THAT MONEY CAN BUY!
WELL-- I GUESS THIS SYNTHESIZER IS ABOUT ALL I'LL NEED, ACTUALLY.
THE NIGHT WEARS ON, THE UPTOWN BARS CLOSE AND THE STREETS CAN ALMOST BE CALLED QUIET-- ALL SEEMS AS USUAL ON THUNDERBOLT TURF.
NO ONE HAILS THE ARRIVAL OF A ROYAL VISITOR...
HARLEM! I DIDN'T REALIZE HOW MUCH I'VE MISSED THIS PART OF THE CITY-- ITS RAW SPIRIT STILL SEEMS TO FILL THE AIR!
HERE, MORE THAN ANYWHERE ELSE, DOES THE THRILL AND HOPE OF LIFE DANCE SIDE BY SIDE WITH DANGER AND DESPAIR!
IT'S ABOMINABLE THAT GROUPS LIKE THE THUNDERBOLTS CHOOSE ONLY TO DEAL IN THE LATTER!
DAREDEVIL AND I FOUGHT THEM ONCE*-- BUT THIS IS APPARENTLY A NEW GENERATION!
*DD #69 --ROG.
THE OLD THUNDERBOLT GANG WAS POLITICALLY ORIENTED-- USING RADICAL RHETORIC TO JUSTIFY THEIR CRIMES!
THE NEW GANG SEEMS EVEN MORE VIOLENT AND MUCH YOUNGER--WITH NO RATIONALIZATION SAVE THEIR OWN MINDLESSNESS!

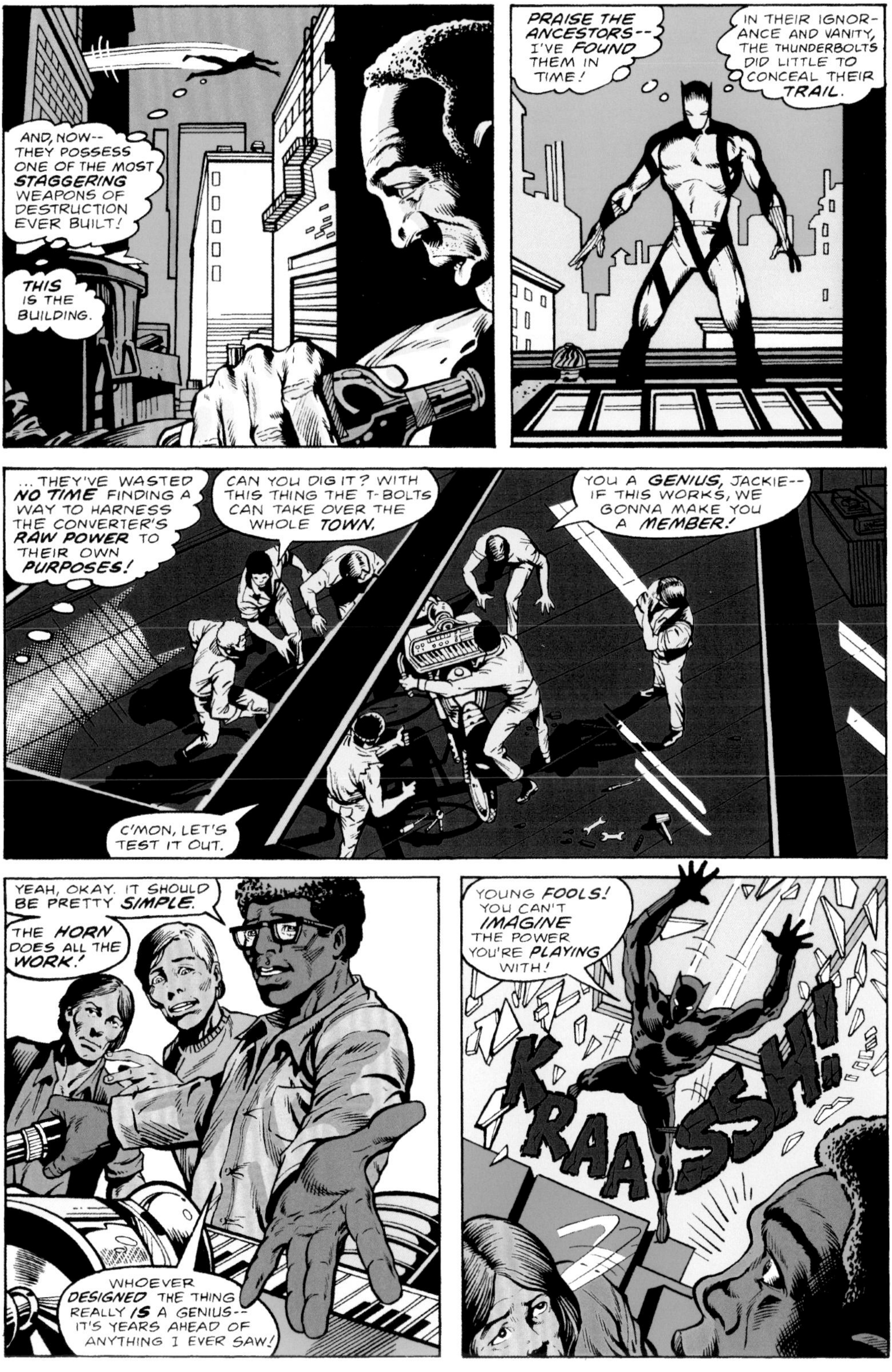
AND, NOW-- THEY POSSESS ONE OF THE MOST STAGGERING WEAPONS OF DESTRUCTION EVER BUILT!
THIS IS THE BUILDING.
PRAISE THE ANCESTORS-- I'VE FOUND THEM IN TIME!
IN THEIR IGNORANCE AND VANITY, THE THUNDERBOLTS DID LITTLE TO CONCEAL THEIR TRAIL.
...THEY'VE WASTED NO TIME FINDING A WAY TO HARNESS THE CONVERTER'S RAW POWER TO THEIR OWN PURPOSES!
CAN YOU DIG IT? WITH THIS THING THE T-BOLTS CAN TAKE OVER THE WHOLE TOWN.
YOU A GENIUS, JACKIE-- IF THIS WORKS, WE GONNA MAKE YOU A MEMBER!
C'MON, LET'S TEST IT OUT.
YEAH, OKAY. IT SHOULD BE PRETTY SIMPLE.
THE HORN DOES ALL THE WORK!
WHOEVER DESIGNED THE THING REALLY IS A GENIUS-- IT'S YEARS AHEAD OF ANYTHING I EVER SAW!
YOUNG FOOLS! YOU CAN'T IMAGINE THE POWER YOU'RE PLAYING WITH!
KRAASSH!!

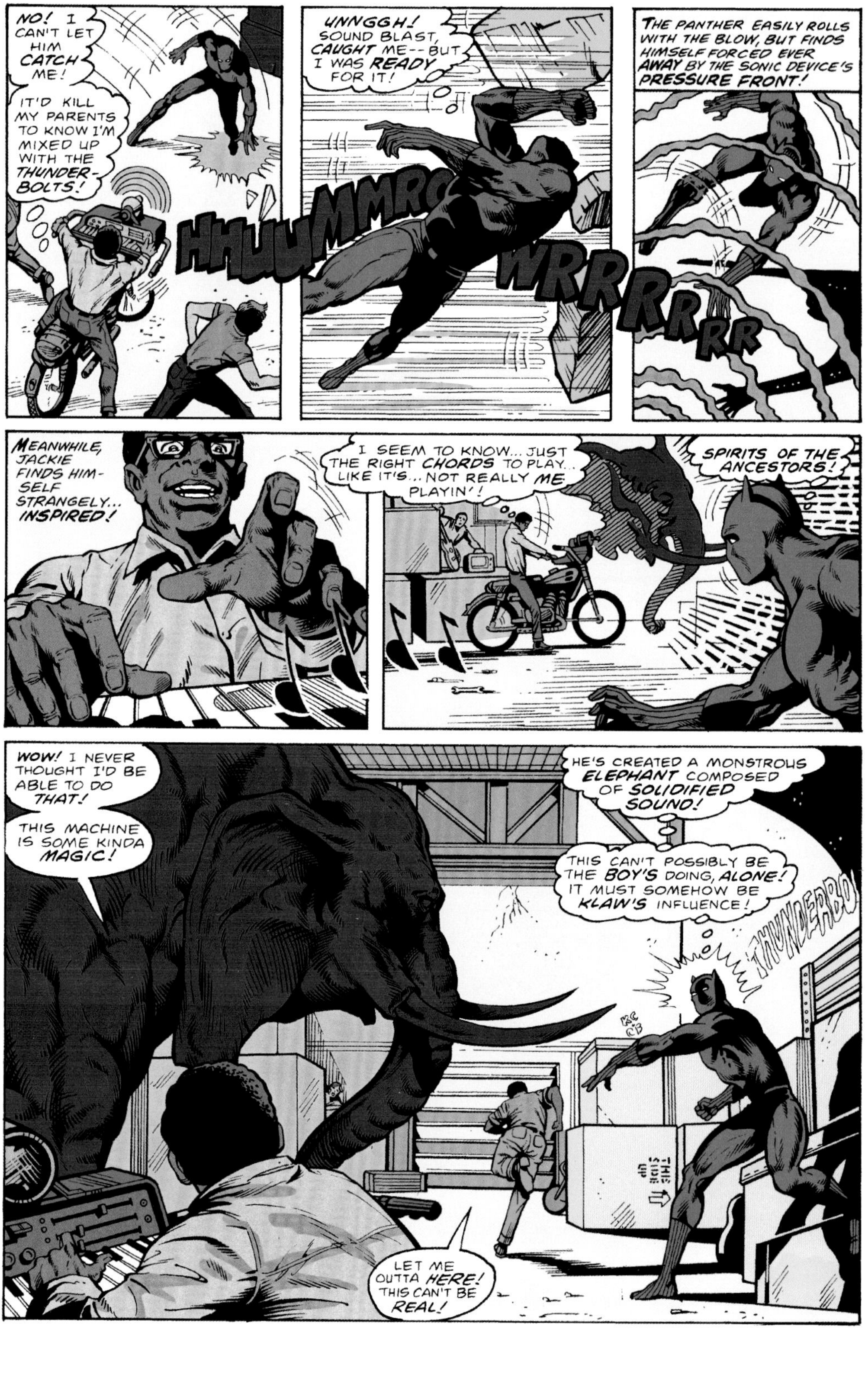
NO! I CAN'T LET HIM CATCH ME!
IT'D KILL MY PARENTS TO KNOW I'M MIXED UP WITH THE THUNDER-BOLTS!
UNNGGH! SOUND BLAST CAUGHT ME-- BUT I WAS READY FOR IT!
HHUUMMRO
WRRRRRRR
THE PANTHER EASILY ROLLS WITH THE BLOW, BUT FINDS HIMSELF FORCED EVER AWAY BY THE SONIC DEVICE'S PRESSURE FRONT!
MEANWHILE, JACKIE FINDS HIM-SELF STRANGELY... INSPIRED!
I SEEM TO KNOW... JUST THE RIGHT CHORDS TO PLAY... LIKE IT'S... NOT REALLY ME PLAYIN'!
SPIRITS OF THE ANCESTORS!
WOW! I NEVER THOUGHT I'D BE ABLE TO DO THAT!
THIS MACHINE IS SOME KINDA MAGIC!
HE'S CREATED A MONSTROUS ELEPHANT COMPOSED OF SOLIDIFIED SOUND!
THIS CAN'T POSSIBLY BE THE BOY'S DOING, ALONE! IT MUST SOMEHOW BE KLAW'S INFLUENCE!
THUNDERBO
THIS SIDE UP
LET ME OUTTA HERE! THIS CAN'T BE REAL!

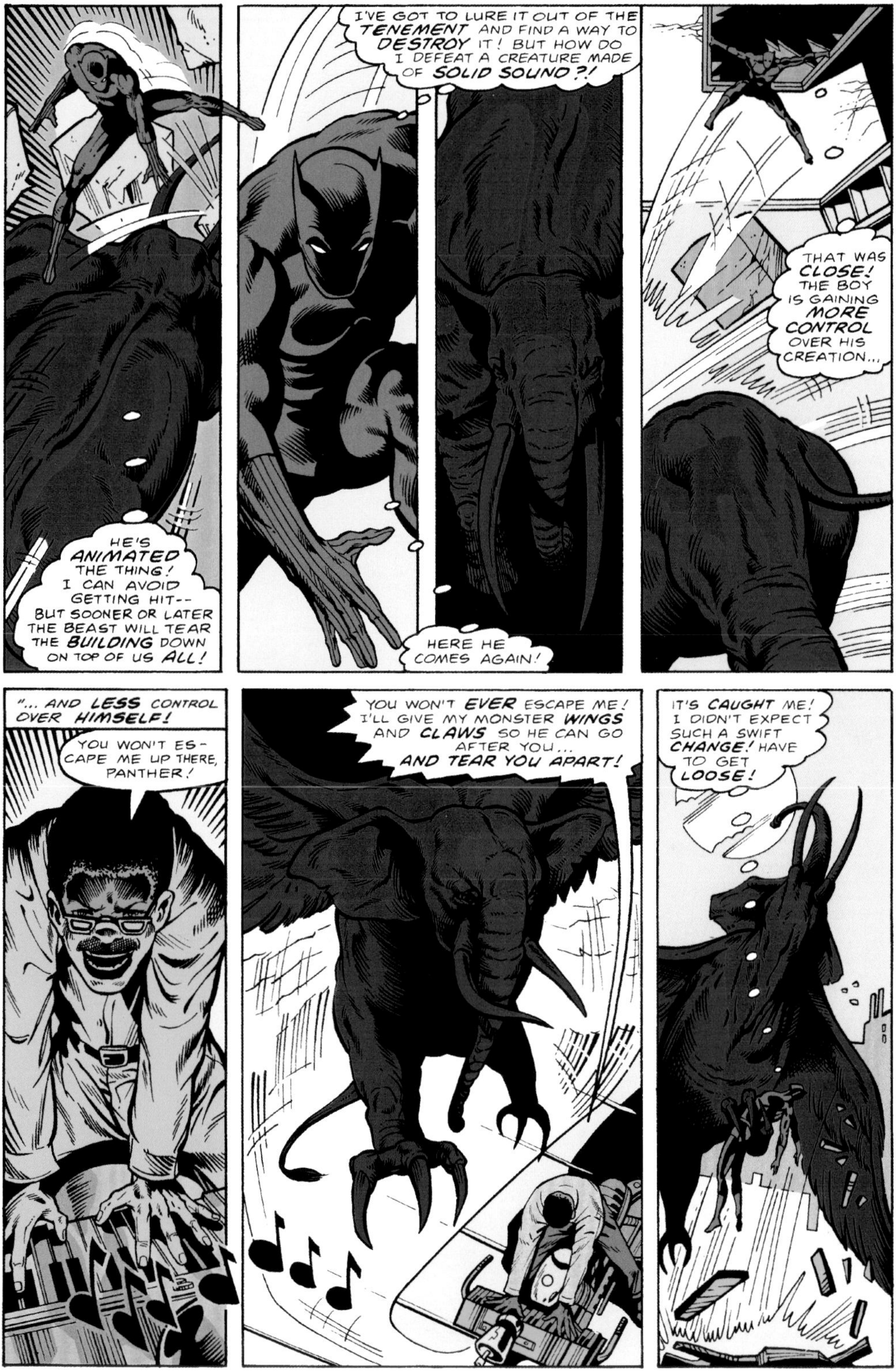
HE'S ANIMATED THE THING! I CAN AVOID GETTING HIT-- BUT SOONER OR LATER THE BEAST WILL TEAR THE BUILDING DOWN ON TOP OF US ALL!
I'VE GOT TO LURE IT OUT OF THE TENEMENT AND FIND A WAY TO DESTROY IT! BUT HOW DO I DEFEAT A CREATURE MADE OF SOLID SOUND?!
HERE HE COMES AGAIN!
THAT WAS CLOSE! THE BOY IS GAINING MORE CONTROL OVER HIS CREATION...
"... AND LESS CONTROL OVER HIMSELF!
YOU WON'T ES-CAPE ME UP THERE, PANTHER!
YOU WON'T EVER ESCAPE ME! I'LL GIVE MY MONSTER WINGS AND CLAWS SO HE CAN GO AFTER YOU... AND TEAR YOU APART!
IT'S CAUGHT ME! I DIDN'T EXPECT SUCH A SWIFT CHANGE! HAVE TO GET LOOSE!

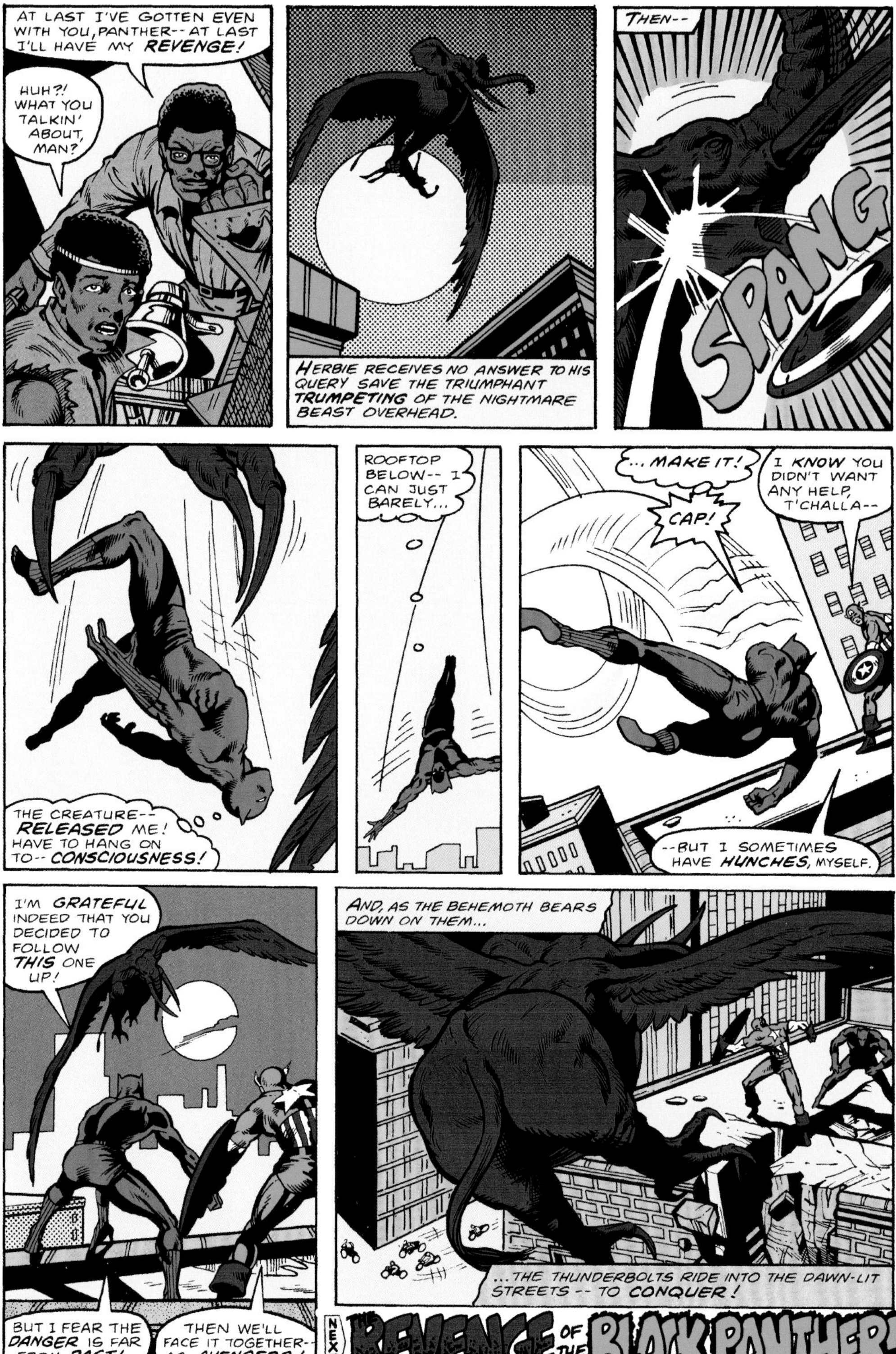

AT LAST I'VE GOTTEN EVEN WITH YOU, PANTHER-- AT LAST I'LL HAVE MY REVENGE!
HUH?! WHAT YOU TALKIN' ABOUT, MAN?
HERBIE RECEIVES NO ANSWER TO HIS QUERY SAVE THE TRIUMPHANT TRUMPETING OF THE NIGHTMARE BEAST OVERHEAD.
THEN--
SPANG
THE CREATURE-- RELEASED ME! HAVE TO HANG ON TO-- CONSCIOUSNESS!
ROOFTOP BELOW-- I CAN JUST BARELY...
...MAKE IT!
CAP!
I KNOW YOU DIDN'T WANT ANY HELP, T'CHALLA--
--BUT I SOMETIMES HAVE HUNCHES, MYSELF.
I'M GRATEFUL INDEED THAT YOU DECIDED TO FOLLOW THIS ONE UP!
BUT I FEAR THE DANGER IS FAR FROM PAST!
THEN WE'LL FACE IT TOGETHER-- AS AVENGERS!
AND, AS THE BEHEMOTH BEARS DOWN ON THEM...
...THE THUNDERBOLTS RIDE INTO THE DAWN-LIT STREETS -- TO CONQUER!
NEXT
THE REVENGE OF THE BLACK PANTHER!

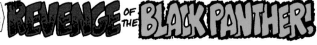

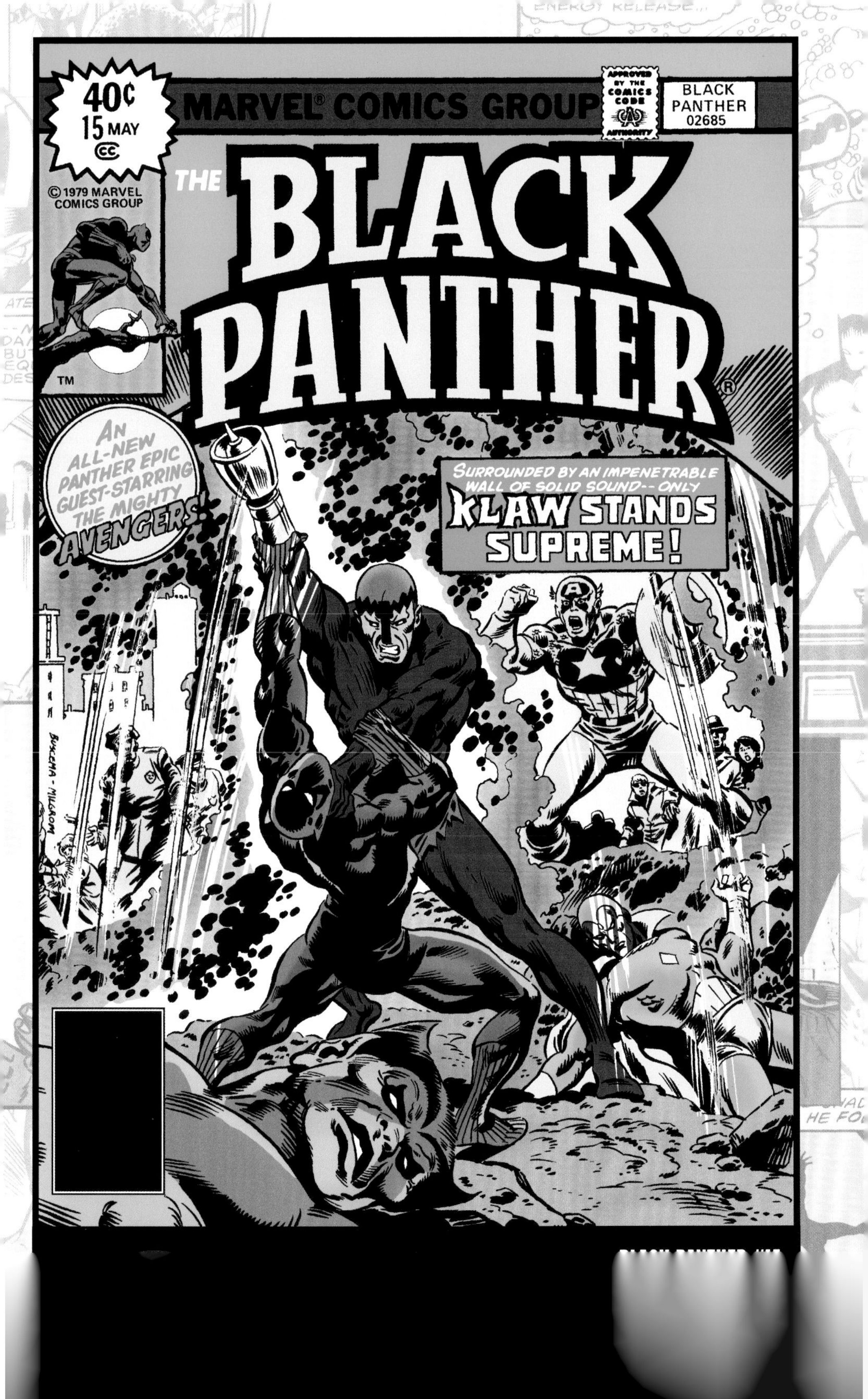

40¢
15 MAY
CC
MARVEL® COMICS GROUP
APPROVED BY THE COMICS CODE AUTHORITY
BLACK PANTHER 02685
© 1979 MARVEL COMICS GROUP
THE BLACK PANTHER®
TM
AN ALL-NEW PANTHER EPIC GUEST-STARRING THE MIGHTY AVENGERS!
SURROUNDED BY AN IMPENETRABLE WALL OF SOLID SOUND-- ONLY KLAW STANDS SUPREME!
BUSCEMA - MILGROM

With the sleekness of the jungle cat whose name he bears, T'Challa— the Prince of Wakanda—stalks both the concrete of the city and the undergrowth of the veldt! So it has been for countless generations of warrior-kings, so it is today— and so shall it be for as long as the law of the jungle dictates that only the swift, the smart, and the strong survive!

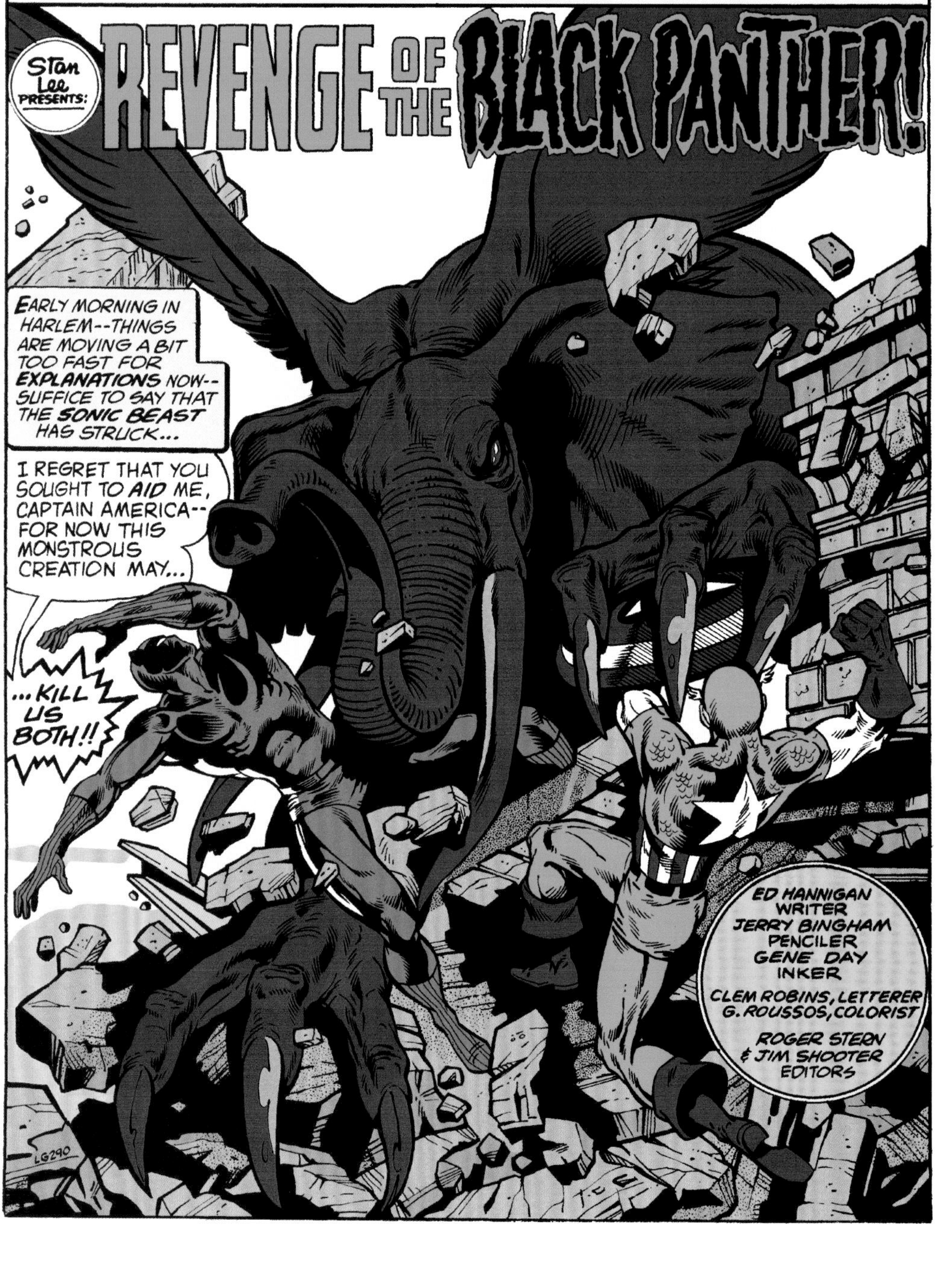

Stan Lee PRESENTS:
REVENGE OF THE BLACK PANTHER!
EARLY MORNING IN HARLEM--THINGS ARE MOVING A BIT TOO FAST FOR EXPLANATIONS NOW--SUFFICE TO SAY THAT THE SONIC BEAST HAS STRUCK...
I REGRET THAT YOU SOUGHT TO AID ME, CAPTAIN AMERICA--FOR NOW THIS MONSTROUS CREATION MAY...
...KILL US BOTH!!
ED HANNIGAN WRITER
JERRY BINGHAM PENCILER
GENE DAY INKER
CLEM ROBINS, LETTERER
G. ROUSSOS, COLORIST
ROGER STERN & JIM SHOOTER EDITORS

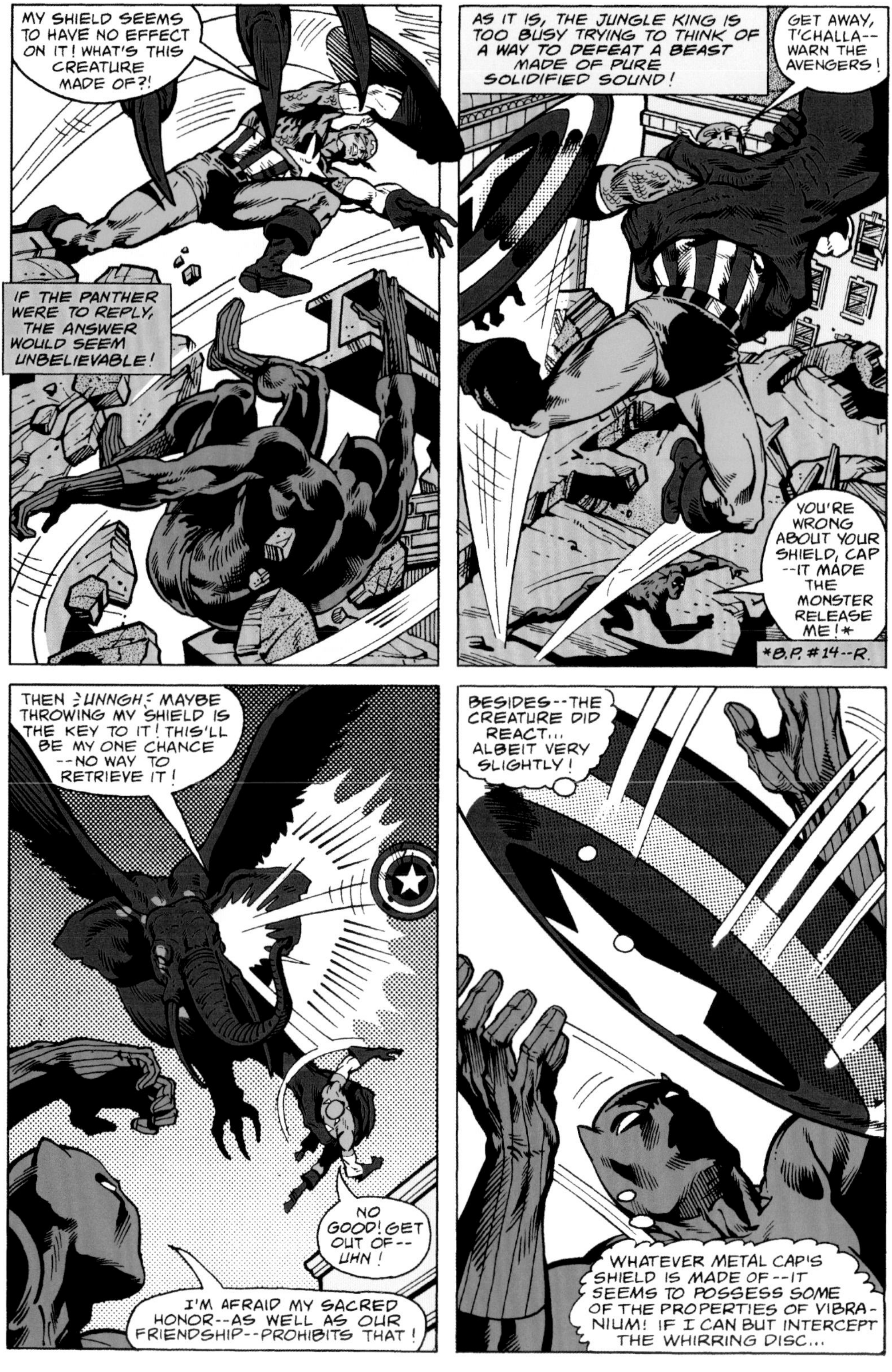
MY SHIELD SEEMS TO HAVE NO EFFECT ON IT! WHAT'S THIS CREATURE MADE OF?!
IF THE PANTHER WERE TO REPLY, THE ANSWER WOULD SEEM UNBELIEVABLE!
AS IT IS, THE JUNGLE KING IS TOO BUSY TRYING TO THINK OF A WAY TO DEFEAT A BEAST MADE OF PURE SOLIDIFIED SOUND!
GET AWAY, T'CHALLA-- WARN THE AVENGERS!
YOU'RE WRONG ABOUT YOUR SHIELD, CAP --IT MADE THE MONSTER RELEASE ME!*
*B.P. #14--R.
THEN ≥UNNGH≤ MAYBE THROWING MY SHIELD IS THE KEY TO IT! THIS'LL BE MY ONE CHANCE --NO WAY TO RETRIEVE IT!
NO GOOD! GET OUT OF-- UHN!
I'M AFRAID MY SACRED HONOR--AS WELL AS OUR FRIENDSHIP--PROHIBITS THAT!
BESIDES--THE CREATURE DID REACT... ALBEIT VERY SLIGHTLY!
WHATEVER METAL CAP'S SHIELD IS MADE OF--IT SEEMS TO POSSESS SOME OF THE PROPERTIES OF VIBRA-NIUM! IF I CAN BUT INTERCEPT THE WHIRRING DISC...

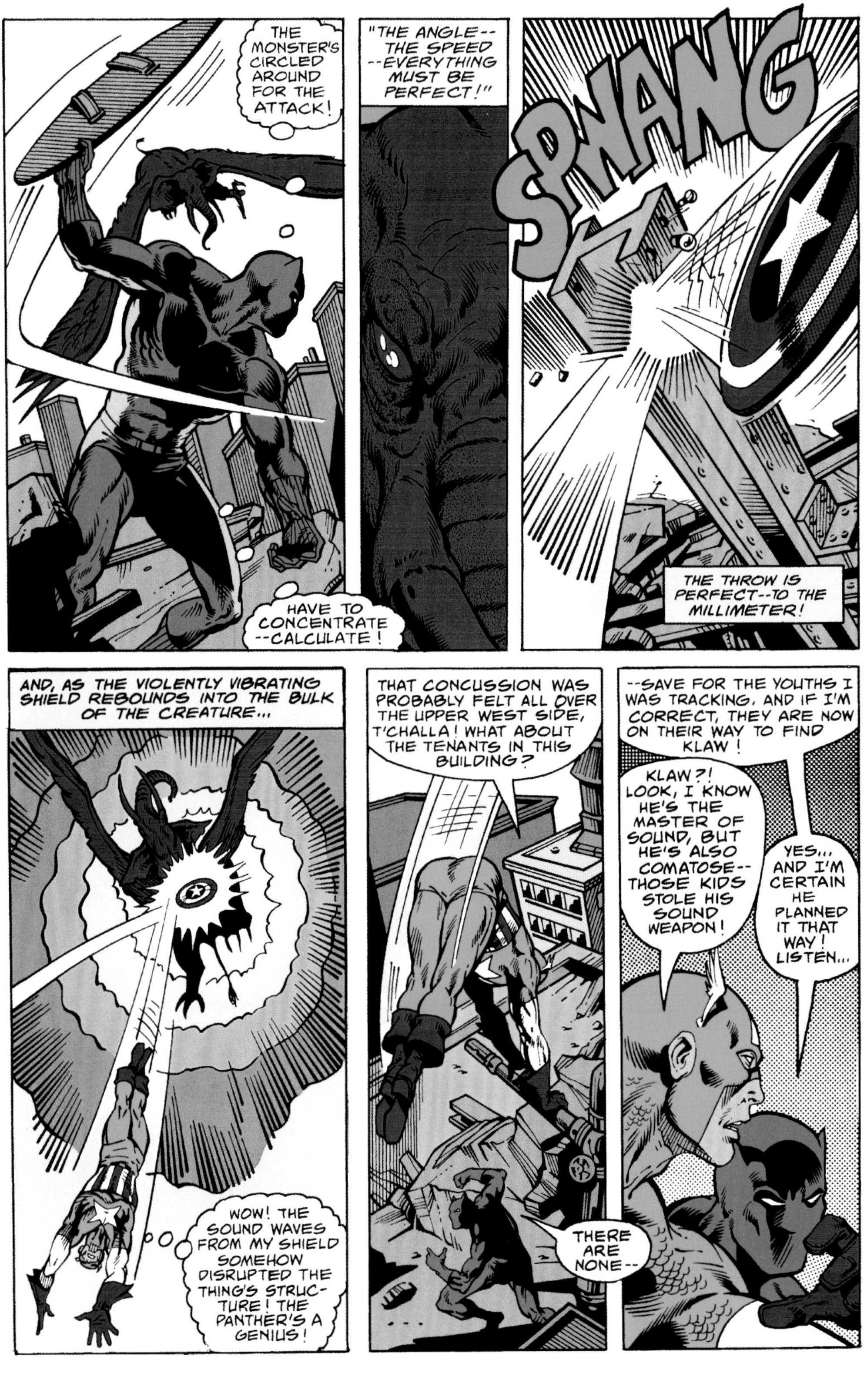
THE MONSTER'S CIRCLED AROUND FOR THE ATTACK!
HAVE TO CONCENTRATE --CALCULATE!
"THE ANGLE-- THE SPEED --EVERYTHING MUST BE PERFECT!"
SPANG
THE THROW IS PERFECT--TO THE MILLIMETER!
AND, AS THE VIOLENTLY VIBRATING SHIELD REBOUNDS INTO THE BULK OF THE CREATURE...
WOW! THE SOUND WAVES FROM MY SHIELD SOMEHOW DISRUPTED THE THING'S STRUC-TURE! THE PANTHER'S A GENIUS!
THAT CONCUSSION WAS PROBABLY FELT ALL OVER THE UPPER WEST SIDE, T'CHALLA! WHAT ABOUT THE TENANTS IN THIS BUILDING?
THERE ARE NONE--
--SAVE FOR THE YOUTHS I WAS TRACKING, AND IF I'M CORRECT, THEY ARE NOW ON THEIR WAY TO FIND KLAW!
KLAW?! LOOK, I KNOW HE'S THE MASTER OF SOUND, BUT HE'S ALSO COMATOSE-- THOSE KIDS STOLE HIS SOUND WEAPON!
YES... AND I'M CERTAIN HE PLANNED IT THAT WAY! LISTEN...

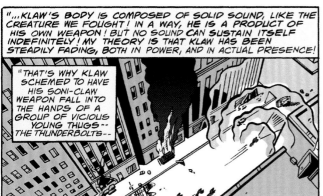

"...KLAW'S BODY IS COMPOSED OF SOLID SOUND, LIKE THE CREATURE WE FOUGHT! IN A WAY, HE IS A PRODUCT OF HIS OWN WEAPON! BUT NO SOUND CAN SUSTAIN ITSELF INDEFINITELY! MY THEORY IS THAT KLAW HAS BEEN STEADILY FADING, BOTH IN POWER, AND IN ACTUAL PRESENCE!

"THAT'S WHY KLAW SCHEMED TO HAVE HIS SONI-CLAW WEAPON FALL INTO THE HANDS OF A GROUP OF VICIOUS YOUNG THUGS-- THE THUNDERBOLTS--

"--WHO ARE EVEN NOW RAMPAGING THROUGH THE CITY, WREAKING DESTRUCTION!"

"THE CURRENT POSSESSOR OF THE WEAPON IS A BOY NAMED JACK--AND SOMEHOW, THE WEAPON IS CONTROLLING HIS MIND!

"HIS DESTINATION, NO DOUBT, IS THE WATERFRONT, WHERE THE VISION AND THE BEAST ARE DELIVERING KLAW'S BODY FOR SHIPMENT TO WAKANDA..."

WELL--WHAT'S THE HOLD UP? IF YOU DON'T ACCEPT AVENGERS' I.D., I'VE GOT DINER'S CLUB...

YOUR PAPERS ARE ALL IN ORDER--FOR CARGO--BUT I CAN'T LOAD HIM 'CAUSE HE'S A PASSENGER! WHERE'S HIS PASSPORT...OR EXTRADITION PAPERS?

WE HAVE EXPLAINED THAT KLAW IS NOT REALLY HUMAN-- HE IS MADE OF SOUND--NO PASSPORT IS NEEDED!

IN ADDITION, THE PANTHER HAS DIPLOMATIC IMMUNITY!

YEAH, YEAH--KING OF WAKANDA, RIGHT? WELL, THIS FREIGHTER IS REGISTERED TO LIBERIA!

BUT EVERYBODY KNOWS THAT THE CARGO IS BOUND FOR WAKANDA!

IF YOU KNOW THE VESSEL'S REGISTRY, THEN YOU MUST KNOW IT IS OWNED BY THE PANTHER'S GOVERNMENT! WE ARE NOT ATTEMPTING TO BREAK THE LAW!

WELL--I'M STILL NOT SURE! I WANT TO TALK TO THIS "PANTHER!" THE STATE DEPARTMENT HAS BEEN WATCHIN' THIS SHIP, AND...

WHAT WILL IT TAKE TO--HEY, WHAT'S THAT WEIRD SOUND?

234.45 CYCLES PER SECOND, BEAST--"A" SHARP! BUT THE PITCH IS STARTING TO CHANGE--

SUDDENLY--

JACKIE-BOY'S STOPPIN', LEVON! AN' LOOK WHAT HE'S DOIN' NOW! THOSE ARE AVENGERS HE'S ATTACKIN'!

WHAT'S THE WORLD COMING TO? I MEAN--PUNK KIDS ON MUSICAL MOTORBIKES, SHOOTING RED LIONS?!

WHILE--

WE'RE ALMOST THERE, CAP--I CAN HEAR THE SOUNDS OF CONFLICT AHEAD!

I JUST HOPE THAT CALL TO YOUR CONSULATE WAS WORTH THE DELAY! WE'RE IN FOR IT IF THOSE KIDS REVIVE KLAW!

"THE SONI-CLAW IS DANGEROUS ENOUGH IN THE HANDS OF AMATEURS!"

THIS CREATURE'S STRUCTURE SEEMS TO BE COMPOSED OF HARMONICS, RATHER THAN ATOMIC PARTICLES!

STILL, MY ANDROID BODY SHOULD BE IMPERVIOUS TO ITS ASSAULT!

BUT... VIZH! WHY'D YOU LET HIM SLIP THROUGH YOU LIKE THAT?!

IT WAS NOT MY DOING, BEAST--I WILLED MY BODY TO DIAMOND HARDNESS! APPARENTLY THE CREATURE IS AS CAPABLE AS I AM OF CONTROLLING ITS SPECIFIC DENSITY!

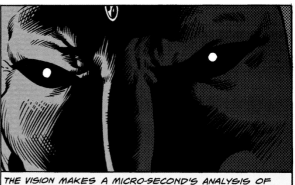

THE VISION MAKES A MICRO-SECOND'S ANALYSIS OF THE SITUATION: THE THREAT OF A SONIC MENAGERIE IS FORMIDABLE, BUT WHAT IS MORE DISTURBING...

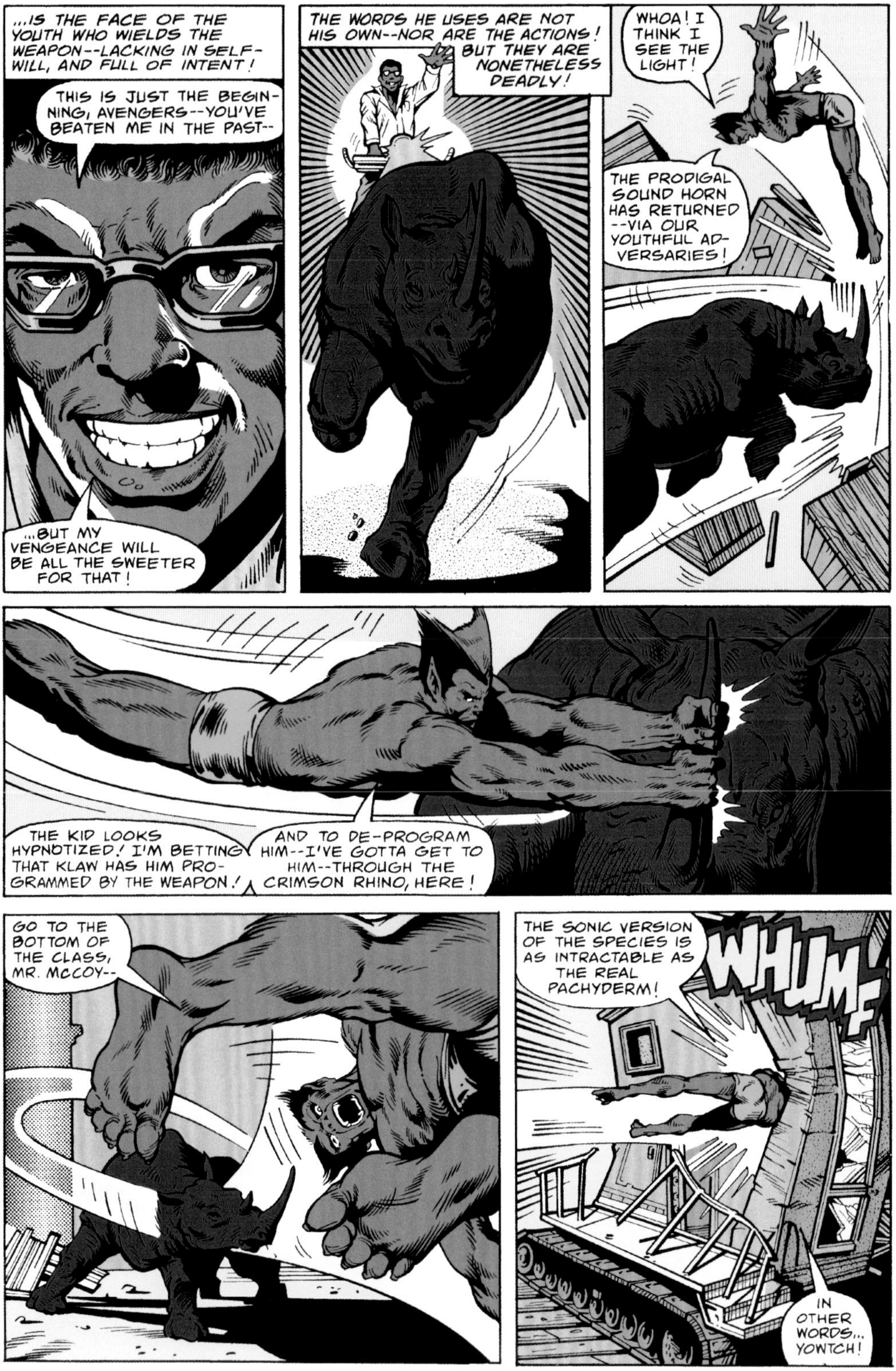
...IS THE FACE OF THE YOUTH WHO WIELDS THE WEAPON--LACKING IN SELF-WILL, AND FULL OF INTENT!
THIS IS JUST THE BEGINNING, AVENGERS--YOU'VE BEATEN ME IN THE PAST--
...BUT MY VENGEANCE WILL BE ALL THE SWEETER FOR THAT!
THE WORDS HE USES ARE NOT HIS OWN--NOR ARE THE ACTIONS!
BUT THEY ARE NONETHELESS DEADLY!
WHOA! I THINK I SEE THE LIGHT!
THE PRODIGAL SOUND HORN HAS RETURNED --VIA OUR YOUTHFUL ADVERSARIES!
THE KID LOOKS HYPNOTIZED! I'M BETTING THAT KLAW HAS HIM PROGRAMMED BY THE WEAPON.
AND TO DE-PROGRAM HIM--I'VE GOTTA GET TO HIM--THROUGH THE CRIMSON RHINO, HERE!
GO TO THE BOTTOM OF THE CLASS, MR. MCCOY--
THE SONIC VERSION OF THE SPECIES IS AS INTRACTABLE AS THE REAL PACHYDERM!
WHUMF
IN OTHER WORDS... YOWTCH!

AT THE SAME MOMENT...

HERBIE-- WHAT ARE WE DOIN' HERE?

I DON'T KNOW, MAN--BUT WHEN I GET MY HANDS ON JACKIE-BOY, WE GONNA FIND OUT!

BUT, EVEN AS THE SELF-STYLED THUNDERBOLTS REACH THE ONCE-TIMID JACKIE--

HOLY CRUD! HE'S MAKIN' A DOME OUTTA SOUND!

AND WE'RE TRAPPED IN HERE WITH 'IM!

MEANWHILE, TWO EVENLY MATCHED SIMU-LOIDS FACE OFF...

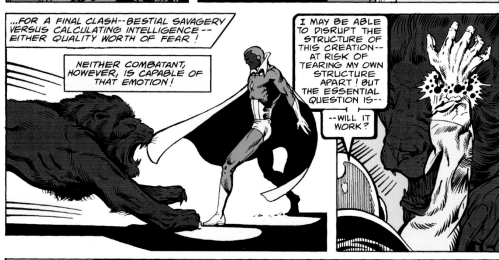

...FOR A FINAL CLASH--BESTIAL SAVAGERY VERSUS CALCULATING INTELLIGENCE-- EITHER QUALITY WORTH OF FEAR!

NEITHER COMBATANT, HOWEVER, IS CAPABLE OF THAT EMOTION!

I MAY BE ABLE TO DISRUPT THE STRUCTURE OF THIS CREATION-- AT RISK OF TEARING MY OWN STRUCTURE APART! BUT THE ESSENTIAL QUESTION IS--

--WILL IT WORK?

WHILE, ON THE OTHER SIDE OF THE IMPROMPTU ARENA...

C'MON, UGLY-- CHARGE, ALREADY, SO I CAN DODGE YOU AGAIN!

THE CREATURE RUMBLES FORWARD, BUT...

NO NEED TO DODGE, BEAST-- I BELIEVE I CAN ERADICATE THIS THREAT!

SWELL, VIZH! WHAT ARE YOU GONNA DO-- WAIT TILL HE TAKES HIS SKIN OFF, AND RUB SAND INTO IT?

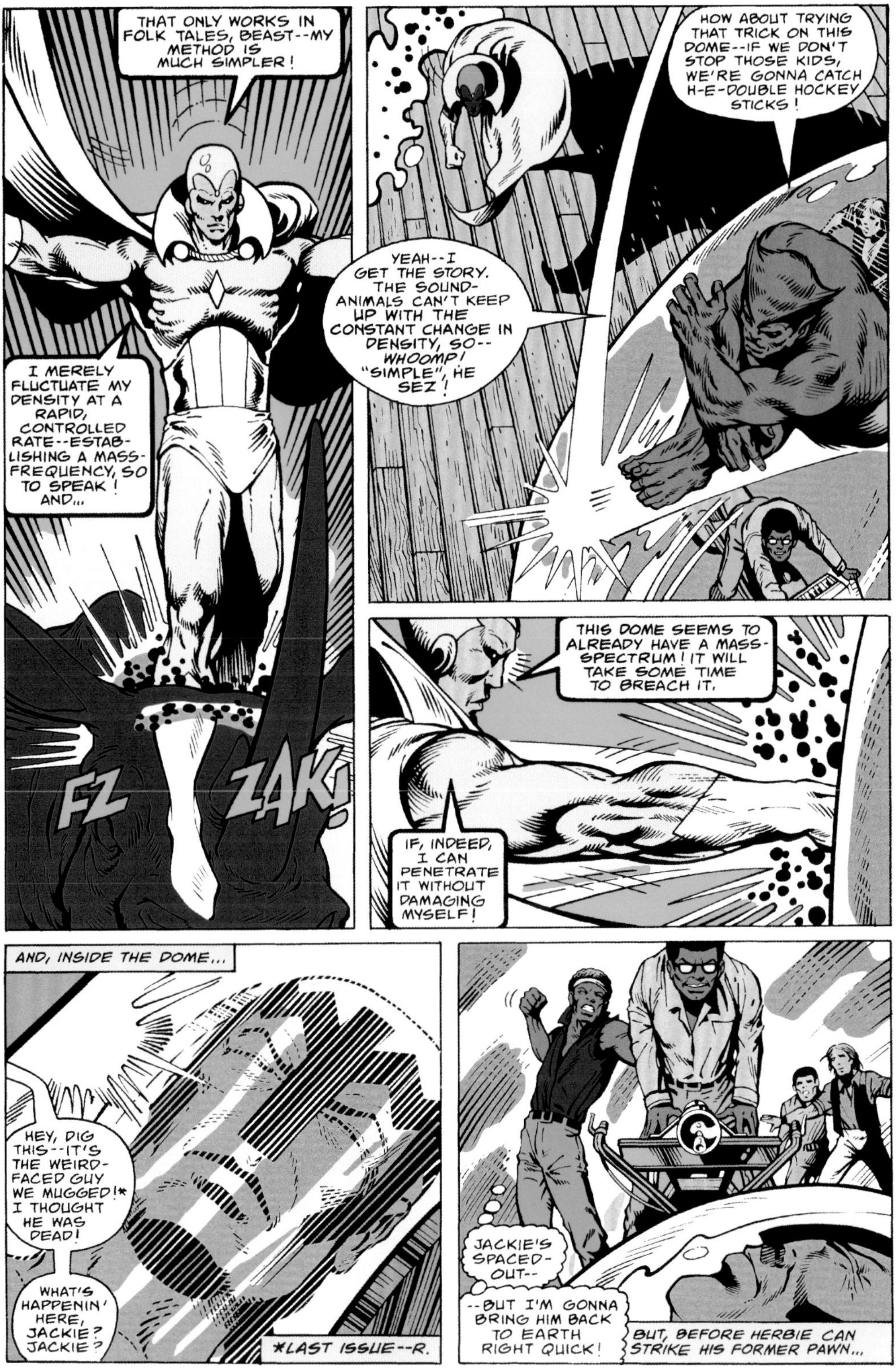
THAT ONLY WORKS IN FOLK TALES, BEAST--MY METHOD IS MUCH SIMPLER!
I MERELY FLUCTUATE MY DENSITY AT A RAPID, CONTROLLED RATE--ESTABLISHING A MASS-FREQUENCY, SO TO SPEAK! AND...
FZ ZAK!
YEAH--I GET THE STORY. THE SOUND-ANIMALS CAN'T KEEP UP WITH THE CONSTANT CHANGE IN DENSITY, SO-- WHOOMP! "SIMPLE", HE SEZ!
HOW ABOUT TRYING THAT TRICK ON THIS DOME--IF WE DON'T STOP THOSE KIDS, WE'RE GONNA CATCH H-E-DOUBLE HOCKEY STICKS!
THIS DOME SEEMS TO ALREADY HAVE A MASS-SPECTRUM! IT WILL TAKE SOME TIME TO BREACH IT.
IF, INDEED, I CAN PENETRATE IT WITHOUT DAMAGING MYSELF!
AND, INSIDE THE DOME...
HEY, DIG THIS--IT'S THE WEIRD-FACED GUY WE MUGGED!* I THOUGHT HE WAS DEAD!
WHAT'S HAPPENIN' HERE, JACKIE? JACKIE?
*LAST ISSUE--R.
JACKIE'S SPACED-OUT--
--BUT I'M GONNA BRING HIM BACK TO EARTH RIGHT QUICK!
BUT, BEFORE HERBIE CAN STRIKE HIS FORMER PAWN...

...JACKIE LASHES OUT WITH A STRENGTH BEYOND THE NATURAL POWER OF HIS LIMBS!

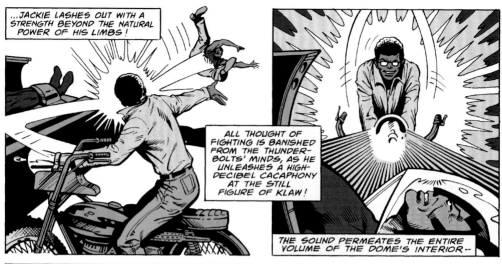

ALL THOUGHT OF FIGHTING IS BANISHED FROM THE THUNDER-BOLTS' MINDS, AS HE UNLEASHES A HIGH-DECIBEL CACAPHONY AT THE STILL FIGURE OF KLAW!

THE SOUND PERMEATES THE ENTIRE VOLUME OF THE DOME'S INTERIOR--

--BUT OUTSIDE, ONLY A LOW RUMBLE CAN BE DISCERNED!

IT LOOKS LIKE WE ARRIVED AT THE CRITICAL MOMENT, T'CHALLA!

I HOPE WE CAN GET THROUGH THAT DOME--THE VISION APPEARS TO BE STYMIED!

I WOULDN'T BE SURPRISED IF IT PROVED TO BE EQUALLY IMPERVIOUS TO YOUR SHIELD'S PECULIAR PROPERTIES, CAP!

PERHAPS HOPE FOR A DIRECT ROUTE INTO THE ENCLOSURE SHOULD BE ABANDONED--IN FAVOR OF A WAY AROUND THE BOUNDS OF THE DOME!

AT ANY RATE, PANTHER-- NOW THAT YOU HAVE ARRIVED--

"--I FEEL THAT YOU SHOULD HAVE COMMAND OF THIS OPERATION. OF ALL THE AVENGERS, YOU HAVE THE MOST EXPERIENCE WITH KLAW--AND THE MOST AT STAKE!"

EVEN AS THE VISION SPEAKS, THE BOUND FORM OF KLAW REGAINS CONSCIOUSNESS--AND, REVITALIZED BY THE FLOOD OF SOUND ENERGY...

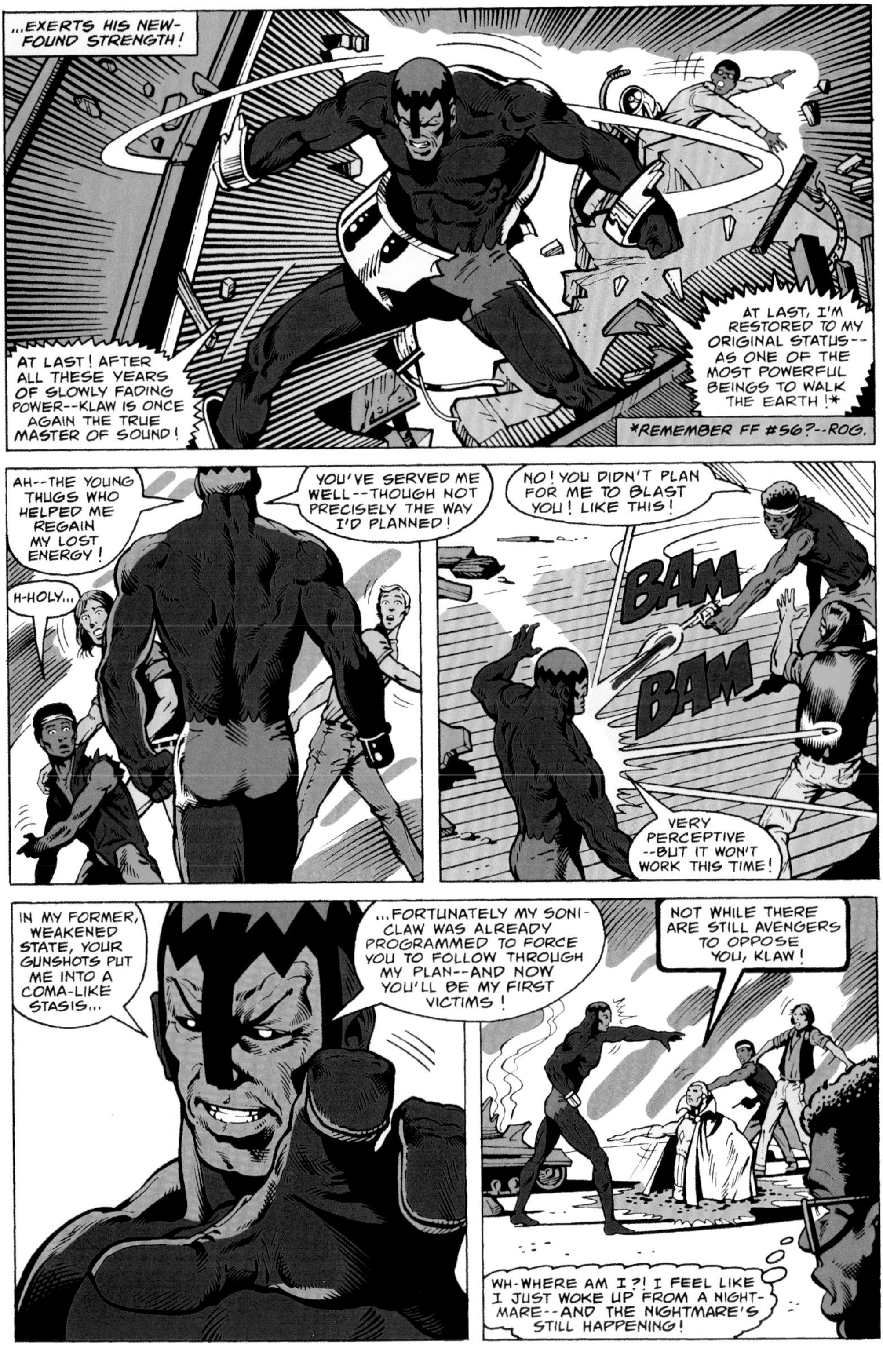
...EXERTS HIS NEW-FOUND STRENGTH!
AT LAST! AFTER ALL THESE YEARS OF SLOWLY FADING POWER--KLAW IS ONCE AGAIN THE TRUE MASTER OF SOUND!
AT LAST, I'M RESTORED TO MY ORIGINAL STATUS--AS ONE OF THE MOST POWERFUL BEINGS TO WALK THE EARTH!*
*REMEMBER FF #56?--ROG.
AH--THE YOUNG THUGS WHO HELPED ME REGAIN MY LOST ENERGY!
YOU'VE SERVED ME WELL--THOUGH NOT PRECISELY THE WAY I'D PLANNED!
H-HOLY...
NO! YOU DIDN'T PLAN FOR ME TO BLAST YOU! LIKE THIS!
BAM
BAM
VERY PERCEPTIVE --BUT IT WON'T WORK THIS TIME!
IN MY FORMER, WEAKENED STATE, YOUR GUNSHOTS PUT ME INTO A COMA-LIKE STASIS...
...FORTUNATELY MY SONI-CLAW WAS ALREADY PROGRAMMED TO FORCE YOU TO FOLLOW THROUGH MY PLAN--AND NOW YOU'LL BE MY FIRST VICTIMS!
NOT WHILE THERE ARE STILL AVENGERS TO OPPOSE YOU, KLAW!
WH-WHERE AM I?! I FEEL LIKE I JUST WOKE UP FROM A NIGHT-MARE--AND THE NIGHTMARE'S STILL HAPPENING!

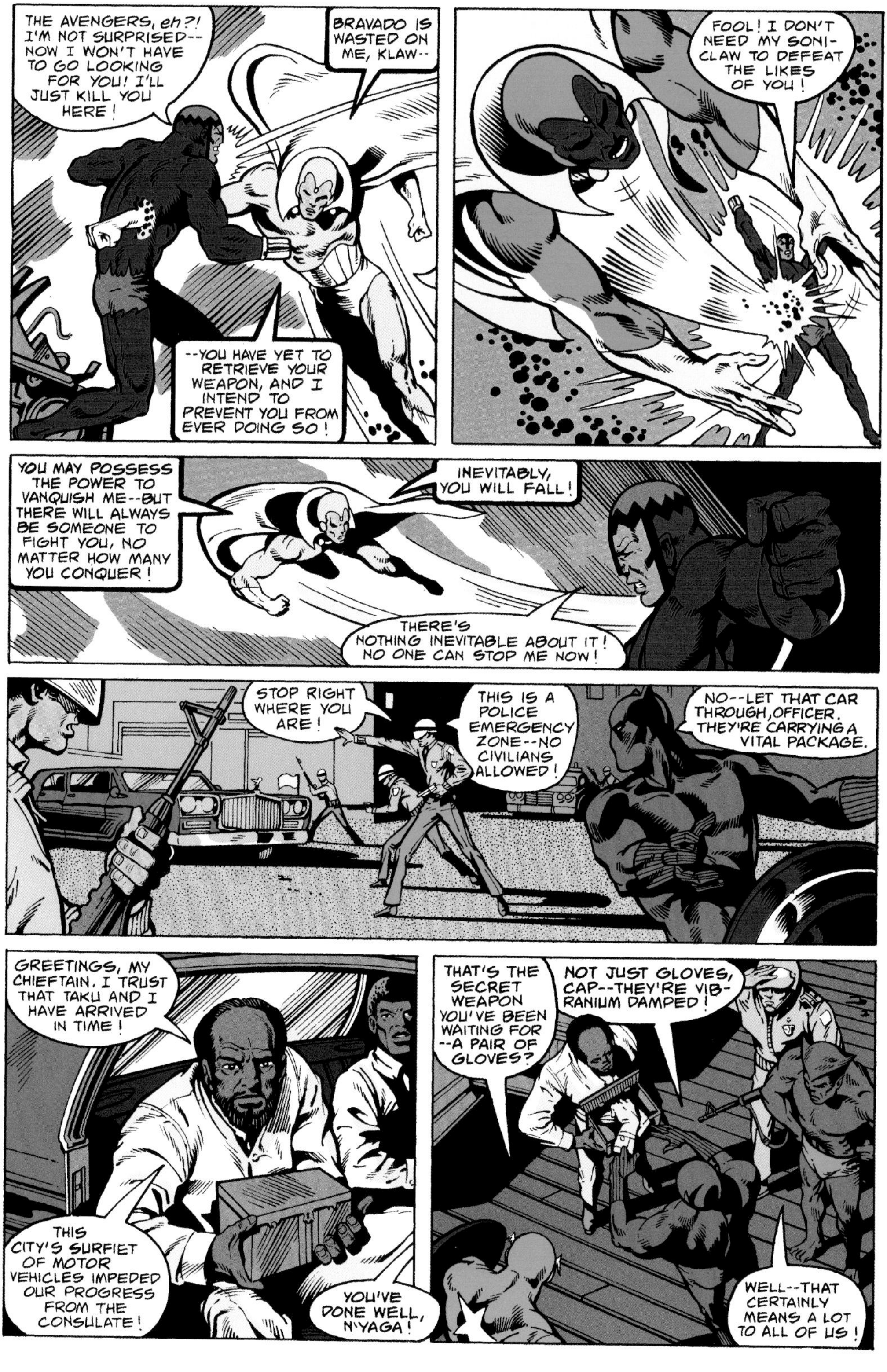
THE AVENGERS, eh?! I'M NOT SURPRISED-- NOW I WON'T HAVE TO GO LOOKING FOR YOU! I'LL JUST KILL YOU HERE!
BRAVADO IS WASTED ON ME, KLAW--
--YOU HAVE YET TO RETRIEVE YOUR WEAPON, AND I INTEND TO PREVENT YOU FROM EVER DOING SO!
FOOL! I DON'T NEED MY SONI-CLAW TO DEFEAT THE LIKES OF YOU!
YOU MAY POSSESS THE POWER TO VANQUISH ME--BUT THERE WILL ALWAYS BE SOMEONE TO FIGHT YOU, NO MATTER HOW MANY YOU CONQUER!
INEVITABLY, YOU WILL FALL!
THERE'S NOTHING INEVITABLE ABOUT IT! NO ONE CAN STOP ME NOW!
STOP RIGHT WHERE YOU ARE!
THIS IS A POLICE EMERGENCY ZONE--NO CIVILIANS ALLOWED!
NO--LET THAT CAR THROUGH, OFFICER. THEY'RE CARRYING A VITAL PACKAGE.
GREETINGS, MY CHIEFTAIN. I TRUST THAT TAKU AND I HAVE ARRIVED IN TIME!
THIS CITY'S SURFIET OF MOTOR VEHICLES IMPEDED OUR PROGRESS FROM THE CONSULATE!
YOU'VE DONE WELL, N'YAGA!
THAT'S THE SECRET WEAPON YOU'VE BEEN WAITING FOR --A PAIR OF GLOVES?
NOT JUST GLOVES, CAP--THEY'RE VIB-RANIUM DAMPED!
WELL--THAT CERTAINLY MEANS A LOT TO ALL OF US!

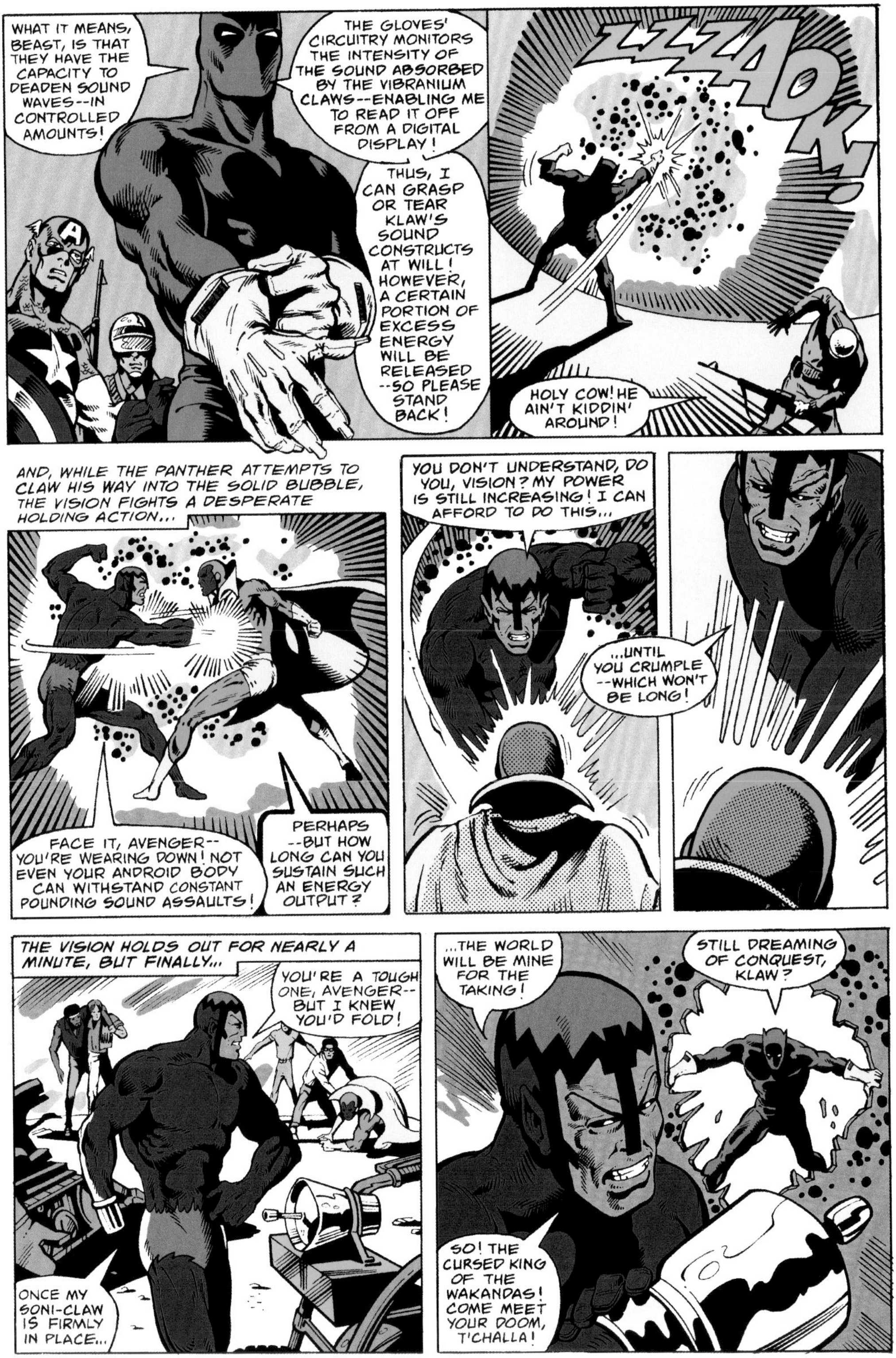
WHAT IT MEANS, BEAST, IS THAT THEY HAVE THE CAPACITY TO DEADEN SOUND WAVES--IN CONTROLLED AMOUNTS!
THE GLOVES' CIRCUITRY MONITORS THE INTENSITY OF THE SOUND ABSORBED BY THE VIBRANIUM CLAWS--ENABLING ME TO READ IT OFF FROM A DIGITAL DISPLAY!
THUS, I CAN GRASP OR TEAR KLAW'S SOUND CONSTRUCTS AT WILL! HOWEVER, A CERTAIN PORTION OF EXCESS ENERGY WILL BE RELEASED --SO PLEASE STAND BACK!
ZZZADK!
HOLY COW! HE AIN'T KIDDIN' AROUND!
AND, WHILE THE PANTHER ATTEMPTS TO CLAW HIS WAY INTO THE SOLID BUBBLE, THE VISION FIGHTS A DESPERATE HOLDING ACTION...
FACE IT, AVENGER-- YOU'RE WEARING DOWN! NOT EVEN YOUR ANDROID BODY CAN WITHSTAND CONSTANT POUNDING SOUND ASSAULTS!
PERHAPS --BUT HOW LONG CAN YOU SUSTAIN SUCH AN ENERGY OUTPUT?
YOU DON'T UNDERSTAND, DO YOU, VISION? MY POWER IS STILL INCREASING! I CAN AFFORD TO DO THIS...
...UNTIL YOU CRUMPLE --WHICH WON'T BE LONG!
THE VISION HOLDS OUT FOR NEARLY A MINUTE, BUT FINALLY...
YOU'RE A TOUGH ONE, AVENGER-- BUT I KNEW YOU'D FOLD!
ONCE MY SONI-CLAW IS FIRMLY IN PLACE...
...THE WORLD WILL BE MINE FOR THE TAKING!
STILL DREAMING OF CONQUEST, KLAW?
SO! THE CURSED KING OF THE WAKANDAS! COME MEET YOUR DOOM, T'CHALLA!

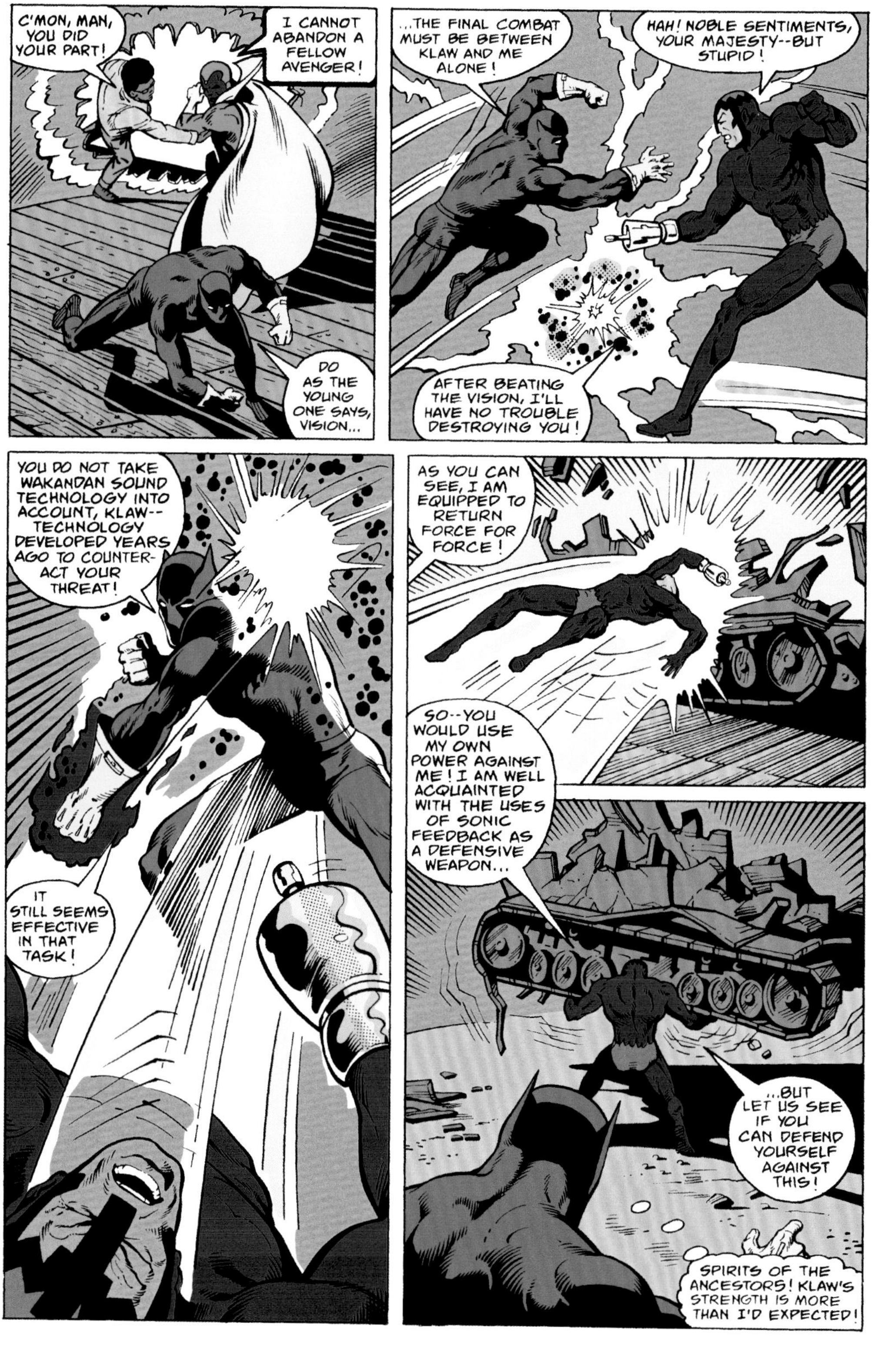
C'MON, MAN, YOU DID YOUR PART!
I CANNOT ABANDON A FELLOW AVENGER!
DO AS THE YOUNG ONE SAYS, VISION...
...THE FINAL COMBAT MUST BE BETWEEN KLAW AND ME ALONE!
HAH! NOBLE SENTIMENTS, YOUR MAJESTY--BUT STUPID!
AFTER BEATING THE VISION, I'LL HAVE NO TROUBLE DESTROYING YOU!
YOU DO NOT TAKE WAKANDAN SOUND TECHNOLOGY INTO ACCOUNT, KLAW--TECHNOLOGY DEVELOPED YEARS AGO TO COUNTER-ACT YOUR THREAT!
IT STILL SEEMS EFFECTIVE IN THAT TASK!
AS YOU CAN SEE, I AM EQUIPPED TO RETURN FORCE FOR FORCE!
SO--YOU WOULD USE MY OWN POWER AGAINST ME! I AM WELL ACQUAINTED WITH THE USES OF SONIC FEEDBACK AS A DEFENSIVE WEAPON...
...BUT LET US SEE IF YOU CAN DEFEND YOURSELF AGAINST THIS!
SPIRITS OF THE ANCESTORS! KLAW'S STRENGTH IS MORE THAN I'D EXPECTED!

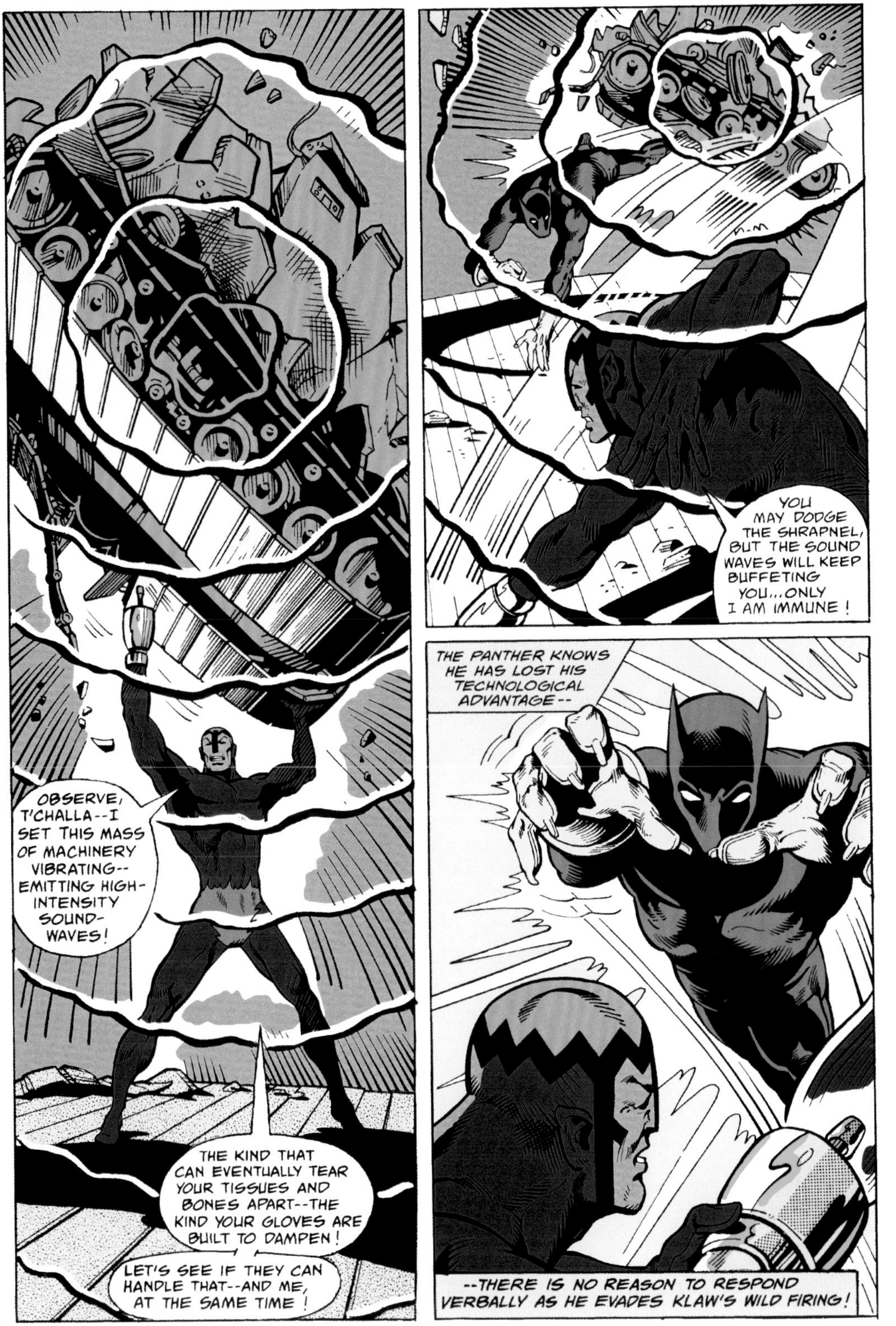
OBSERVE, T'CHALLA--I SET THIS MASS OF MACHINERY VIBRATING--EMITTING HIGH-INTENSITY SOUND-WAVES!
THE KIND THAT CAN EVENTUALLY TEAR YOUR TISSUES AND BONES APART--THE KIND YOUR GLOVES ARE BUILT TO DAMPEN!
LET'S SEE IF THEY CAN HANDLE THAT--AND ME, AT THE SAME TIME!
YOU MAY DODGE THE SHRAPNEL, BUT THE SOUND WAVES WILL KEEP BUFFETING YOU...ONLY I AM IMMUNE!
THE PANTHER KNOWS HE HAS LOST HIS TECHNOLOGICAL ADVANTAGE--
--THERE IS NO REASON TO RESPOND VERBALLY AS HE EVADES KLAW'S WILD FIRING!

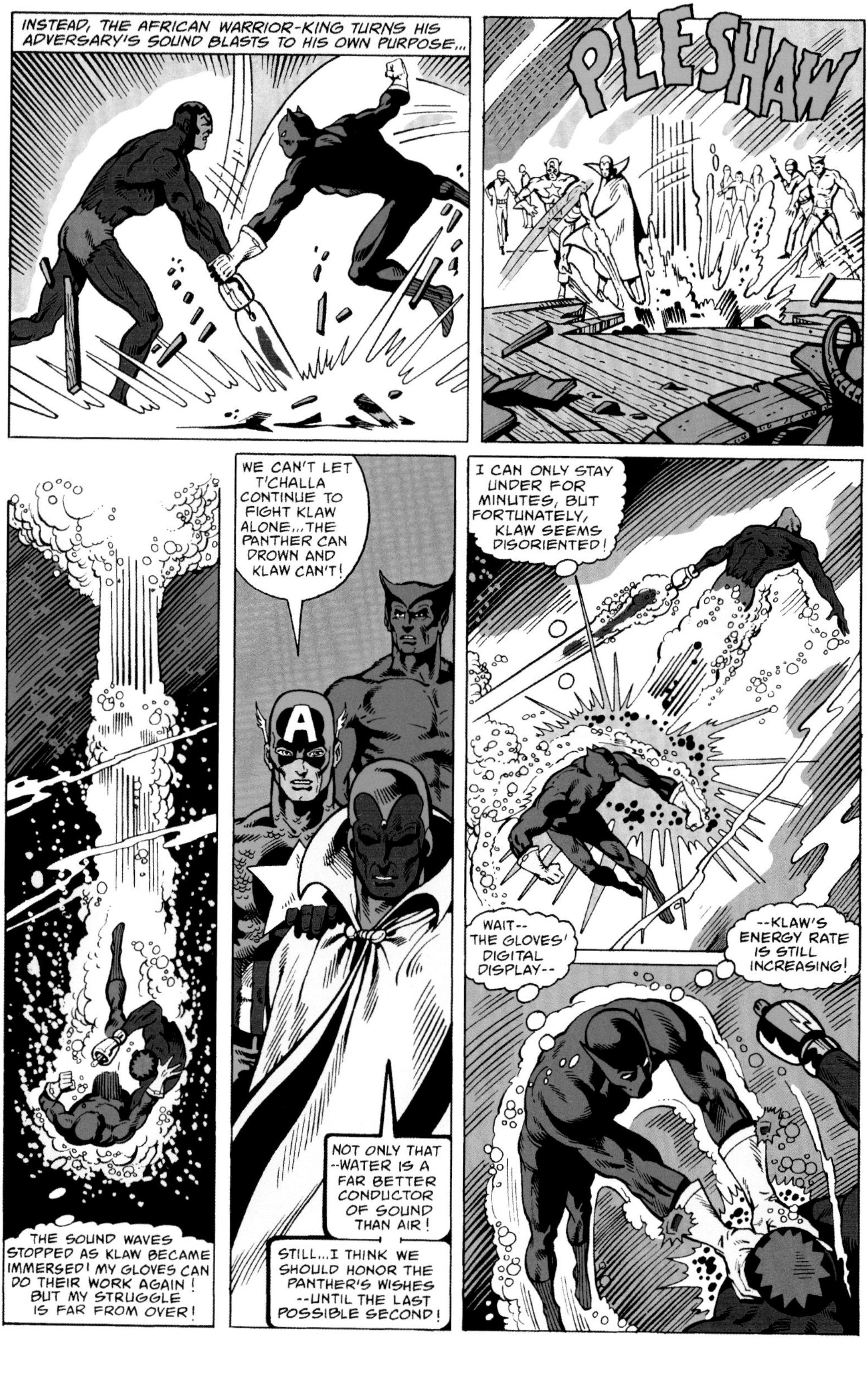
INSTEAD, THE AFRICAN WARRIOR-KING TURNS HIS ADVERSARY'S SOUND BLASTS TO HIS OWN PURPOSE...
PLESHAW
THE SOUND WAVES STOPPED AS KLAW BECAME IMMERSED! MY GLOVES CAN DO THEIR WORK AGAIN! BUT MY STRUGGLE IS FAR FROM OVER!
WE CAN'T LET T'CHALLA CONTINUE TO FIGHT KLAW ALONE... THE PANTHER CAN DROWN AND KLAW CAN'T!
NOT ONLY THAT --WATER IS A FAR BETTER CONDUCTOR OF SOUND THAN AIR!
STILL... I THINK WE SHOULD HONOR THE PANTHER'S WISHES --UNTIL THE LAST POSSIBLE SECOND!
I CAN ONLY STAY UNDER FOR MINUTES, BUT FORTUNATELY, KLAW SEEMS DISORIENTED!
WAIT-- THE GLOVES' DIGITAL DISPLAY--
--KLAW'S ENERGY RATE IS STILL INCREASING!

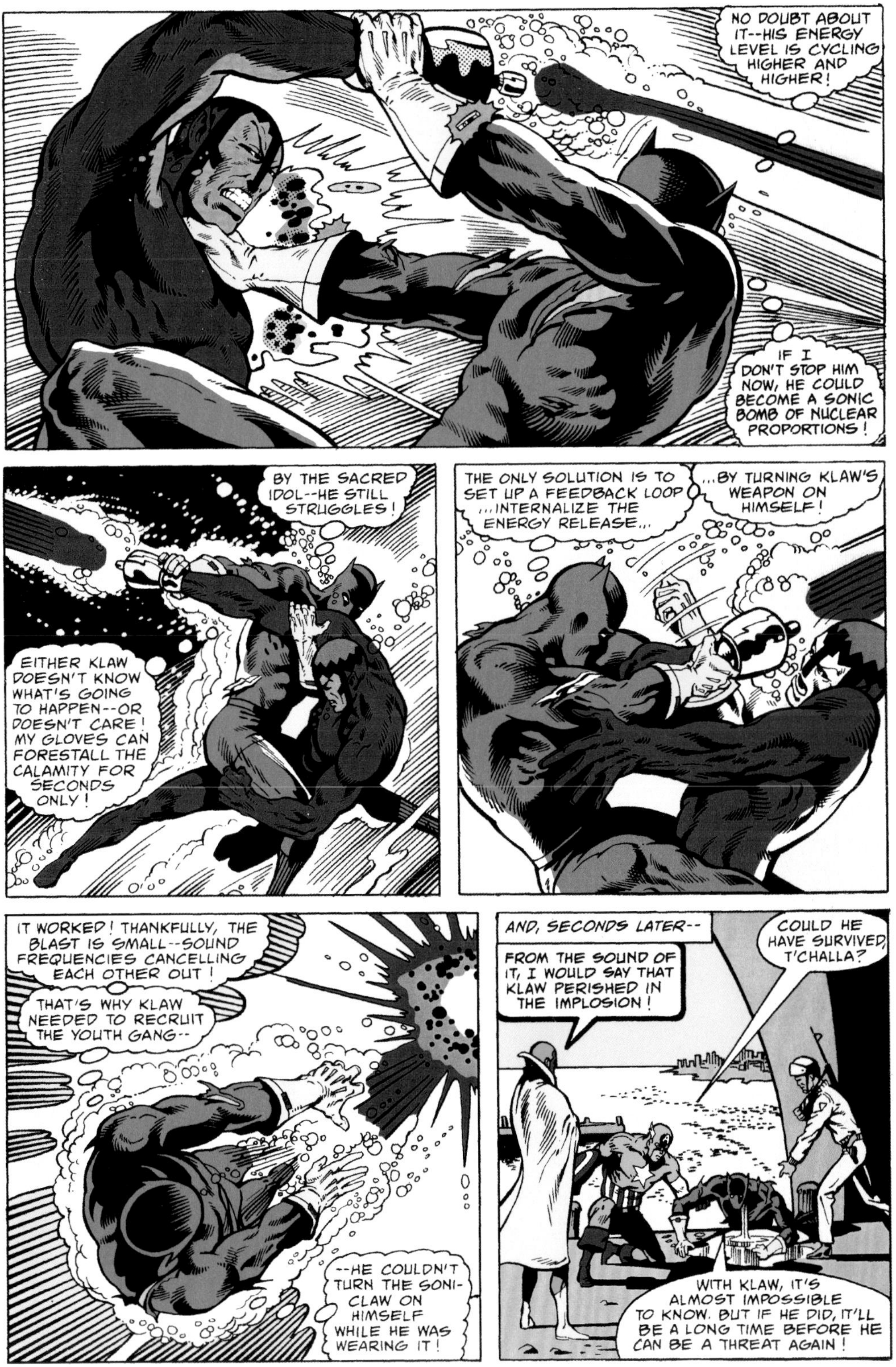
NO DOUBT ABOUT IT--HIS ENERGY LEVEL IS CYCLING HIGHER AND HIGHER!
IF I DON'T STOP HIM NOW, HE COULD BECOME A SONIC BOMB OF NUCLEAR PROPORTIONS!
BY THE SACRED IDOL--HE STILL STRUGGLES!
EITHER KLAW DOESN'T KNOW WHAT'S GOING TO HAPPEN--OR DOESN'T CARE! MY GLOVES CAN FORESTALL THE CALAMITY FOR SECONDS ONLY!
THE ONLY SOLUTION IS TO SET UP A FEEDBACK LOOP ...INTERNALIZE THE ENERGY RELEASE...
...BY TURNING KLAW'S WEAPON ON HIMSELF!
IT WORKED! THANKFULLY, THE BLAST IS SMALL--SOUND FREQUENCIES CANCELLING EACH OTHER OUT!
THAT'S WHY KLAW NEEDED TO RECRUIT THE YOUTH GANG--
--HE COULDN'T TURN THE SONI-CLAW ON HIMSELF WHILE HE WAS WEARING IT!
AND, SECONDS LATER--
FROM THE SOUND OF IT, I WOULD SAY THAT KLAW PERISHED IN THE IMPLOSION!
COULD HE HAVE SURVIVED, T'CHALLA?
WITH KLAW, IT'S ALMOST IMPOSSIBLE TO KNOW. BUT IF HE DID, IT'LL BE A LONG TIME BEFORE HE CAN BE A THREAT AGAIN!

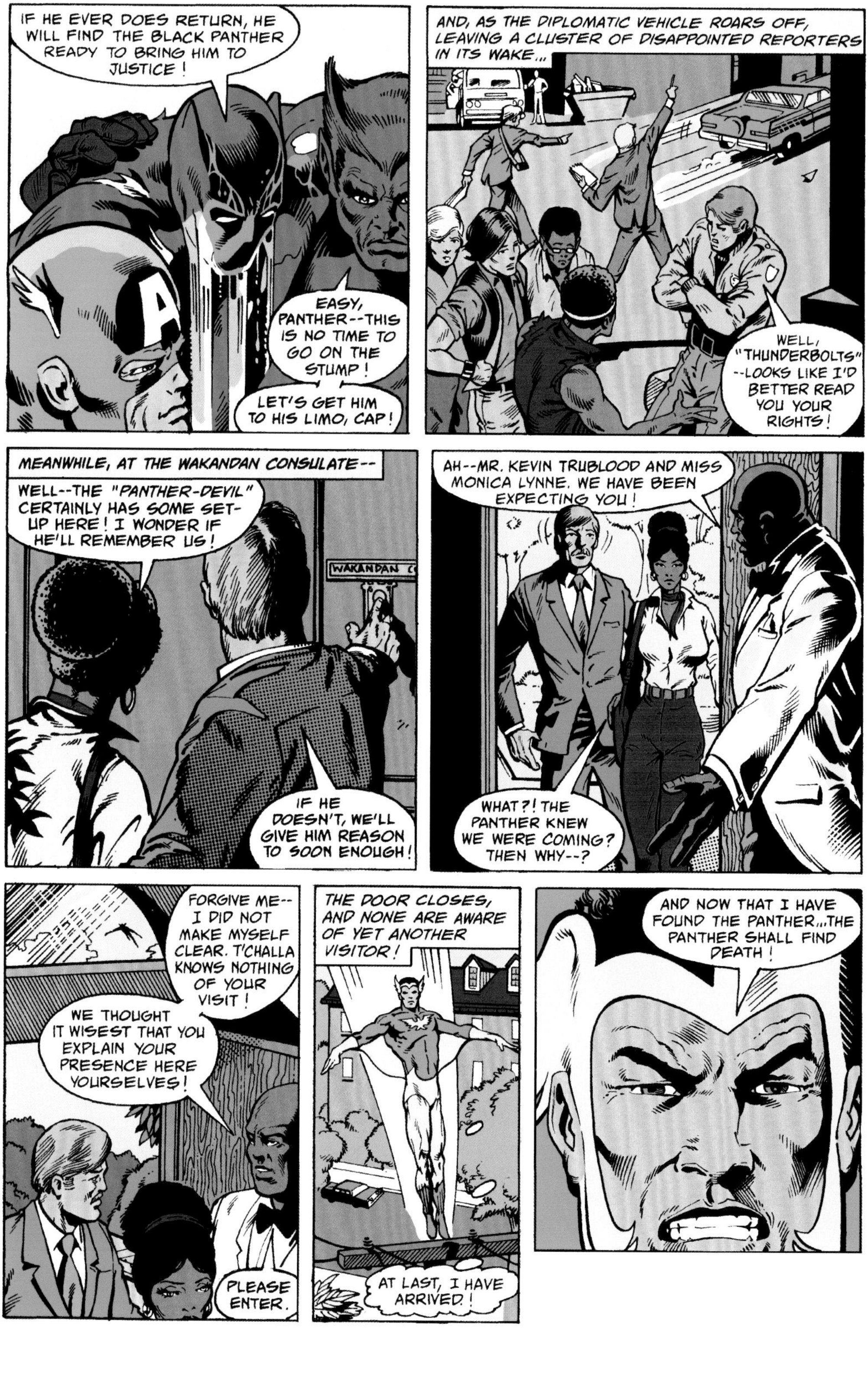
IF HE EVER DOES RETURN, HE WILL FIND THE BLACK PANTHER READY TO BRING HIM TO JUSTICE!
EASY, PANTHER--THIS IS NO TIME TO GO ON THE STUMP!
LET'S GET HIM TO HIS LIMO, CAP!
AND, AS THE DIPLOMATIC VEHICLE ROARS OFF, LEAVING A CLUSTER OF DISAPPOINTED REPORTERS IN ITS WAKE...
WELL, "THUNDERBOLTS" --LOOKS LIKE I'D BETTER READ YOU YOUR RIGHTS!
MEANWHILE, AT THE WAKANDAN CONSULATE--
WELL--THE "PANTHER-DEVIL" CERTAINLY HAS SOME SET-UP HERE! I WONDER IF HE'LL REMEMBER US!
IF HE DOESN'T, WE'LL GIVE HIM REASON TO SOON ENOUGH!
AH--MR. KEVIN TRUBLOOD AND MISS MONICA LYNNE. WE HAVE BEEN EXPECTING YOU!
WHAT?! THE PANTHER KNEW WE WERE COMING? THEN WHY--?
FORGIVE ME--I DID NOT MAKE MYSELF CLEAR. T'CHALLA KNOWS NOTHING OF YOUR VISIT!
WE THOUGHT IT WISEST THAT YOU EXPLAIN YOUR PRESENCE HERE YOURSELVES!
PLEASE ENTER.
THE DOOR CLOSES, AND NONE ARE AWARE OF YET ANOTHER VISITOR!
AT LAST, I HAVE ARRIVED!
AND NOW THAT I HAVE FOUND THE PANTHER...THE PANTHER SHALL FIND DEATH!

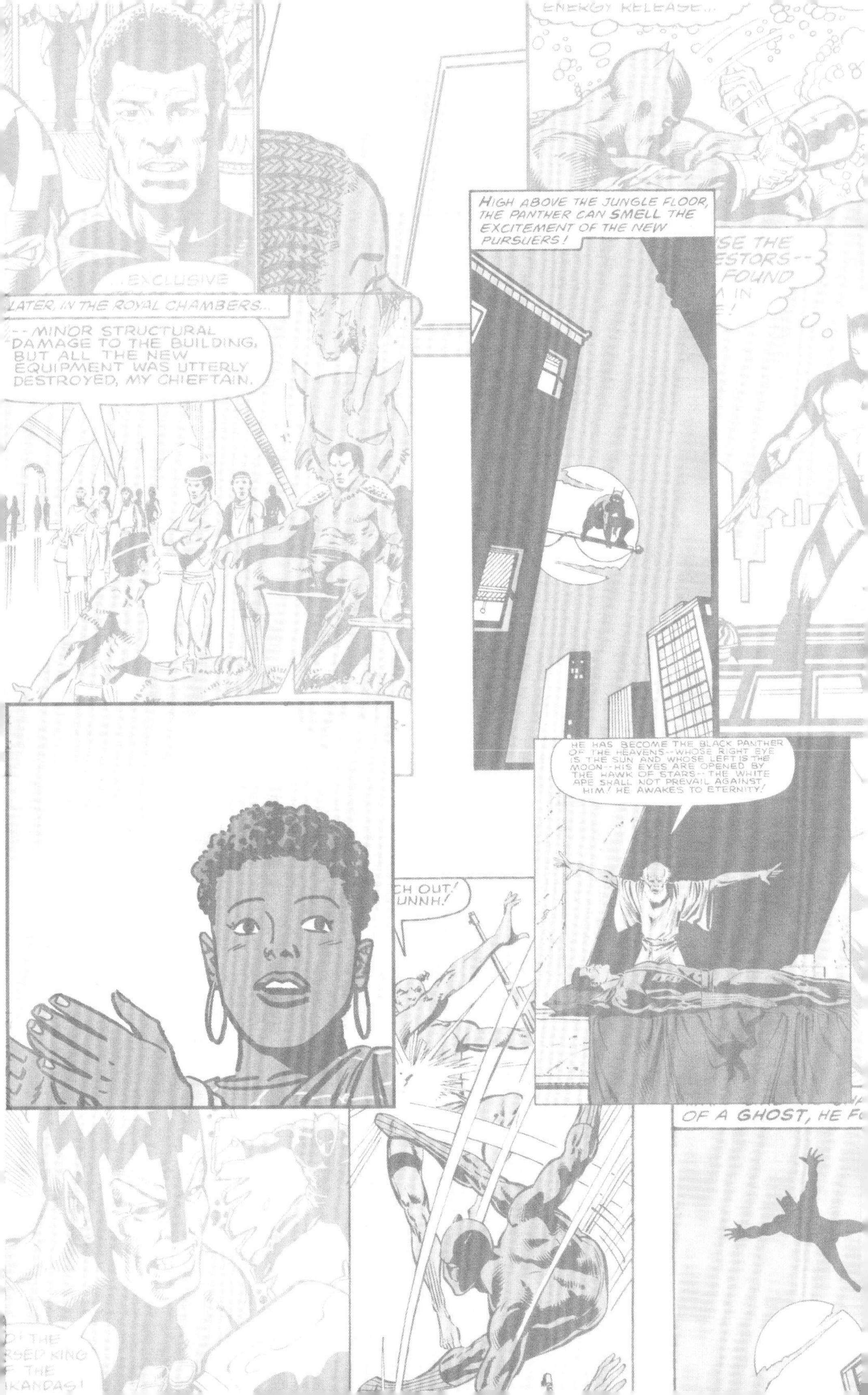

ENERGY RELEASE...
...EXCLUSIVE
LATER, IN THE ROYAL CHAMBERS...
--MINOR STRUCTURAL DAMAGE TO THE BUILDING, BUT ALL THE NEW EQUIPMENT WAS UTTERLY DESTROYED, MY CHIEFTAIN.
HIGH ABOVE THE JUNGLE FLOOR, THE PANTHER CAN SMELL THE EXCITEMENT OF THE NEW PURSUERS!
HE HAS BECOME THE BLACK PANTHER OF THE HEAVENS--WHOSE RIGHT EYE IS THE SUN AND WHOSE LEFT IS THE MOON--HIS EYES ARE OPENED BY THE HAWK OF STARS--THE WHITE APE SHALL NOT PREVAIL AGAINST HIM! HE AWAKES TO ETERNITY!

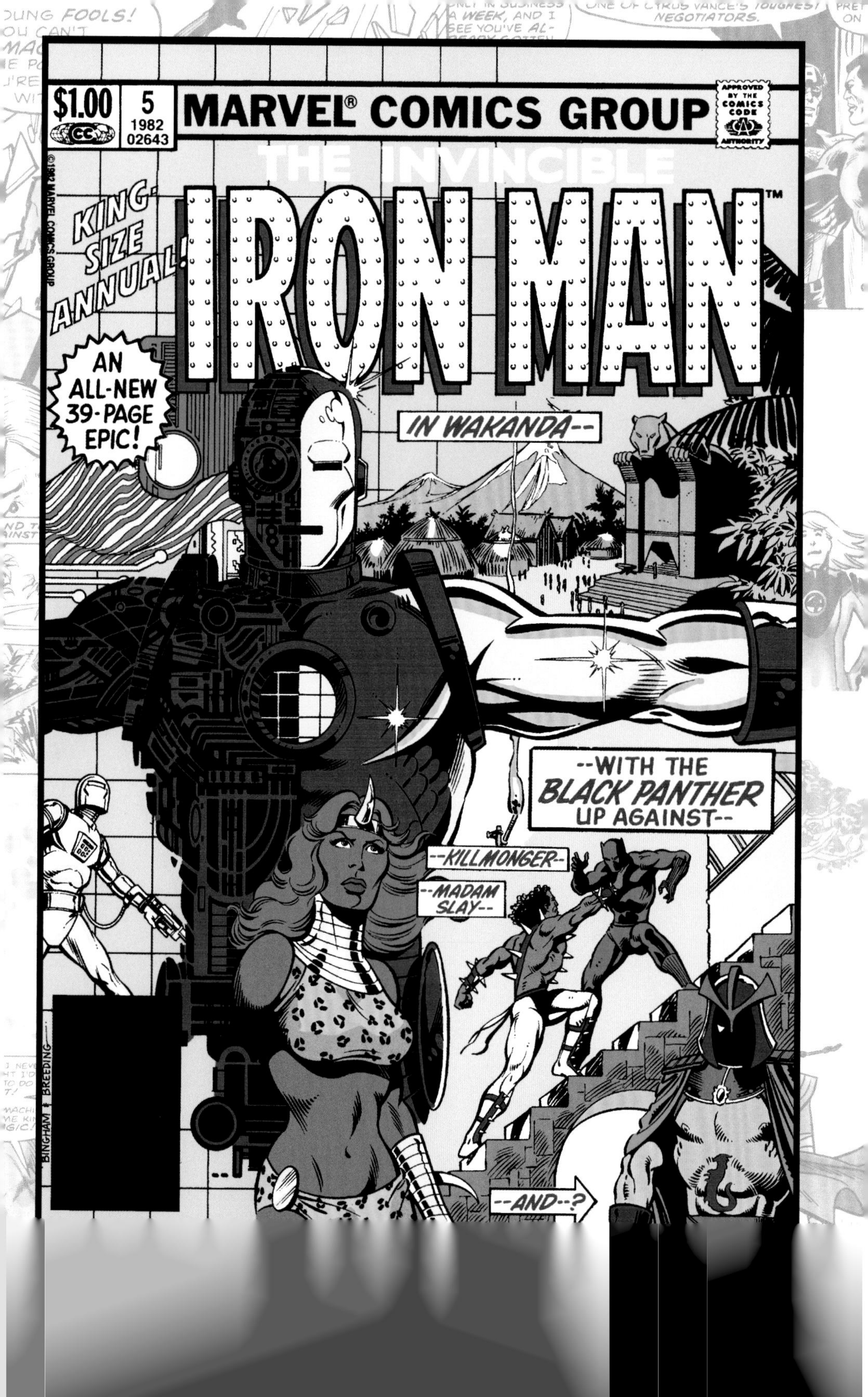
$1.00
5
1982
02643
MARVEL® COMICS GROUP
APPROVED BY THE COMICS CODE AUTHORITY
THE INVINCIBLE
IRON MAN™
KING-SIZE ANNUAL!
AN ALL-NEW 39-PAGE EPIC!
IN WAKANDA--
--WITH THE BLACK PANTHER UP AGAINST--
--KILLMONGER--
--MADAM SLAY--
--AND--?
©1982 MARVEL COMICS GROUP
BINGHAM & BREEDING

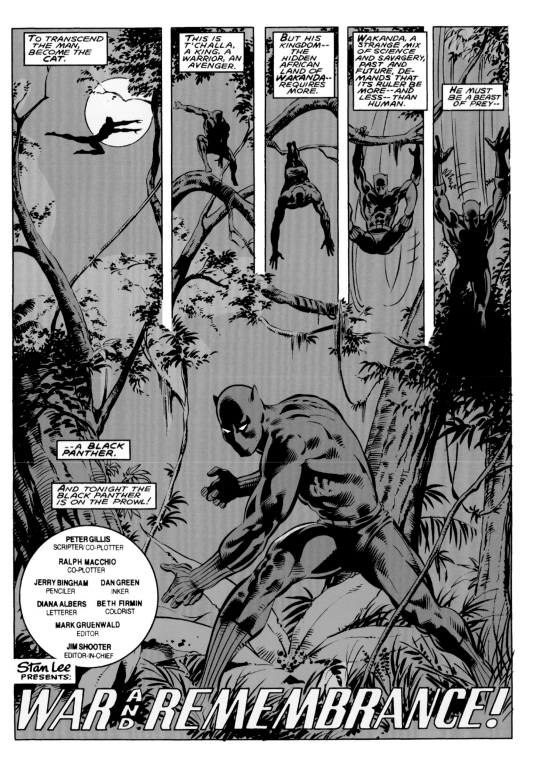

TO TRANSCEND THE MAN, BECOME THE CAT.

THIS IS T'CHALLA, A KING, A WARRIOR, AN AVENGER.

BUT HIS KINGDOM-- THE HIDDEN AFRICAN LAND OF WAKANDA-- REQUIRES MORE.

WAKANDA, A STRANGE MIX OF SCIENCE AND SAVAGERY, PAST AND FUTURE, DE-MANDS THAT ITS RULER BE MORE--AND LESS--THAN HUMAN.

HE MUST BE A BEAST OF PREY--

--A BLACK PANTHER.

AND TONIGHT THE BLACK PANTHER IS ON THE PROWL!

**PETER GILLIS**
SCRIPTER/CO-PLOTTER

**RALPH MACCHIO**
CO-PLOTTER

**JERRY BINGHAM**        **DAN GREEN**
PENCILER                            INKER

**DIANA ALBERS**        **BETH FIRMIN**
LETTERER                          COLORIST

**MARK GRUENWALD**
EDITOR

**JIM SHOOTER**
EDITOR-IN-CHIEF

Stan Lee
PRESENTS:

WAR AND REMEMBRANCE!

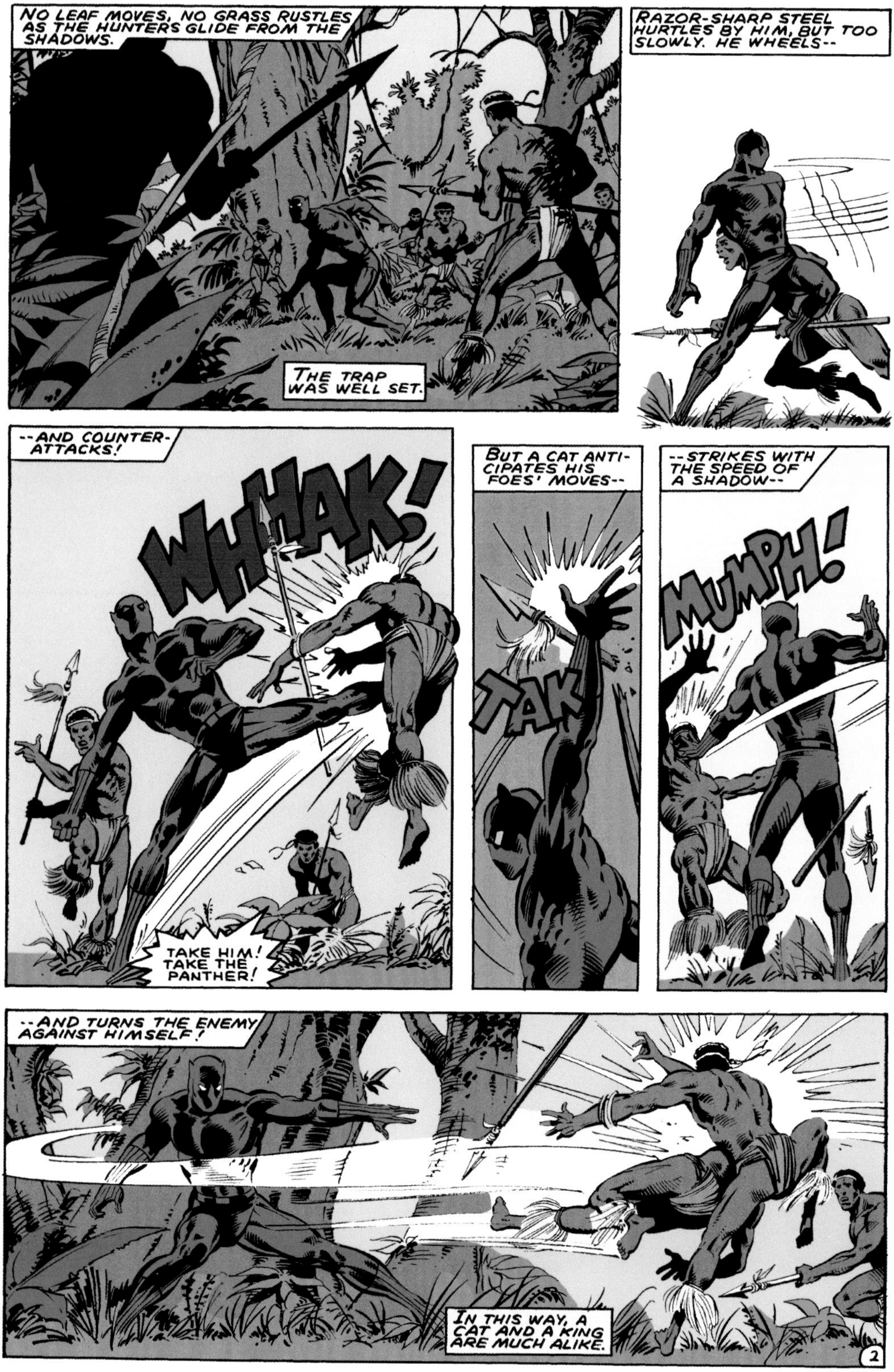
NO LEAF MOVES, NO GRASS RUSTLES AS THE HUNTERS GLIDE FROM THE SHADOWS.
THE TRAP WAS WELL SET.
RAZOR-SHARP STEEL HURTLES BY HIM, BUT TOO SLOWLY. HE WHEELS--
--AND COUNTER-ATTACKS!
WHHAK!
TAKE HIM! TAKE THE PANTHER!
BUT A CAT ANTICIPATES HIS FOES' MOVES--
TAK
--STRIKES WITH THE SPEED OF A SHADOW--
MUMPH!
--AND TURNS THE ENEMY AGAINST HIMSELF!
IN THIS WAY, A CAT AND A KING ARE MUCH ALIKE.
2

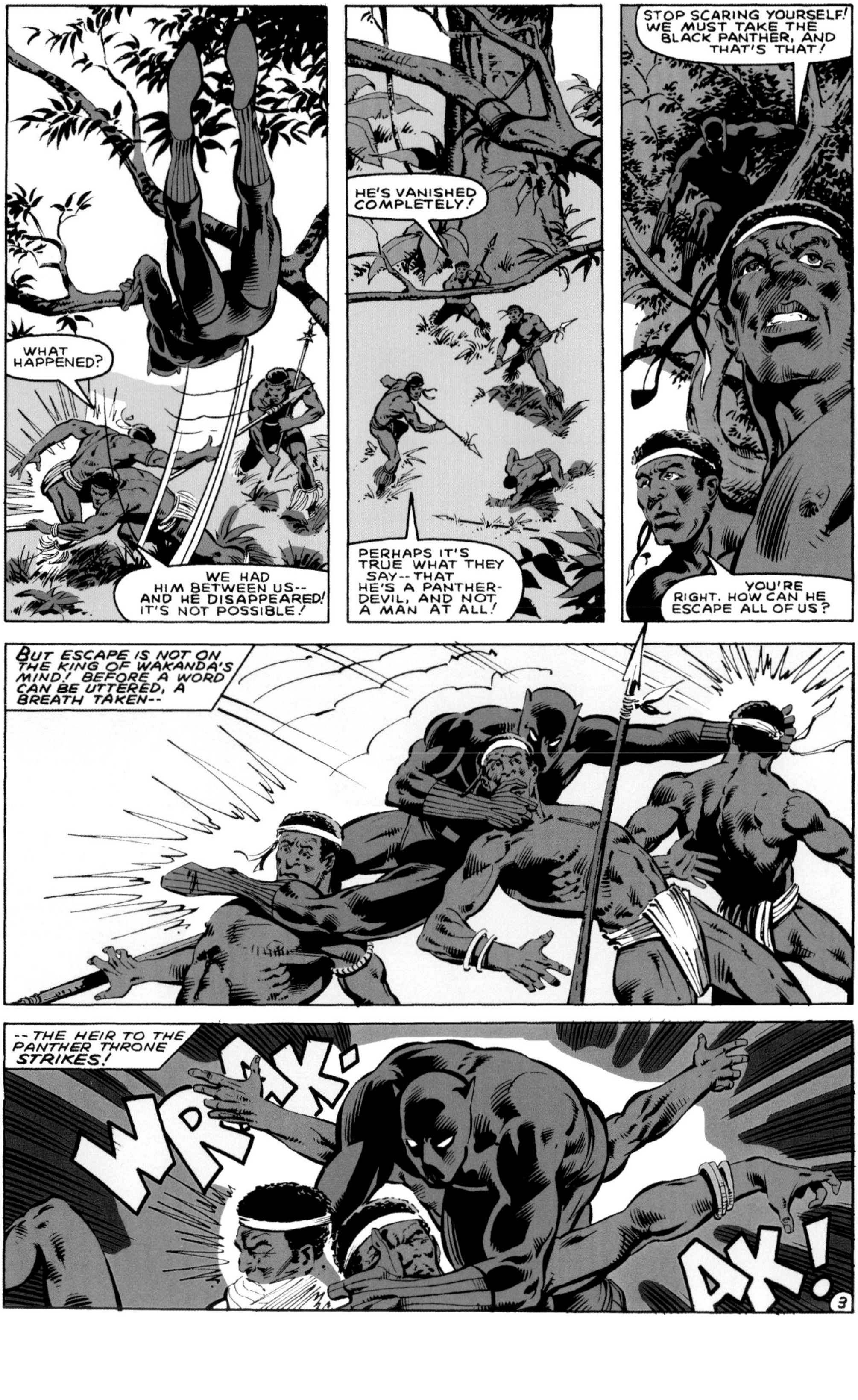
WHAT HAPPENED?
WE HAD HIM BETWEEN US-- AND HE DISAPPEARED! IT'S NOT POSSIBLE!
HE'S VANISHED COMPLETELY!
PERHAPS IT'S TRUE WHAT THEY SAY--THAT HE'S A PANTHER-DEVIL, AND NOT A MAN AT ALL!
STOP SCARING YOURSELF! WE MUST TAKE THE BLACK PANTHER, AND THAT'S THAT!
YOU'RE RIGHT. HOW CAN HE ESCAPE ALL OF US?
BUT ESCAPE IS NOT ON THE KING OF WAKANDA'S MIND! BEFORE A WORD CAN BE UTTERED, A BREATH TAKEN--
--THE HEIR TO THE PANTHER THRONE STRIKES!
WHAK!
AX!
3

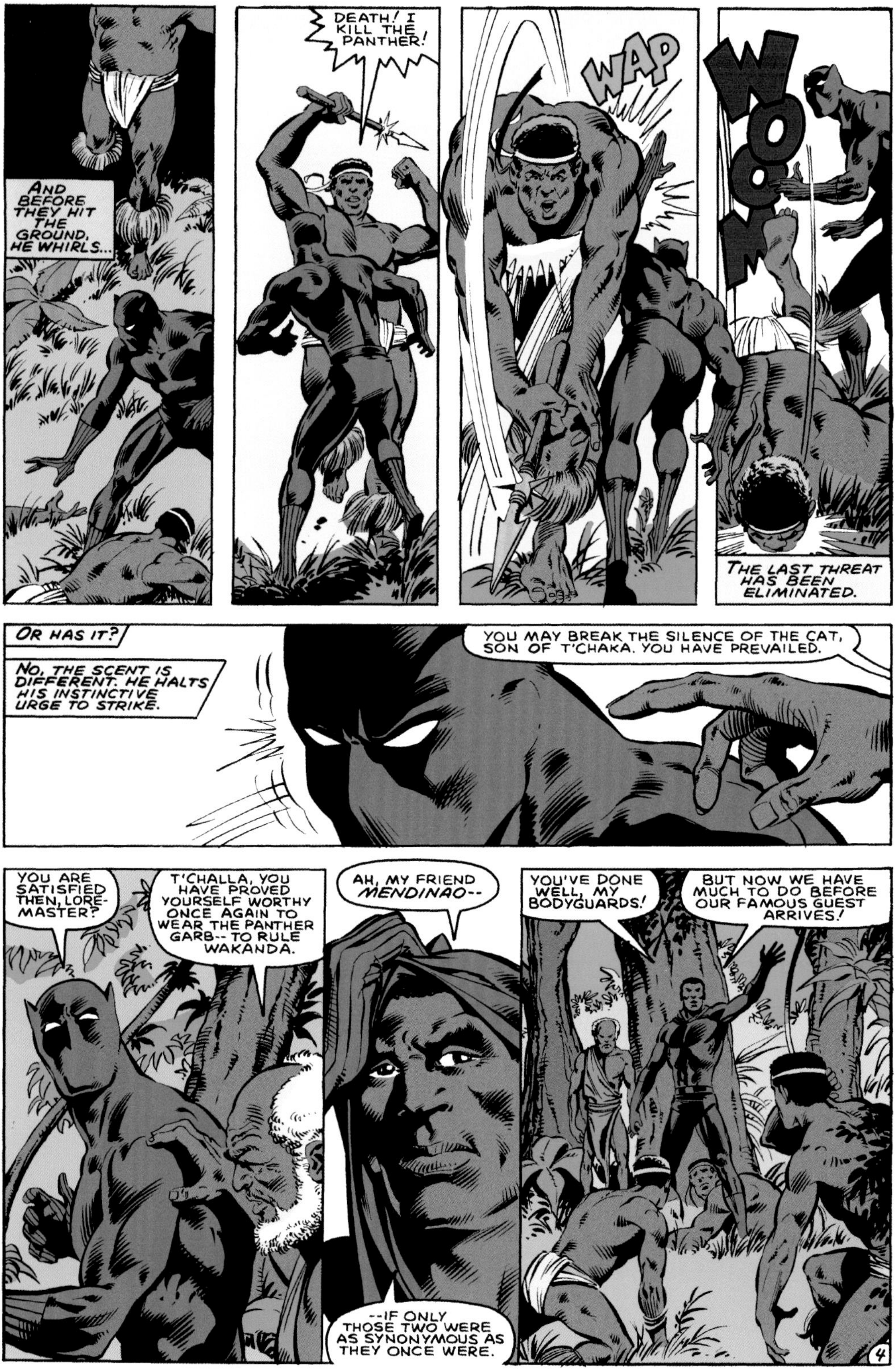
AND BEFORE THEY HIT THE GROUND, HE WHIRLS...
DEATH! I KILL THE PANTHER!
WAP
WOOM
THE LAST THREAT HAS BEEN ELIMINATED.
OR HAS IT?
NO, THE SCENT IS DIFFERENT. HE HALTS HIS INSTINCTIVE URGE TO STRIKE.
YOU MAY BREAK THE SILENCE OF THE CAT, SON OF T'CHAKA. YOU HAVE PREVAILED.
YOU ARE SATISFIED THEN, LORE-MASTER?
T'CHALLA, YOU HAVE PROVED YOURSELF WORTHY ONCE AGAIN TO WEAR THE PANTHER GARB-- TO RULE WAKANDA.
AH, MY FRIEND MENDINAO--
--IF ONLY THOSE TWO WERE AS SYNONYMOUS AS THEY ONCE WERE.
YOU'VE DONE WELL, MY BODYGUARDS!
BUT NOW WE HAVE MUCH TO DO BEFORE OUR FAMOUS GUEST ARRIVES!
4

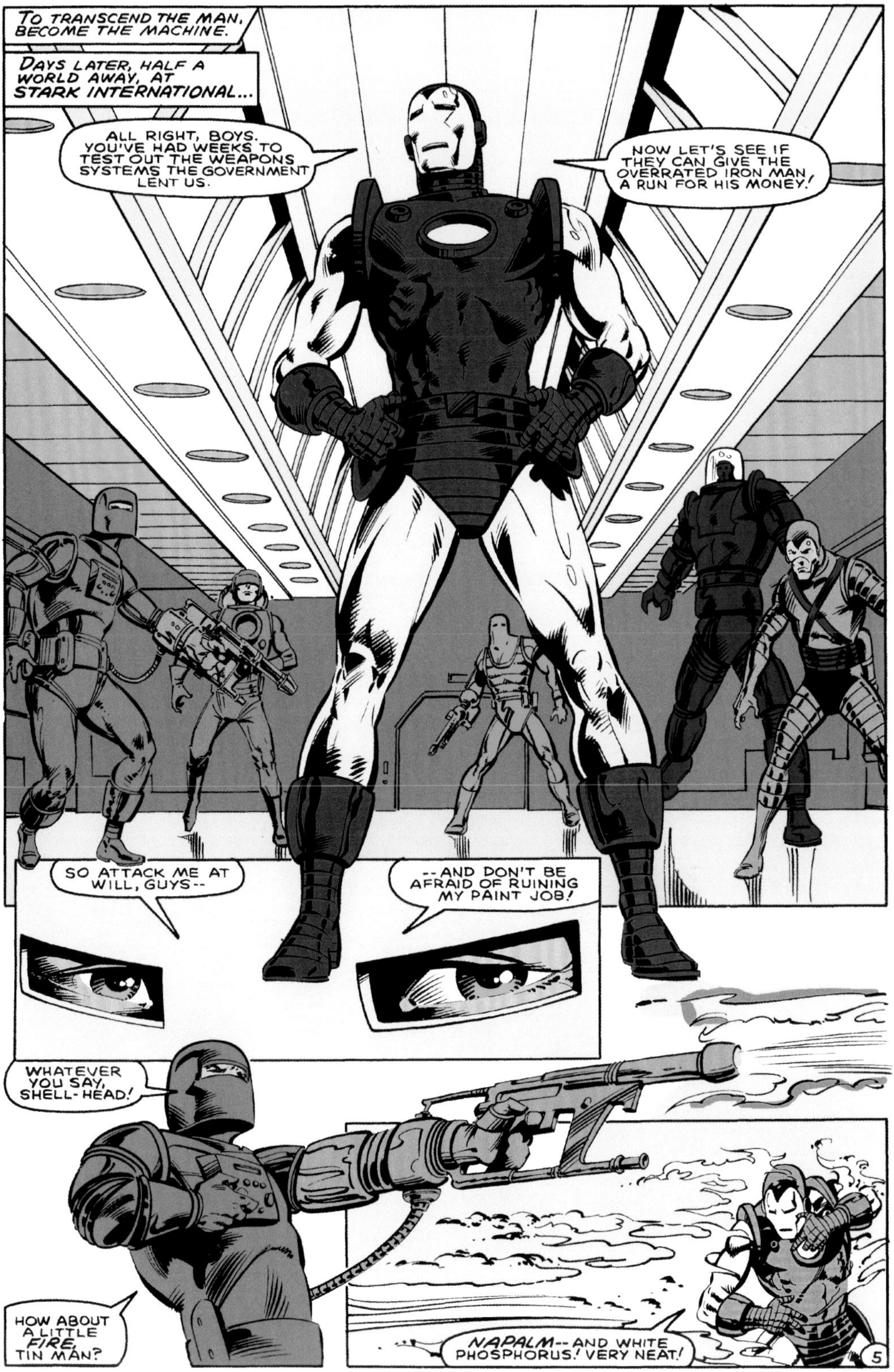
TO TRANSCEND THE MAN, BECOME THE MACHINE.
DAYS LATER, HALF A WORLD AWAY, AT STARK INTERNATIONAL...
ALL RIGHT, BOYS. YOU'VE HAD WEEKS TO TEST OUT THE WEAPONS SYSTEMS THE GOVERNMENT LENT US.
NOW LET'S SEE IF THEY CAN GIVE THE OVERRATED IRON MAN A RUN FOR HIS MONEY!
SO ATTACK ME AT WILL, GUYS--
--AND DON'T BE AFRAID OF RUINING MY PAINT JOB!
WHATEVER YOU SAY, SHELL-HEAD!
HOW ABOUT A LITTLE FIRE, TIN MAN?
NAPALM--AND WHITE PHOSPHORUS! VERY NEAT!

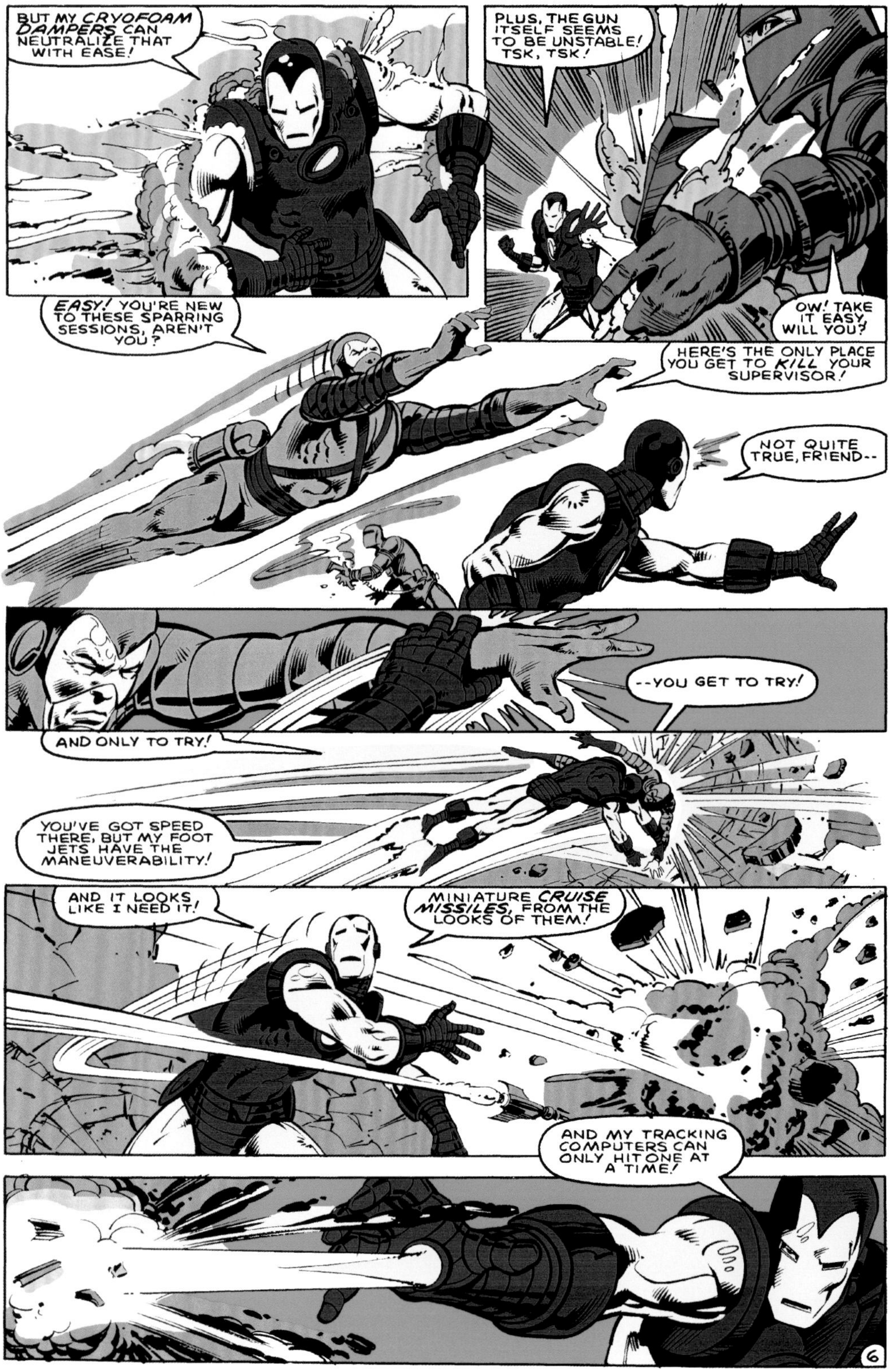
BUT MY CRYOFOAM DAMPERS CAN NEUTRALIZE THAT WITH EASE!
PLUS, THE GUN ITSELF SEEMS TO BE UNSTABLE! TSK, TSK!
OW! TAKE IT EASY, WILL YOU?
EASY! YOU'RE NEW TO THESE SPARRING SESSIONS, AREN'T YOU?
HERE'S THE ONLY PLACE YOU GET TO KILL YOUR SUPERVISOR!
NOT QUITE TRUE, FRIEND--
--YOU GET TO TRY!
AND ONLY TO TRY!
YOU'VE GOT SPEED THERE, BUT MY FOOT JETS HAVE THE MANEUVERABILITY!
AND IT LOOKS LIKE I NEED IT!
MINIATURE CRUISE MISSILES, FROM THE LOOKS OF THEM!
AND MY TRACKING COMPUTERS CAN ONLY HIT ONE AT A TIME!
6

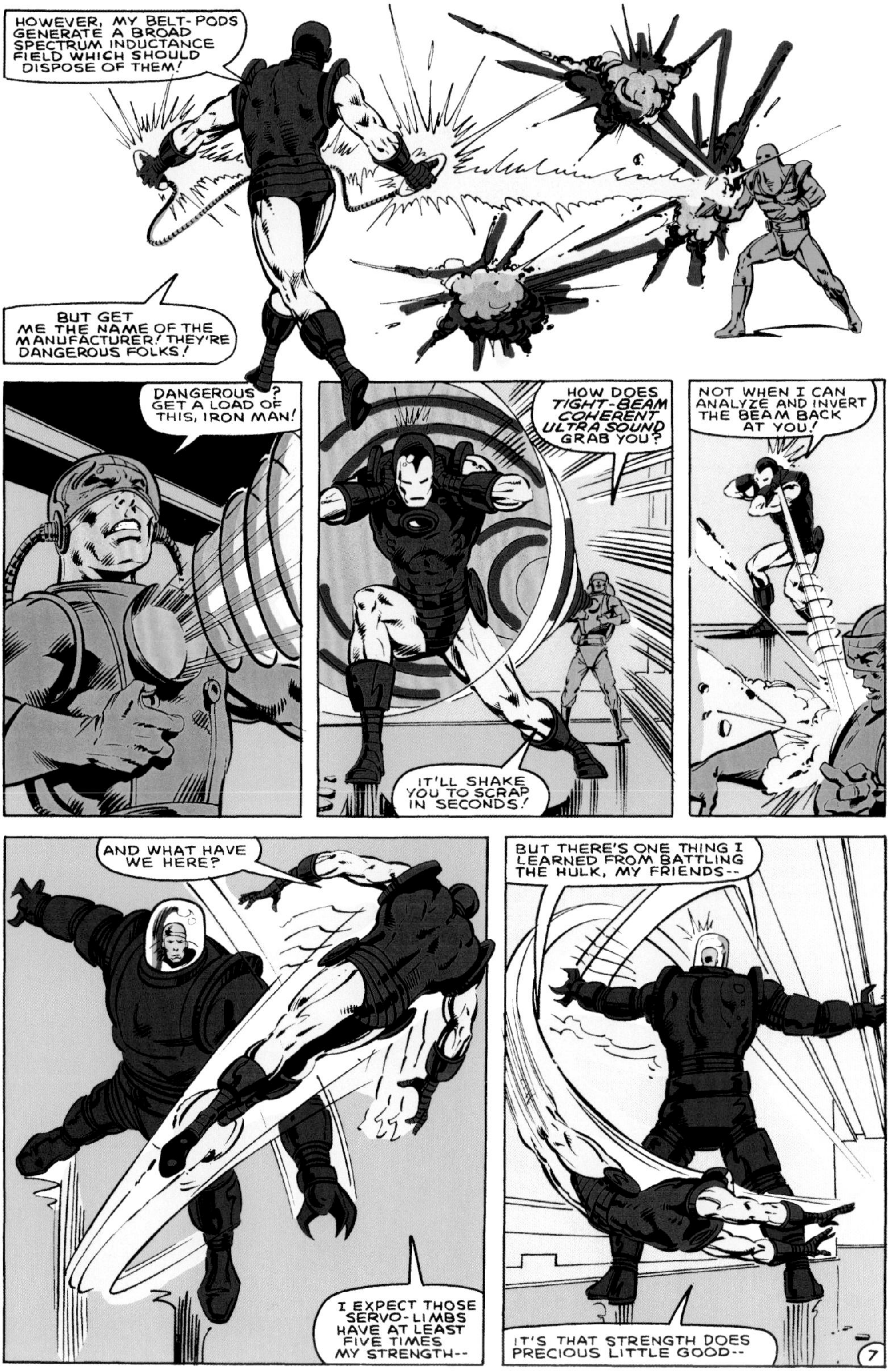
HOWEVER, MY BELT-PODS GENERATE A BROAD SPECTRUM INDUCTANCE FIELD WHICH SHOULD DISPOSE OF THEM!
BUT GET ME THE NAME OF THE MANUFACTURER! THEY'RE DANGEROUS FOLKS!
DANGEROUS ? GET A LOAD OF THIS, IRON MAN!
HOW DOES TIGHT-BEAM COHERENT ULTRA SOUND GRAB YOU?
IT'LL SHAKE YOU TO SCRAP IN SECONDS!
NOT WHEN I CAN ANALYZE AND INVERT THE BEAM BACK AT YOU!
AND WHAT HAVE WE HERE?
I EXPECT THOSE SERVO-LIMBS HAVE AT LEAST FIVE TIMES MY STRENGTH--
BUT THERE'S ONE THING I LEARNED FROM BATTLING THE HULK, MY FRIENDS--
IT'S THAT STRENGTH DOES PRECIOUS LITTLE GOOD--

--IF I DON'T GIVE YOU A CHANCE TO USE IT!

OR, 'THE BIGGER THEY ARE, THE HARDER THEY FALL!'

Y'KNOW, IRON MAN, ALL THIS WILL DO IS PUT MORE PRESSURE ON STARK INTER-NATIONAL TO GET BACK INTO ARMAMENTS AGAIN!

WELL, BOYS, THAT'S *TONY STARK'S* HEADACHE--NOT YOURS AND MINE!

BUT YOU DID FINE, AND THE TIN SUIT GOT A REAL WORKOUT!

SO GO LICK YOUR WOUNDS, WHILE I LICK MINE!

*ONCE ALONE, HE PONDERS THE PARADOX: THE COMPANY WHICH MADE AND SUSTAINS THE WORLD'S MOST ADVANCED FIGHTING MACHINE--*

*--IS A COMPANY WHICH NO LONGER MAKES WEAPONS! AND THE ANSWER HE GAVE THE MEN WAS AN EVASION...*

*SINCE TONY STARK'S HEAD-ACHES AND IRON MAN'S ARE ONE AND THE SAME!*

*STILL, THERE ARE REASONS...*

BOSS, THIS IS RHODEY! WE'RE SCHEDULED TO LEAVE FOR WAKANDA IN AN HOUR!

*WAKANDA AFTER MIDNIGHT--*

WAKANDA RESEA... FACILITY AUTHORIZED PERSO...

*--AND A RESEARCH PLANT OPERATED BY WAKANDA IN CONJUNCTION WITH STARK INTERNATIONAL.*

8

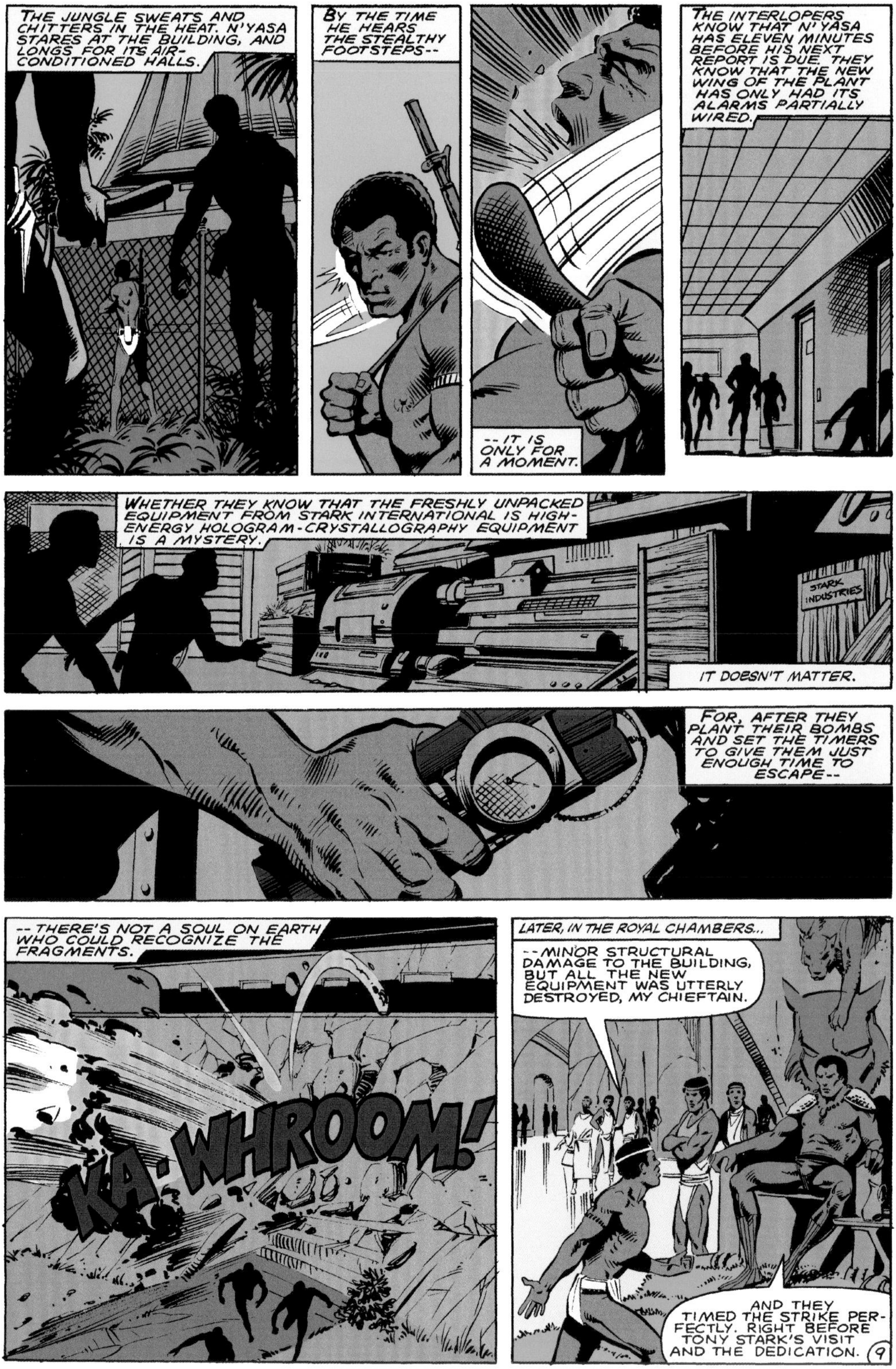

THE JUNGLE SWEATS AND CHITTERS IN THE HEAT. N'YASA STARES AT THE BUILDING, AND LONGS FOR ITS AIR-CONDITIONED HALLS.
BY THE TIME HE HEARS THE STEALTHY FOOTSTEPS--
--IT IS ONLY FOR A MOMENT.
THE INTERLOPERS KNOW THAT N'YASA HAS ELEVEN MINUTES BEFORE HIS NEXT REPORT IS DUE. THEY KNOW THAT THE NEW WING OF THE PLANT HAS ONLY HAD ITS ALARMS PARTIALLY WIRED.
WHETHER THEY KNOW THAT THE FRESHLY UNPACKED EQUIPMENT FROM STARK INTERNATIONAL IS HIGH-ENERGY HOLOGRAM-CRYSTALLOGRAPHY EQUIPMENT IS A MYSTERY.
STARK INDUSTRIES
IT DOESN'T MATTER.
FOR, AFTER THEY PLANT THEIR BOMBS AND SET THE TIMERS TO GIVE THEM JUST ENOUGH TIME TO ESCAPE--
--THERE'S NOT A SOUL ON EARTH WHO COULD RECOGNIZE THE FRAGMENTS.
KA-WHROOM!
LATER, IN THE ROYAL CHAMBERS...
--MINOR STRUCTURAL DAMAGE TO THE BUILDING, BUT ALL THE NEW EQUIPMENT WAS UTTERLY DESTROYED, MY CHIEFTAIN.
AND THEY TIMED THE STRIKE PERFECTLY. RIGHT BEFORE TONY STARK'S VISIT AND THE DEDICATION.
9

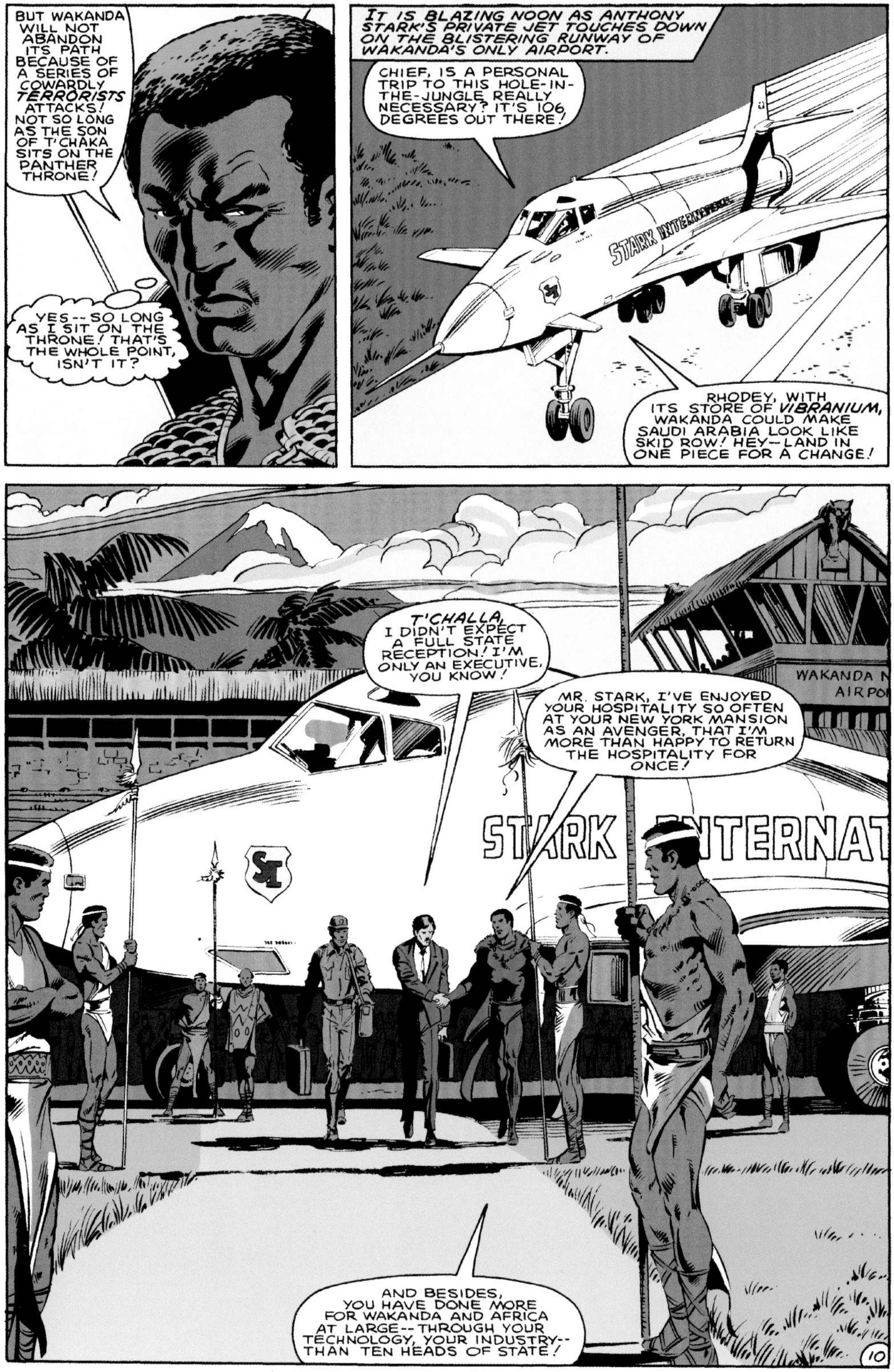
BUT WAKANDA WILL NOT ABANDON ITS PATH BECAUSE OF A SERIES OF COWARDLY TERRORISTS ATTACKS! NOT SO LONG AS THE SON OF T'CHAKA SITS ON THE PANTHER THRONE!
YES--SO LONG AS I SIT ON THE THRONE! THAT'S THE WHOLE POINT, ISN'T IT?
IT IS BLAZING NOON AS ANTHONY STARK'S PRIVATE JET TOUCHES DOWN ON THE BLISTERING RUNWAY OF WAKANDA'S ONLY AIRPORT.
CHIEF, IS A PERSONAL TRIP TO THIS HOLE-IN-THE-JUNGLE REALLY NECESSARY? IT'S 106 DEGREES OUT THERE!
STARK INTERNATIONAL
RHODEY, WITH ITS STORE OF VIBRANIUM, WAKANDA COULD MAKE SAUDI ARABIA LOOK LIKE SKID ROW! HEY--LAND IN ONE PIECE FOR A CHANGE!
T'CHALLA, I DIDN'T EXPECT A FULL STATE RECEPTION! I'M ONLY AN EXECUTIVE, YOU KNOW!
WAKANDA N
AIRPO
MR. STARK, I'VE ENJOYED YOUR HOSPITALITY SO OFTEN AT YOUR NEW YORK MANSION AS AN AVENGER, THAT I'M MORE THAN HAPPY TO RETURN THE HOSPITALITY FOR ONCE!
STARK INTERNAT
AND BESIDES, YOU HAVE DONE MORE FOR WAKANDA AND AFRICA AT LARGE--THROUGH YOUR TECHNOLOGY, YOUR INDUSTRY--THAN TEN HEADS OF STATE!
10

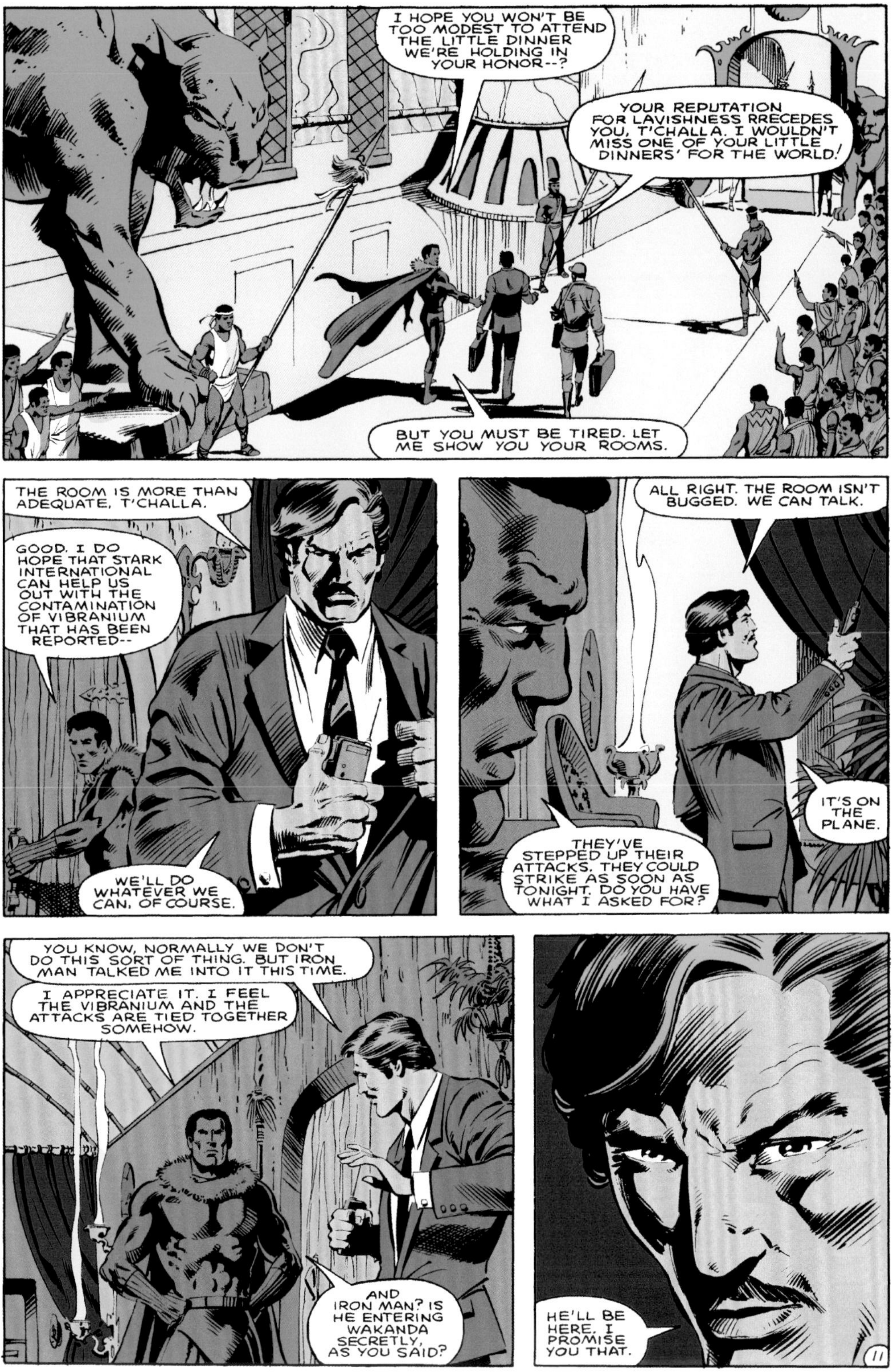
I HOPE YOU WON'T BE TOO MODEST TO ATTEND THE LITTLE DINNER WE'RE HOLDING IN YOUR HONOR--?
YOUR REPUTATION FOR LAVISHNESS RRECEDES YOU, T'CHALLA. I WOULDN'T MISS ONE OF YOUR LITTLE DINNERS' FOR THE WORLD!
BUT YOU MUST BE TIRED. LET ME SHOW YOU YOUR ROOMS.
THE ROOM IS MORE THAN ADEQUATE, T'CHALLA.
GOOD. I DO HOPE THAT STARK INTERNATIONAL CAN HELP US OUT WITH THE CONTAMINATION OF VIBRANIUM THAT HAS BEEN REPORTED--
WE'LL DO WHATEVER WE CAN, OF COURSE.
ALL RIGHT. THE ROOM ISN'T BUGGED. WE CAN TALK.
THEY'VE STEPPED UP THEIR ATTACKS. THEY COULD STRIKE AS SOON AS TONIGHT. DO YOU HAVE WHAT I ASKED FOR?
IT'S ON THE PLANE.
YOU KNOW, NORMALLY WE DON'T DO THIS SORT OF THING. BUT IRON MAN TALKED ME INTO IT THIS TIME.
I APPRECIATE IT. I FEEL THE VIBRANIUM AND THE ATTACKS ARE TIED TOGETHER SOMEHOW.
AND IRON MAN? IS HE ENTERING WAKANDA SECRETLY, AS YOU SAID?
HE'LL BE HERE. I PROMISE YOU THAT.
11

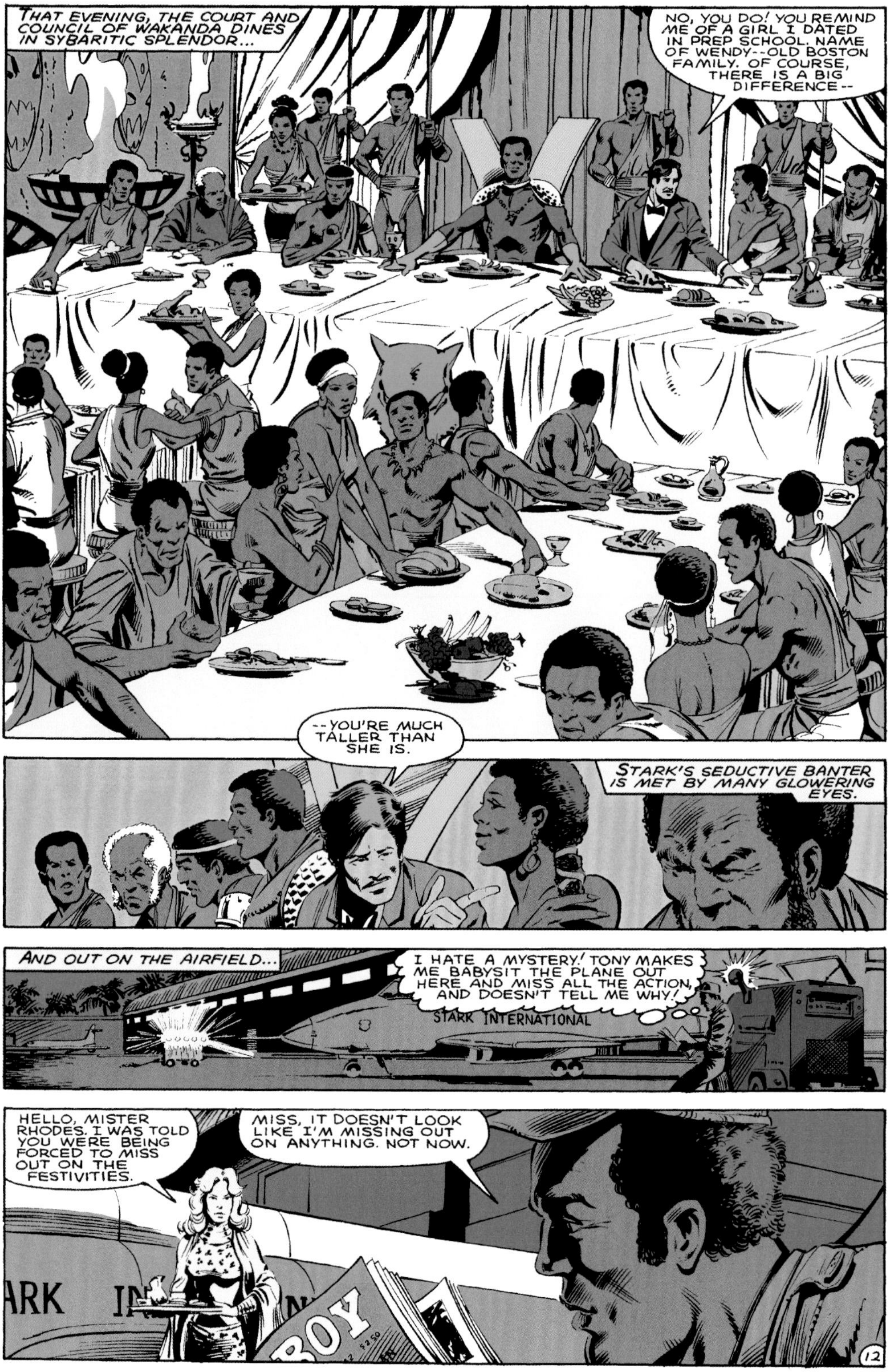
THAT EVENING, THE COURT AND COUNCIL OF WAKANDA DINES IN SYBARITIC SPLENDOR...
NO, YOU DO! YOU REMIND ME OF A GIRL I DATED IN PREP SCHOOL. NAME OF WENDY--OLD BOSTON FAMILY. OF COURSE, THERE IS A BIG DIFFERENCE--
--YOU'RE MUCH TALLER THAN SHE IS.
STARK'S SEDUCTIVE BANTER IS MET BY MANY GLOWERING EYES.
AND OUT ON THE AIRFIELD...
I HATE A MYSTERY! TONY MAKES ME BABYSIT THE PLANE OUT HERE AND MISS ALL THE ACTION, AND DOESN'T TELL ME WHY!
STARK INTERNATIONAL
HELLO, MISTER RHODES. I WAS TOLD YOU WERE BEING FORCED TO MISS OUT ON THE FESTIVITIES.
MISS, IT DOESN'T LOOK LIKE I'M MISSING OUT ON ANYTHING. NOT NOW.
ARK
BOY

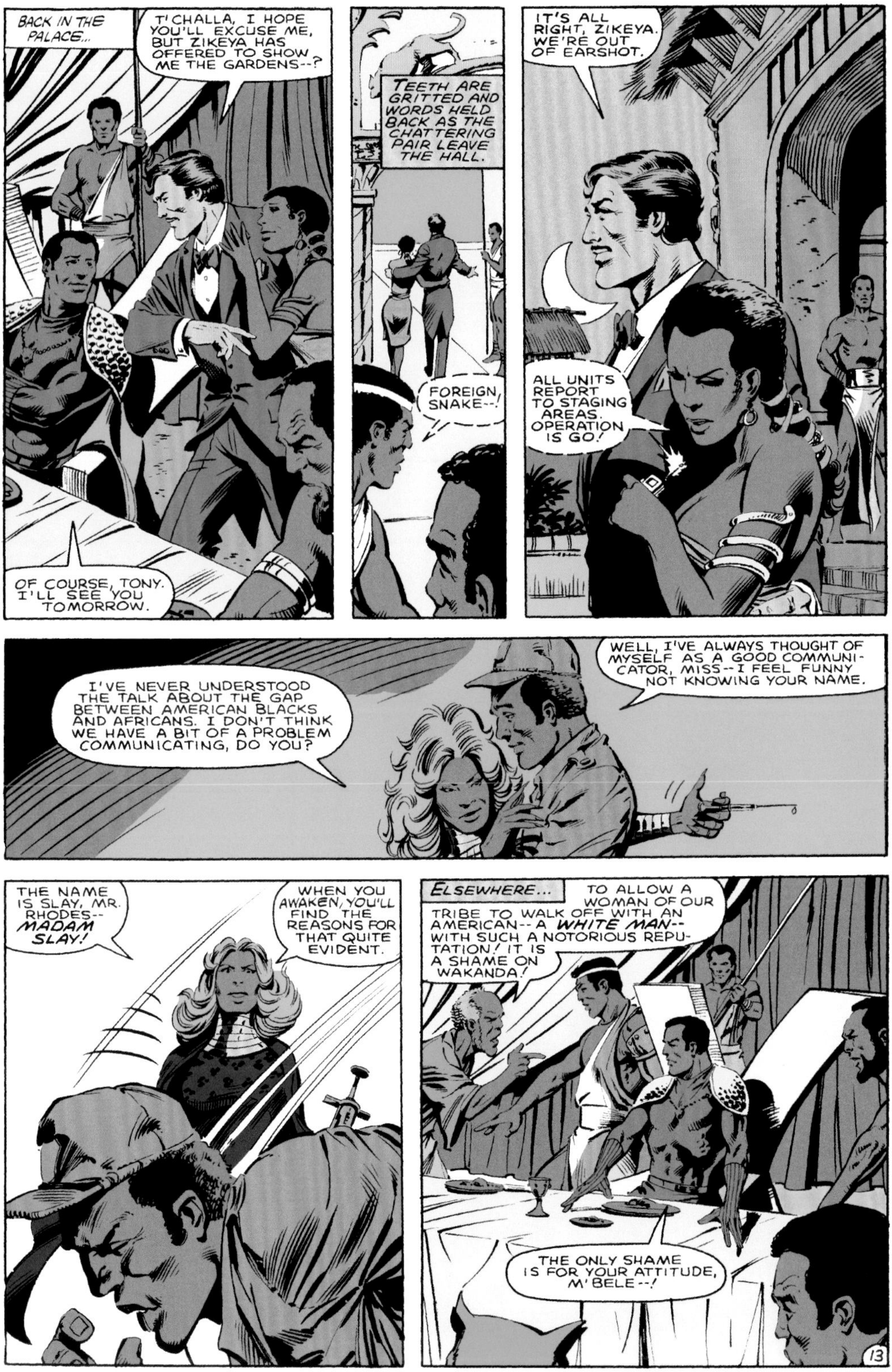
BACK IN THE PALACE...
T'CHALLA, I HOPE YOU'LL EXCUSE ME, BUT ZIKEYA HAS OFFERED TO SHOW ME THE GARDENS--?
OF COURSE, TONY. I'LL SEE YOU TOMORROW.
TEETH ARE GRITTED AND WORDS HELD BACK AS THE CHATTERING PAIR LEAVE THE HALL.
FOREIGN SNAKE--!
IT'S ALL RIGHT, ZIKEYA. WE'RE OUT OF EARSHOT.
ALL UNITS REPORT TO STAGING AREAS. OPERATION IS GO!
I'VE NEVER UNDERSTOOD THE TALK ABOUT THE GAP BETWEEN AMERICAN BLACKS AND AFRICANS. I DON'T THINK WE HAVE A BIT OF A PROBLEM COMMUNICATING, DO YOU?
WELL, I'VE ALWAYS THOUGHT OF MYSELF AS A GOOD COMMUNICATOR, MISS--I FEEL FUNNY NOT KNOWING YOUR NAME.
THE NAME IS SLAY, MR. RHODES-- MADAM SLAY!
WHEN YOU AWAKEN, YOU'LL FIND THE REASONS FOR THAT QUITE EVIDENT.
ELSEWHERE...
TO ALLOW A WOMAN OF OUR TRIBE TO WALK OFF WITH AN AMERICAN-- A WHITE MAN-- WITH SUCH A NOTORIOUS REPUTATION! IT IS A SHAME ON WAKANDA!
THE ONLY SHAME IS FOR YOUR ATTITUDE, M'BELE--!
13

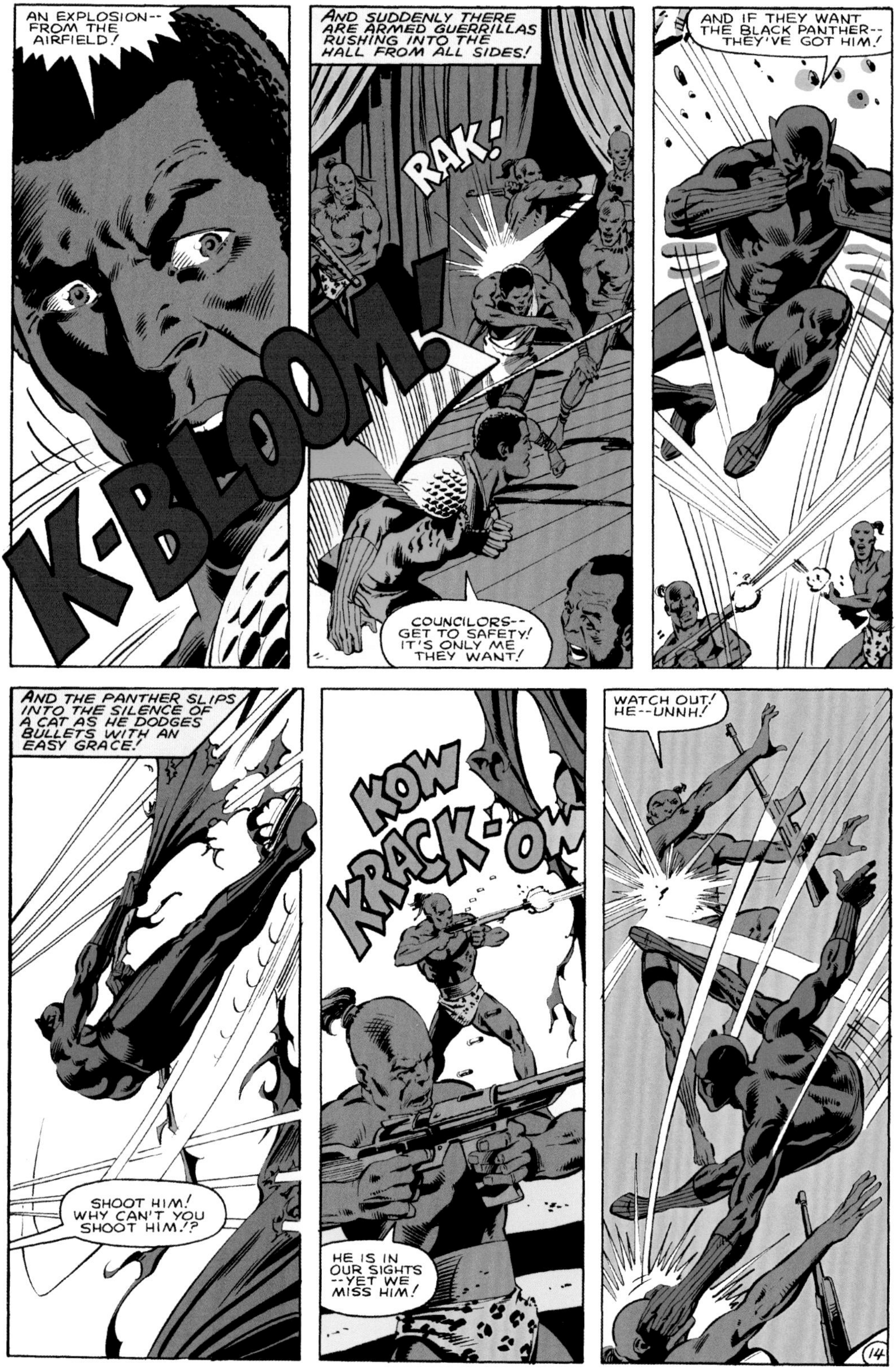

AN EXPLOSION-- FROM THE AIRFIELD!
K-BLOOM!
AND SUDDENLY THERE ARE ARMED GUERRILLAS RUSHING INTO THE HALL FROM ALL SIDES!
RAK!
COUNCILORS-- GET TO SAFETY! IT'S ONLY ME THEY WANT!
AND IF THEY WANT THE BLACK PANTHER-- THEY'VE GOT HIM!
AND THE PANTHER SLIPS INTO THE SILENCE OF A CAT AS HE DODGES BULLETS WITH AN EASY GRACE!
SHOOT HIM! WHY CAN'T YOU SHOOT HIM!?
KOW
KRACK-OW
HE IS IN OUR SIGHTS --YET WE MISS HIM!
WATCH OUT! HE--UNNH!
14

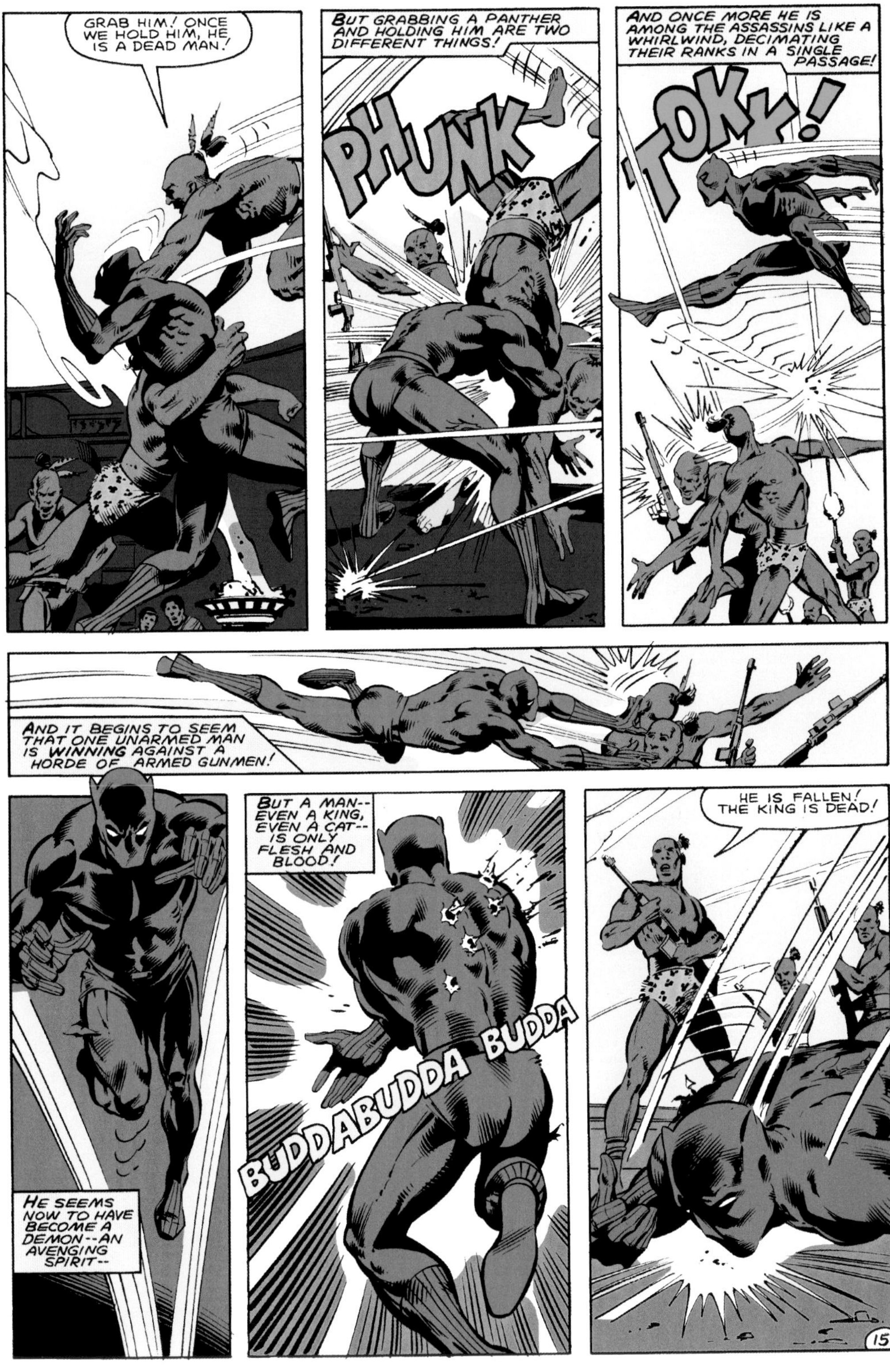
GRAB HIM! ONCE WE HOLD HIM, HE IS A DEAD MAN!
BUT GRABBING A PANTHER AND HOLDING HIM ARE TWO DIFFERENT THINGS!
PHUNK
AND ONCE MORE HE IS AMONG THE ASSASSINS LIKE A WHIRLWIND, DECIMATING THEIR RANKS IN A SINGLE PASSAGE!
TOKK!
AND IT BEGINS TO SEEM THAT ONE UNARMED MAN IS WINNING AGAINST A HORDE OF ARMED GUNMEN!
HE SEEMS NOW TO HAVE BECOME A DEMON--AN AVENGING SPIRIT--
BUT A MAN--EVEN A KING, EVEN A CAT--IS ONLY FLESH AND BLOOD!
BUDDABUDDA BUDDA
HE IS FALLEN! THE KING IS DEAD!
15

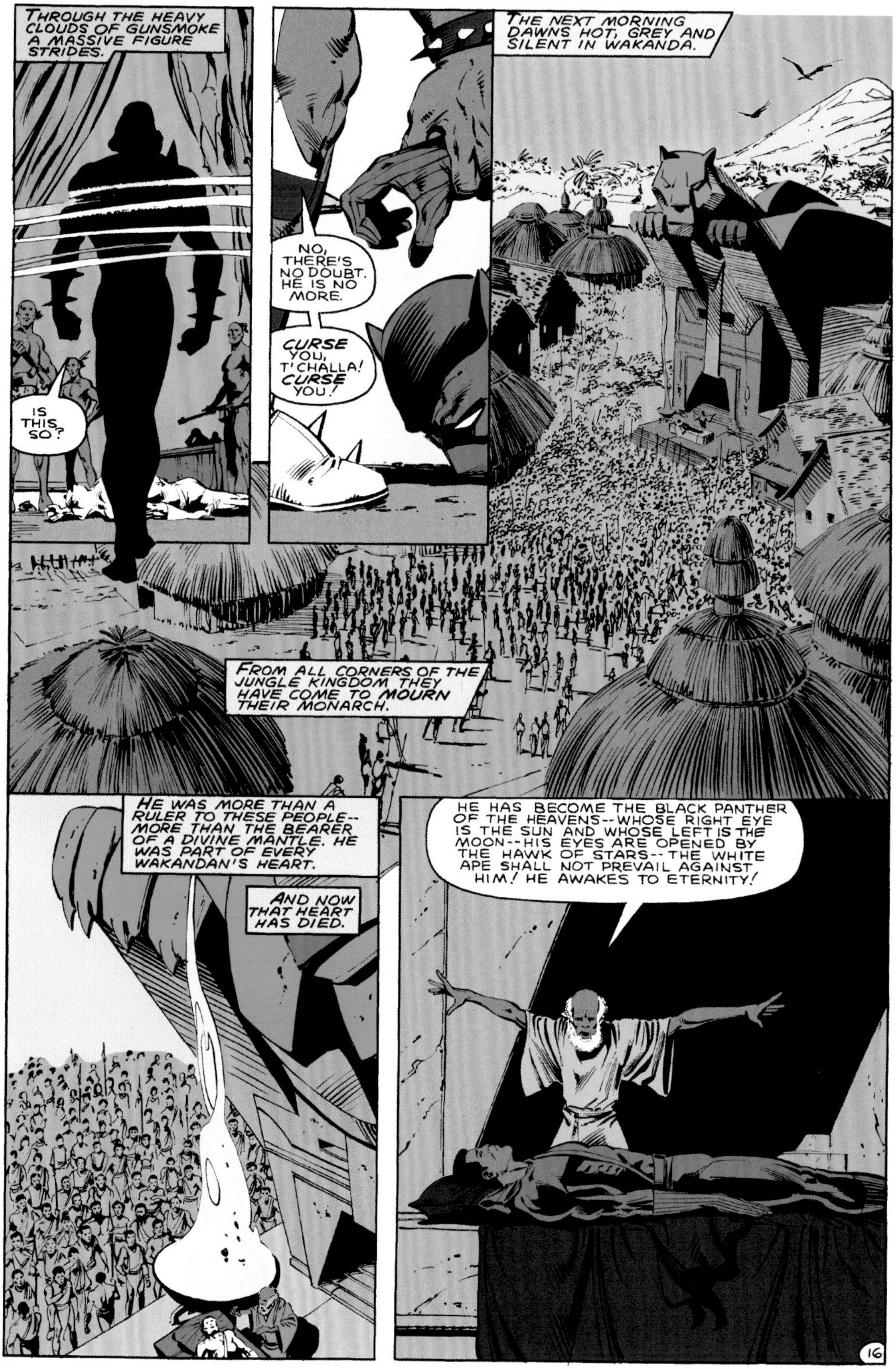
THROUGH THE HEAVY CLOUDS OF GUNSMOKE A MASSIVE FIGURE STRIDES.
IS THIS SO?
NO, THERE'S NO DOUBT. HE IS NO MORE.
CURSE YOU, T'CHALLA! CURSE YOU!
THE NEXT MORNING DAWNS HOT, GREY AND SILENT IN WAKANDA.
FROM ALL CORNERS OF THE JUNGLE KINGDOM THEY HAVE COME TO MOURN THEIR MONARCH.
HE WAS MORE THAN A RULER TO THESE PEOPLE-- MORE THAN THE BEARER OF A DIVINE MANTLE. HE WAS PART OF EVERY WAKANDAN'S HEART.
AND NOW THAT HEART HAS DIED.
HE HAS BECOME THE BLACK PANTHER OF THE HEAVENS--WHOSE RIGHT EYE IS THE SUN AND WHOSE LEFT IS THE MOON--HIS EYES ARE OPENED BY THE HAWK OF STARS--THE WHITE APE SHALL NOT PREVAIL AGAINST HIM! HE AWAKES TO ETERNITY!
16

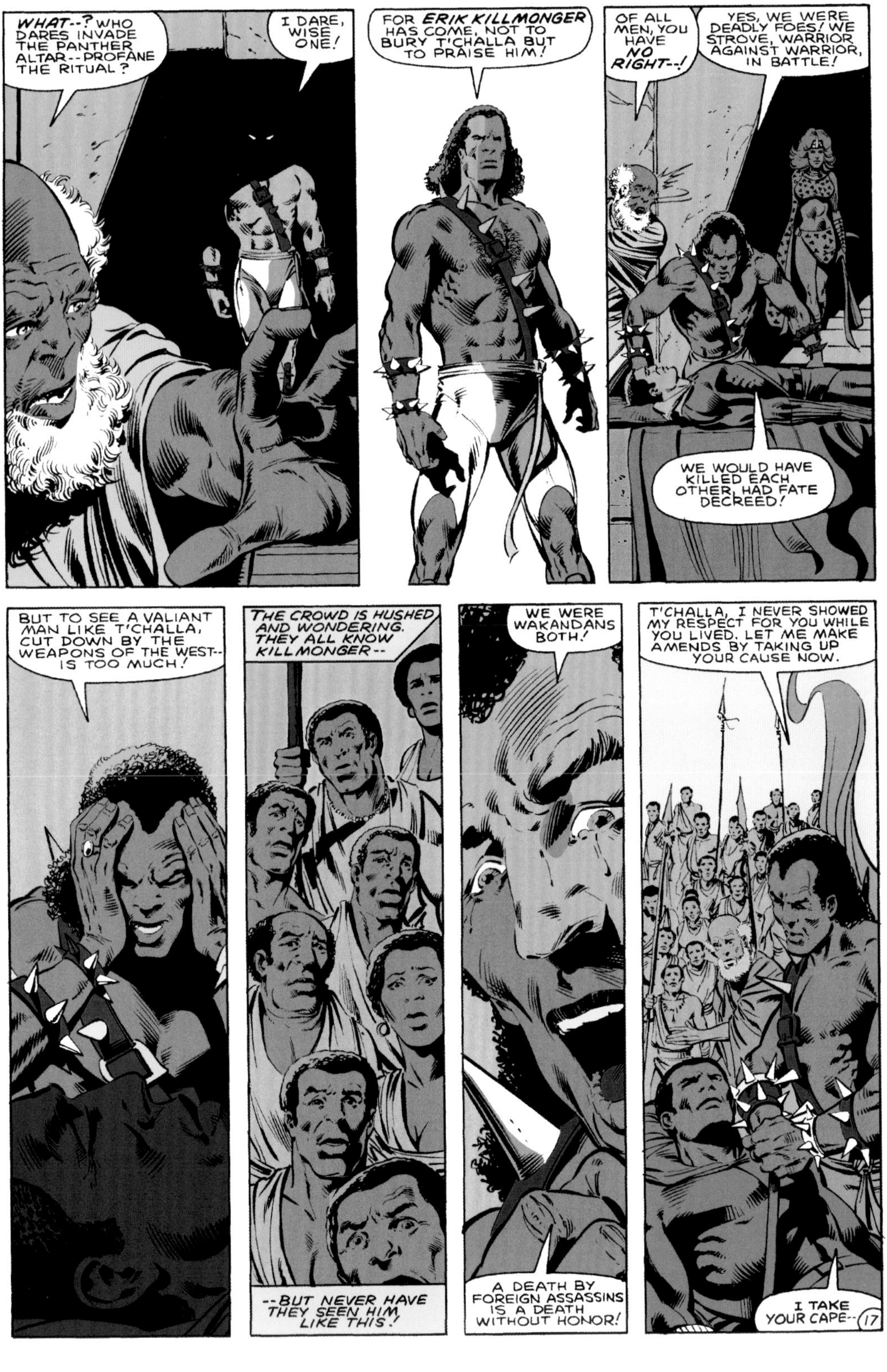
WHAT--? WHO DARES INVADE THE PANTHER ALTAR--PROFANE THE RITUAL?
I DARE, WISE ONE!
FOR ERIK KILLMONGER HAS COME, NOT TO BURY T'CHALLA BUT TO PRAISE HIM!
OF ALL MEN, YOU HAVE NO RIGHT--!
YES, WE WERE DEADLY FOES! WE STROVE, WARRIOR AGAINST WARRIOR, IN BATTLE!
WE WOULD HAVE KILLED EACH OTHER, HAD FATE DECREED!
BUT TO SEE A VALIANT MAN LIKE T'CHALLA, CUT DOWN BY THE WEAPONS OF THE WEST--IS TOO MUCH!
THE CROWD IS HUSHED AND WONDERING. THEY ALL KNOW KILLMONGER--
--BUT NEVER HAVE THEY SEEN HIM LIKE THIS!
WE WERE WAKANDANS BOTH!
A DEATH BY FOREIGN ASSASSINS IS A DEATH WITHOUT HONOR!
T'CHALLA, I NEVER SHOWED MY RESPECT FOR YOU WHILE YOU LIVED. LET ME MAKE AMENDS BY TAKING UP YOUR CAUSE NOW.
I TAKE YOUR CAPE--
17

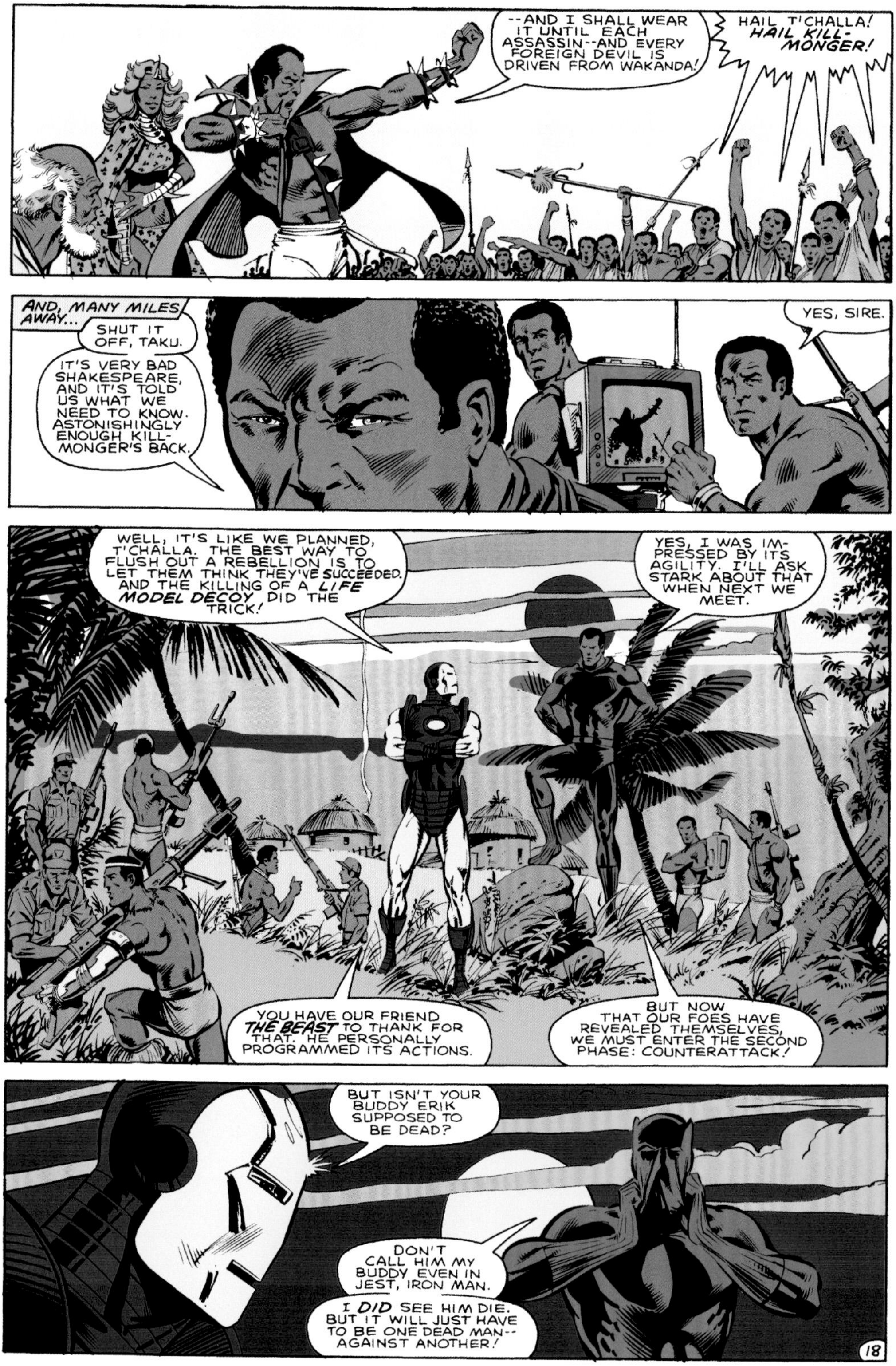
--AND I SHALL WEAR IT UNTIL EACH ASSASSIN--AND EVERY FOREIGN DEVIL IS DRIVEN FROM WAKANDA!
HAIL T'CHALLA! HAIL KILL-MONGER!
AND, MANY MILES AWAY...
SHUT IT OFF, TAKU.
IT'S VERY BAD SHAKESPEARE, AND IT'S TOLD US WHAT WE NEED TO KNOW. ASTONISHINGLY ENOUGH KILL-MONGER'S BACK.
YES, SIRE.
WELL, IT'S LIKE WE PLANNED, T'CHALLA. THE BEST WAY TO FLUSH OUT A REBELLION IS TO LET THEM THINK THEY'VE SUCCEEDED. AND THE KILLING OF A LIFE MODEL DECOY DID THE TRICK!
YES, I WAS IM-PRESSED BY ITS AGILITY. I'LL ASK STARK ABOUT THAT WHEN NEXT WE MEET.
YOU HAVE OUR FRIEND THE BEAST TO THANK FOR THAT. HE PERSONALLY PROGRAMMED ITS ACTIONS.
BUT NOW THAT OUR FOES HAVE REVEALED THEMSELVES, WE MUST ENTER THE SECOND PHASE: COUNTERATTACK!
BUT ISN'T YOUR BUDDY ERIK SUPPOSED TO BE DEAD?
DON'T CALL HIM MY BUDDY EVEN IN JEST, IRON MAN.
I DID SEE HIM DIE. BUT IT WILL JUST HAVE TO BE ONE DEAD MAN--AGAINST ANOTHER!

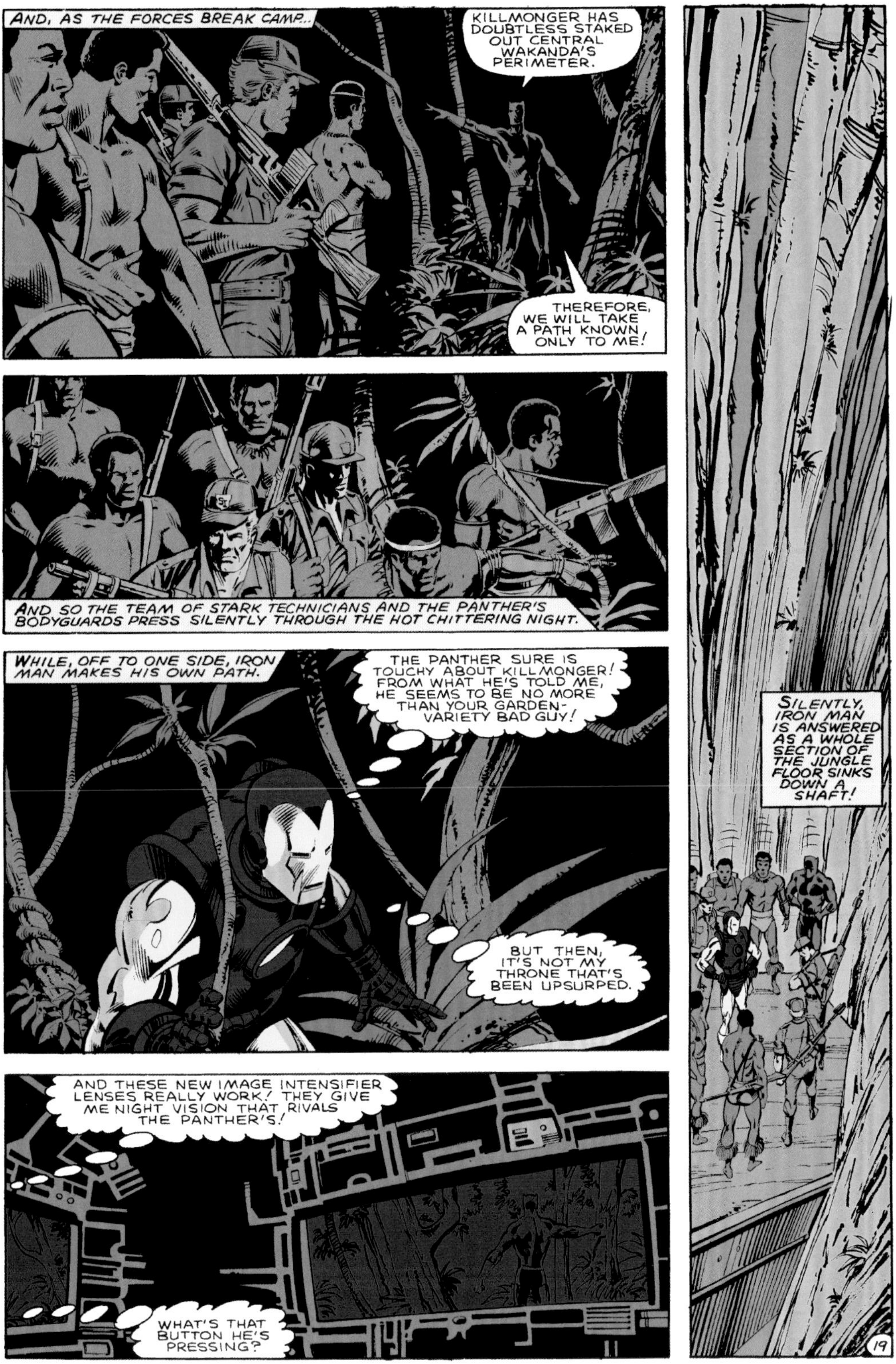
AND, AS THE FORCES BREAK CAMP...
KILLMONGER HAS DOUBTLESS STAKED OUT CENTRAL WAKANDA'S PERIMETER.
THEREFORE, WE WILL TAKE A PATH KNOWN ONLY TO ME!
AND SO THE TEAM OF STARK TECHNICIANS AND THE PANTHER'S BODYGUARDS PRESS SILENTLY THROUGH THE HOT CHITTERING NIGHT.
WHILE, OFF TO ONE SIDE, IRON MAN MAKES HIS OWN PATH.
THE PANTHER SURE IS TOUCHY ABOUT KILLMONGER! FROM WHAT HE'S TOLD ME, HE SEEMS TO BE NO MORE THAN YOUR GARDEN-VARIETY BAD GUY!
BUT THEN, IT'S NOT MY THRONE THAT'S BEEN UPSURPED.
AND THESE NEW IMAGE INTENSIFIER LENSES REALLY WORK! THEY GIVE ME NIGHT VISION THAT RIVALS THE PANTHER'S!
WHAT'S THAT BUTTON HE'S PRESSING?
SILENTLY, IRON MAN IS ANSWERED AS A WHOLE SECTION OF THE JUNGLE FLOOR SINKS DOWN A SHAFT!

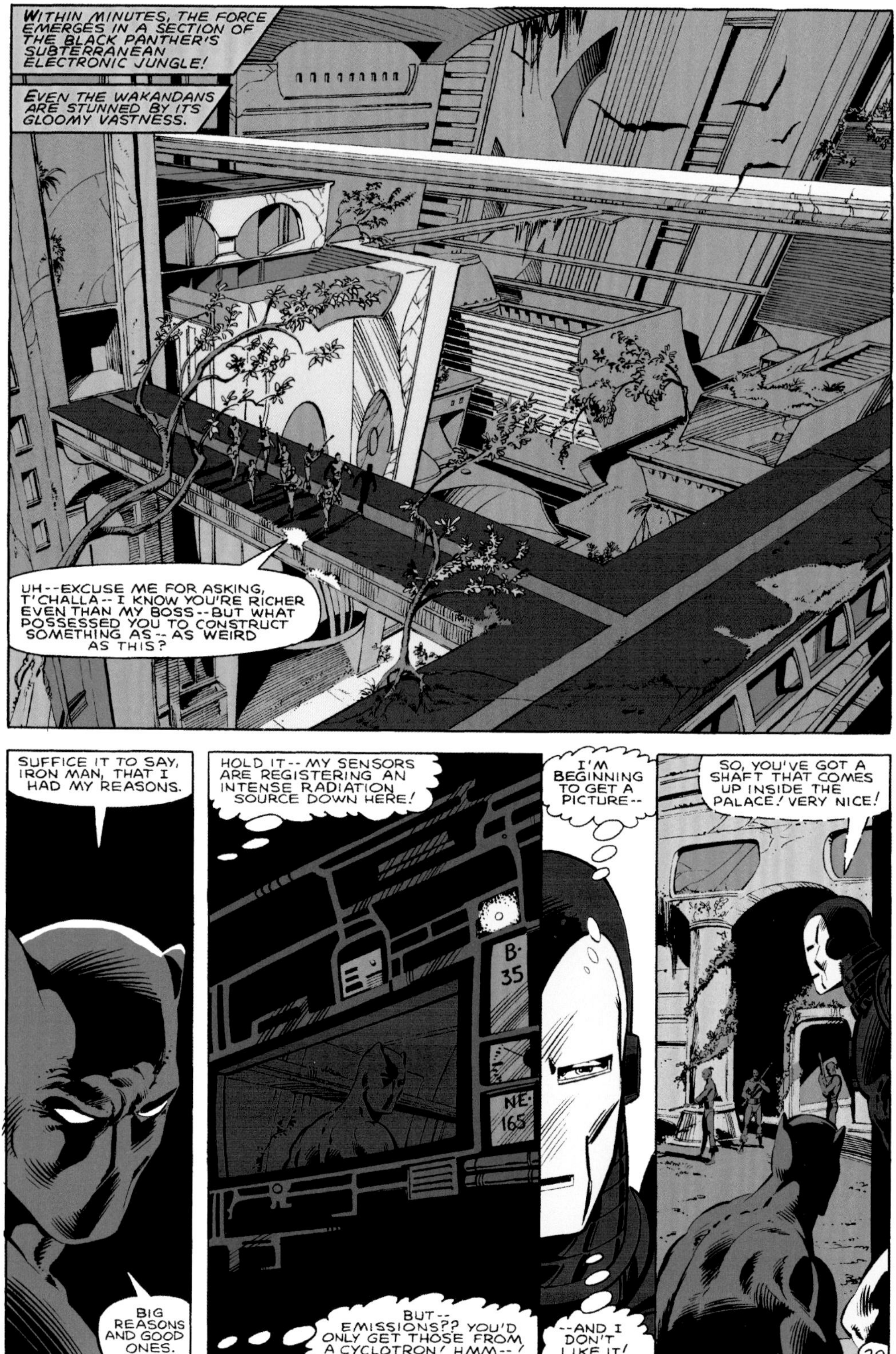
WITHIN MINUTES, THE FORCE EMERGES IN A SECTION OF THE BLACK PANTHER'S SUBTERRANEAN ELECTRONIC JUNGLE!
EVEN THE WAKANDANS ARE STUNNED BY ITS GLOOMY VASTNESS.
UH--EXCUSE ME FOR ASKING, T'CHALLA-- I KNOW YOU'RE RICHER EVEN THAN MY BOSS--BUT WHAT POSSESSED YOU TO CONSTRUCT SOMETHING AS--AS WEIRD AS THIS?
SUFFICE IT TO SAY, IRON MAN, THAT I HAD MY REASONS.
BIG REASONS AND GOOD ONES.
HOLD IT--MY SENSORS ARE REGISTERING AN INTENSE RADIATION SOURCE DOWN HERE!
B-35
NE-165
BUT--EMISSIONS?? YOU'D ONLY GET THOSE FROM A CYCLOTRON! HMM--!
I'M BEGINNING TO GET A PICTURE--
--AND I DON'T LIKE IT!
SO, YOU'VE GOT A SHAFT THAT COMES UP INSIDE THE PALACE! VERY NICE!

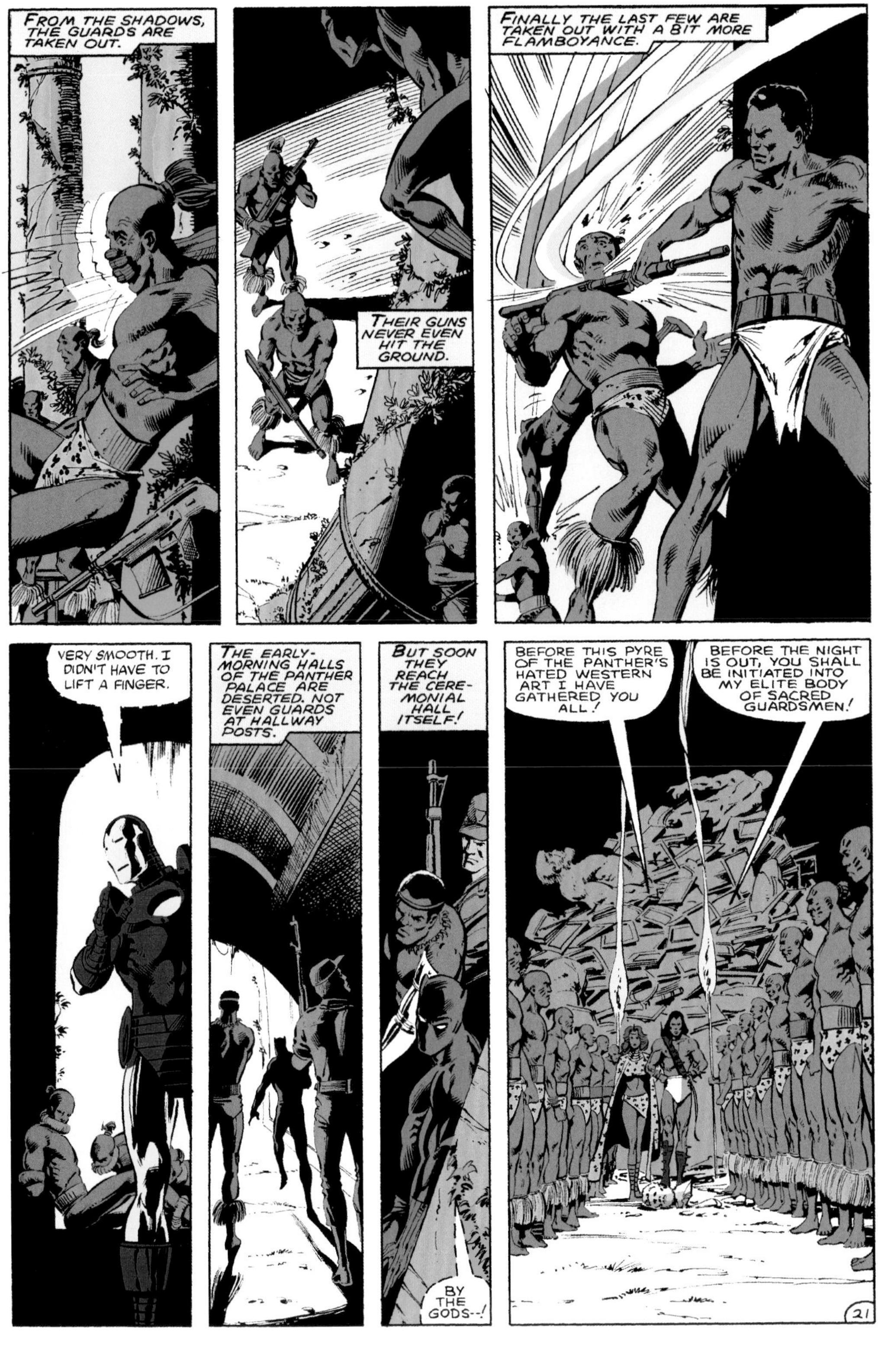
FROM THE SHADOWS, THE GUARDS ARE TAKEN OUT.
THEIR GUNS NEVER EVEN HIT THE GROUND.
FINALLY THE LAST FEW ARE TAKEN OUT WITH A BIT MORE FLAMBOYANCE.
VERY SMOOTH. I DIDN'T HAVE TO LIFT A FINGER.
THE EARLY-MORNING HALLS OF THE PANTHER PALACE ARE DESERTED. NOT EVEN GUARDS AT HALLWAY POSTS.
BUT SOON THEY REACH THE CERE-MONIAL HALL ITSELF!
BY THE GODS--!
BEFORE THIS PYRE OF THE PANTHER'S HATED WESTERN ART I HAVE GATHERED YOU ALL!
BEFORE THE NIGHT IS OUT, YOU SHALL BE INITIATED INTO MY ELITE BODY OF SACRED GUARDSMEN!
21

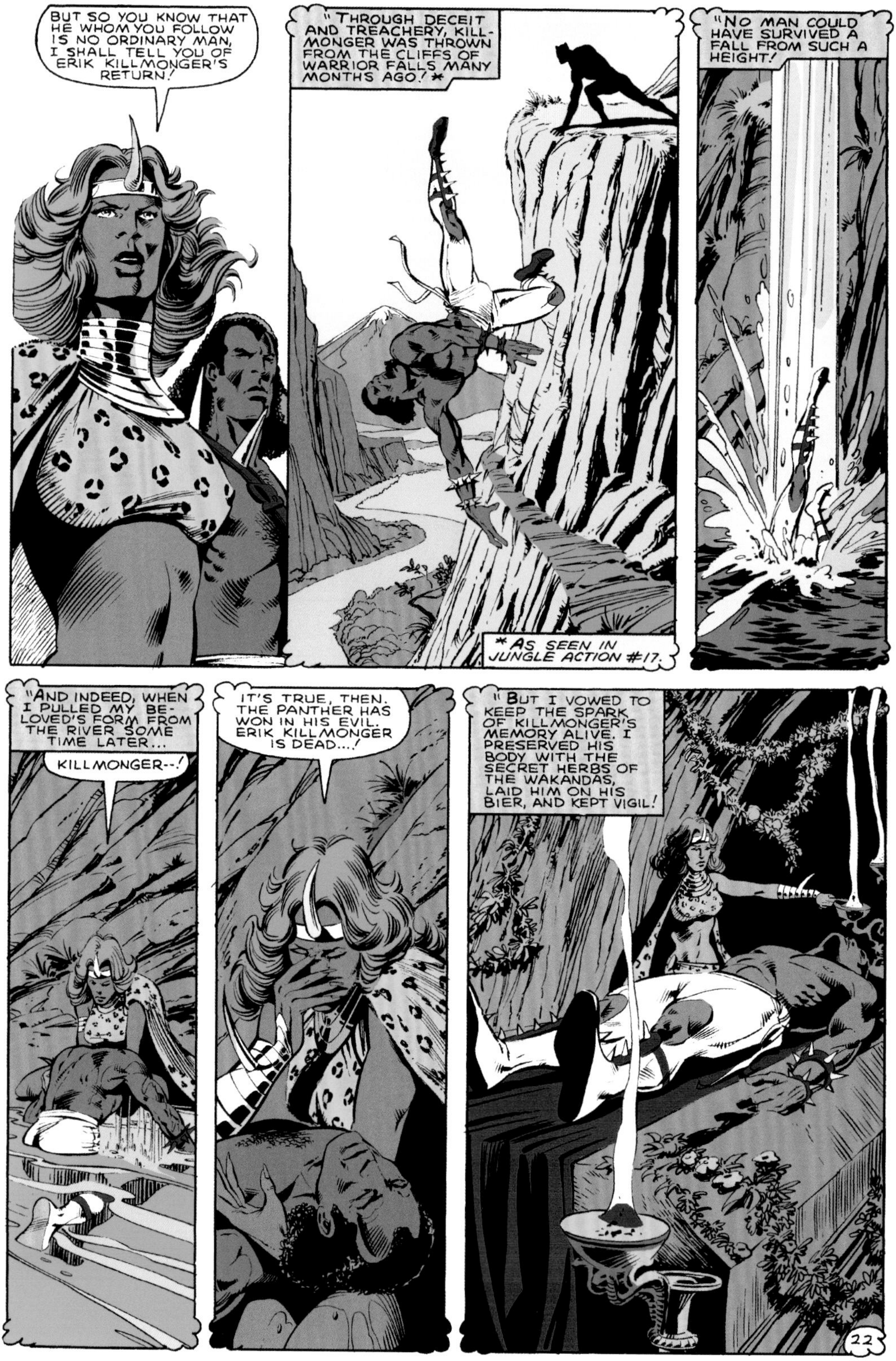
BUT SO YOU KNOW THAT HE WHOM YOU FOLLOW IS NO ORDINARY MAN, I SHALL TELL YOU OF ERIK KILLMONGER'S RETURN!
"THROUGH DECEIT AND TREACHERY, KILLMONGER WAS THROWN FROM THE CLIFFS OF WARRIOR FALLS MANY MONTHS AGO!*
*AS SEEN IN JUNGLE ACTION #17.
"NO MAN COULD HAVE SURVIVED A FALL FROM SUCH A HEIGHT!
"AND INDEED, WHEN I PULLED MY BELOVED'S FORM FROM THE RIVER SOME TIME LATER...
KILLMONGER--!
IT'S TRUE, THEN. THE PANTHER HAS WON IN HIS EVIL. ERIK KILLMONGER IS DEAD...!
"BUT I VOWED TO KEEP THE SPARK OF KILLMONGER'S MEMORY ALIVE. I PRESERVED HIS BODY WITH THE SECRET HERBS OF THE WAKANDAS, LAID HIM ON HIS BIER, AND KEPT VIGIL!

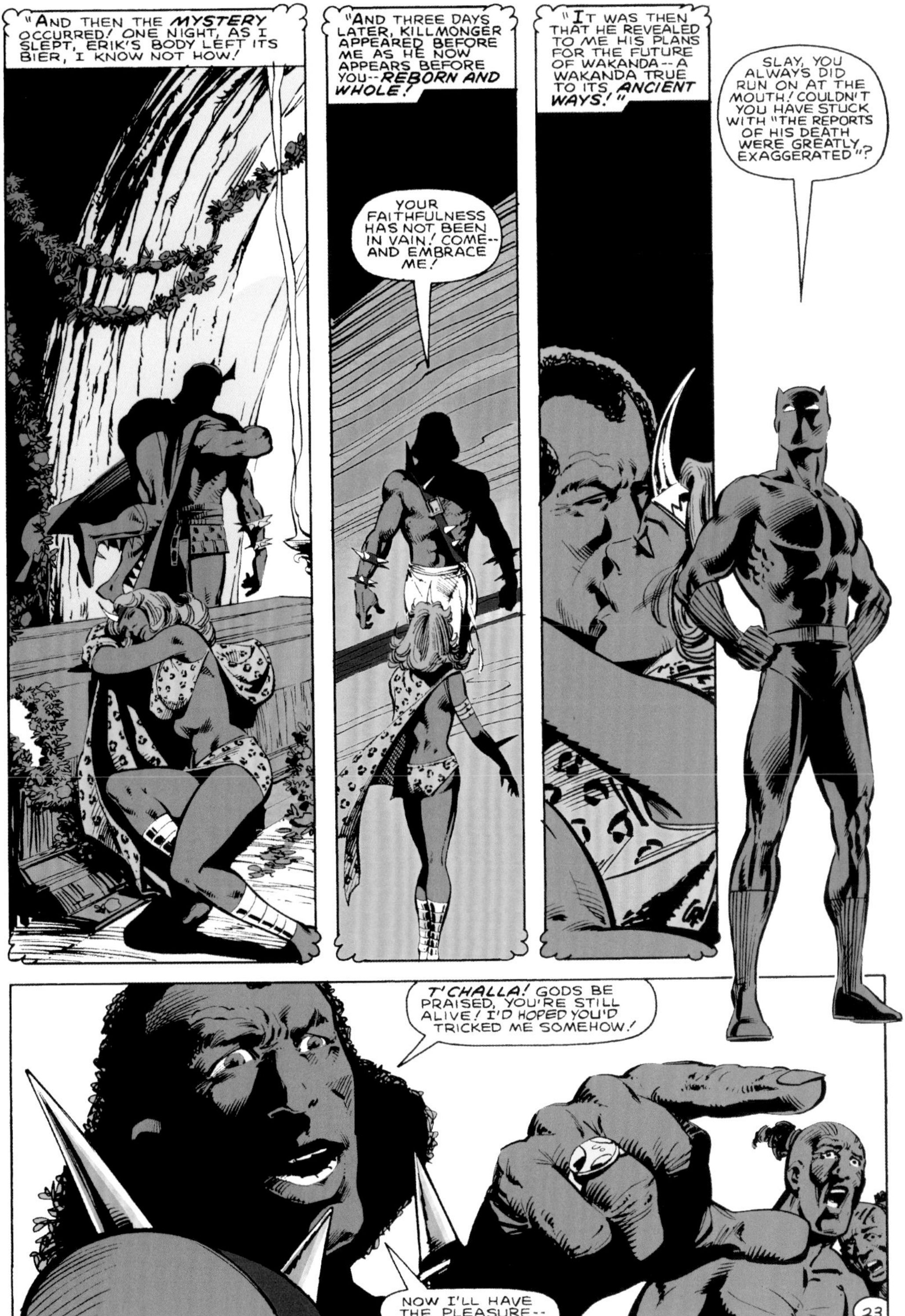
"AND THEN THE MYSTERY OCCURRED! ONE NIGHT, AS I SLEPT, ERIK'S BODY LEFT ITS BIER, I KNOW NOT HOW!
"AND THREE DAYS LATER, KILLMONGER APPEARED BEFORE ME AS HE NOW APPEARS BEFORE YOU--REBORN AND WHOLE!
YOUR FAITHFULNESS HAS NOT BEEN IN VAIN! COME--AND EMBRACE ME!
"IT WAS THEN THAT HE REVEALED TO ME HIS PLANS FOR THE FUTURE OF WAKANDA--A WAKANDA TRUE TO ITS ANCIENT WAYS!"
SLAY, YOU ALWAYS DID RUN ON AT THE MOUTH! COULDN'T YOU HAVE STUCK WITH "THE REPORTS OF HIS DEATH WERE GREATLY EXAGGERATED"?
T'CHALLA! GODS BE PRAISED, YOU'RE STILL ALIVE! I'D HOPED YOU'D TRICKED ME SOMEHOW!
NOW I'LL HAVE THE PLEASURE--
23

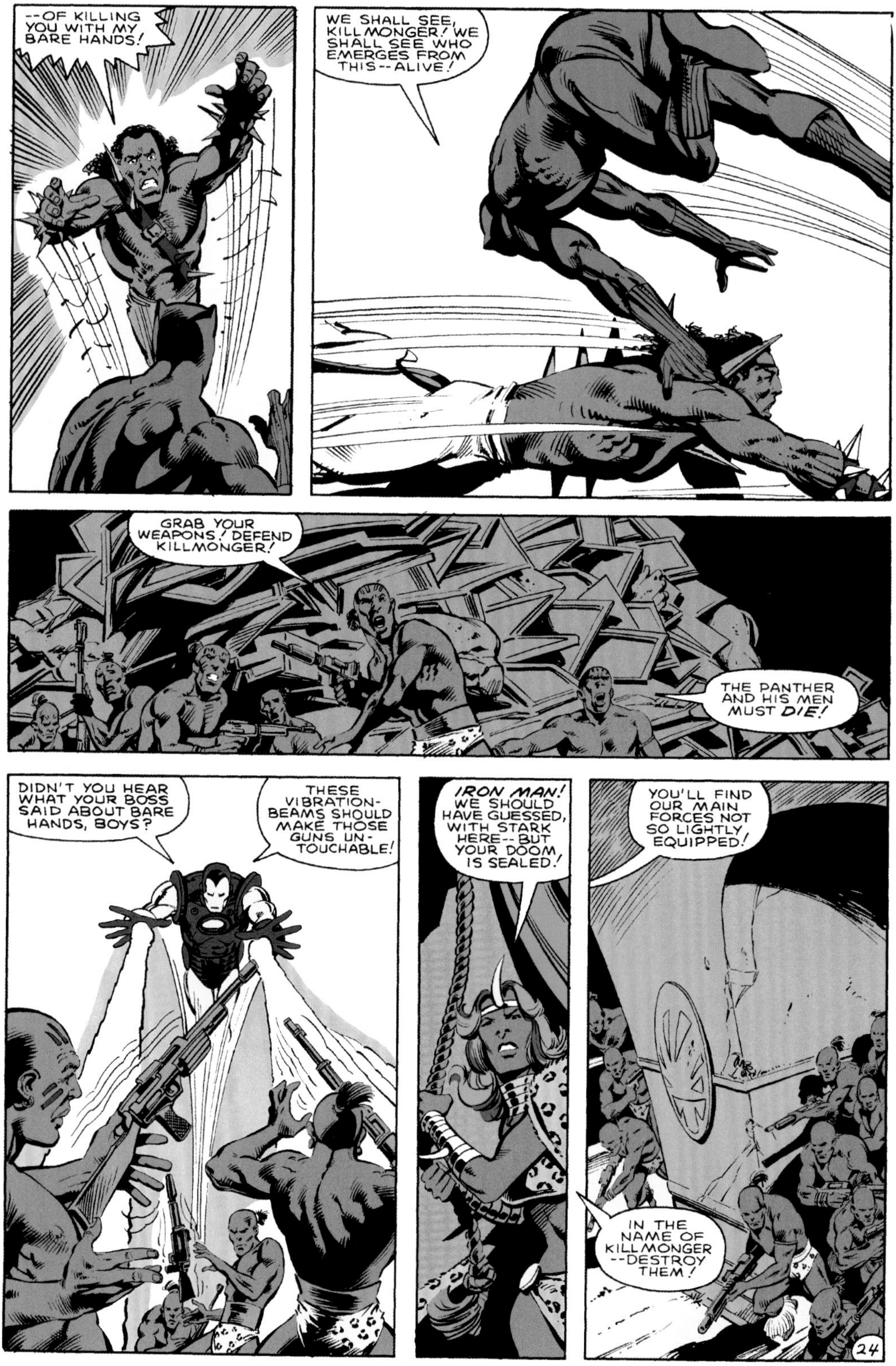
--OF KILLING YOU WITH MY BARE HANDS!
WE SHALL SEE, KILLMONGER! WE SHALL SEE WHO EMERGES FROM THIS--ALIVE!
GRAB YOUR WEAPONS! DEFEND KILLMONGER!
THE PANTHER AND HIS MEN MUST DIE!
DIDN'T YOU HEAR WHAT YOUR BOSS SAID ABOUT BARE HANDS, BOYS?
THESE VIBRATION-BEAMS SHOULD MAKE THOSE GUNS UN-TOUCHABLE!
IRON MAN! WE SHOULD HAVE GUESSED, WITH STARK HERE--BUT YOUR DOOM IS SEALED!
YOU'LL FIND OUR MAIN FORCES NOT SO LIGHTLY EQUIPPED!
IN THE NAME OF KILLMONGER--DESTROY THEM!
24

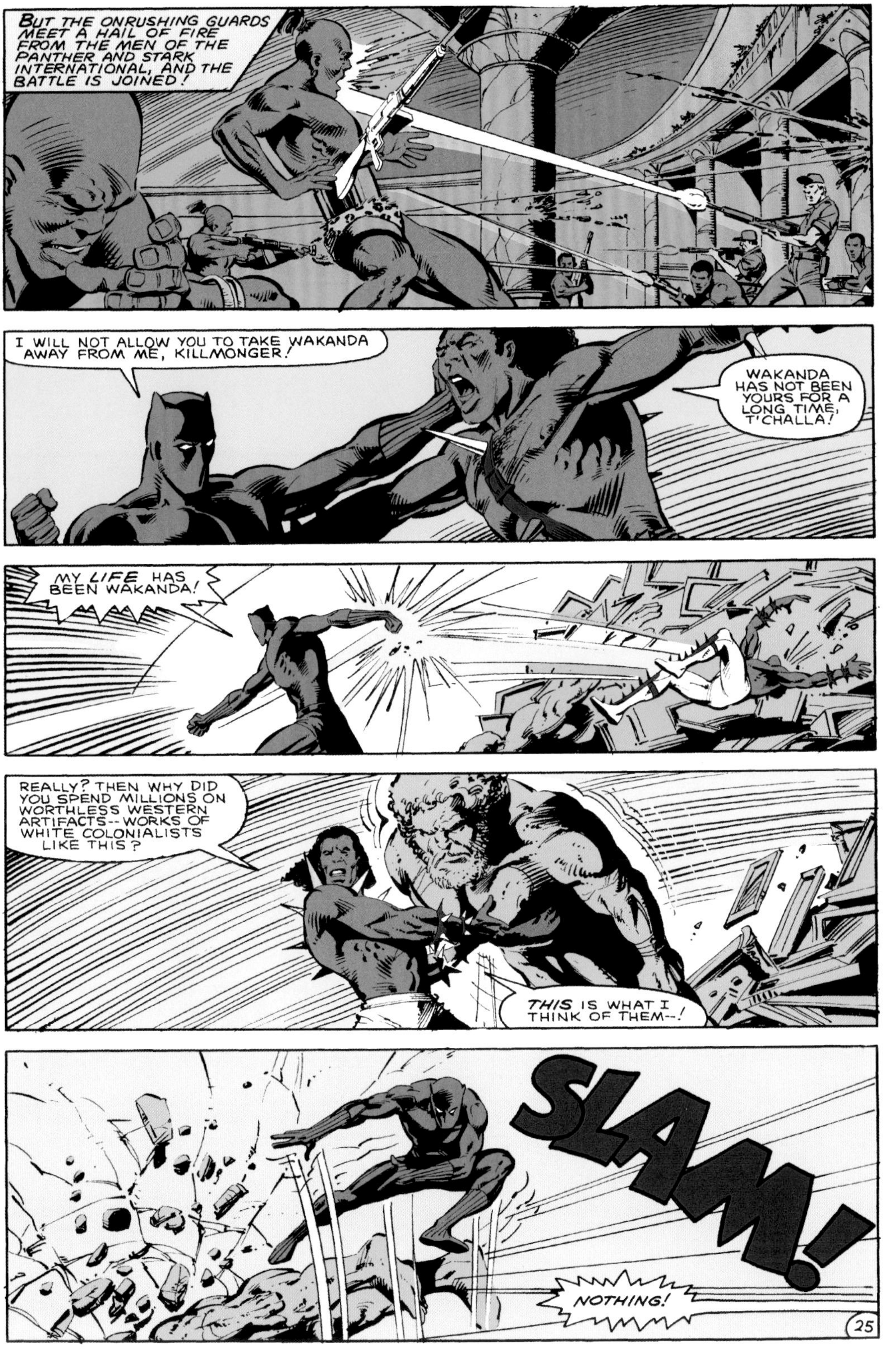

BUT THE ONRUSHING GUARDS MEET A HAIL OF FIRE FROM THE MEN OF THE PANTHER AND STARK INTERNATIONAL, AND THE BATTLE IS JOINED!
I WILL NOT ALLOW YOU TO TAKE WAKANDA AWAY FROM ME, KILLMONGER!
WAKANDA HAS NOT BEEN YOURS FOR A LONG TIME, T'CHALLA!
MY LIFE HAS BEEN WAKANDA!
REALLY? THEN WHY DID YOU SPEND MILLIONS ON WORTHLESS WESTERN ARTIFACTS-- WORKS OF WHITE COLONIALISTS LIKE THIS?
THIS IS WHAT I THINK OF THEM--!
SLAM!
NOTHING!
25

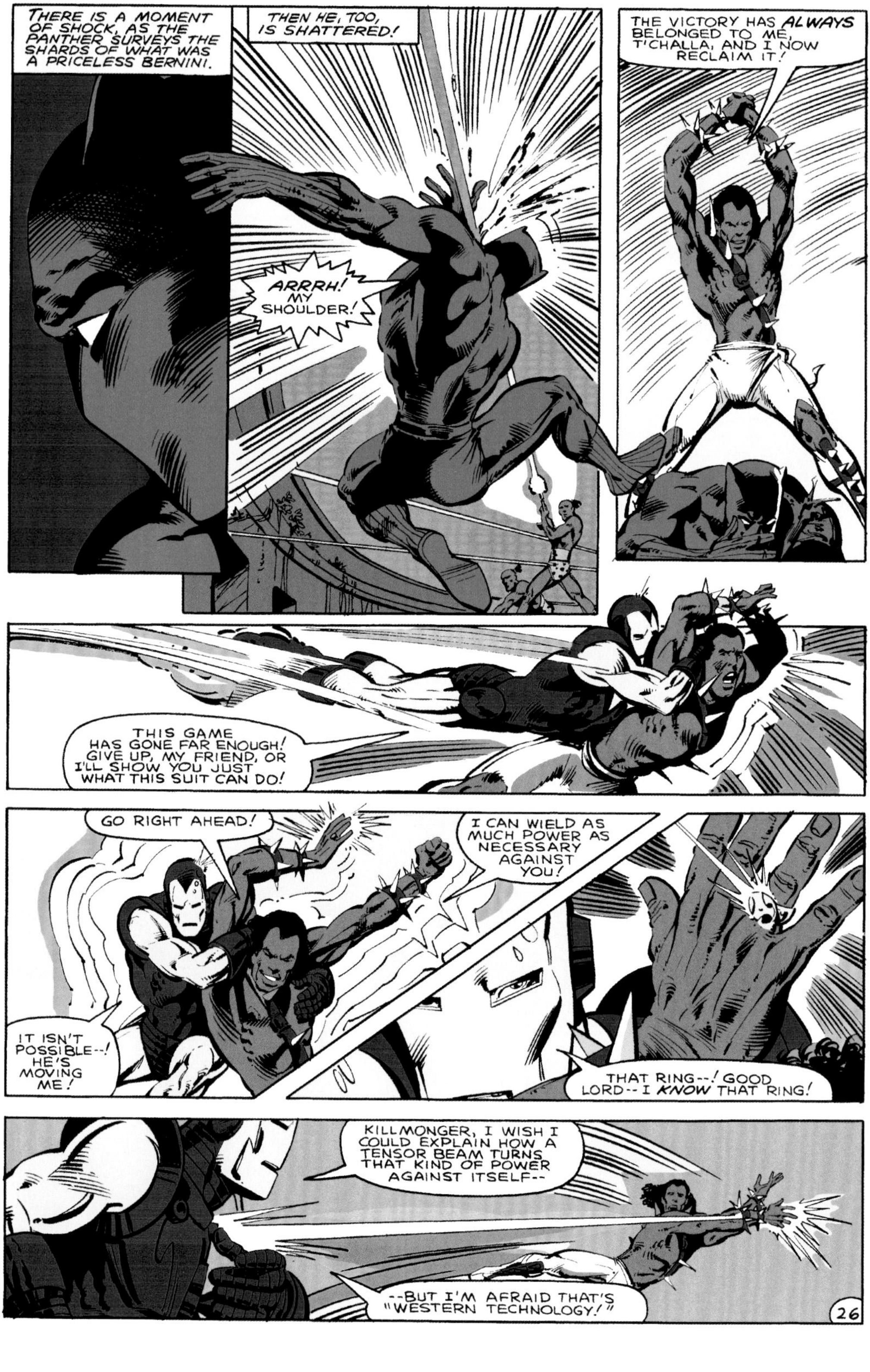
THERE IS A MOMENT OF SHOCK, AS THE PANTHER SURVEYS THE SHARDS OF WHAT WAS A PRICELESS BERNINI.
THEN HE, TOO, IS SHATTERED!
ARRRH! MY SHOULDER!
THE VICTORY HAS ALWAYS BELONGED TO ME, T'CHALLA, AND I NOW RECLAIM IT!
THIS GAME HAS GONE FAR ENOUGH! GIVE UP, MY FRIEND, OR I'LL SHOW YOU JUST WHAT THIS SUIT CAN DO!
GO RIGHT AHEAD!
I CAN WIELD AS MUCH POWER AS NECESSARY AGAINST YOU!
IT ISN'T POSSIBLE--! HE'S MOVING ME!
THAT RING--! GOOD LORD-- I KNOW THAT RING!
KILLMONGER, I WISH I COULD EXPLAIN HOW A TENSOR BEAM TURNS THAT KIND OF POWER AGAINST ITSELF--
--BUT I'M AFRAID THAT'S "WESTERN TECHNOLOGY!"

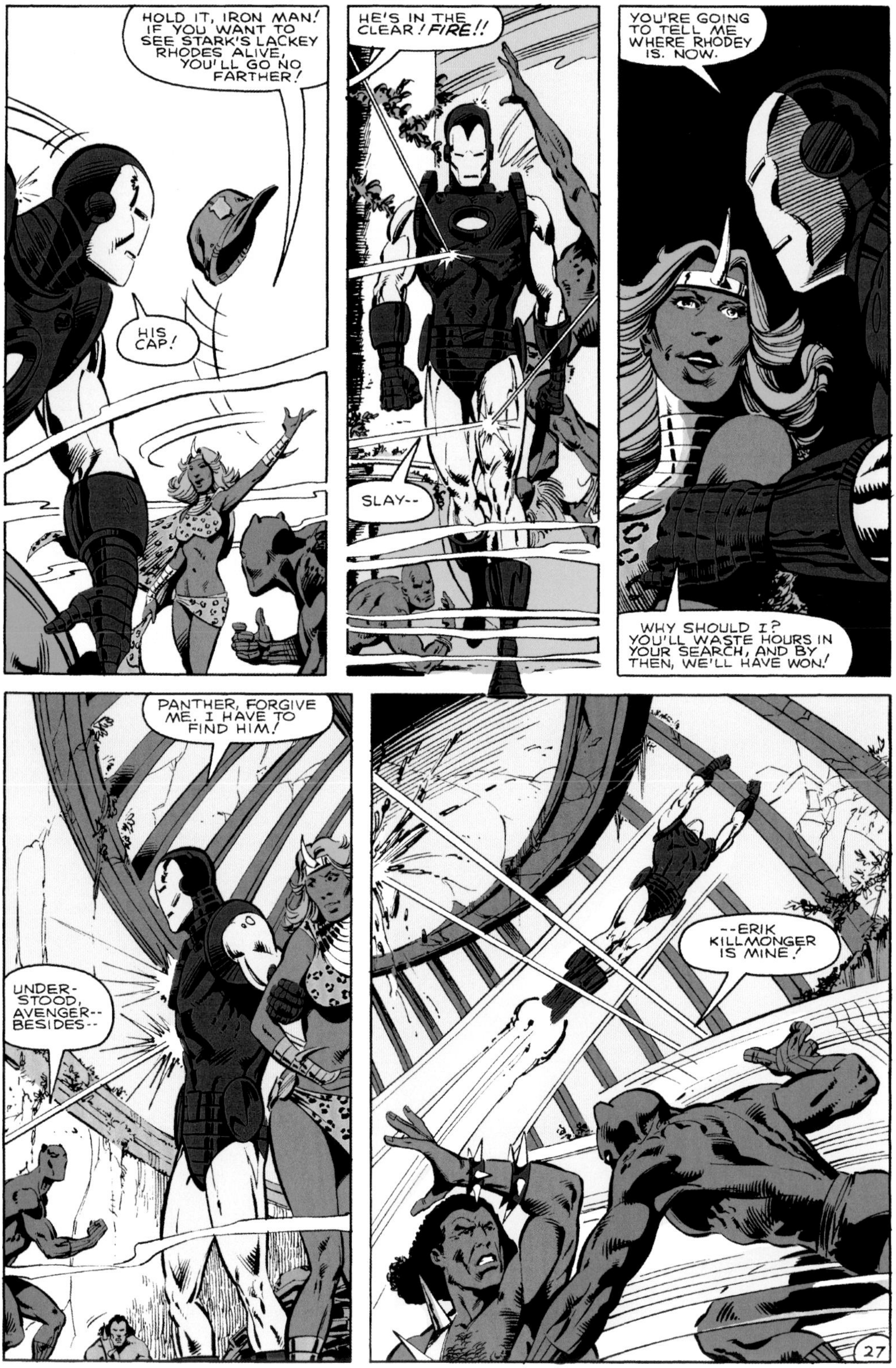
HOLD IT, IRON MAN! IF YOU WANT TO SEE STARK'S LACKEY RHODES ALIVE, YOU'LL GO NO FARTHER!
HIS CAP!
HE'S IN THE CLEAR! FIRE!!
SLAY--
YOU'RE GOING TO TELL ME WHERE RHODEY IS. NOW.
WHY SHOULD I? YOU'LL WASTE HOURS IN YOUR SEARCH, AND BY THEN, WE'LL HAVE WON!
PANTHER, FORGIVE ME. I HAVE TO FIND HIM!
UNDER-STOOD, AVENGER-- BESIDES--
--ERIK KILLMONGER IS MINE!
27

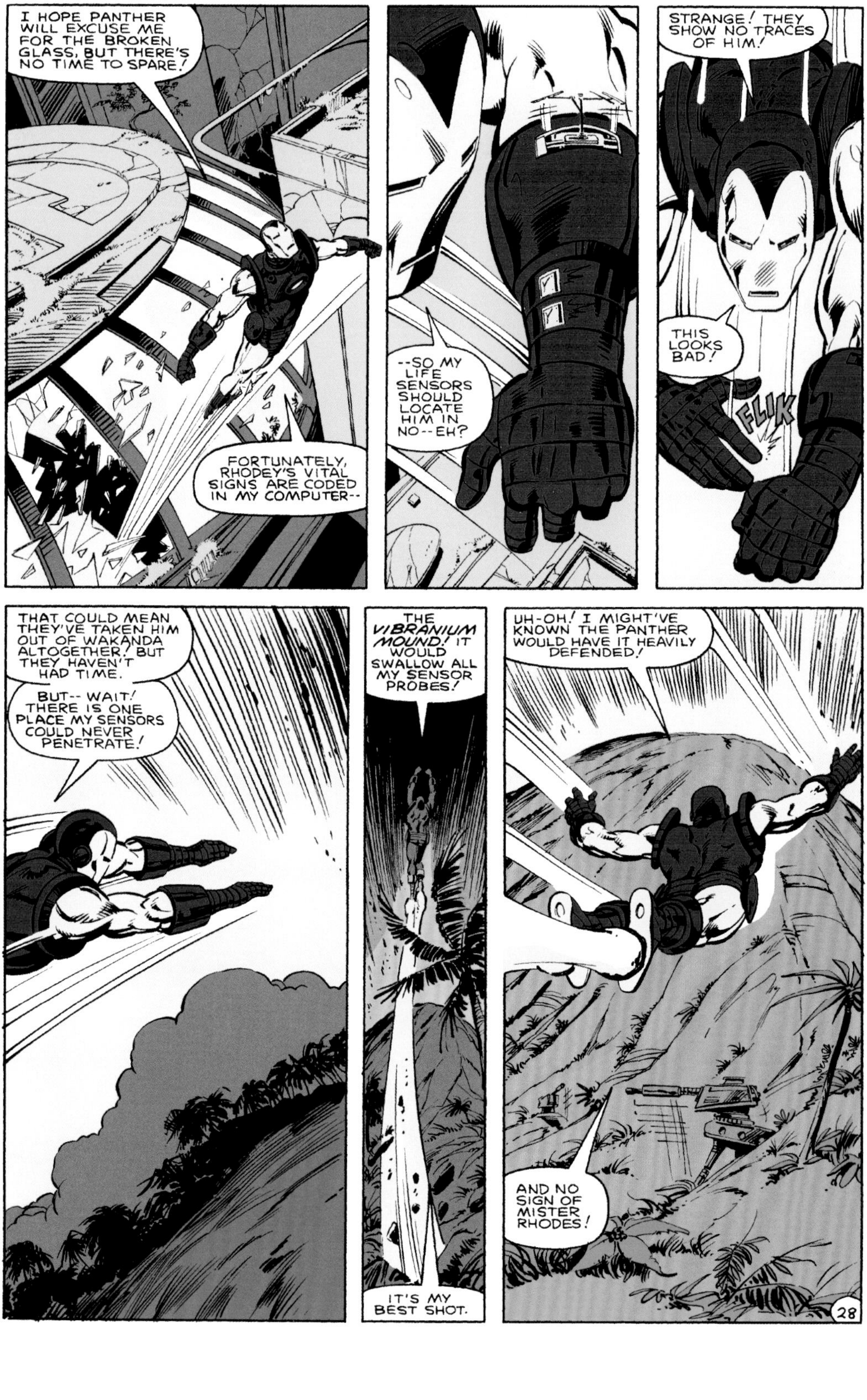

I HOPE PANTHER WILL EXCUSE ME FOR THE BROKEN GLASS, BUT THERE'S NO TIME TO SPARE!
FORTUNATELY, RHODEY'S VITAL SIGNS ARE CODED IN MY COMPUTER--
--SO MY LIFE SENSORS SHOULD LOCATE HIM IN NO--EH?
STRANGE! THEY SHOW NO TRACES OF HIM!
THIS LOOKS BAD!
FLIK
THAT COULD MEAN THEY'VE TAKEN HIM OUT OF WAKANDA ALTOGETHER! BUT THEY HAVEN'T HAD TIME.
BUT-- WAIT! THERE IS ONE PLACE MY SENSORS COULD NEVER PENETRATE!
THE *VIBRANIUM MOUND!* IT WOULD SWALLOW ALL MY SENSOR PROBES!
IT'S MY BEST SHOT.
UH-OH! I MIGHT'VE KNOWN THE PANTHER WOULD HAVE IT HEAVILY DEFENDED!
AND NO SIGN OF MISTER RHODES!

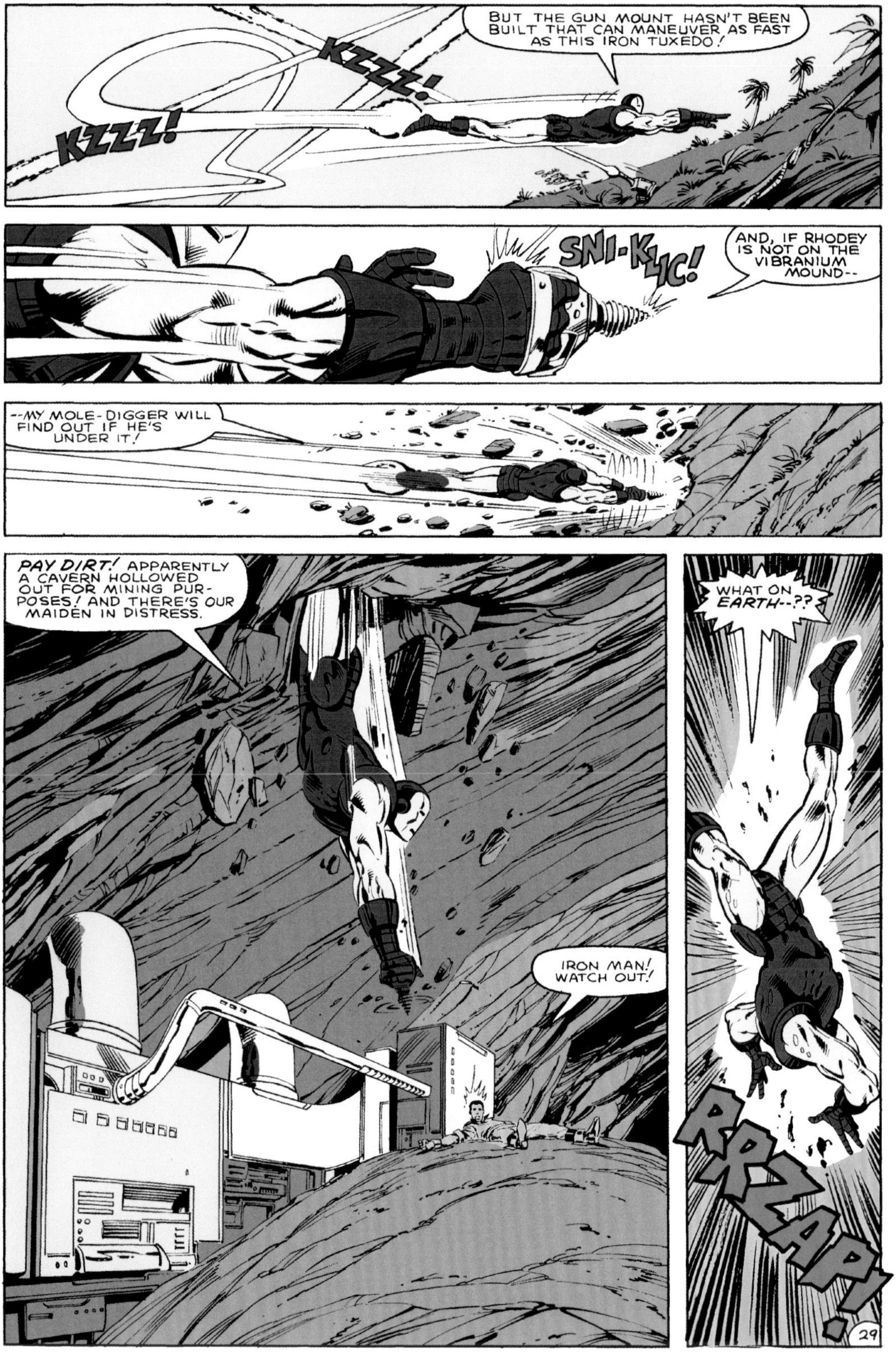

BUT THE GUN MOUNT HASN'T BEEN BUILT THAT CAN MANEUVER AS FAST AS THIS IRON TUXEDO!
KZZZZ!
KZZZ!
SNI-KLIC!
AND, IF RHODEY IS NOT ON THE VIBRANIUM MOUND--
--MY MOLE-DIGGER WILL FIND OUT IF HE'S UNDER IT!
PAY DIRT! APPARENTLY A CAVERN HOLLOWED OUT FOR MINING PURPOSES! AND THERE'S OUR MAIDEN IN DISTRESS.
IRON MAN! WATCH OUT!
WHAT ON EARTH--??
RRZAP!

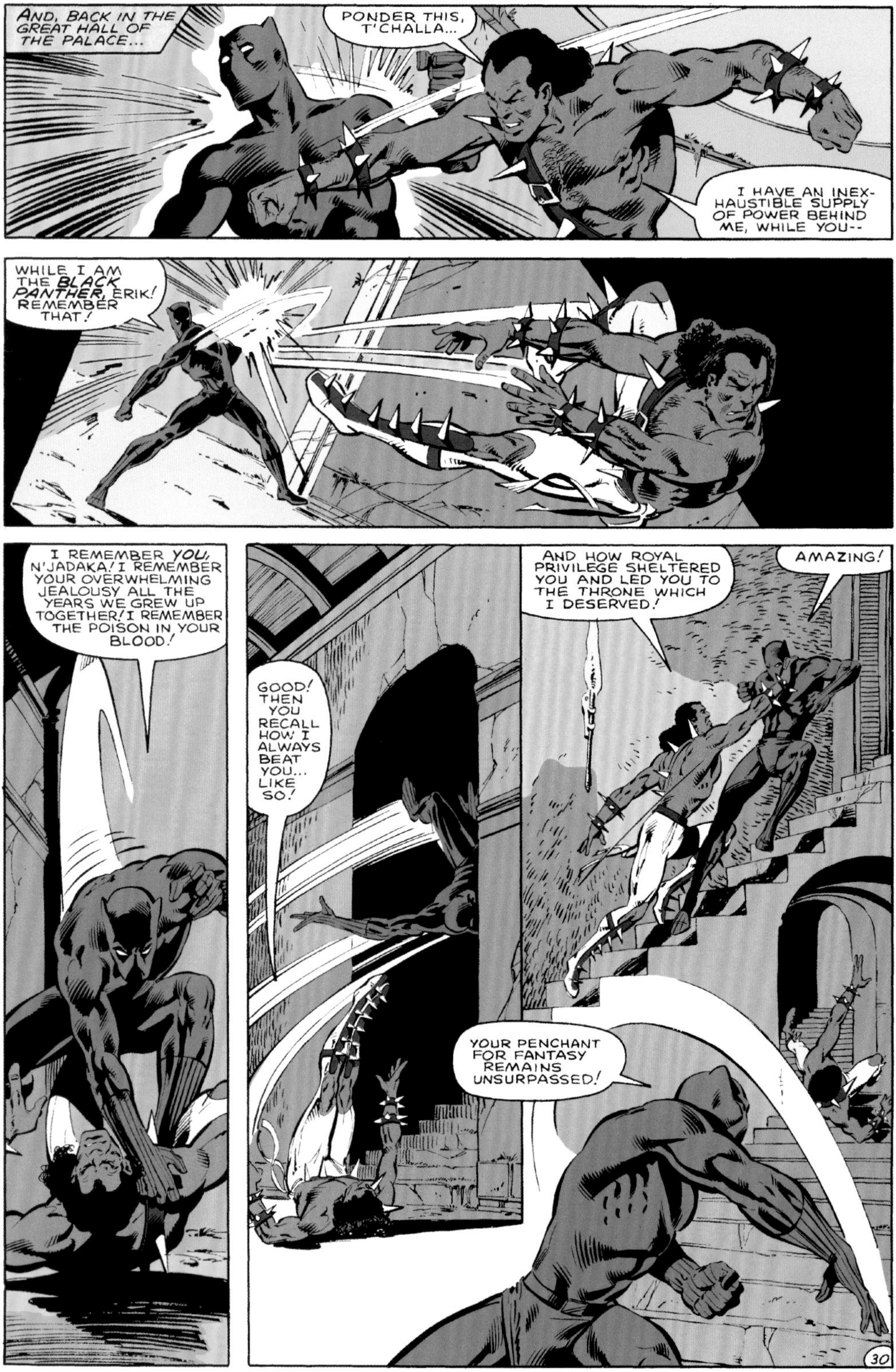
AND, BACK IN THE GREAT HALL OF THE PALACE...
PONDER THIS, T'CHALLA...
I HAVE AN INEXHAUSTIBLE SUPPLY OF POWER BEHIND ME, WHILE YOU--
WHILE I AM THE BLACK PANTHER, ERIK! REMEMBER THAT!
I REMEMBER YOU, N'JADAKA! I REMEMBER YOUR OVERWHELMING JEALOUSY ALL THE YEARS WE GREW UP TOGETHER! I REMEMBER THE POISON IN YOUR BLOOD!
GOOD! THEN YOU RECALL HOW I ALWAYS BEAT YOU... LIKE SO!
AND HOW ROYAL PRIVILEGE SHELTERED YOU AND LED YOU TO THE THRONE WHICH I DESERVED!
AMAZING!
YOUR PENCHANT FOR FANTASY REMAINS UNSURPASSED!

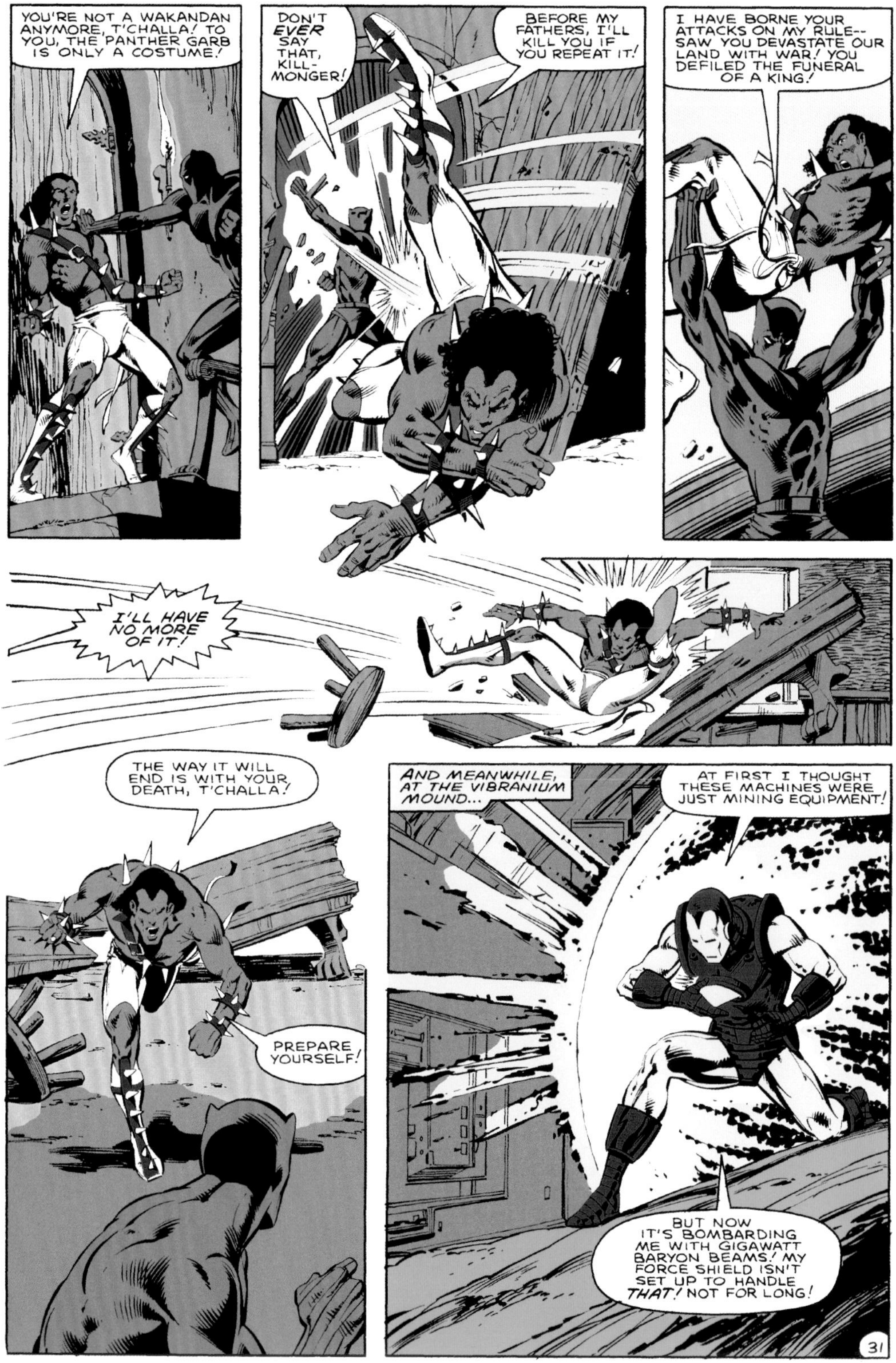
YOU'RE NOT A WAKANDAN ANYMORE, T'CHALLA! TO YOU, THE PANTHER GARB IS ONLY A COSTUME!
DON'T *EVER* SAY THAT, KILL-MONGER!
BEFORE MY FATHERS, I'LL KILL YOU IF YOU REPEAT IT!
I HAVE BORNE YOUR ATTACKS ON MY RULE-- SAW YOU DEVASTATE OUR LAND WITH WAR! YOU DEFILED THE FUNERAL OF A KING!
*I'LL HAVE NO MORE OF IT!*
THE WAY IT WILL END IS WITH YOUR DEATH, T'CHALLA!
PREPARE YOURSELF!
*AND MEANWHILE, AT THE VIBRANIUM MOUND...*
AT FIRST I THOUGHT THESE MACHINES WERE JUST MINING EQUIPMENT!
BUT NOW IT'S BOMBARDING ME WITH GIGAWATT BARYON BEAMS! MY FORCE SHIELD ISN'T SET UP TO HANDLE *THAT*! NOT FOR LONG!

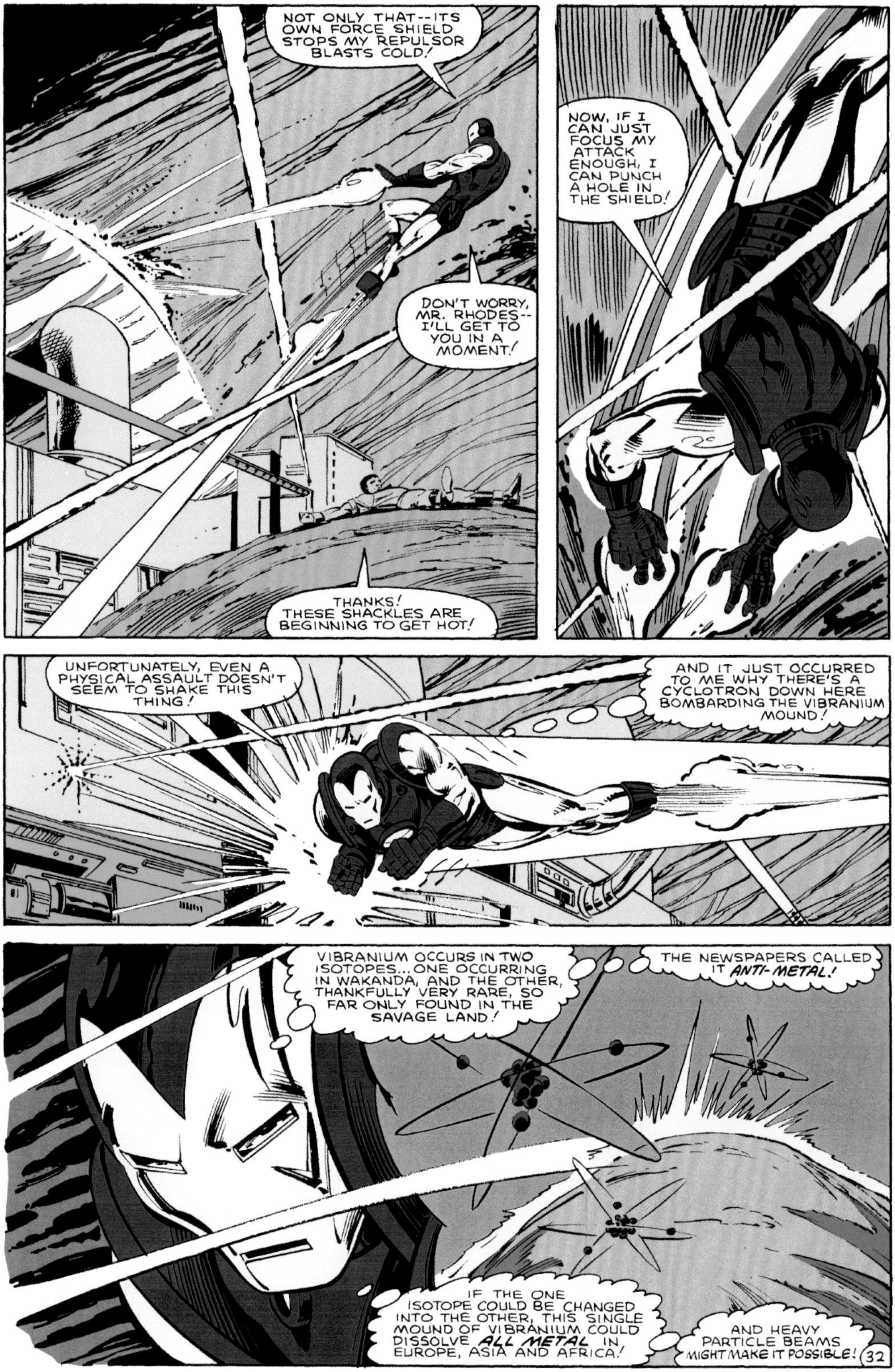
NOT ONLY THAT--ITS OWN FORCE SHIELD STOPS MY REPULSOR BLASTS COLD!
DON'T WORRY, MR. RHODES-- I'LL GET TO YOU IN A MOMENT!
THANKS! THESE SHACKLES ARE BEGINNING TO GET HOT!
NOW, IF I CAN JUST FOCUS MY ATTACK ENOUGH, I CAN PUNCH A HOLE IN THE SHIELD!
UNFORTUNATELY, EVEN A PHYSICAL ASSAULT DOESN'T SEEM TO SHAKE THIS THING!
AND IT JUST OCCURRED TO ME WHY THERE'S A CYCLOTRON DOWN HERE BOMBARDING THE VIBRANIUM MOUND!
VIBRANIUM OCCURS IN TWO ISOTOPES... ONE OCCURRING IN WAKANDA, AND THE OTHER, THANKFULLY VERY RARE, SO FAR ONLY FOUND IN THE SAVAGE LAND!
THE NEWSPAPERS CALLED IT ANTI-METAL!
IF THE ONE ISOTOPE COULD BE CHANGED INTO THE OTHER, THIS SINGLE MOUND OF VIBRANIUM COULD DISSOLVE ALL METAL IN EUROPE, ASIA AND AFRICA!
AND HEAVY PARTICLE BEAMS MIGHT MAKE IT POSSIBLE!

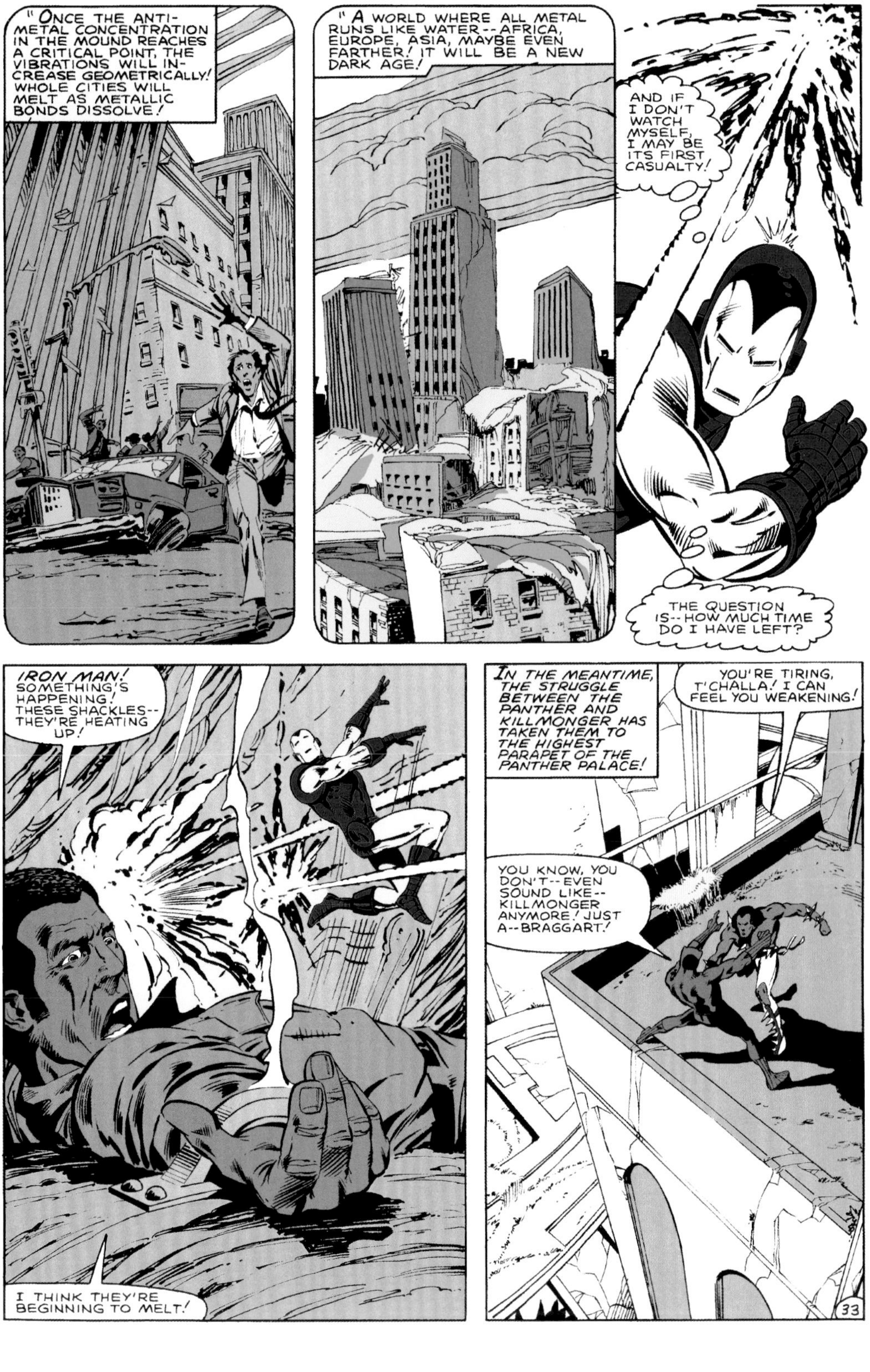
"ONCE THE ANTI-METAL CONCENTRATION IN THE MOUND REACHES A CRITICAL POINT, THE VIBRATIONS WILL INCREASE GEOMETRICALLY! WHOLE CITIES WILL MELT AS METALLIC BONDS DISSOLVE!
"A WORLD WHERE ALL METAL RUNS LIKE WATER--AFRICA, EUROPE, ASIA, MAYBE EVEN FARTHER! IT WILL BE A NEW DARK AGE!
AND IF I DON'T WATCH MYSELF, I MAY BE ITS FIRST CASUALTY!
THE QUESTION IS--HOW MUCH TIME DO I HAVE LEFT?
IRON MAN! SOMETHING'S HAPPENING! THESE SHACKLES--THEY'RE HEATING UP!
I THINK THEY'RE BEGINNING TO MELT!
IN THE MEANTIME, THE STRUGGLE BETWEEN THE PANTHER AND KILLMONGER HAS TAKEN THEM TO THE HIGHEST PARAPET OF THE PANTHER PALACE!
YOU'RE TIRING, T'CHALLA! I CAN FEEL YOU WEAKENING!
YOU KNOW, YOU DON'T--EVEN SOUND LIKE--KILLMONGER ANYMORE! JUST A--BRAGGART!
33

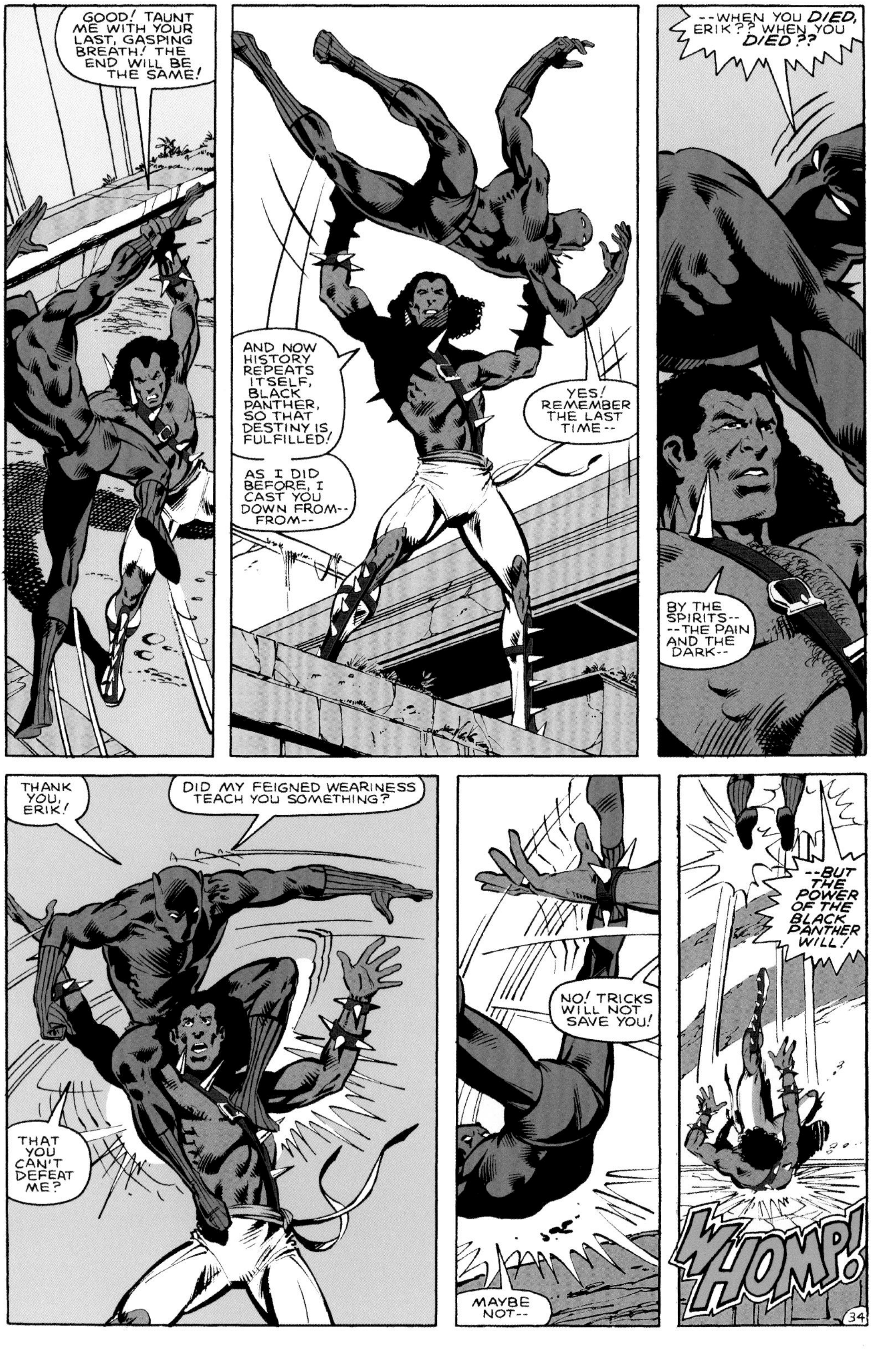
GOOD! TAUNT ME WITH YOUR LAST, GASPING BREATH! THE END WILL BE THE SAME!
AND NOW HISTORY REPEATS ITSELF, BLACK PANTHER, SO THAT DESTINY IS FULFILLED!
AS I DID BEFORE, I CAST YOU DOWN FROM-- FROM--
YES! REMEMBER THE LAST TIME--
--WHEN YOU DIED, ERIK?? WHEN YOU DIED??
BY THE SPIRITS-- --THE PAIN AND THE DARK--
THANK YOU, ERIK!
DID MY FEIGNED WEARINESS TEACH YOU SOMETHING?
THAT YOU CAN'T DEFEAT ME?
NO! TRICKS WILL NOT SAVE YOU!
MAYBE NOT--
--BUT THE POWER OF THE BLACK PANTHER WILL!
WHOMP!
34

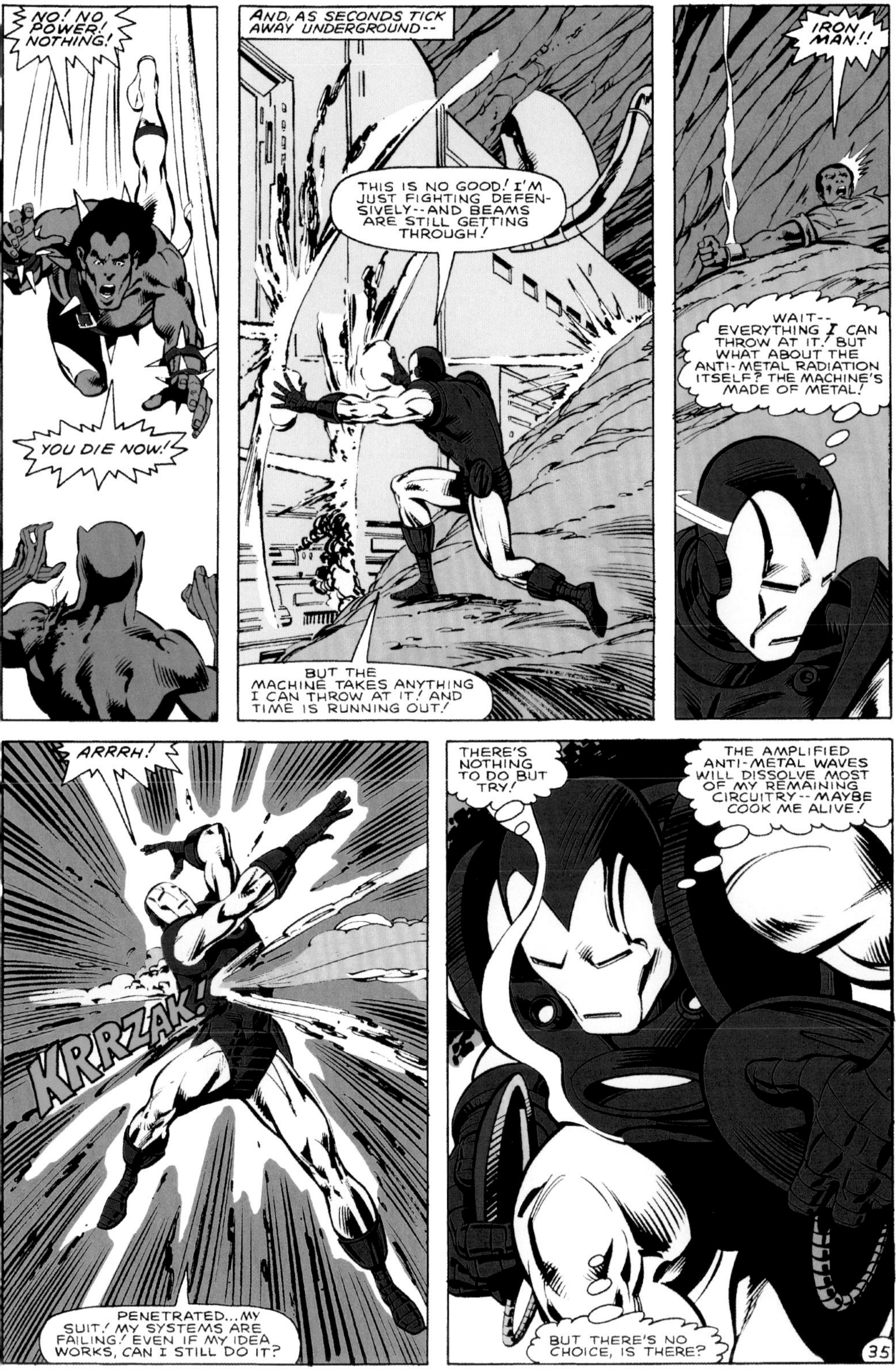
NO! NO POWER! NOTHING!
YOU DIE NOW!
AND, AS SECONDS TICK AWAY UNDERGROUND--
THIS IS NO GOOD! I'M JUST FIGHTING DEFENSIVELY--AND BEAMS ARE STILL GETTING THROUGH!
BUT THE MACHINE TAKES ANYTHING I CAN THROW AT IT! AND TIME IS RUNNING OUT!
IRON MAN!!
WAIT-- EVERYTHING I CAN THROW AT IT! BUT WHAT ABOUT THE ANTI-METAL RADIATION ITSELF? THE MACHINE'S MADE OF METAL!
ARRRH!
KRRZAK!
PENETRATED... MY SUIT! MY SYSTEMS ARE FAILING! EVEN IF MY IDEA WORKS, CAN I STILL DO IT?
THERE'S NOTHING TO DO BUT TRY!
THE AMPLIFIED ANTI-METAL WAVES WILL DISSOLVE MOST OF MY REMAINING CIRCUITRY--MAYBE COOK ME ALIVE!
BUT THERE'S NO CHOICE, IS THERE?

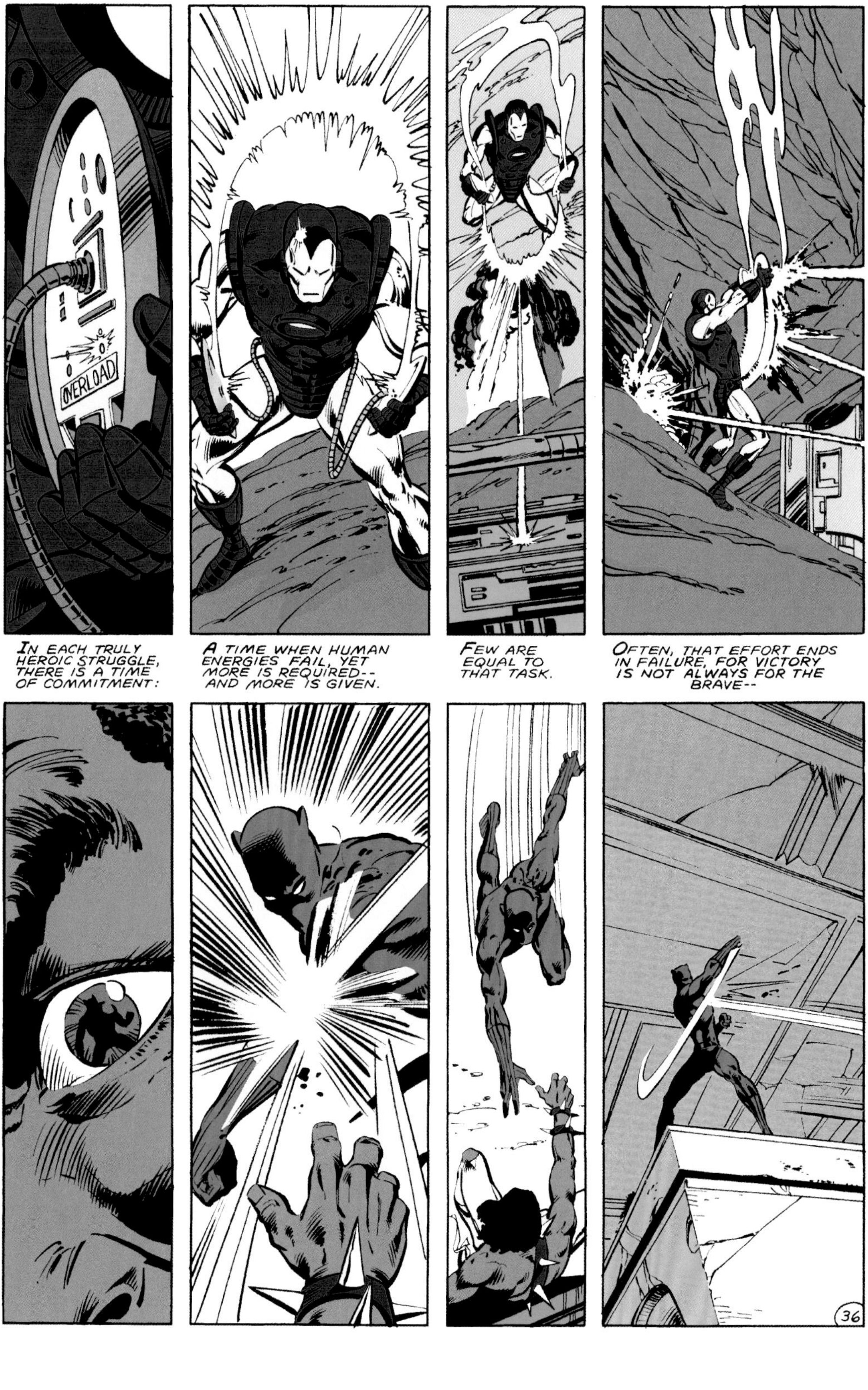
OVERLOAD
IN EACH TRULY HEROIC STRUGGLE, THERE IS A TIME OF COMMITMENT:
A TIME WHEN HUMAN ENERGIES FAIL, YET MORE IS REQUIRED-- AND MORE IS GIVEN.
FEW ARE EQUAL TO THAT TASK.
OFTEN, THAT EFFORT ENDS IN FAILURE, FOR VICTORY IS NOT ALWAYS FOR THE BRAVE--
36

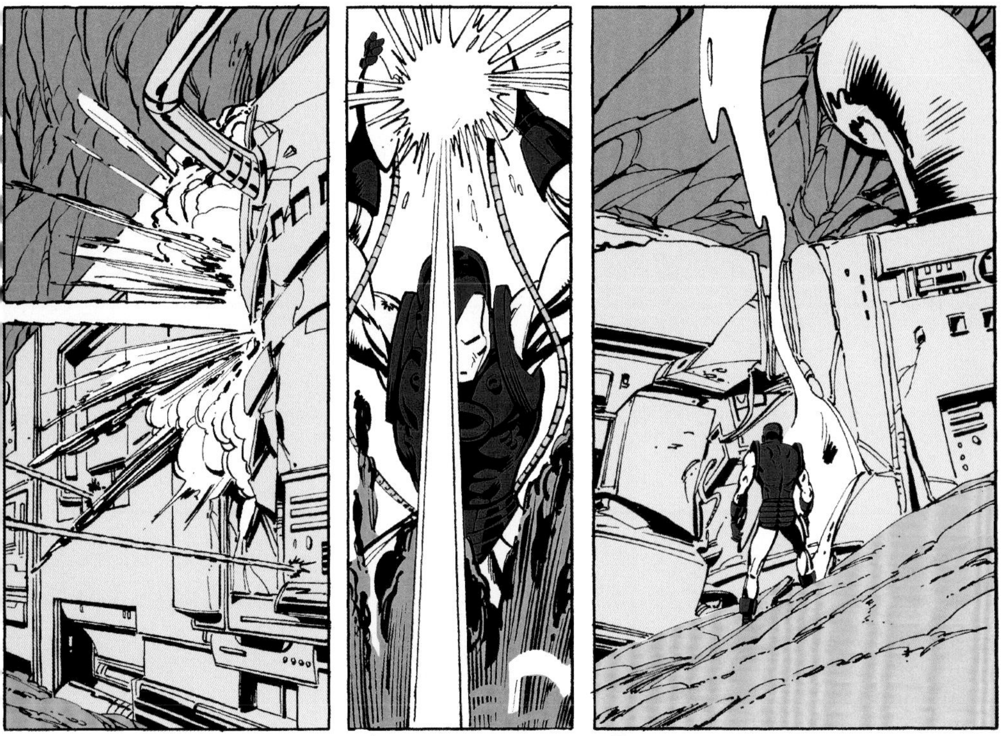
--BUT WHERE A MAN MIGHT FALTER, THESE ONES DO NOT. NOT WHILE LIFE AND SPIRIT ENDURE.
NOT UNTIL THE LAST MEASURE IS GIVEN.
TO TRANSCEND THE MAN, BECOME THE HERO.

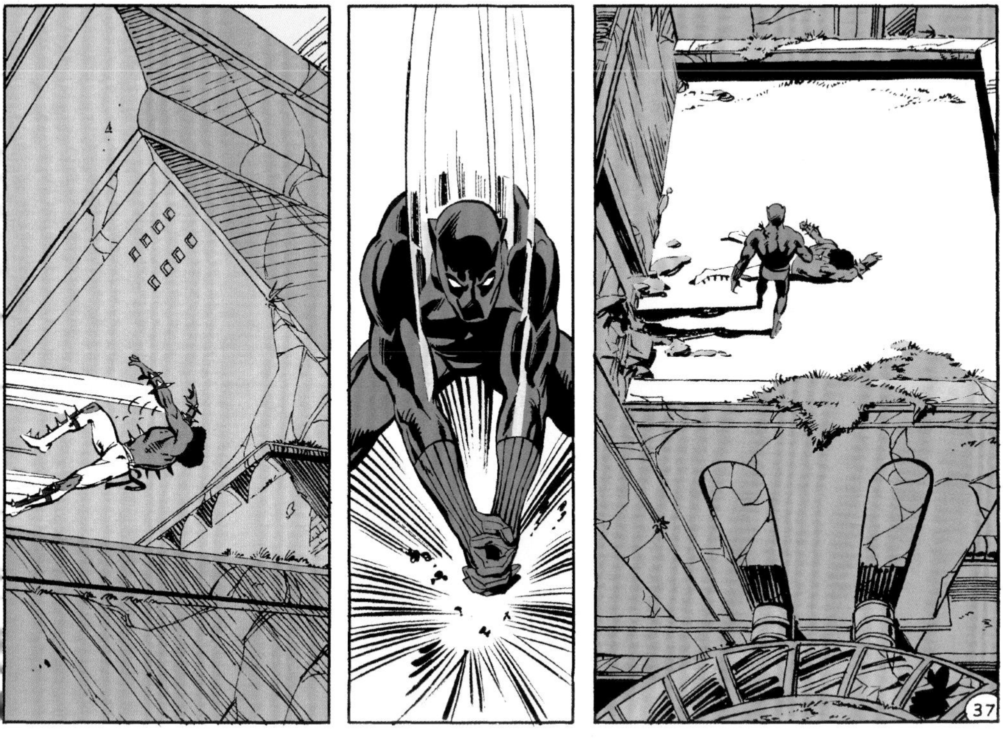

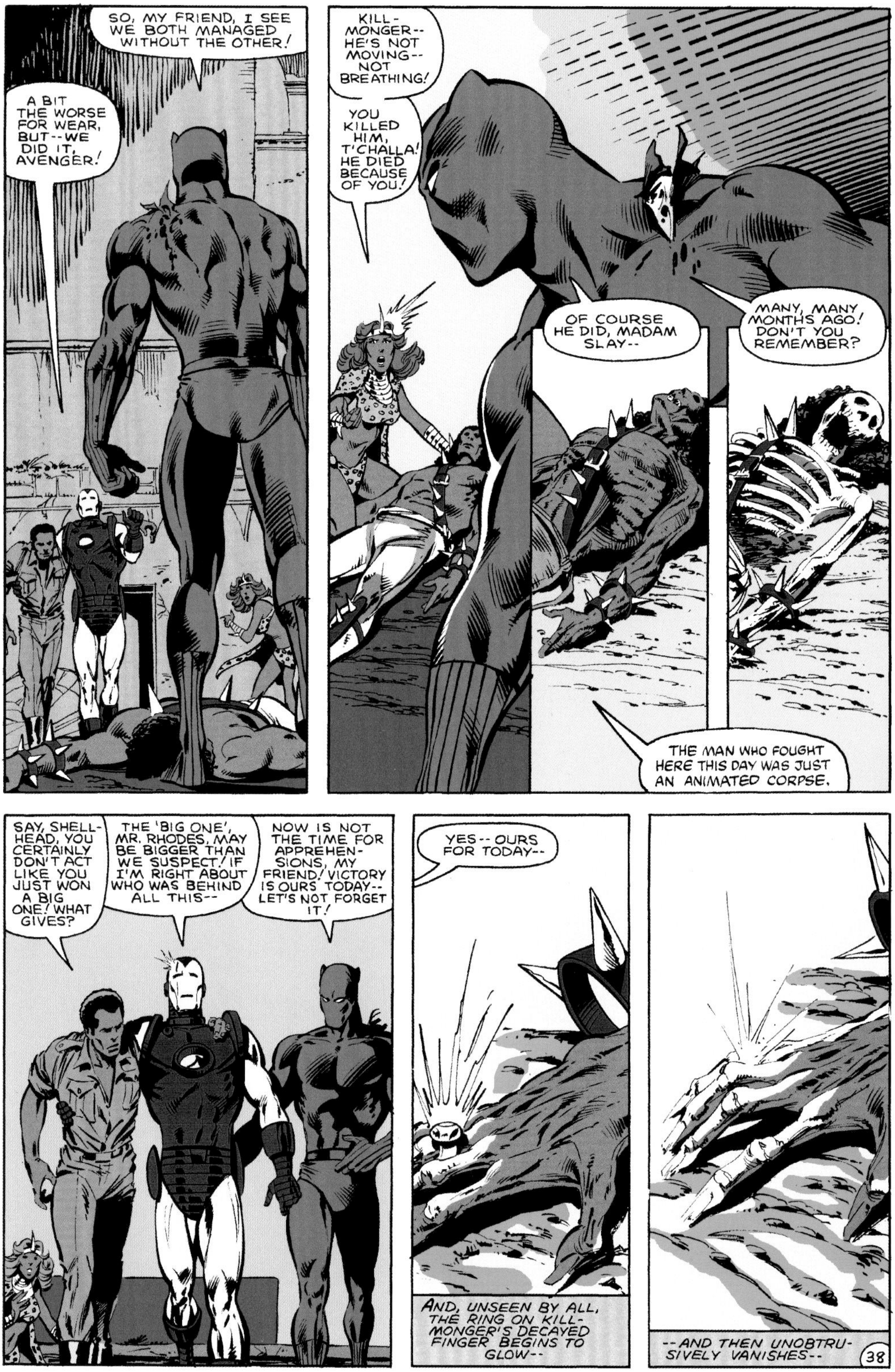

SO, MY FRIEND, I SEE WE BOTH MANAGED WITHOUT THE OTHER!
A BIT THE WORSE FOR WEAR, BUT--WE DID IT, AVENGER!
KILL-MONGER--HE'S NOT MOVING--NOT BREATHING!
YOU KILLED HIM, T'CHALLA! HE DIED BECAUSE OF YOU!
OF COURSE HE DID, MADAM SLAY--
MANY, MANY MONTHS AGO! DON'T YOU REMEMBER?
THE MAN WHO FOUGHT HERE THIS DAY WAS JUST AN ANIMATED CORPSE.
SAY, SHELL-HEAD, YOU CERTAINLY DON'T ACT LIKE YOU JUST WON A BIG ONE! WHAT GIVES?
THE 'BIG ONE', MR. RHODES, MAY BE BIGGER THAN WE SUSPECT! IF I'M RIGHT ABOUT WHO WAS BEHIND ALL THIS--
NOW IS NOT THE TIME FOR APPREHENSIONS, MY FRIEND! VICTORY IS OURS TODAY--LET'S NOT FORGET IT!
YES--OURS FOR TODAY--
AND, UNSEEN BY ALL, THE RING ON KILL-MONGER'S DECAYED FINGER BEGINS TO GLOW--
--AND THEN UNOBTRU-SIVELY VANISHES--

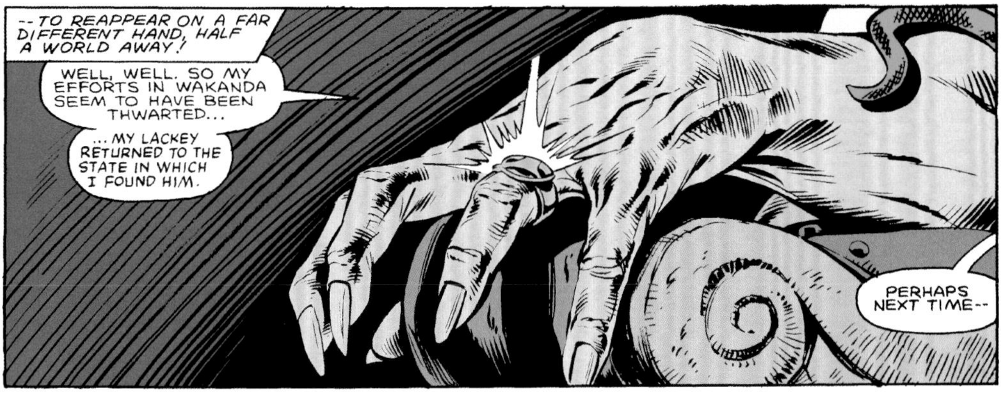
--TO REAPPEAR ON A FAR DIFFERENT HAND, HALF A WORLD AWAY!
WELL, WELL. SO MY EFFORTS IN WAKANDA SEEM TO HAVE BEEN THWARTED...
...MY LACKEY RETURNED TO THE STATE IN WHICH I FOUND HIM.
PERHAPS NEXT TIME--

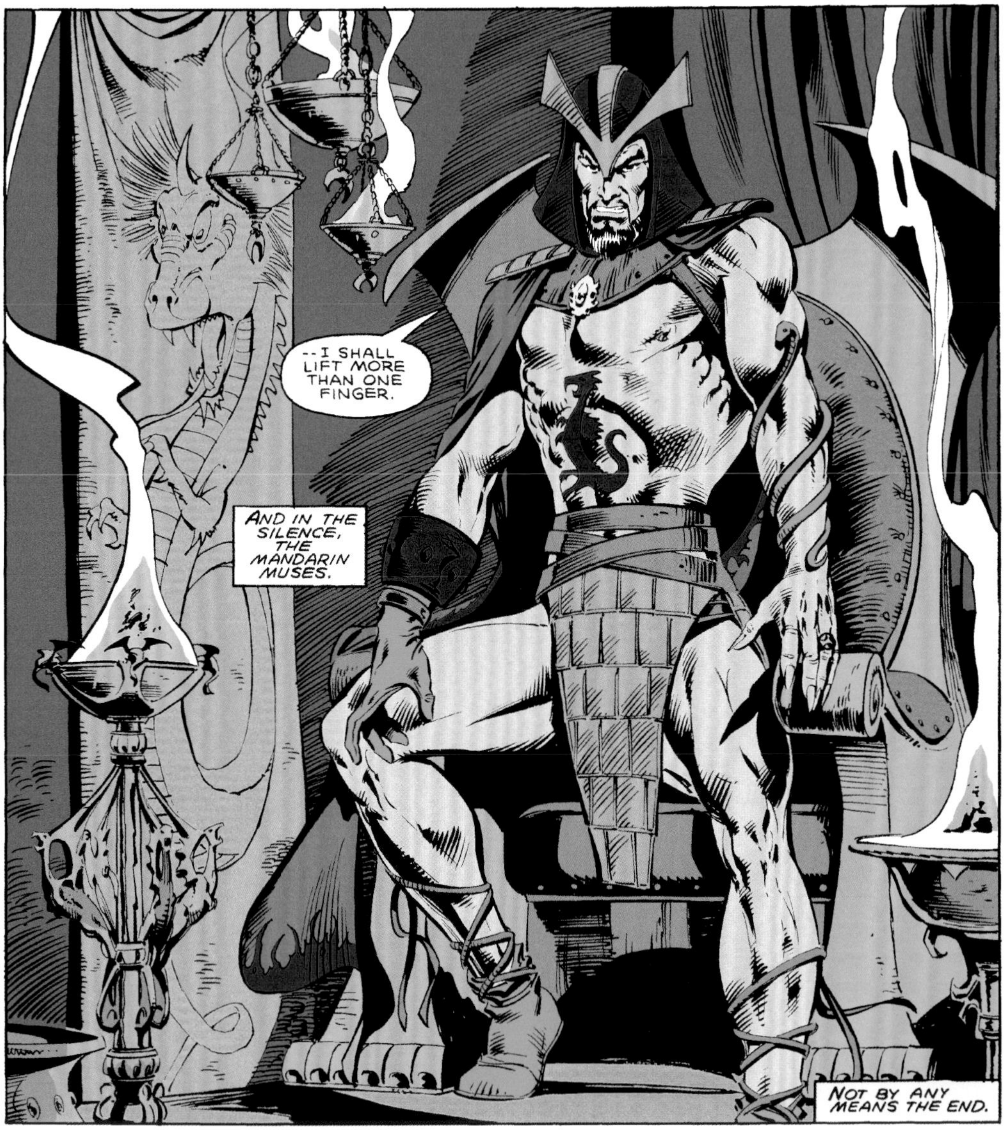
--I SHALL LIFT MORE THAN ONE FINGER.
AND IN THE SILENCE, THE MANDARIN MUSES.
NOT BY ANY MEANS THE END.

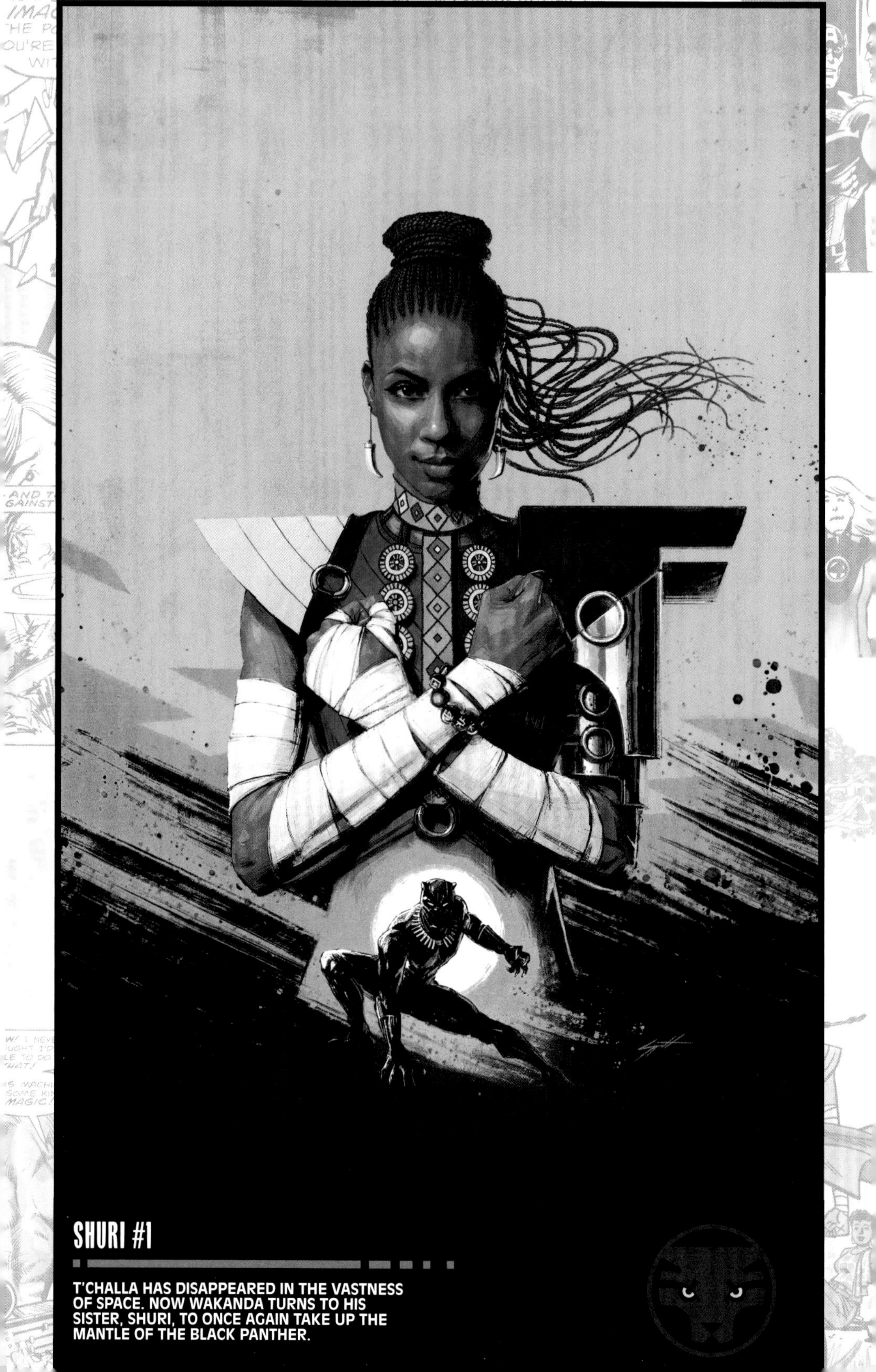

## SHURI #1

T'CHALLA HAS DISAPPEARED IN THE VASTNESS OF SPACE. NOW WAKANDA TURNS TO HIS SISTER, SHURI, TO ONCE AGAIN TAKE UP THE MANTLE OF THE BLACK PANTHER.

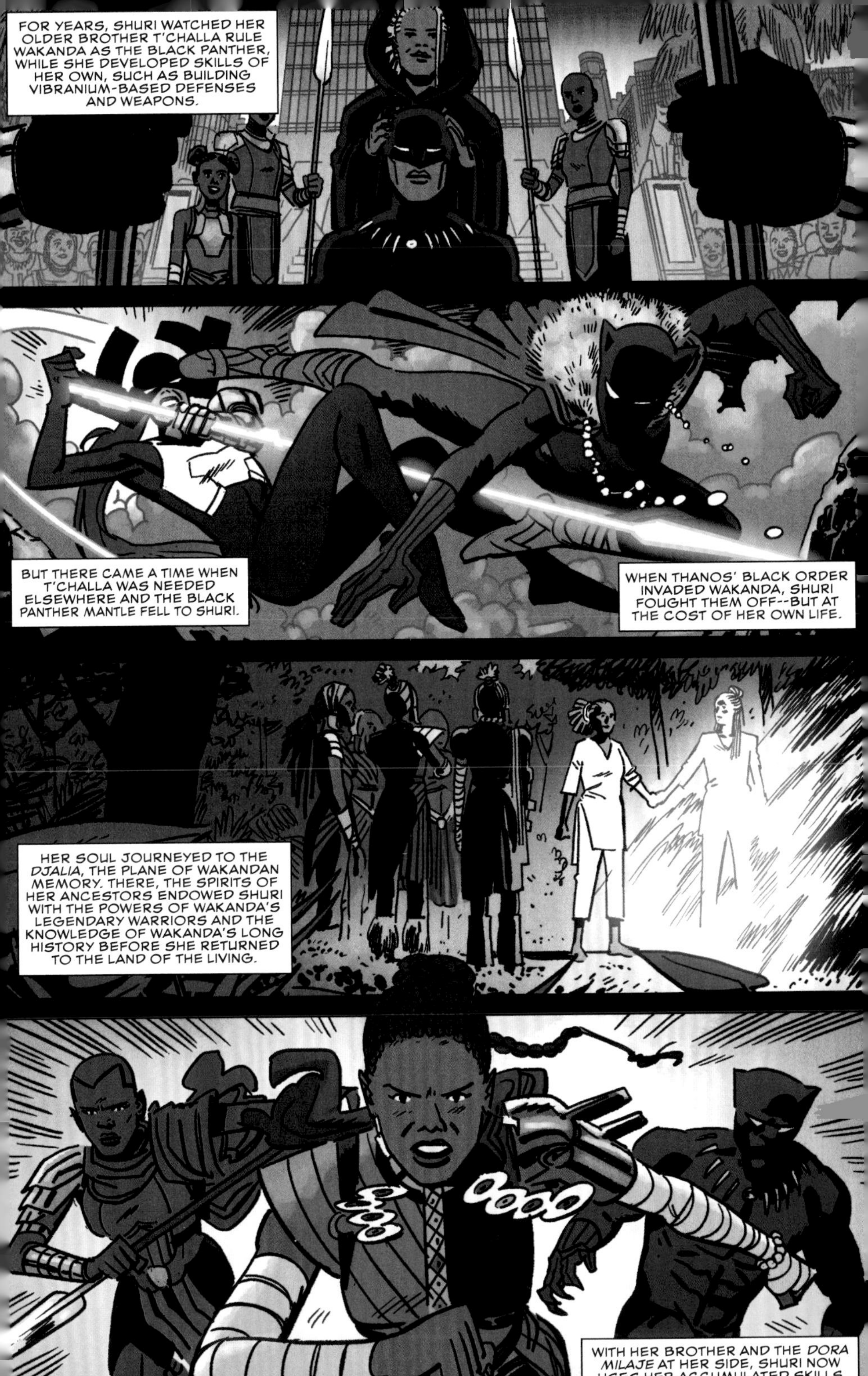
FOR YEARS, SHURI WATCHED HER OLDER BROTHER T'CHALLA RULE WAKANDA AS THE BLACK PANTHER, WHILE SHE DEVELOPED SKILLS OF HER OWN, SUCH AS BUILDING VIBRANIUM-BASED DEFENSES AND WEAPONS.
BUT THERE CAME A TIME WHEN T'CHALLA WAS NEEDED ELSEWHERE AND THE BLACK PANTHER MANTLE FELL TO SHURI.
WHEN THANOS' BLACK ORDER INVADED WAKANDA, SHURI FOUGHT THEM OFF--BUT AT THE COST OF HER OWN LIFE.
HER SOUL JOURNEYED TO THE *DJALIA*, THE PLANE OF WAKANDAN MEMORY. THERE, THE SPIRITS OF HER ANCESTORS ENDOWED SHURI WITH THE POWERS OF WAKANDA'S LEGENDARY WARRIORS AND THE KNOWLEDGE OF WAKANDA'S LONG HISTORY BEFORE SHE RETURNED TO THE LAND OF THE LIVING.
WITH HER BROTHER AND THE *DORA MILAJE* AT HER SIDE, SHURI NOW USES HER ACCUMULATED SKILLS AND WISDOM TO HELP SAFEGUARD HER NATION. WAKANDA FOREVER.

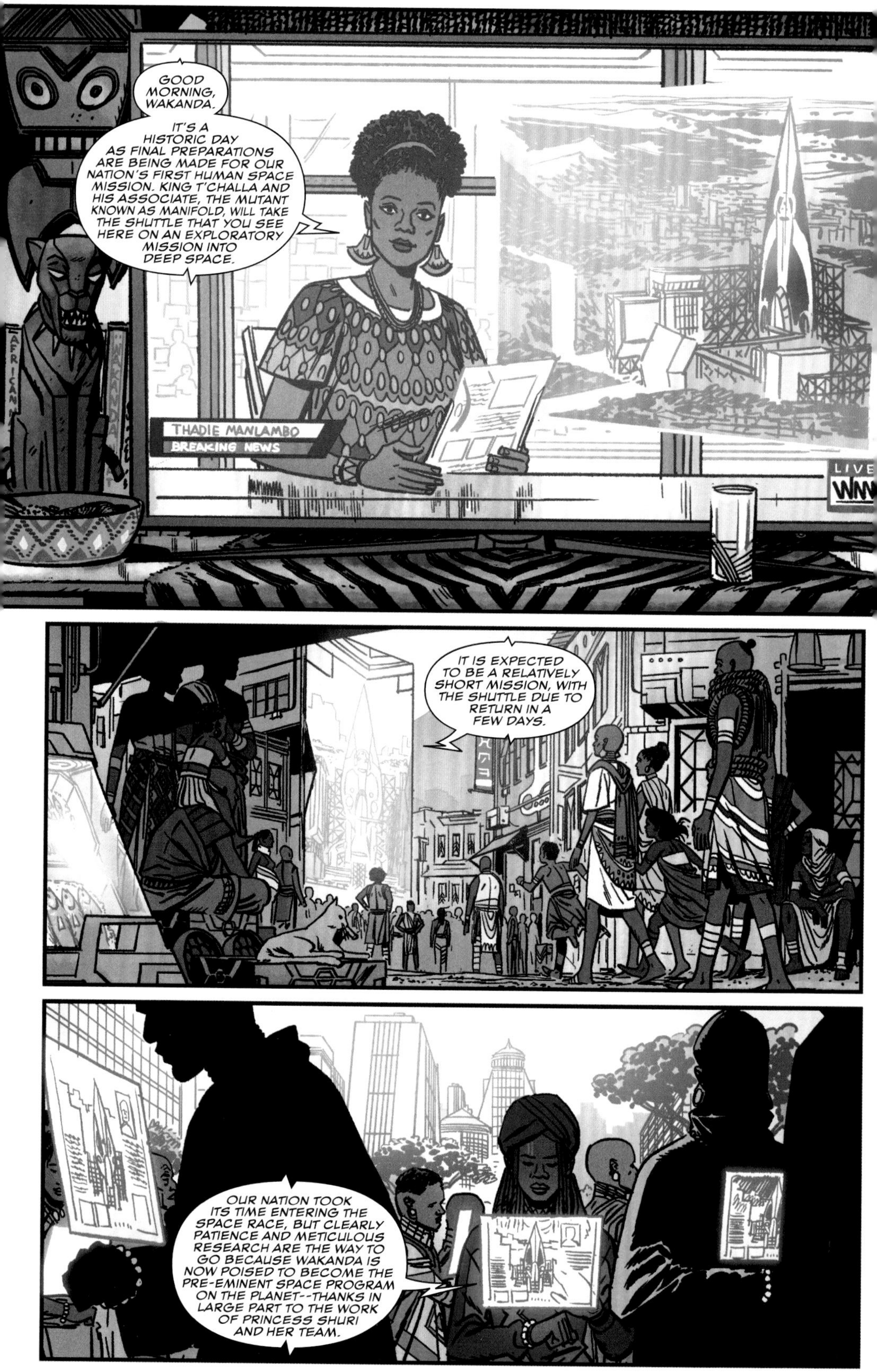
GOOD MORNING, WAKANDA.
IT'S A HISTORIC DAY AS FINAL PREPARATIONS ARE BEING MADE FOR OUR NATION'S FIRST HUMAN SPACE MISSION. KING T'CHALLA AND HIS ASSOCIATE, THE MUTANT KNOWN AS MANIFOLD, WILL TAKE THE SHUTTLE THAT YOU SEE HERE ON AN EXPLORATORY MISSION INTO DEEP SPACE.
THADIE MANLAMBO
BREAKING NEWS
LIVE
IT IS EXPECTED TO BE A RELATIVELY SHORT MISSION, WITH THE SHUTTLE DUE TO RETURN IN A FEW DAYS.
OUR NATION TOOK ITS TIME ENTERING THE SPACE RACE, BUT CLEARLY PATIENCE AND METICULOUS RESEARCH ARE THE WAY TO GO BECAUSE WAKANDA IS NOW POISED TO BECOME THE PRE-EMINENT SPACE PROGRAM ON THE PLANET--THANKS IN LARGE PART TO THE WORK OF PRINCESS SHURI AND HER TEAM.

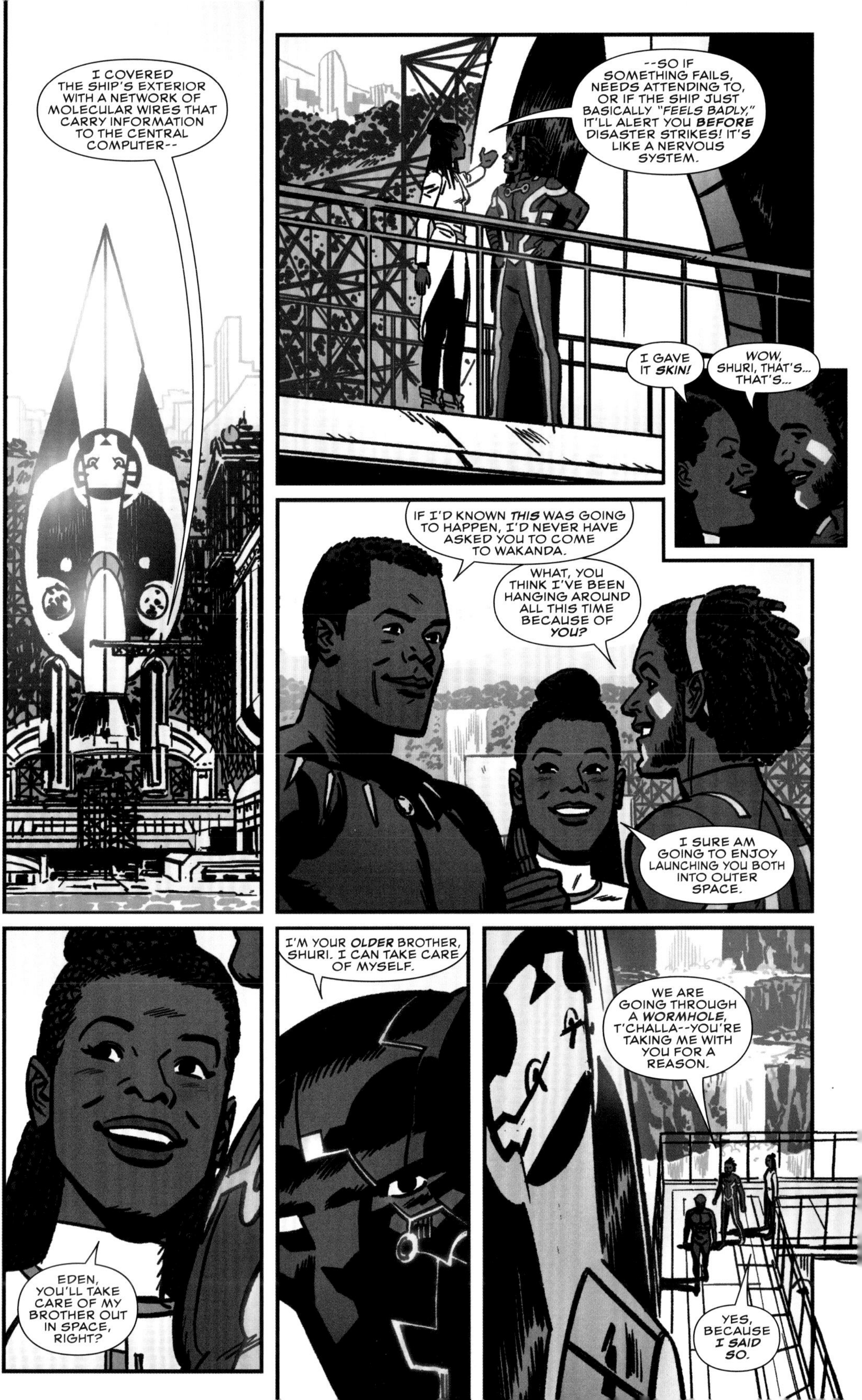
I COVERED THE SHIP'S EXTERIOR WITH A NETWORK OF MOLECULAR WIRES THAT CARRY INFORMATION TO THE CENTRAL COMPUTER--
--SO IF SOMETHING FAILS, NEEDS ATTENDING TO, OR IF THE SHIP JUST BASICALLY "FEELS BADLY," IT'LL ALERT YOU BEFORE DISASTER STRIKES! IT'S LIKE A NERVOUS SYSTEM.
I GAVE IT SKIN!
WOW, SHURI, THAT'S... THAT'S...
IF I'D KNOWN THIS WAS GOING TO HAPPEN, I'D NEVER HAVE ASKED YOU TO COME TO WAKANDA.
WHAT, YOU THINK I'VE BEEN HANGING AROUND ALL THIS TIME BECAUSE OF YOU?
I SURE AM GOING TO ENJOY LAUNCHING YOU BOTH INTO OUTER SPACE.
EDEN, YOU'LL TAKE CARE OF MY BROTHER OUT IN SPACE, RIGHT?
I'M YOUR OLDER BROTHER, SHURI. I CAN TAKE CARE OF MYSELF.
WE ARE GOING THROUGH A WORMHOLE, T'CHALLA--YOU'RE TAKING ME WITH YOU FOR A REASON.
YES, BECAUSE I SAID SO.

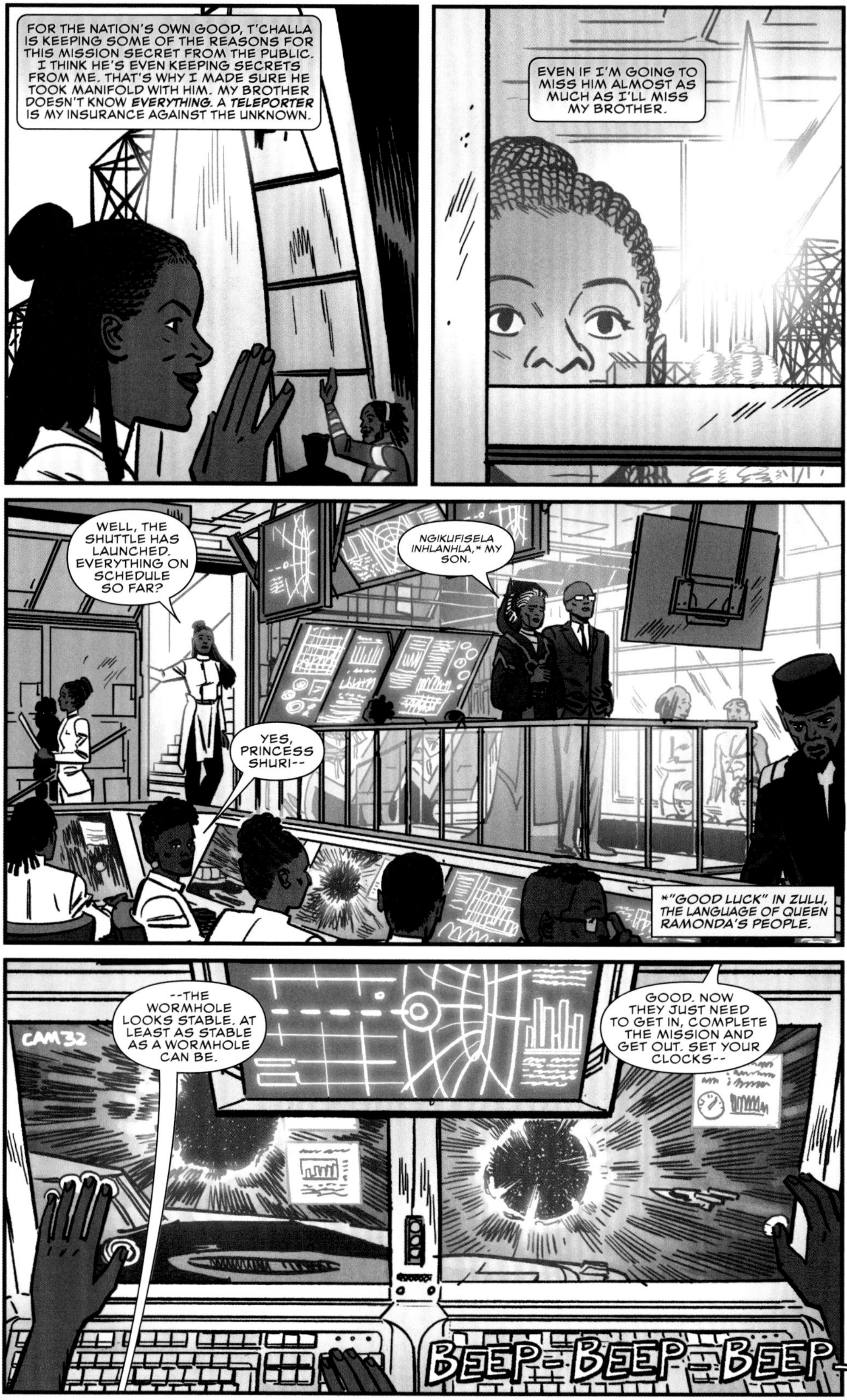
FOR THE NATION'S OWN GOOD, T'CHALLA IS KEEPING SOME OF THE REASONS FOR THIS MISSION SECRET FROM THE PUBLIC. I THINK HE'S EVEN KEEPING SECRETS FROM ME. THAT'S WHY I MADE SURE HE TOOK MANIFOLD WITH HIM. MY BROTHER DOESN'T KNOW *EVERYTHING*. A *TELEPORTER* IS MY INSURANCE AGAINST THE UNKNOWN.
EVEN IF I'M GOING TO MISS HIM ALMOST AS MUCH AS I'LL MISS MY BROTHER.
WELL, THE SHUTTLE HAS LAUNCHED. EVERYTHING ON SCHEDULE SO FAR?
*NGIKUFISELA INHLANHLA,** MY SON.
YES, PRINCESS SHURI--
*"GOOD LUCK" IN ZULU, THE LANGUAGE OF QUEEN RAMONDA'S PEOPLE.
CAM 32
--THE WORMHOLE LOOKS STABLE. AT LEAST AS STABLE AS A WORMHOLE CAN BE.
GOOD. NOW THEY JUST NEED TO GET IN, COMPLETE THE MISSION AND GET OUT. SET YOUR CLOCKS--
BEEP-BEEP-BEEP-

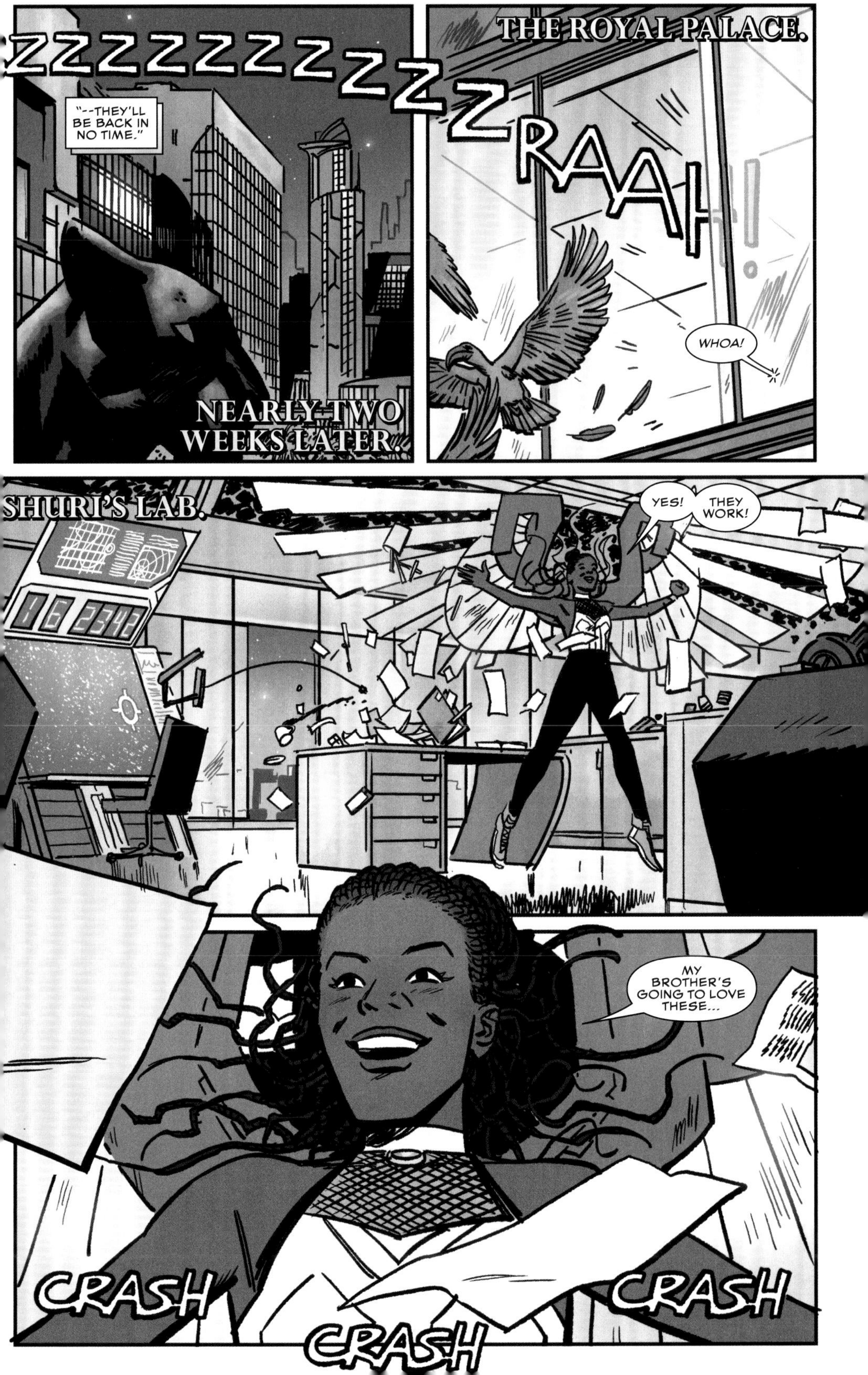
ZZZZZZZZZZZRAAH
"--THEY'LL BE BACK IN NO TIME."
NEARLY TWO WEEKS LATER.
THE ROYAL PALACE.
WHOA!
SHURI'S LAB.
YES!
THEY WORK!
MY BROTHER'S GOING TO LOVE THESE...
CRASH
CRASH
CRASH

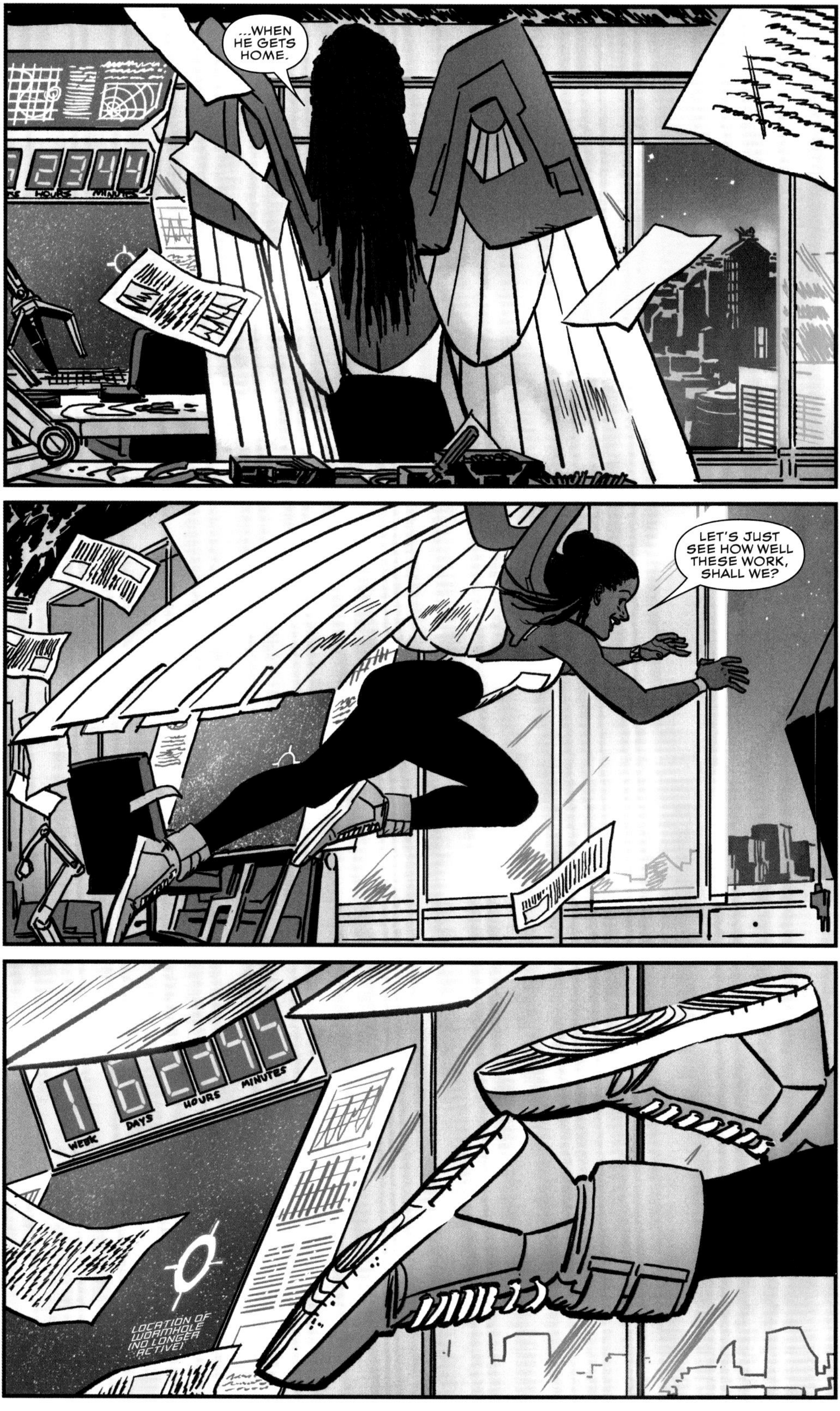
...WHEN HE GETS HOME.
HOURS
MINUTES
LET'S JUST SEE HOW WELL THESE WORK, SHALL WE?
WEEK
DAYS
HOURS
MINUTES
LOCATION OF WORMHOLE (NO LONGER ACTIVE)

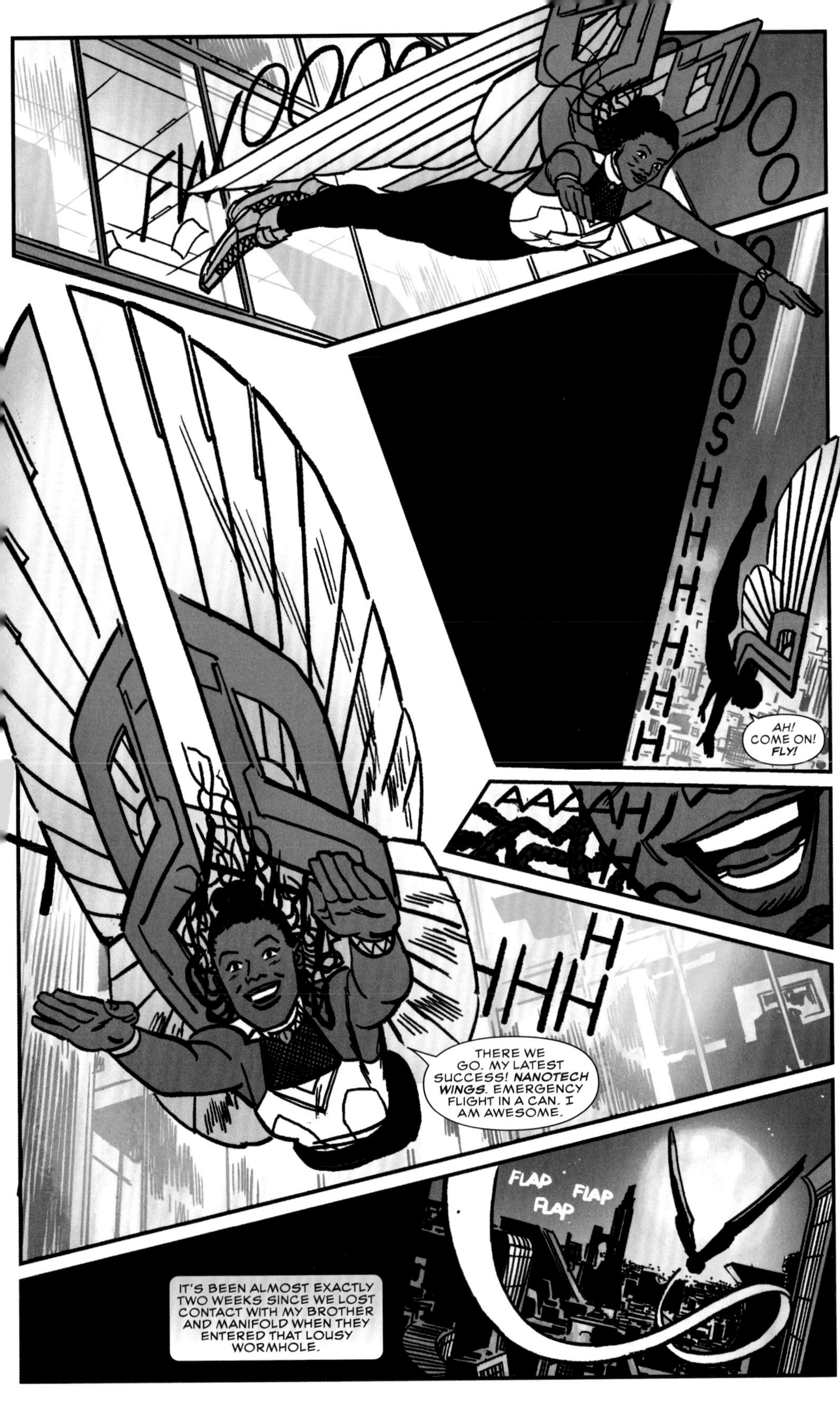
FWOOOOOOOOOOOOOOOSHHHHHHHHH
AH! COME ON! FLY!
AAAAHHHHHHHH
THERE WE GO. MY LATEST SUCCESS! NANOTECH WINGS. EMERGENCY FLIGHT IN A CAN. I AM AWESOME.
FLAP FLAP FLAP
IT'S BEEN ALMOST EXACTLY TWO WEEKS SINCE WE LOST CONTACT WITH MY BROTHER AND MANIFOLD WHEN THEY ENTERED THAT LOUSY WORMHOLE.

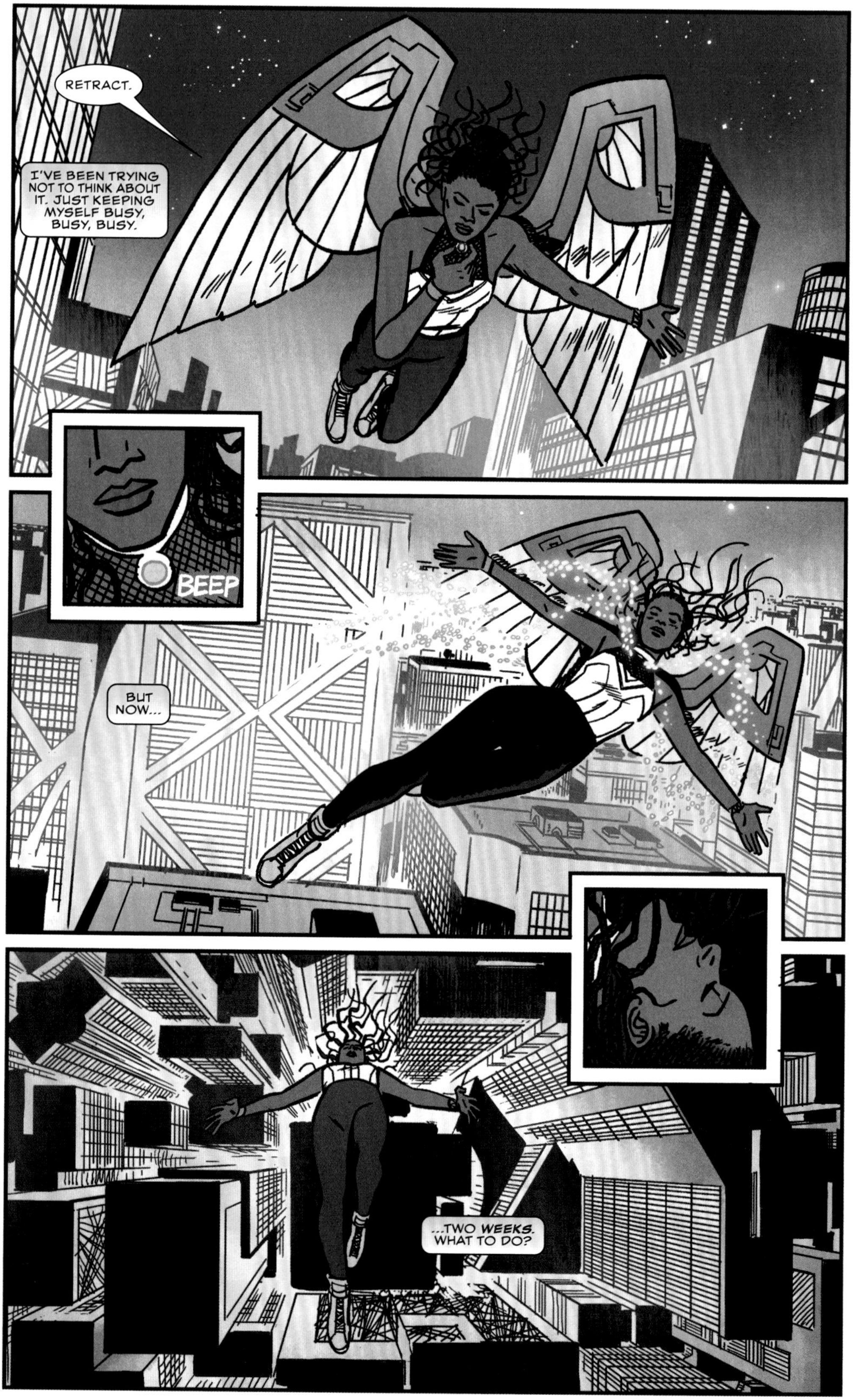
RETRACT.
I'VE BEEN TRYING NOT TO THINK ABOUT IT. JUST KEEPING MYSELF BUSY, BUSY, BUSY.
BEEP
BUT NOW...
...TWO WEEKS. WHAT TO DO?

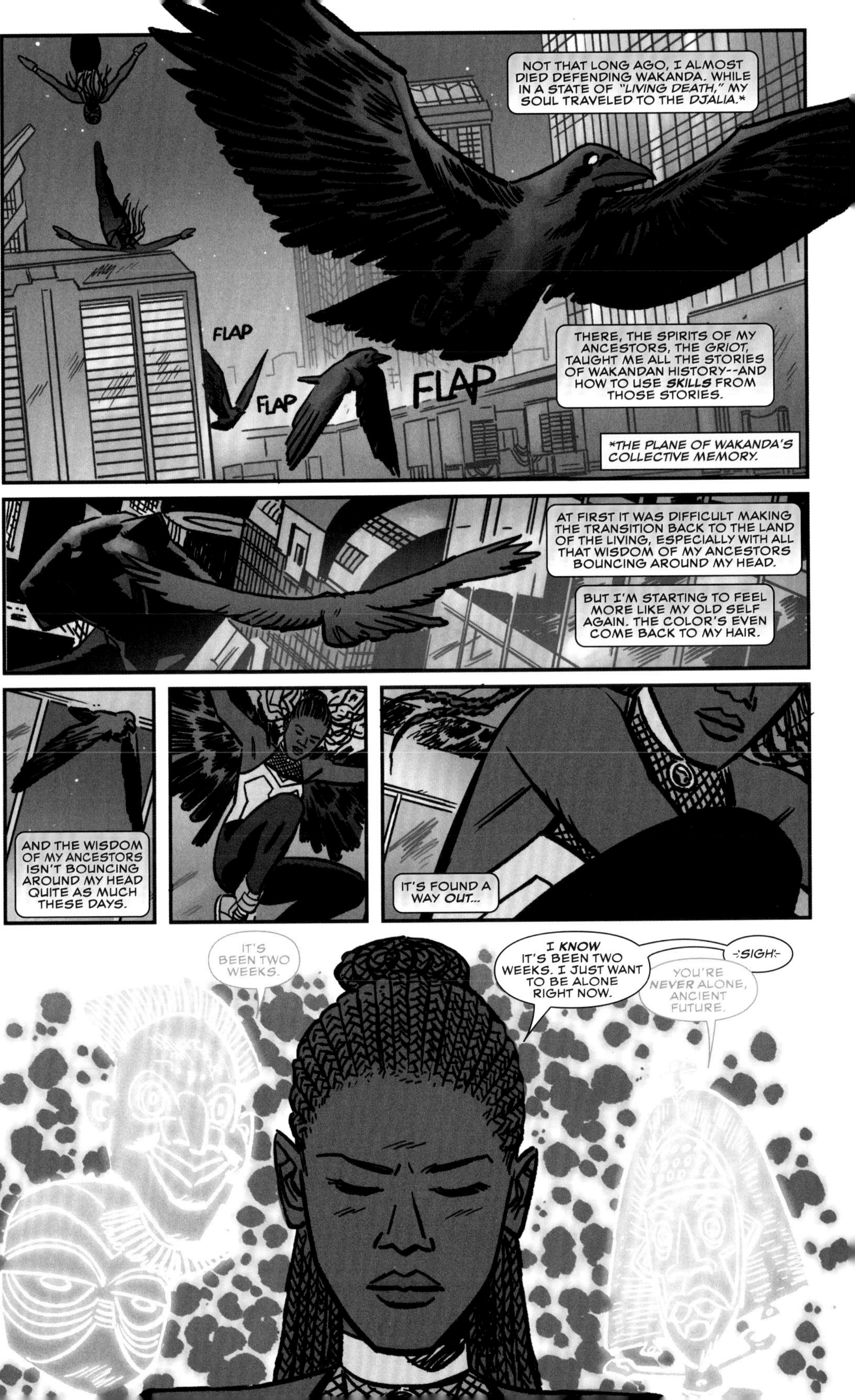
NOT THAT LONG AGO, I ALMOST DIED DEFENDING WAKANDA. WHILE IN A STATE OF "LIVING DEATH," MY SOUL TRAVELED TO THE DJALIA.*
FLAP
FLAP
FLAP
THERE, THE SPIRITS OF MY ANCESTORS, THE GRIOT, TAUGHT ME ALL THE STORIES OF WAKANDAN HISTORY--AND HOW TO USE SKILLS FROM THOSE STORIES.
*THE PLANE OF WAKANDA'S COLLECTIVE MEMORY.
AT FIRST IT WAS DIFFICULT MAKING THE TRANSITION BACK TO THE LAND OF THE LIVING, ESPECIALLY WITH ALL THAT WISDOM OF MY ANCESTORS BOUNCING AROUND MY HEAD.
BUT I'M STARTING TO FEEL MORE LIKE MY OLD SELF AGAIN. THE COLOR'S EVEN COME BACK TO MY HAIR.
AND THE WISDOM OF MY ANCESTORS ISN'T BOUNCING AROUND MY HEAD QUITE AS MUCH THESE DAYS.
IT'S FOUND A WAY OUT...
IT'S BEEN TWO WEEKS.
I KNOW IT'S BEEN TWO WEEKS. I JUST WANT TO BE ALONE RIGHT NOW.
-SIGH-
YOU'RE NEVER ALONE, ANCIENT FUTURE.

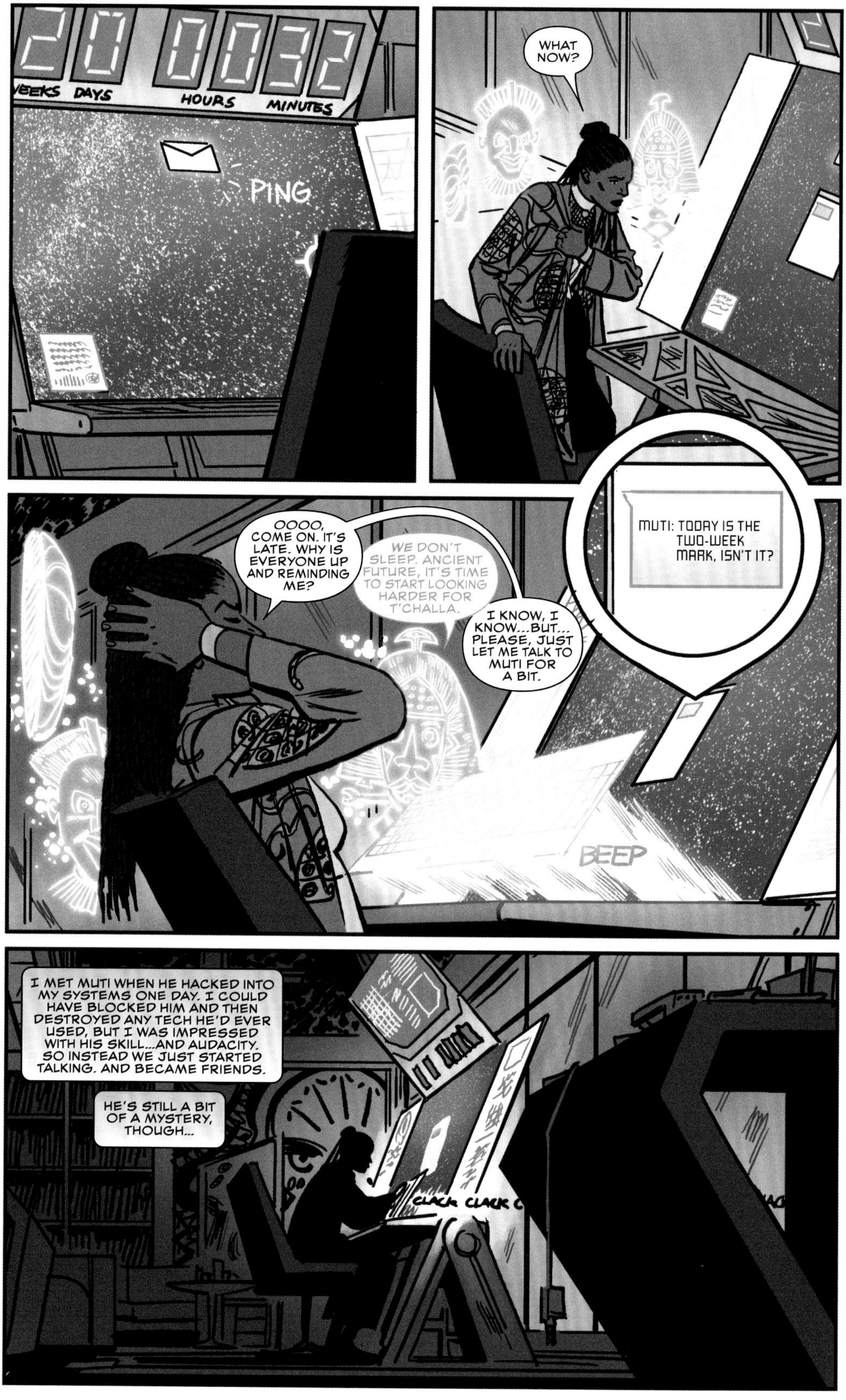

WEEKS DAYS HOURS MINUTES
PING
WHAT NOW?
OOOO, COME ON. IT'S LATE. WHY IS EVERYONE UP AND REMINDING ME?
WE DON'T SLEEP. ANCIENT FUTURE, IT'S TIME TO START LOOKING HARDER FOR T'CHALLA.
I KNOW, I KNOW...BUT... PLEASE, JUST LET ME TALK TO MUTI FOR A BIT.
MUTI: TODAY IS THE TWO-WEEK MARK, ISN'T IT?
BEEP
I MET MUTI WHEN HE HACKED INTO MY SYSTEMS ONE DAY. I COULD HAVE BLOCKED HIM AND THEN DESTROYED ANY TECH HE'D EVER USED, BUT I WAS IMPRESSED WITH HIS SKILL...AND AUDACITY. SO INSTEAD WE JUST STARTED TALKING. AND BECAME FRIENDS.
HE'S STILL A BIT OF A MYSTERY, THOUGH...
CLACK CLACK

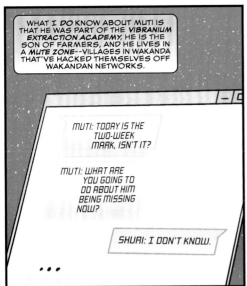

WHAT I *DO* KNOW ABOUT MUTI IS THAT HE WAS PART OF THE *VIBRANIUM EXTRACTION ACADEMY*, HE IS THE SON OF FARMERS, AND HE LIVES IN A *MUTE ZONE*--VILLAGES IN WAKANDA THAT'VE HACKED THEMSELVES OFF WAKANDAN NETWORKS.

MUTI: TODAY IS THE TWO-WEEK MARK, ISN'T IT?

MUTI: WHAT ARE YOU GOING TO DO ABOUT HIM BEING MISSING NOW?

SHURI: I DON'T KNOW.

. . .

SHURI: I DON'T KNOW.

MUTI: NO PRESSURE. JUST CHECKING ON YOU.

THE PART THAT *REALLY* MATTERS TO ME, THOUGH?

MUTI'S THE ONLY PERSON WHO DOESN'T CALL ME "PRINCESS."

WEEKS   DAYS   HOURS   MINUTES

WHERE ARE YOU, BROTHER? WHAT ARE YOU REALLY UP TO? AND WHAT AM I GONNA DO?

CLACKITY-CLACK-CLACK

PRESSURE. ...T CHECKING ...OU.

SHURI: WHEN I WAS SEVEN, I SAVED MY BROTHER FROM A SNAKE...

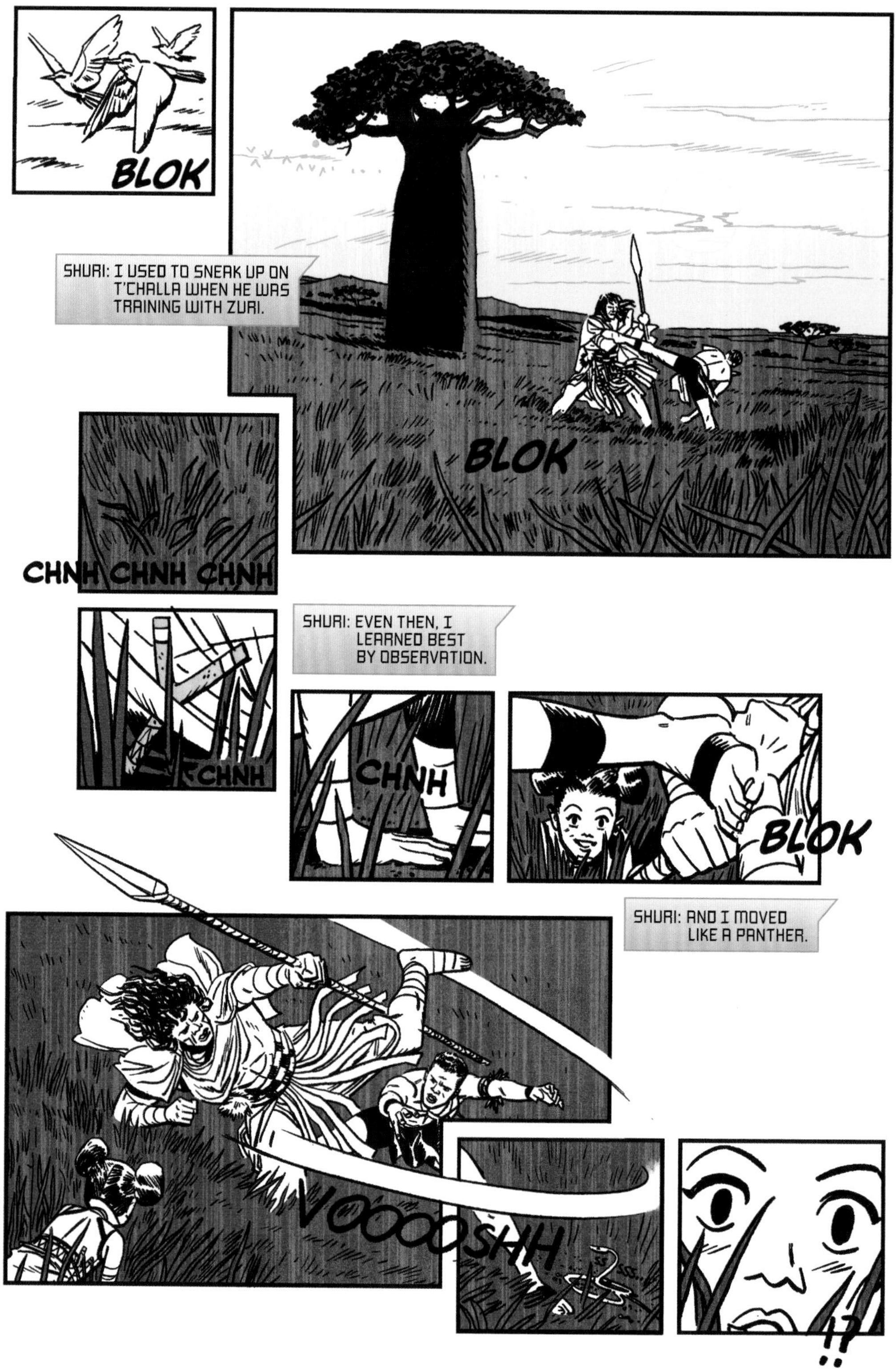
BLOK
SHURI: I USED TO SNEAK UP ON T'CHALLA WHEN HE WAS TRAINING WITH ZURI.
BLOK
CHNH CHNH CHNH
CHNH
SHURI: EVEN THEN, I LEARNED BEST BY OBSERVATION.
CHNH
BLOK
SHURI: AND I MOVED LIKE A PANTHER.
VOOOOSHH
!?

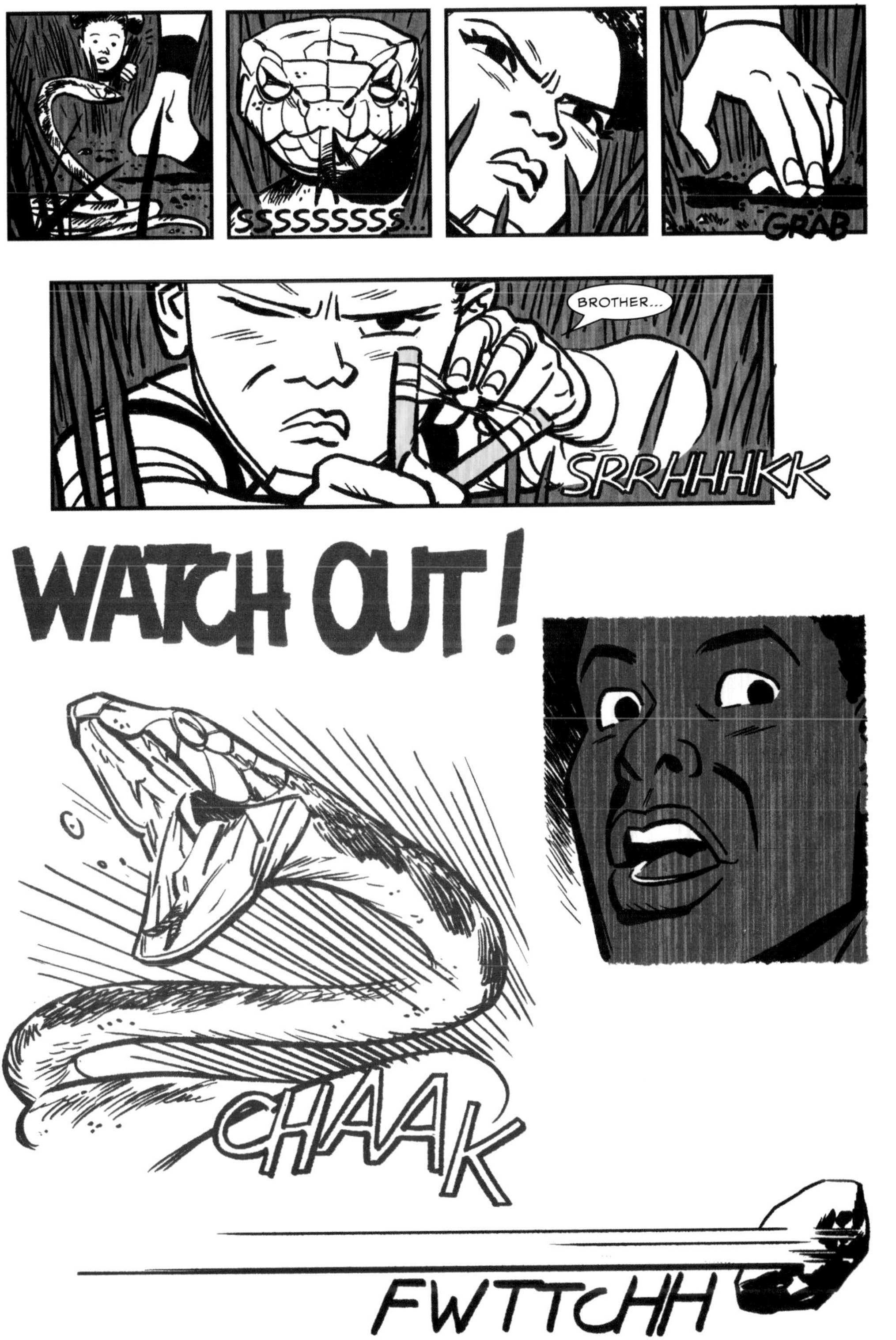
SSSSSSSSSS...
GRAB
BROTHER...
SRRHHHKK
WATCH OUT!
CHAAK
FWTTCHH

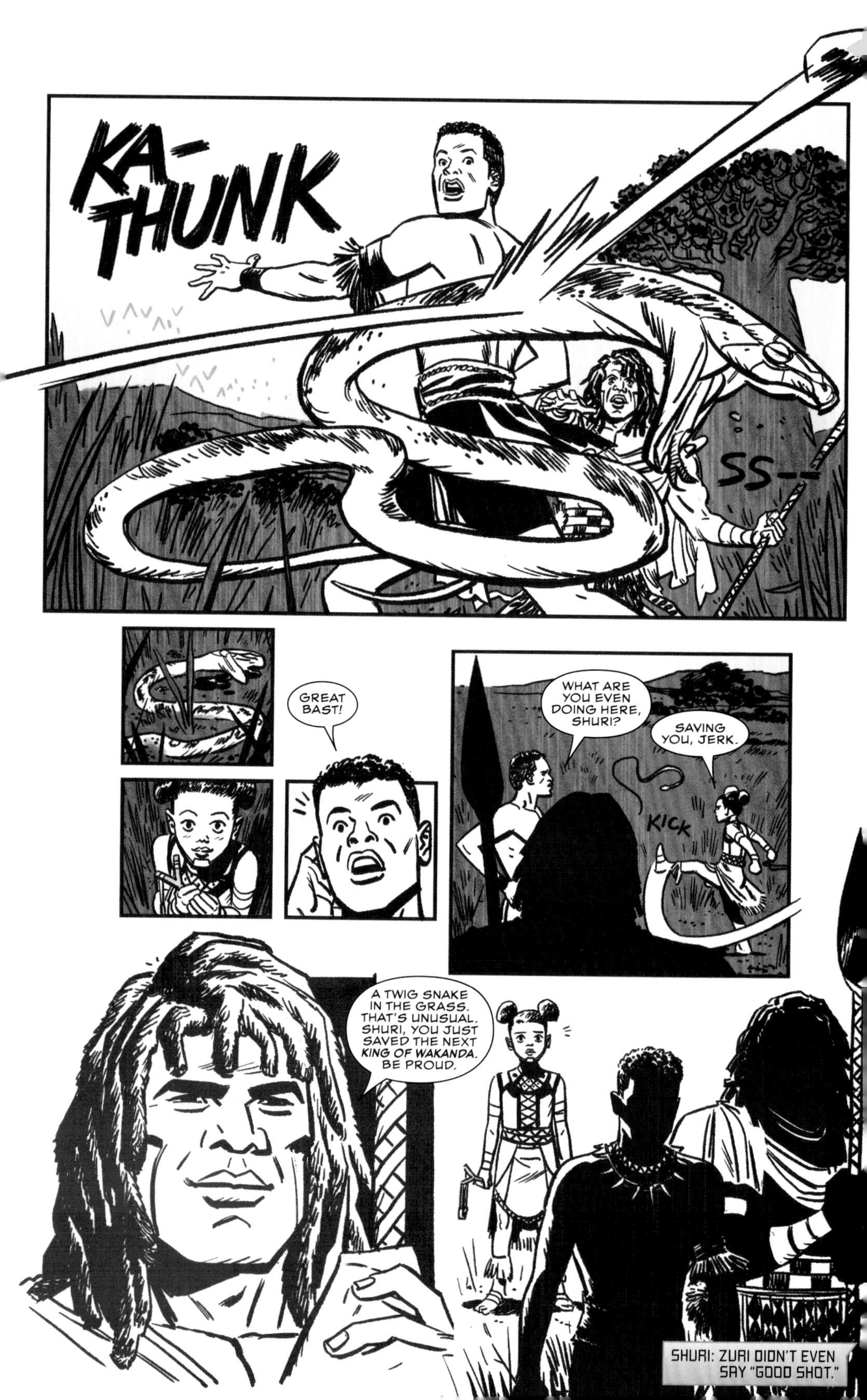
KA-THUNK
SS--
GREAT BAST!
WHAT ARE YOU EVEN DOING HERE, SHURI?
SAVING YOU, JERK.
KICK
A TWIG SNAKE IN THE GRASS. THAT'S UNUSUAL. SHURI, YOU JUST SAVED THE NEXT KING OF WAKANDA. BE PROUD.
SHURI: ZURI DIDN'T EVEN SAY "GOOD SHOT."

SHURI: IT WAS ALWAYS ABOUT MY BROTHER FIRST. HE WAS THE RIGHT GENDER, PLUS HE WAS THE OLDEST. NOW HE'S FLOWN OFF AND I CAN'T FIND HIM...AND I BUILT THAT SHIP...WHAT IF IT'S MY FAULT?

SEE? ALWAYS ABOUT MY BROTHER. I'M GOING TO BED.

WEEKS    DAYS

AND YOU SHOULDN'T BE TALKING TO STRANGERS ON A COMPUTER.

SHURI: IT WAS ABOUT FIRST. RIGHT G HE WAS NOW HE AND I CA HIM...AN THAT SHI IF IT'S MY

MUTI: MAYBE HE'S LOST.

MUTI: MAYBE HE'S LOST.

SHURI: I GUESS I SHOULD BE LOOKING FOR HIM INSTEAD OF TALKING TO YOU, RIGHT? TTYL.

MUTI: ♥ LATER.

THE NEXT DAY.

THE BIRNIN ZANA MARKET.

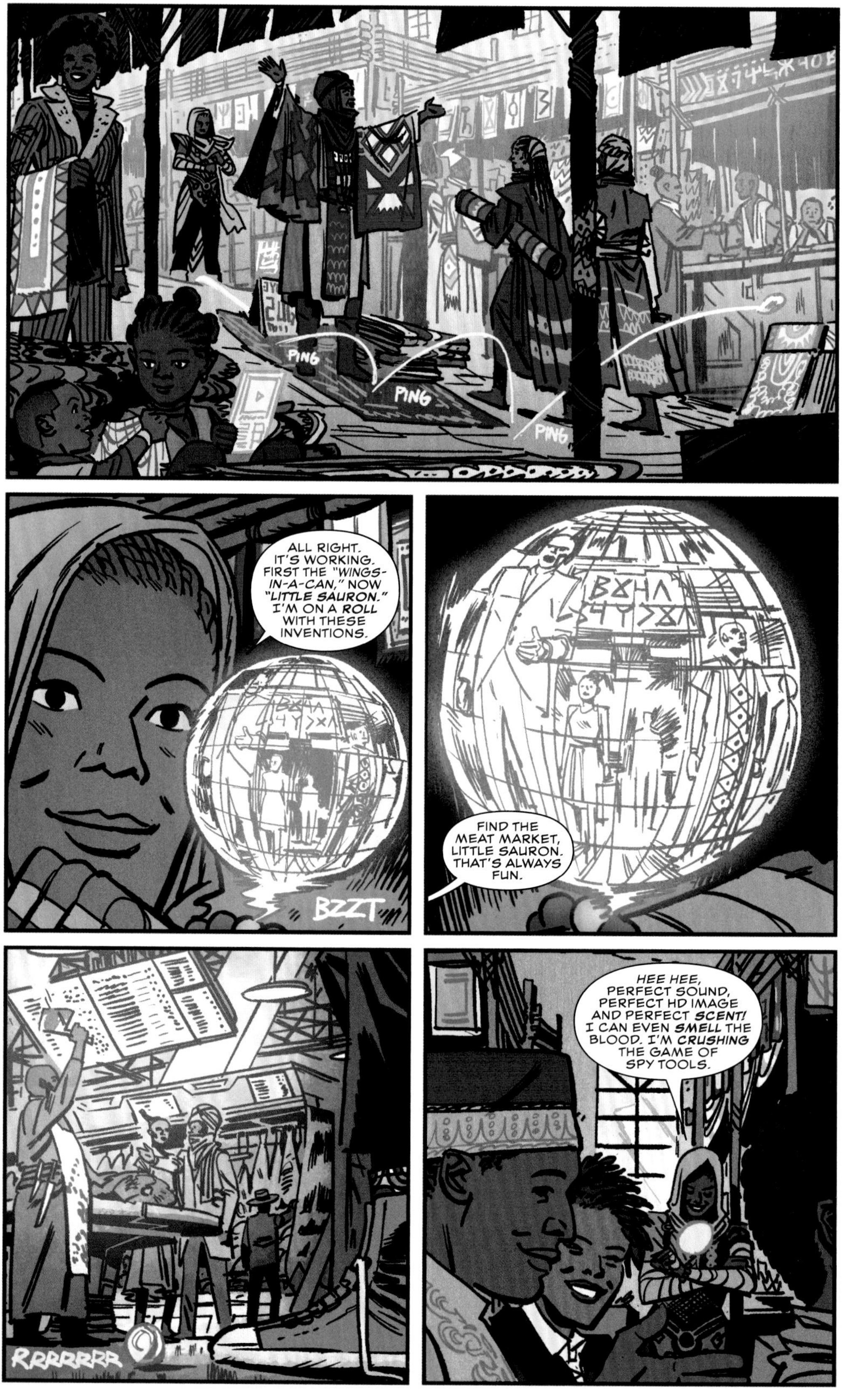
PING
PING
PING
ALL RIGHT. IT'S WORKING. FIRST THE "WINGS-IN-A-CAN," NOW "LITTLE SAURON." I'M ON A ROLL WITH THESE INVENTIONS.
BZZT
FIND THE MEAT MARKET, LITTLE SAURON. THAT'S ALWAYS FUN.
RRRRRRR
HEE HEE, PERFECT SOUND, PERFECT HD IMAGE AND PERFECT SCENT! I CAN EVEN SMELL THE BLOOD. I'M CRUSHING THE GAME OF SPY TOOLS.

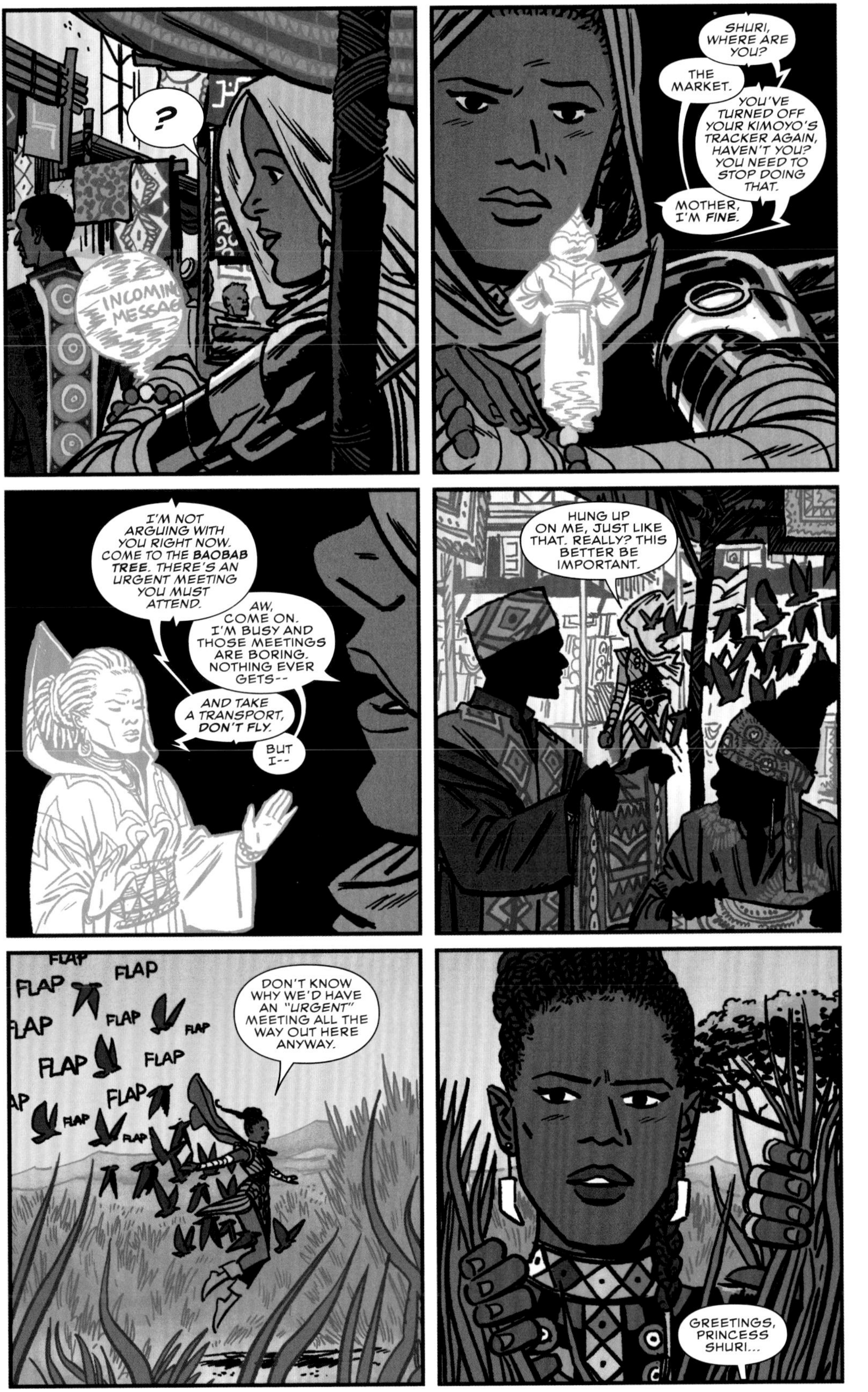
?
INCOMING MESSAGE
SHURI, WHERE ARE YOU?
THE MARKET.
YOU'VE TURNED OFF YOUR KIMOYO'S TRACKER AGAIN, HAVEN'T YOU? YOU NEED TO STOP DOING THAT.
MOTHER, I'M FINE.
I'M NOT ARGUING WITH YOU RIGHT NOW. COME TO THE BAOBAB TREE. THERE'S AN URGENT MEETING YOU MUST ATTEND.
AW, COME ON. I'M BUSY AND THOSE MEETINGS ARE BORING. NOTHING EVER GETS--
AND TAKE A TRANSPORT, DON'T FLY.
BUT I--
HUNG UP ON ME, JUST LIKE THAT. REALLY? THIS BETTER BE IMPORTANT.
FLAP FLAP FLAP FLAP FLAP FLAP FLAP FLAP FLAP FLAP FLAP FLAP
DON'T KNOW WHY WE'D HAVE AN "URGENT" MEETING ALL THE WAY OUT HERE ANYWAY.
GREETINGS, PRINCESS SHURI...

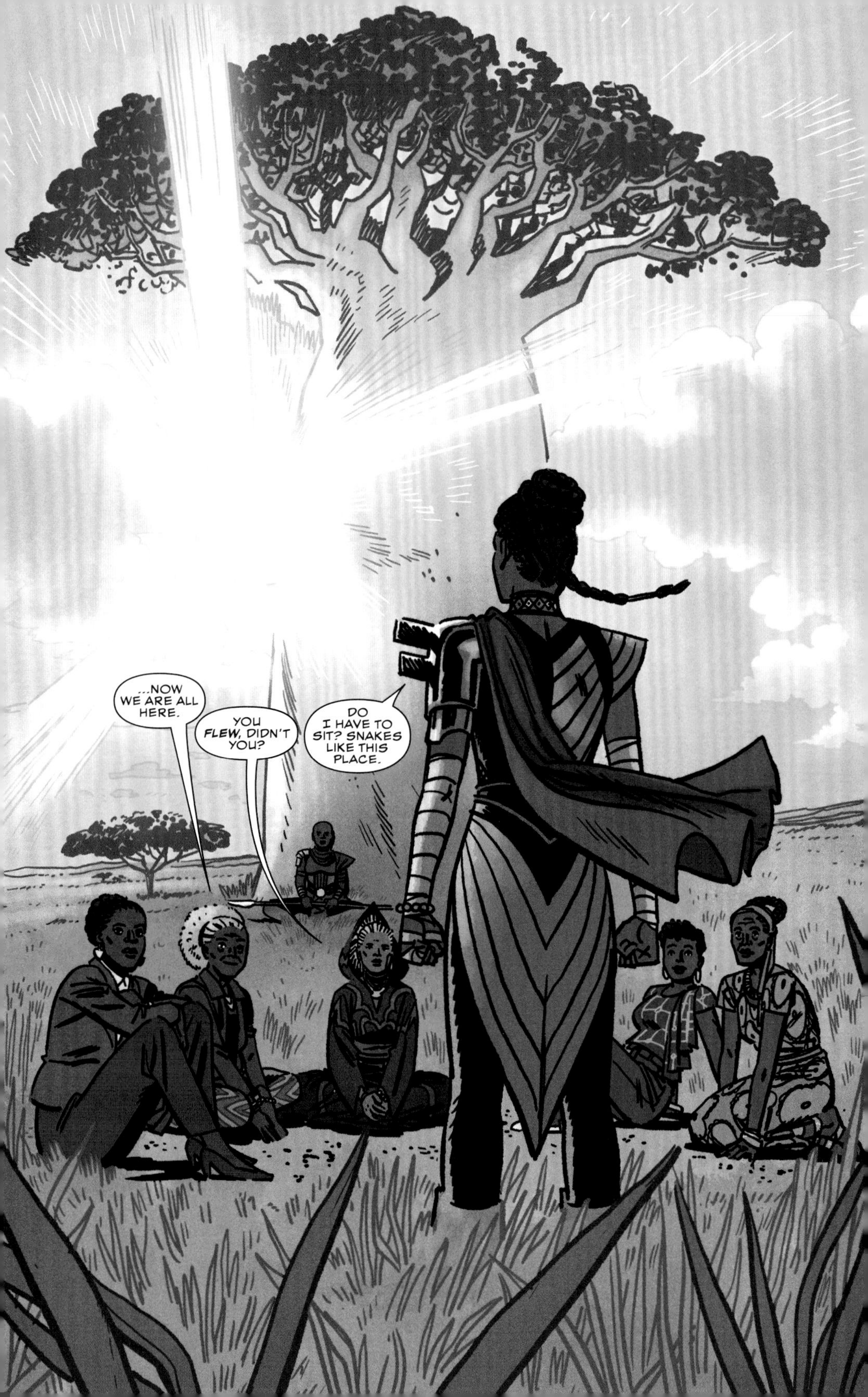

...NOW WE ARE ALL HERE.
YOU *FLEW*, DIDN'T YOU?
DO I HAVE TO SIT? SNAKES LIKE THIS PLACE.

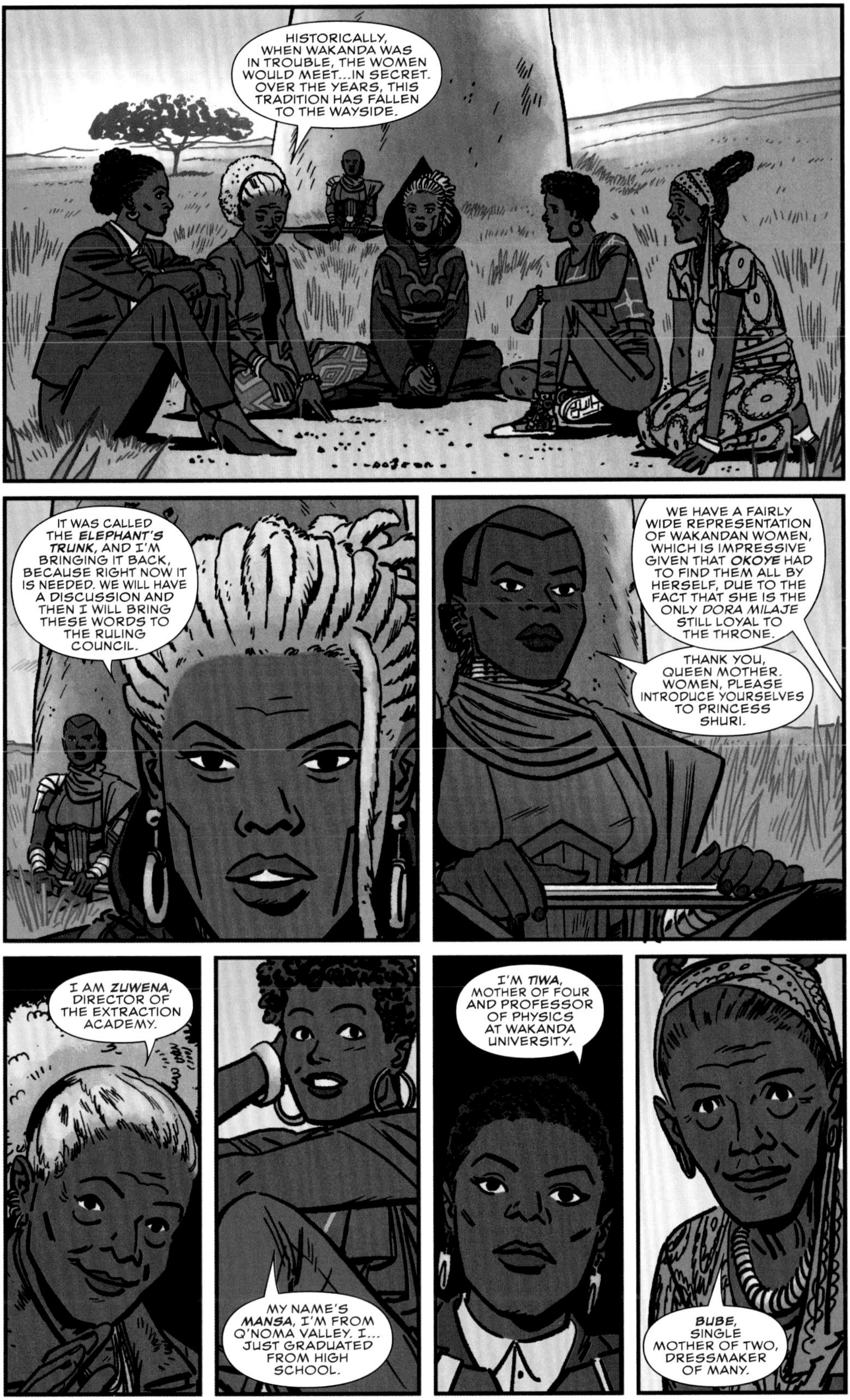
HISTORICALLY, WHEN WAKANDA WAS IN TROUBLE, THE WOMEN WOULD MEET...IN SECRET. OVER THE YEARS, THIS TRADITION HAS FALLEN TO THE WAYSIDE.
IT WAS CALLED THE ELEPHANT'S TRUNK, AND I'M BRINGING IT BACK, BECAUSE RIGHT NOW IT IS NEEDED. WE WILL HAVE A DISCUSSION AND THEN I WILL BRING THESE WORDS TO THE RULING COUNCIL.
WE HAVE A FAIRLY WIDE REPRESENTATION OF WAKANDAN WOMEN, WHICH IS IMPRESSIVE GIVEN THAT OKOYE HAD TO FIND THEM ALL BY HERSELF, DUE TO THE FACT THAT SHE IS THE ONLY DORA MILAJE STILL LOYAL TO THE THRONE.
THANK YOU, QUEEN MOTHER. WOMEN, PLEASE INTRODUCE YOURSELVES TO PRINCESS SHURI.
I AM ZUWENA, DIRECTOR OF THE EXTRACTION ACADEMY.
MY NAME'S MANSA, I'M FROM Q'NOMA VALLEY. I... JUST GRADUATED FROM HIGH SCHOOL.
I'M TIWA, MOTHER OF FOUR AND PROFESSOR OF PHYSICS AT WAKANDA UNIVERSITY.
BUBE, SINGLE MOTHER OF TWO, DRESSMAKER OF MANY.

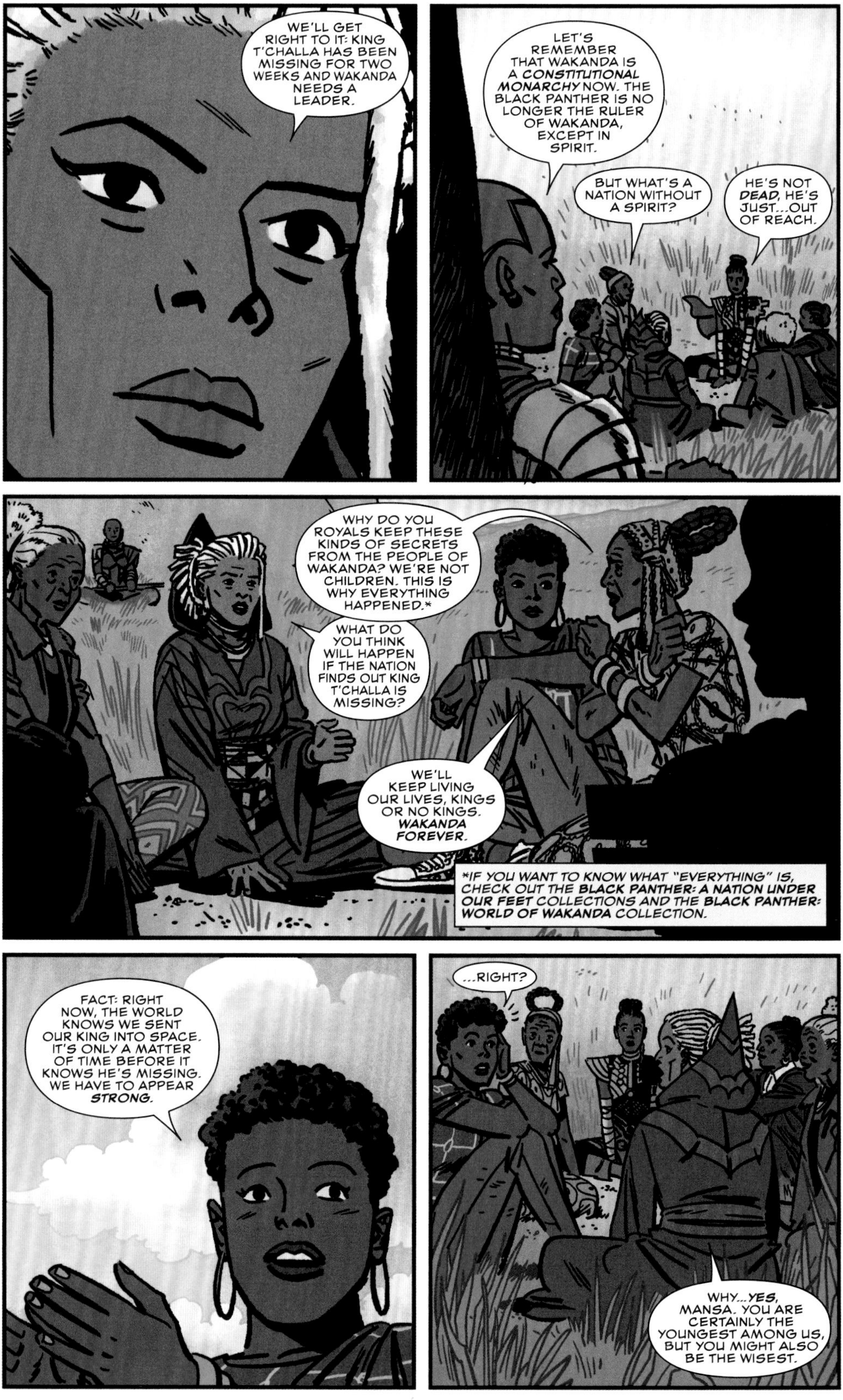
WE'LL GET RIGHT TO IT: KING T'CHALLA HAS BEEN MISSING FOR TWO WEEKS AND WAKANDA NEEDS A LEADER.
LET'S REMEMBER THAT WAKANDA IS A CONSTITUTIONAL MONARCHY NOW. THE BLACK PANTHER IS NO LONGER THE RULER OF WAKANDA, EXCEPT IN SPIRIT.
BUT WHAT'S A NATION WITHOUT A SPIRIT?
HE'S NOT DEAD, HE'S JUST...OUT OF REACH.
WHY DO YOU ROYALS KEEP THESE KINDS OF SECRETS FROM THE PEOPLE OF WAKANDA? WE'RE NOT CHILDREN. THIS IS WHY EVERYTHING HAPPENED.*
WHAT DO YOU THINK WILL HAPPEN IF THE NATION FINDS OUT KING T'CHALLA IS MISSING?
WE'LL KEEP LIVING OUR LIVES, KINGS OR NO KINGS. WAKANDA FOREVER.
*IF YOU WANT TO KNOW WHAT "EVERYTHING" IS, CHECK OUT THE BLACK PANTHER: A NATION UNDER OUR FEET COLLECTIONS AND THE BLACK PANTHER: WORLD OF WAKANDA COLLECTION.
FACT: RIGHT NOW, THE WORLD KNOWS WE SENT OUR KING INTO SPACE. IT'S ONLY A MATTER OF TIME BEFORE IT KNOWS HE'S MISSING. WE HAVE TO APPEAR STRONG.
...RIGHT?
WHY...YES, MANSA. YOU ARE CERTAINLY THE YOUNGEST AMONG US, BUT YOU MIGHT ALSO BE THE WISEST.

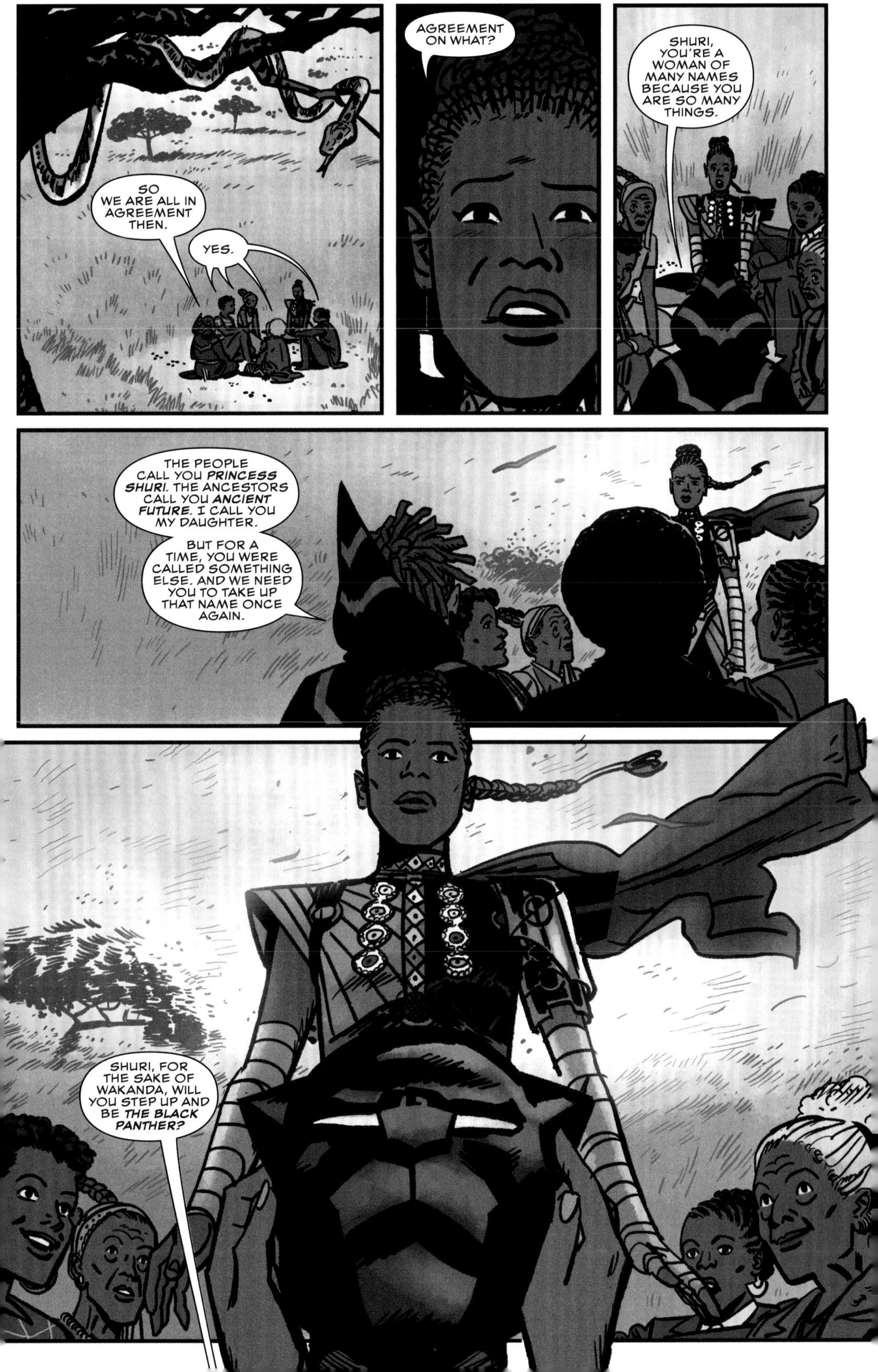

SO WE ARE ALL IN AGREEMENT THEN.
YES.
AGREEMENT ON WHAT?
SHURI, YOU'RE A WOMAN OF MANY NAMES BECAUSE YOU ARE SO MANY THINGS.
THE PEOPLE CALL YOU *PRINCESS SHURI*. THE ANCESTORS CALL YOU *ANCIENT FUTURE*. I CALL YOU MY DAUGHTER.
BUT FOR A TIME, YOU WERE CALLED SOMETHING ELSE. AND WE NEED YOU TO TAKE UP THAT NAME ONCE AGAIN.
SHURI, FOR THE SAKE OF WAKANDA, WILL YOU STEP UP AND BE *THE BLACK PANTHER?*

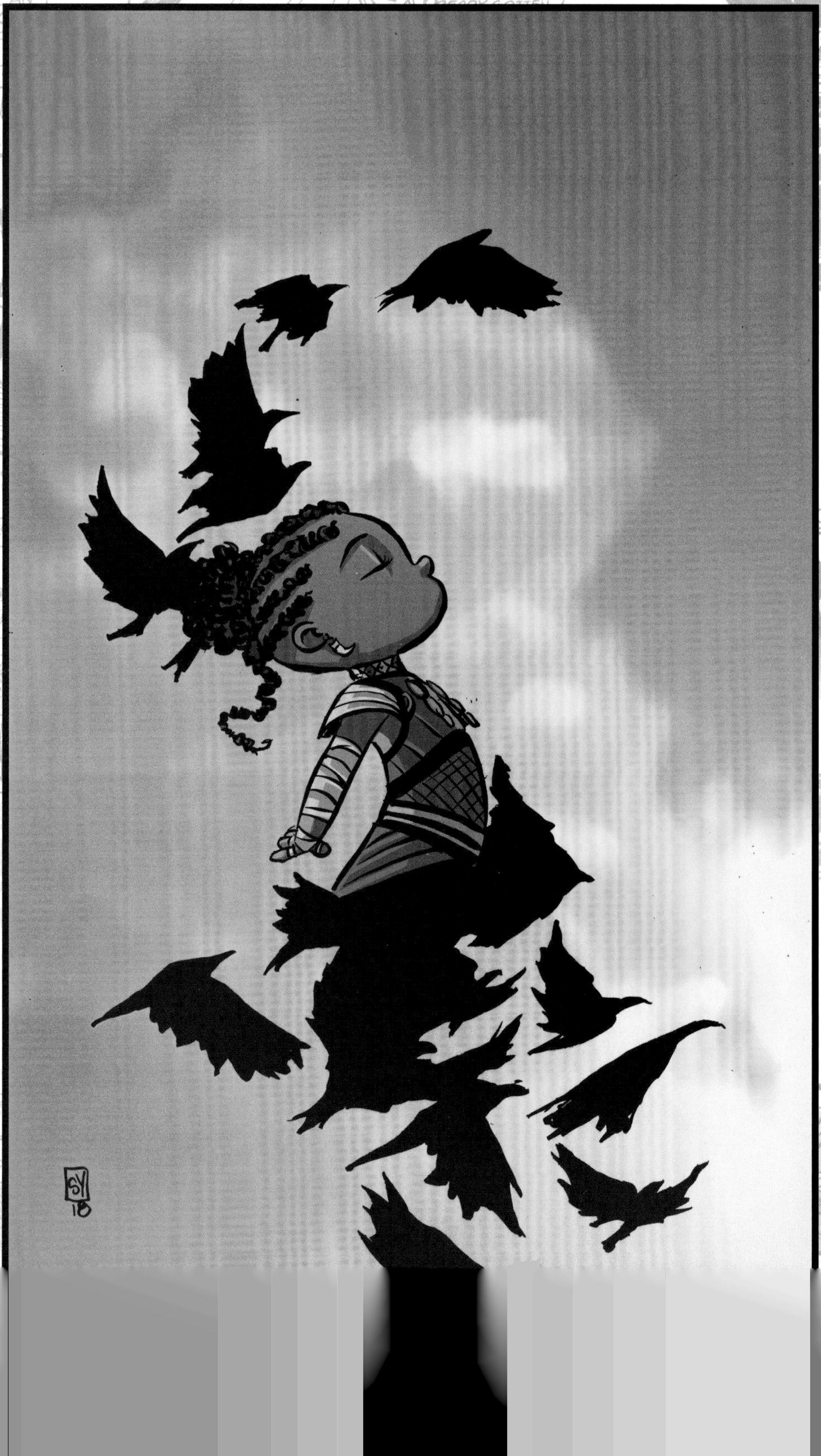